The Sea And The Stars

The Sea
And
The Stars

*

ROBERT WILDER

G. P. Putnam's Sons
New York

To
THE CLANTONS
*Robert and Jean. Leslie, John and
Cameron. Present and Future.
With deep affection.*

The Sea And The Stars

* I * *

THE warm sun of late afternoon slanted across the balcony's corner where he lay on a padded deck chair and watched the golf carts as they traced a pattern of erratic beetles over the shining fairways. A few players walked with their caddies but not many. Golf was taken as a leisurely diversion with a minimum of exercise.

By turning a little he could look out over the Sound. The water rippled like poured copper. Beyond it the shoreline of the beach side held back the ocean's constant thrust. It was crested with the tall, feathered tops of cocoanut palms; massed with the color of bougainvillaea and flame vine. The slender trunks of the palms were the silvered white of an ancient's beard and they all inclined gracefully to the west, bent so by the prevailing winds.

Concealed within the groves and behind the flowers, accessible only through gates where watchmen were on duty through both the day and night, were the homes of the very wealthy. They were occupied no more than three months or so out of the year by their owners. They walled their estates, marked out their private stretches of beach with latticed fences, barricaded themselves against each other. This, despite the fact they shared a common social life with cocktail parties, dinners and dances. They played tennis on each other's courts, fished and golfed together, sat over a bridge table. There were marriages between their children and associations in corporate industries. But, this was a secluded world and they guarded themselves against intrusion more out of habit than necessity.

Moored to the piers or within the jettied marinas were sloops, cabin cruisers, open cockpit speedboats, auxiliary powered schooners and yachts of ninety-eight feet or over. They were not often used although the beautiful cruising waters of the Bahamas were less than one hundred miles away. The youngsters played with the speedboats, tearing the Sound into strips of foaming water. Their parents gave cocktail parties aboard the larger craft without an anchor being raised. In an hour or so the lights would go on and portholes make small, yellow cats' eyes in the gathering darkness.

Stoddard Lathrop looked at the beach side from his place on the mainland and thought, with a dry humor, God must have felt this way when he gazed upon the world and found it good. Unlike God, Lathrop hadn't rested on the seventh day. Sometimes he imagined he had torn the slimy mangrove from its roots, leveled the dunes and set the palms with his own hands. He had built it all; this and more—from Cocoa Beach to Miami; from Key Largo to Eluthera, in the Bahamas—the Stalath Corporation had reached out to grasp and hold.

The balcony where he rested now was a section of the south wing of the club. He had created this, also. The Copa de Oro Club, named for the lovely flower which grows so profusely in Mexico. Cup of Gold. It was a fitting name. While in the planning stage and these acres of flat, palmetto scrub and thin stands of pine bordered by heavy marsh were being torn at by bulldozers and men, a feature writer for a pictorial weekly was sent down from New York to interview him.

"What, exactly, do you intend doing here, Mr. Lathrop?"

"Well," he had drawled the reply, "I'm going to build a club for rich millionaires. After all, they've gotta have some place to hide."

The redundancy amused the writer as Stoddard intended it should. In the article the designation of *rich millionaires* had been placed in italics. It was picked up by Florida's east coast papers and passed along on the wire services. It pleased Lathrop's fancy to cast himself in the role of a gallus-snapping Cracker who, by the mysterious combination of luck and drive, had become one of the ten wealthiest men in the United States. He had played at the character for so long now he sometimes believed it himself.

In designing the Copa de Oro he had tossed away the first, conventional drawings submitted by the architects and landscaping artists. A half dozen men had been simultaneously employed on the project. With minor variations they all came up with unimaginative, bastardized neo-Spanish or Moorish structures. They were stiffly ugly, laced with long, arched corridors and somber, high-ceilinged rooms. They were theatrical and shallow in concept.

"Here." He had impatiently snatched a pencil from a drawing board. "Can't you fellows see what we have to work with?" He scrawled a flowing, half-S curve. "After we get it filled and with a seawall and landscaping this will be the line of shore. Give me a building to follow it. I don't want any goddamned surprises. I'm not going to have anyone come down that long drive between the lane of Australian pines, take one look at this place and say to himself: How the hell did the Alhambra get here? What we put up has grown from the land, the water and the air. It is part of the whole. When someone sees it for the first time I don't want him to know he's seeing it. You understand what I mean?

Only one, a young man by the name of Clint Rickards, seemed touched by Lathrop's creative flame. What finally came from his board had grace and beauty, open to the sparkling waters of the Sound, the sun, the sweep of the fairways and gardens. There was no obtrusive note here. It was, as Lathrop wanted it to be, a part of the whole. He turned it over to Rickards and had retained him ever since for all his other building.

There were only four apartments in the Clubhouse itself. One of eight rooms with its own kitchen, a French staff and chef. Lathrop was convinced well-trained Frenchmen made the best servants. A smaller apartment provided quarters for his secretary, Sharon Ward. The remaining two were leased to New York firms which used them for their executives and clients. On the ground floor were bars, billiard, card and reading rooms; a large dining room and several smaller ones where the members could have complete privacy when they wished it. Spaced about the grounds were twenty cottages, each an architectural gem of design and convenience. No two were alike and they rented for five hundred dollars a day. They were fully staffed from chef to houseboy. If it suited their pleasure none of the resident members ever had to enter the central Clubhouse. The initiation fee of the Copa de Oro was fifty thousand dollars; the dues five thousand. This gave the members nothing more than the distinction of belonging—flying the Club's burgee from their yachts, moored in the marina, and the wearing of the Club's flowered crest on their jackets.

On a small table near his chair was an ebony and silver box lined with cedar. From it he took a slender cigar of panatela shape. He still had, perhaps, five hundred of these in hermetically sealed containers. Before Castro had seized Cuba they were made to his order on the island in a small establishment specializing in the finest of Havana leaf. Each month they were sent to him in regular consignments. As he touched a flame to the fragrant tobacco he thought that by the time those he had on hand were gone someone would have deposed Fidel. This failing, he mused, he just might get a few friends together and buy Cuba. This would solve a great many problems for everyone and his cigar makers could go back to their craft instead of parading around with their damn silly banners.

He stretched out his long legs in their tailored slacks of white flannel. No one wore white flannel anymore. When he had been young a wardrobe wasn't complete without a pair of white flannels and a blue coat. They were what you wore to the dances on Saturday night. Now he had the cloth especially woven in England, tailored there to his measurements. It was a hell of a note when you couldn't buy white flannel in the United States. He wondered why? He recalled, also, there had been a time in the 20's when all the young men wore gray flannel trousers. They were called "bags." Some damn British nonsense. The visit of the Prince of Wales had something to do with it. Bags and golf knickerbockers; "plus fours," they fell below the calf and were common street wear, even in New York City. Now the kids wore denim Levi's, plastered across their skinny rumps and sagging below the navel in front.

He allowed the smoke to roll from his tongue and relaxed. He was a large man and the years had made but a slight impression upon a heavy frame. Oh, there were changes! He was aware of them. There were lines and wrinkles, a crepelike texture to the skin on his hands and about his throat. The elasticity, the bounce, were no longer there but he was tough, tough and weathered the way a good piece of leather grows when cared for. Well, hell, you didn't come to the age of seventy-one without it showing.

It would have astonished him if anyone had suggested he'd spent a busy day for a man of his age. For him it had been normal. He had bought a building on Flagler Street, in Miami; flown in a pontoon-equipped light plane over to Lake Harney and closed a deal for 40,000 acres of land. Then he and his pilot returned to the Copa de Oro, transferred to the heavier twin-engine job he kept there and winged over to Eluthera, in the Bahamas. His agents had been putting together some 20,000 acres of land on the southern tip of the island. It was just about in one piece now and on it he planned an extension of the Copa de Oro Club. From Eluthera he had gone to Nassau where he was half owner in a bank, full owner of two warehouses and a hotel. He'd had lunch with friends, a couple of drinks and then flown back here to the Club.

He scratched at his head where the hair was the color and texture of white silk thread. It threw into sharp contrast the deep tan of his skin. A small grin played about his lips. He knew what they said about him in Miami and other places: "Stoddard Lathrop is an island of money completely surrounded by Florida." In a way, maybe, it was true. But what was he supposed to do? Retire? No one wanted to understand it was a game; always had been. Some men played golf, went big game hunting or fishing. They devoted their lives to these pursuits and no one seemed to think this at all unusual. But to keep making money when the need for it was long past made you an eccentric.

He had put $20,000,000 into the Copa de Oro Club. With the surrounding land he owned, the development planned, it would all come back with a few additional millions sticking to it. Sometimes he would shut his eyes and see the entire State of Florida spread out like a map in relief. Wherever he looked there was a Stalath Corporation project.

He rarely left the state now although he owned and maintained a vast, sprawling, bluestone lodge in the mountains near Asheville; a fifteen-room apartment in New York City; the house in Coral Gables outside Miami. He laughed softly to himself thinking of Coral Gables.

It was a magnificent estate with its gardens, rare tropical flora, a hot-house and an aviary. He divided his time between Coral Gables and the Copa de Oro. It was the recollection of the Dade County commissioners which caused the chuckle. They thought he was crazy. The main highway was a half a mile or so away but he liked his privacy and the traffic sounds sometimes annoyed him. So, he had purchased all the land on the opposite side and spent two million dollars to have the road rerouted. It was, he thought, a damn sight better road than the State and County had built.

There was a light step on the balcony and he turned in his chair. Sharon Ward came toward him. As always, her beauty and the free, swinging stride delighted him. She was tall for a girl and her hair, a natural reddish-bronze, framed a face of surpassing loveliness. Sharon, he thought, must be about twenty-six now and she had been with him for seven years. He had gone to his offices in the Stalath Building, in Miami, one morning. Ordinarily he paid scant attention to the typists, file clerks and minor executives in the large central room. They were part of the complex machinery necessary to the corporation's operation; did their jobs from nine to five and then disappeared. He rarely entered this room and wasn't quite sure what prompted him to do so now. He looked about for a moment and realized he didn't know the name of a single person employed here. There was the briefest pause in the whisper of typewriters, the crisp sound of the IBM machines. Then the rhythm reasserted itself.

He walked down the middle aisle and the glint of sunlight on red hair caught his attention. A girl at a desk near a window was stapling documents together and placing them in indexed cardboard folders. Then she went to a file and put them in their proper slots. Watching her he caught himself wondering if this monotonous, stultifying routine occupied her full time. He went to stand beside her desk.

"That's a hell of a job."

"Yes, it is." She didn't add "sir" or "Mr. Lathrop" but there was no impertinence in her manner or the reply. "It's a hell of a job."

"If I were you I'm damned if I'd keep doing it."

She halted in the act of hitting the small lever of the stapling machine with the heel of her hand. Then, unhurriedly, she opened a drawer, took out her bag and stood up.

"You're right, Mr. Lathrop. I'm damned if I will. Good morning." She walked away.

He waited until she was halfway across the room and then yelled, much louder than was necessary.

"Hey! You! Come back here."

The hundred or more persons in the room froze at their tasks. There was not even a murmur of sound. If complete silence was possible, this was it. The girl halted, turned but made no move to obey the shouted command. She simply waited. It was a small contest of wills. He understood this, and also, that it was one in which he must come out second. She was poised but not arrogant; surprised but not defiant or alarmed. Finally, as he knew he would, he crossed toward her, hiding the smile threatening to break over his face.

"What's your name?"

"Sharon Ward."

"Well, Sharon Ward, you come along with me."

He touched her elbow with his hand, guiding her from the room. They went down the long corridor together, past the cubicles with their frosted glass partitions. Massive double doors opened upon a softly lighted, heavily carpeted reception room. He nodded to the trim young woman at a desk.

"Good morning."

"Good morning, Mr. Lathrop." She stood up.

His secretary, Madeline Perry, waited just inside the doors of his office. She was, as always, formally and efficiently correct, holding a pad of memoranda.

"Good morning, Mr. Lathrop."

"Good morning, Miss Perry. I don't want to be disturbed."

"Yes, sir." She left, closing the door.

The office, occupying a corner of the building with windows overlooking Biscayne Bay, was paneled in native cypress with dividing strips of dark, waxed cedar. Oatmeal-colored drapes fell from ceiling to floor. The furniture was comfortable, upholstered in soft, glove leather. The lighting was subdued. It was a room reflecting taste and an appreciation for beauty.

15 ★

"Sit down, Miss Ward."

She took a chair. It was deep and comfortable, made for lounging, but she sat with dignity; looking up to study him with an alert, and possibly amused, interest.

"Were you really going to walk out; quit, just like that?"

"Yes."

"Why?"

"Because, as you said, it's a hell of a job."

"Do you have another, something in mind?"

"No."

He sat on a corner of the desk, an unusual thing for him to do, and regarded her with a slight frown of perplexity. She was so completely self-assured. Was it a pose? He decided not.

"Tell me something about yourself."

"Do you mind if I smoke?"

"Yes!" It was sharply impatient.

The cigarettes, half out of her bag, were replaced without a trace of embarrassment.

"I'm nineteen years old. Born in New York. My parents live there. He, my father, is a minister in Yonkers. I finished high school and had a freshman year at Barnard College. I had to leave because we didn't have enough money to keep me there. I went to a secretarial school and came to Miami a year ago with a television show as a script girl. The producer kept making passes and I was tired of dodging. So, I quit. I've been working as a file clerk for Stalath for seven months. I type well, can take dictation fast and accurately. I can also spell."

"Would you like to work for me?"

"I was," the green eyes fired with humor, "or I did, until a few minutes ago."

"I mean for me not the Stalath Corporation."

"Is there a distinction?"

"Yes, although it may not seem so. Miss Perry has been with me for several years but the job has outgrown her capacity to absorb it. Anyhow, she is leaving next month to be married. I don't want to take someone from the secretarial pool because I'm pretty sure no one there would fit the position."

"What makes you think I will?"

"I don't know," he confessed, puzzled himself. "I honestly don't know. It's a hunch. I get them. They pay off." He slid from the desk. "Suppose you follow Miss Perry around for a week or so and get the feel of things here." He reached over and pressed a button on the intercommunication system.

"Yes, sir?" the voice replied immediately.

"I'm sending Miss Sharon Ward in to see you, Miss Perry. She'll be working for me after you leave. Show her what you can of the operations here. This will be a new position so I'll still need someone to take your place."

"Yes, sir." There was surprise and doubt in the statement. "I'll interview some applicants."

Sharon Ward stood up. "Thank you, Mr. Lathrop." She wasn't overawed by what had happened to her within the space of a few minutes.

"You haven't asked about salary."

"You'll pay me what I'm worth."

"Are you being deliberately impudent or is this your normal manner?"

"It hadn't occurred to me I was impudent, Mr. Lathrop. You offered me a position and I said thank you. You mentioned salary. I said you would pay me what I am worth. That makes sense to me. Certainly you're not going to pay me more than I'm worth."

"Or less?" He studied her quizzically.

"Or less. Why should you?"

"Do you know?" He went around and sat in his chair now, leaning back and putting his feet on the desk. "You are either going to have a job with me for the rest of your life or as long as you want it, or get fired the first week. I'm damned if I can tell you now which it will be."

"I think I'll be around, Mr. Lathrop. You see," a gamin's grin appeared, "I get hunches, also."

That was the way it had happened seven years ago. Since then she had become invaluable. The title *Secretary* meant little. Confidante. Companion. Aide. Friend. All were better words. She had two secretaries of her own and they were flown from the Miami offices to wherever they happened to be. He rarely had to give her instructions. It was enough, for the most part, to say: Take care of this. Handle it for me. You know what I'd do. She had never made a mistake in judgment of men or a situation. At Coral Gables she had her own suite in the big house. When he entertained, which was often, she was the hostess. When they were alone she was the best of all possible confidantes. She played a fair game of chess, was a tough opponent at gin rummy and made the best martini he had ever drunk. There was never any constraint between them. They were both well aware that the close association was a matter of whispered gossip. This amused him. Sometimes he almost wished it were true. Looking at her he caught himself wondering how it would be between them if he were forty, or even thirty, years younger.

Following her now was a white-coated houseboy carrying a frosted silver bucket. The neck of a champagne bottle was neatly wrapped in a napkin. Glasses were chilling with the wine.

"Hello." Sharon pulled a chair around for herself. "I thought maybe you'd spend the night in Nassau. Don't get up."

He had made no move to rise and her knuckles played across her lips to hide a smile.

"I wasn't going to. I'm seventy-one years old. You should stand when I come into a room. It's a matter of respect for your elders. Why don't you do it?"

"Good afternoon, sir." The boy placed the bucket between them.

"Afternoon, Manuel. Leave it there. I'll open it."

The boy left them and Lathrop reached over to give the bottle a twirl in its bed of ice.

Sharon lit a cigarette. "You make it pretty hard for anyone to remember you're seventy-one. As a matter of fact, if you weren't sure you didn't look or act seventy-one I don't think you'd ever admit to the age."

He grunted, knowing there was a little truth in what she said. There was a small vanity about the way he kept himself in shape. He played golf in the middle eighties and still walked the course. Actually, he never thought much about the years. Although, and this disturbed him a trifle, in her company, lately, he sometimes found himself measuring the span separating them.

"You usually make martinis. What's the champagne for?"

"It's my birthday."

"The hell it is?"

"Don't pretend you forgot or didn't know. You never remember anyhow. Let's open the booze."

She lay back, turning her face to the waning sun which still held a caressing warmth. Even in repose there was a suggestion of the vibrant, flashing quality of her youth. He stripped the foil from the bottle, untwisted the wire and eased the cork out with the faintest of whispers.

"There's a new car in your garage." He poured the wine. "A Rolls Silver Cloud. You once admired one. It's a birthday present."

"You're a fraud." She reached over to place her hand on his. "A fake, a phony who pretends he's without sentiment; who shouts, pounds the table, scaring most persons into doing what he wants. You even try it with me sometimes. Why?"

"Habit. Never give the other fellow a chance to yell first. It puts you on the defensive. Always get in the first lick." He sipped the wine appreciatively. "It's never worked with you, though. You don't scare worth a damn, never have."

This was the golden part of the day with the first indigo shadows beginning to creep upon the water. The sun moved toward the darkness of distant pines. A flight of ducks came down upon the Sound, skidding like water skiers on their webbed feet. Then they gathered into a small, bobbing knot. Watching them he could remember how, once long ago, the rivers would be covered from shore to shore with the waterfowl migrating South for the winter. The murmur of the ocean, now, came in a muted bass note and there was a magic spell upon the land.

"Why the hell don't you get married?" He broke the silence rudely.

"I suppose because I'm in love with you." The reply was so simply, so directly made it could not possibly carry a suggestion of banter. "I guess that's the reason."

"That's one hell of a thing to say."

"Yes, isn't it?"

"I don't know what I'd do without you." He refilled their glasses. "But it sure doesn't have a damn thing to do with love."

"I never assumed it did."

"Then why the hell did you say a crazy thing like that?"

"You asked a question. I answered it."

"You're young, beautiful, intelligent." He snorted his impatience. "Those things in a girl add up to the need for a man. Don't tell me you've never felt it."

"Of course I've felt it but I'm not frustrated. I don't lie awake at night with erotic fancies. I sleep fine and without disturbing dreams. When those things begin to get to me, I'll do something about them."

"You'll end up as a desiccated old maid. Then it will be too late. No one will want you."

"Oh, I don't know about that!" She was airily unconcerned. "You just don't read the right fiction. There's always a gardener's boy, a chauffeur or a groom around for the sex-starved spinster who has some money and influence. They're mostly in British novels for some reason. So, when I'm really dried-up maybe I'll go to England. Better still, since you're so interested, we'll go together. You can supply the money and influence. I'll say: Please, sir, Mr. Lathrop, will you buy me a fine, strong hostler's lad because I'm so desiccated." She threw back her head and shouted with laughter.

He eyed her sourly for a moment and then a slow smile responded to her gaiety. Often he wondered how she managed to combine the disciplined efficiency of her duties with a nature which seemed inherently mocking and insouciant.

"All right, but don't ever say I didn't try to warn you."

"I wouldn't think of it." They sat in companionable silence, both enjoying the brief interlude of twilight, sharing the best of all possible associations—that of complete understanding and the pleasure of knowing there was no need for words. It was he who spoke first and what he said was so completely irrelevant that she had to fight down a second burst of laughter. But from long experience she understood this was the way his mind worked. Even when he seemed relaxed it was restless, probing, searching constantly for new ideas for his limitless energy.

"Did you know more people eat ice cream than drink milk?"

"No."

"Well, they do. Barton and Tanner made a survey for me. So, do you know what I'm going to do?" He didn't wait for a reply. "I'm going to buy another dairy to go with the one I picked up in Homestead. Then I'm going to build an ice cream plant. Funny thing." He was momentarily puzzled. "People eat more chocolate ice cream than any other flavor. That was in the survey too."

"Get some chocolate-giving cows and you'll have it made."

He ignored the flippant remark. "Damn curious thing. That fellow Hershey, in Pennsylvania, who started making milk chocolate. He must have known what he was doing right from the start. There weren't any surveys in those days to tell him what people liked." He spoke, not with envy but only a small regret he hadn't been the one to think of milk chocolate first. "They never spent a penny advertising but the public bought it. All they had to say was: Give me a Hershey bar. Everyone knew what they meant. Hershey bar became part of the language. It might even be in the dictionary. Look it up for me sometime."

Despite his rambling musings she didn't doubt for one second he intended to add ice cream making to the already staggering number of enterprises carrying the name of Stalath Corporation. He was a juggler, constantly increasing the number of balls he kept in the air. Now and then he dropped one. When this happened he simply marked it off as a failure and selected a new sphere.

"Ought to have a good name." He had forgotten Hershey and was back to the ice cream. "Something rich, a thing people would like to say. It should create an image in their minds."

"Gold Cup." She tossed it off.

He squinted at her, frowned and then nodded with satisfaction. "I knew damn well there was a reason why I pay you twenty-five thousand dollars a year and all expenses. Gold Cup." He tasted the name. "That's it." He refilled their glasses. "Gold Cup Ice Cream. Hell, you can just see it in a dish; a big, yellow glob." He winked at her in pleased agreement.

"Even when it's chocolate," she teased.

"The flavor won't make a damn bit of difference. It's the picture they get in their mind, the idea. You always need a hinge to sell a product. Do you know something? When I was a boy all through the South people called Coca-Cola 'Dope.' They'd go into a fountain and say to the soda jerk: 'Give me a Dope.' It was whispered around that Coca-Cola had some sort of narcotic stimulant in it. I guess the word coca had something to do with it; like short, maybe, for cocaine. I don't know. Anyhow the idea, the picture, got into people's minds. It was the hinge and it sold Coca-Cola like hell and gone. Maybe someone real smart in the company started the rumor. If so he was a genius." There was an admiring tribute in the admission.

"How was it in Florida?" She always liked to listen when he was in a reminiscent humor. His memory was an incredible storehouse. "I mean, when you were a boy."

"Florida?" He half closed his eyes. "It was sort of ragged. I guess that's a good word; ragged, wild and wonderful before men started putting their hands on it."

"Men like you?"

"In a way you could say so, I guess." He wasn't offended. "It's still wonderful and beautiful but in a different way. Take this east coast. From Jacksonville there wasn't a damn thing but miles of pine flats, palmetto scrub and sand dunes all the way to St. Augustine. Then from St. Augustine the same thing. The scrub was like a great, motionless, heather-colored sea. There just wasn't any end to it. Henry Flagler did have his hotel at Ormond. He built a bridge across the river and ran his trains over it, right to the hotel so the guests wouldn't be inconvenienced. You could almost step from the railroad cars right into the lobby. I think he wanted to make Ormond another Palm Beach, which was just getting started. He had big wicker chairs and Negro boys to pedal them so the guests could enjoy the sea breeze without the effort of walking. Then there was nothing but tangle and scrub to Daytona and on down. Miles and miles of scrub palmetto, sand dunes and the sea oats growing on them with a heavy, gold color like great stands of wheat. There were a few small towns scattered along the mainland but almost nothing on the beach side. No one thought it was worth a damn. It's hard to figure out now. I've often wondered about it. Oh, people would go across the river to have a picnic on the beach and maybe go wading. But that was something they did for a day's outing. They built their homes on the mainland. Looking back, I think maybe they were afraid of the ocean. Most of the early people came from Ohio, Pennsylvania, the Midwest. They weren't used to anything bigger than a river or a lake. The Atlantic Ocean made them uneasy. It might just make up its mind some day to roll right over the dunes. So I guess they felt safer on the other side.

★　22

You could have probably bought all of Merrit Island for five or ten thousand dollars." He chuckled. "When I was a boy, Daytona was my home. There were really sort of three communities. Daytona on the mainland; then Daytona Beach, across the river with maybe a dozen cottages and a store or two. Then there was Seabreeze, kind of an extension of Daytona Beach. Seabreeze was sort of ultra, I guess you'd call it, with two big hotels, the Clarendon and Colonnades. I guess there was the Princess Isena there, too, at that time." He was reaching back into the years, trying to recapture time. "There was a real line of demarcation between Daytona and Daytona Beach. The folks living on the mainland didn't think the beach was quite respectable. That's why they made the distinction in names. Maybe it wasn't. The hotels in Seabreeze used to bring down their winter help, girls from Boston and New York, as waitresses. I tell you the sand of those dunes used to fly at night after the girls finished work. It was hard to walk without stepping on someone's back in the dark. It's hard to remember just when the beach began to lose its rakish character. There was a banker by the name of Conrad. He built a big house over there. I guess that changed everything. People said if it's all right for banker Conrad then it must be good enough for us. There's nothing like money to put a polish on a place." He rose, stretched and looked down at her. "I talk too damn much. It makes me remember how old I am." He put out his hand and she took it, rising lightly from the chair.

"I'd like to hear the whole story sometime."

"It would be hard to know where to begin." He dismissed the idea. "Have dinner with me tonight, downstairs. I'll meet you at the bar. Seven thirty."

They walked together down the balcony. Twilight had faded quickly. Now there was a scattering of lights across the Sound on the boats; small fireflies in the distance.

"You know something?" A sheepish smile appeared and was gone. "I'd like to say I came to Florida in an ox cart, hacking our way through the wilderness, beating off marauding Seminole Indians. It wasn't like that at all. I was seven years old and we came in one of Mr. Pullman's cars. How the hell can you have the story of a pioneer who rode in a Pullman?"

At the sliding glass doors of his apartment he released her hand,

23   ★

watched for a moment as she strode toward the opposite end of the wing to her own quarters. Then he sighed a little, envious of the buoyancy of spirit and body. One of these days she would get married and he didn't know how in the hell he would get along without her.

II

STODDARD had been his mother's family name and so, for reasons of pride, sentiment or vanity, he had been christened Stoddard Lathrop. Little thought was given to how a boy might be expected to bear up under the weight of such an unwieldy combination. Sometime in his first or second year, his father began calling him Tod. His mother employed the affectionate diminutive, Toddy. And, as he grew older this filled him with an unutterable nausea and he sometimes refused to answer, pretending he hadn't heard. Generally, though, Tod stuck and in time most persons forgot or ignored the Stoddard. In school, and later in college, he was Tod Lathrop.

Lately, and this he wryly put down to approaching senility, he caught himself thinking of his childhood; trying to resolve some of his very first recollections. These musings usually occurred at bedtime when he put aside whatever it was he had been reading and turned off the light. Then he would lie for awhile in the darkness and allow his mind to stray and rove where it would. Odd fragments gathered then but he could not always relate them to time.

He had been born in Rochester, New York. Of his home he remembered only that it had a bay window with a cushioned seat of faded red velvet. In the backyard there were some apple trees bearing a sour, dwarfed fruit. Dimly recalled was a period when he attended a kindergarten. Of this, one thing stood apart. For some reason it was considered a privilege and honor beyond measuring to pass out the small lunch boxes the children brought with them for the noon recess. If you were especially well behaved and did your crayon work neatly this distinction was accorded you to the envy of the others. There was, also, a small cottage set in a grove of trees on a high bank above Lake Ontario some twelve miles from Rochester. On the narrow beach a rowboat was tied and from this, on Sundays, his father fished. Sometimes he was taken along and permitted to dangle a line from a homemade pole. He couldn't remember ever having caught anything and went only because his father seemed to enjoy his company. He was restless, charged with a boundless energy. Sitting quietly in a boat became a mild form of torture. The real excitement came when the catch was cleaned on the cottage's narrow back porch with its cast-iron pump which always had to be primed with water from a can before it would draw. Under a saw-toothed knife the scales would fly like brilliant sequins in the sunlight. Then came the gutting of the fish; the slash down the belly and a mysterious combination of entrials drawn. Once his father extended a grayish-white handful.

"With certain variations, improvements and complications, Tod, this is what you look like inside here." A finger had poked at his belly to indicate the spot.

He had been quite certain his father was joking, but just the same, it gave him an uneasy feeling to think he might be stuffed with such a slimy mess.

Then there were the weekly oranges. Why should this custom be retained? He had no idea. His father brought a dozen home each Saturday and they were carried in a sack of slick, purple color. The fruit was a treat, made more so by the fact his father never failed to say:

"When I was a young man and went home to Florida, where your grandfather and grandmother live, for Christmas holiday, I used to pick oranges like this right off the trees. Oranges and we had bananas, also, but they weren't very good eating unless they were fried and sprinkled with brown sugar. One of these days we're all going down to Florida to live."

Tod was impressed by his father's feat of picking oranges right off the trees and the possibility of going to Florida; although he hadn't the slightest idea where or what it was. He could think of no appropriate comment. His mother, though, always murmured a sound of astonishment and quiet excitement.

"Do you really think we will, Dennis? Go to Florida sometime?"

"You bet we'll go. You can bet your bottom dollar on it."

It was an expression which his father used frequently and it never failed to mystify Tod. What was a bottom dollar? In the bathroom he often climbed on a chair, twisted about until he could examine himself in the mirror, and searched his buttocks for a *bottom dollar*. Maybe only grown-ups had them. He was disappointed and waited hopefully for the time when one would appear.

Dennis Lathrop was a lawyer and not a particularly good one. In his heart he knew why. He had no patience with the ritual of court, the wordy circumlocutions, the tangle of legalities through which one must hack his way in even the simplest of litigations. His intolerance of the stylized procedure frequently brought him into sharp conflict with the bench and he was always on the verge of being cited for contempt. When he thought about his career it was with a certain astonishment. Why had he decided to be a lawyer? He could find no valid reason beyond the fact that the Lathrops had always been lawyers, doctors or missionaries. It just hadn't occurred to him to break the pattern and he chose law as the least oppressive of the selection. None of the Lathrops had been able to make much money. The one exception was his father, a physician, who married the daughter of a wealthy Ohio merchant who dealt in feed and grain in addition to a substantial coal and coke operation near Cincinnati. After his wife came into her full inheritance he treated medicine as an avocation and, finally, gave it up entirely. It was his opinion that only an idiot would work when the necessity for making money no longer existed. Now he led a leisurely, sun-soaked life in Florida and found the world very good indeed.

Dennis Lathrop was a man of tremendous physical and mental energy and always gave the impression of being in a hurry. Despite his faults as an attorney he had built a fair practice in Rochester. He had his quirks, was far from brilliant, but he tore into every case with such animation and zeal that he frequently overwhelmed his opponents with the sheer force of his personality. The juries delighted in his histrionic exhibitions, considering them as performances for their especial benefit. Despite a moderate success he was never really happy in his profession. His nature demanded a conflict of body against body. He often imagined himself as an engineer, ripping tunnels through mountains, stringing bridges from peak to peak in the Andes and, perhaps, marrying an Incan princess. In college he had been on both the boxing and wrestling teams. They were elemental sports; the pitting of man against man appealed to him far more than a contest of minds.

Often of late he found himself inclined to uproot his life. Turn his back upon all familiar things and strike out in a new direction. Rochester was not the most pleasant place in which to live. The winters were bitter, marrow-chilling, the summers frequently unbearably oppressive. He was only thirty-two years old; still young enough to make a change. The Lathrops and Stoddards were among the town's first families. He was burdened with numberless relatives on both sides. They all took their relationship seriously with dreary dinners and mammoth gatherings at Christmas and Thanksgiving. And they all regarded Dennis as an oddity; never quite comfortable in his presence. He was given to heretical ideas and shocking blasphemies, refusing to take the law as a calling handed down from Heaven. He did not attend church, went fishing on Sunday, took off his coat and played baseball with the youngsters on the block. He had no patience with the family dinners. In his opinion, frequently and loudly voiced, they were damned dull affairs. The uncles, aunts and cousins gathered to talk of business conditions, the servant problem, the deplorable state of the Government. They ate themselves into a near stupor and then the men stretched out in chairs, couches and hammocks like so many gorged anacondas and slept the afternoon away. By God, he told himself, I will not become one of them! More and more he began to think of Florida.

The year was 1900. William McKinley was President. In New York the first electric automobile omnibus began operating on the Fifth Avenue Line, and the Chippewa Indians, in Minnesota, went on the war path. Flushed with his success at Manila, Admiral Dewey announced he would be a candidate for the Presidency, and Dr. Walter Reed was appointed to find out what caused yellow fever in Havana. His report that it was spread solely by a female mosquito occasioned some skepticism from his colleagues and a few indignant protests from the women, who considered the announcement a reflection on their sex. Laborers on the Croton Dam, in New York, struck for a wage of $1.50 a day, and troops were sent to preserve order. In San Francisco there was a mass meeting to extend the Chinese Exclusion Act to include the Japanese, and in St. Louis 2,000 "deputies" took over the operation of the streetcars. Throughout the country most persons of means brooded gloomily on the future.

One night, with the house silent, Dennis lay in bed beside his wife Alice. Abruptly he spoke of what had been on his mind for a long time.

"We're going to get the hell out of here."

"Please, Dennis," she whispered. "I do wish you wouldn't swear so much. Little Toddy is picking it up. Yesterday he said 'Goddamn that cat.' "

"Hell and God aren't swearing. Your minister talks about them every Sunday. Anyhow, did you hear what I said?"

"Yes, Dennis. You said we were going to get the hell out of here." She smothered an embarrassed giggle, pressing her face into his shoulder.

"We're going to Florida. I've always wanted to live there. Now I've made up my mind. To hell with this place."

She sat up, staring down at him incredulously. He really meant it. This was no longer idle talk.

"Florida." She repeated the word, making of it a wailing sound of dismay. "Florida is so far away, Dennis."

"Far away from what?"

"Why, far away from Rochester, the family, all our friends and the people we know."

"You're damn right it is." He made a popping sound of satisfaction with his lips. "It's about as far away as any place I can think of."

"But"—she was alarmed now over the idea of the impending uprooting—"it isn't really civilized and filled with savages, wild Indians, crocodiles; things like that."

"There aren't things like Indians or crocodiles," he corrected her. "They are either Indians or crocodiles or they are something else. Besides, what few, poor Indians we left all ran away to hide in a place called the Everglades. Maybe there are some alligators in the swamps. My mother and father have been living there for years. They still have their scalps and haven't lost a toe to an alligator. When I was at Columbia University I used to go down at vacation time. You'll like it. I promise." He stretched out an arm and gathered her to him.

"But," she was appalled, "our home here, everything we own, Toddy going to school now."

"There are schools in Florida. We can sell the house and ship the things you want to keep. I'm sick of Rochester, the people in it, my office and what I'm doing."

Stoddard Lathrop's recollection now of what actually happened was vague. It was a time, he remembered, of confusion. His mother frequently burst into tears. She walked about the house forlornly, patting the arm of a favorite chair or wistfully touching a sofa. All about them men came and went, hammering and sawing. Linens and china were packed and crated. The furniture was auctioned off in the front yard. Trunks were packed. There was noise and excitement for a boy of seven and he could barely wait for a day to begin to see what was going to happen next. His father whistled all the time, superintending everything, getting in everyone's way; laughing and joking with the workmen, stopping them to tell a funny story. Tod followed him about, proud of this boisterous, energetic man who had suddenly become wonderful and, somehow, different. It was almost like having a big brother instead of a parent.

Then came the train ride, the first leg of the long trip southward. From the engine the smoke poured in black clouds and whorls. Cinders flew against the window with the sound of scattering pebbles. The countryside raced past, and now and then Tod would catch a glimpse of other boys standing near the tracks and gazing with envy. The cars swayed and rumbled and he wondered what kept them on the rails at a curve.

Every hour or so a man, wearing a smudged white coat and carrying a tray suspended on a strap from his neck, came through their car selling fruit, candy and sandwiches. His father bought him a small box of soft, varicolored, gummy sweets. These, he explained gravely, were called Turkish Delight. The Sultans in a faraway place called Turkey fed them to their favorite houris.

"Dennis Lathrop." Even now he could remember the outraged tone of her voice, the mortified objection. "How can you say such a thing in front of a young boy? Suppose someone heard you?"

"Houri?" Lathrop deliberately repeated the word and louder this time. "A houri is a Mohammedan maid of paradise, a nymph. And," his eyes were filled with laughter, "I have no idea how a lady, such as yourself, gently reared, knows the other word which has a similar sound."

The exchange was completely mystifying to Tod. But sixty-five years later he could recall it vividly. His father's booming laughter while his mother hid her face in a wisp of a handkerchief and then pretended to stare fixedly out of the window.

New York City was overwhelming. Carriages, drays, streetcars, handcarts, and what must be a million persons, jostled and dodged each other in a scrambling confusion. The din was constant. Hand in hand Tod walked with his father up Broadway from Herald Square, past the theatres, hotels, amusement parlors and stores. He wondered where all the people went at night for there didn't seem to be any room for the houses he was accustomed to in Rochester. They stopped at the Claridge bar while his father had a whisky and filled a plate for Tod from the buffet of hams, turkey, sausages and cold meats. That afternoon they all went to a vaudeville show and later had supper in their hotel's dining room with its great crystal chandeliers, red carpets, and waiters in full dress suits. The hotel was on Fifth Avenue and his father said it was one of the most famous in the world.

"The Waldorf. You can always say you stopped at the Waldorf, Tod. It's something to remember. When you get older make it a rule never to go second class. If you can't afford first class, stay home."

The following day they boarded a second train. This time they rode in what his father said was a "sleeping car." He even called the porter to explain to the boy how the berths were made up at night.

As they traveled southward Dennis Lathrop spread an atlas on his lap and with a finger traced for Tod the route their train followed. Pennsylvania. "There is where they fought the battle of Gettysburg. Virginia. General Lee was a fine soldier but Grant was tougher and took Richmond. North Carolina. I can't remember exactly what happened there but over here is Tennessee. Your grandfather was there with Joe Hooker when they chased the Rebs off Lookout

Mountain." Tod had no idea who Joe Hooker was but from his father's emphatic tone of satisfaction it seemed as though Grandfather Lathrop and Joe Hooker assaulted and took the mountaintop by themselves. "Georgia," his father continued. "Sherman burned Atlanta and went to the sea. That was just about the end. When you're older in school and study history you can say you've been through all these places. Now"—he paused and then put a fingertip on a yellow-colored projection on the map—"this is Florida where we are going to live. If I'd had any sense we would have come down here long ago."

Jacksonville.

"They named it for Andy Jackson." His father seemed to know everything. "He was a real cutter that Andy Jackson. They call this town the Gateway to Florida and I guess it is."

They spent a day and a night in the hustling port city. Below it, down the peninsula, lay the scattered towns made possible by Henry Flagler's railroad. From 1890 Flagler had pushed steadily southward. At St. Augustine he had built the magnificent Ponce de Leon Hotel. It was an all but incredible structure of Moorish design with palm-girthed fountains, minarets, domes, spires, and colorful gardens covering six acres. Later Flagler was to extend his rails farther and farther, to Ormond, Daytona, Palm Beach, Miami, until they finally spanned the sea to reach Key West.

While his mother rested at the hotel Tod and his father strolled along Bay Street where the docks were piled high with casks of turpentine, resin, lumber. Coastwise steamers were moored at the piers alongside a few schooners. Young as he was Tod could sense a vitality here although he had no name for it. He and his father stopped to buy a paper of freshly boiled shrimps and sat on a stack of freshly cut pine, shelling and eating the sweet, pink-white morsels still warm from the boiling kettle. Beyond the docks the St. Johns River flowed darkly. A small ferry carried passengers, wagons and an occasional rig to the opposite shore. Here, backed by the heavy, massed bluish-green of the pines and the gray of live oak, a little settlement was strung along the shore. They were calling it South Jacksonville as though Jacksonville proper had already expanded to its full size.

"I come from haunt of coot and tern," Dennis Lathrop recited softly.

"What, Father?"

"Oh!" He was brought back to the moment. "It's part of a poem I learned a long time ago in school. Longfellow or Wordsworth, I think. Something about a river. I don't remember it too well. 'I come from haunt of coot and tern.' Those are waterfowl. Then there is something about making a sudden sally and trickling down a valley." He lit a cigar. The air was spiced with the odors of the river marsh, the smell of turpentine and resin oozing from newly sliced pine. Over the scene was the plaintive rhythm of the Negro work gangs as they loaded or unloaded cargo. "This is the St. Johns River. It flows through the lake country in the interior. We'll go and see it. I'm going to have time to do a lot of things I never could before." He stared at the current thoughtfully. "We'll do them together. I wish I knew more about boys of seven. I try to remember how it was with me at your age but I can't."

Tod wasn't at all certain what his father meant. What was there to know about boys? He'd like to be a man right now with a man's freedom.

"Maybe, down here, we'll have a chance to find out something about each other. It's going to be a different life for us all. I may not even practice law again. Right now I'm walking around stark-naked in a new world. Sooner or later I'll have to decide what kind of clothes I am going to wear. You don't know what the hell I'm talking about, do you?" An arm went affectionately around the hunched shoulders.

"No, sir." Tod was completely mystified.

"Maybe I don't either. It's like there was a well in me, bubbling over. I have to find a place to let it run. Do you know, I haven't seen my mother or father in ten years. They usually go to the mountains in North Carolina for the summer when it gets too hot here in Florida. I'll be getting to know them all over, too. Your grandfather, Willard Lathrop, is what you might call a character. Oh"—he recognized Tod's baffled expression—"he looks, walks and talks like other men but he really isn't one of them. He told me once he had to fight his way through school with boys who thought Willard was a la-de-da name and called him that. Every time he'd whip a boy he'd say, 'My name's Will Lathrop. Now, don't you forget it or I'll come back and do this all over again.' I guess they remembered because I never heard anyone call him anything but Will; even your grandmother."

"Did he beat Grandmother Lathrop, too?" This facet of his grand-father's character was interesting. "Is that why she calls him Will?"

"I'm not sure." His father laughed and wadded the damp paper poke into a ball, tossing it away. "But she calls him Will. So maybe he did at that in a nice sort of way." Dennis took off his hat, leaned back on one elbow and elevated his face into the sun's heat. His smile was one of pleasant reminiscence. "You'll find out about your grandfather in your own way. When I said he was a character I meant he just doesn't think like other people." He drew appreciatively on the cigar.

Tod covertly studied his father. This was a mood with which he was unfamiliar but it was nice here, just sitting and listening to him talk.

"You take how it was when he married your grandmother. All this, of course, I heard about and learned when I began to grow up. Your grandmother's father was very wealthy. I guess it was the first real money any of the Lathrops ever got close to. Now," there was pride in his voice, "most men, when they marry a girl with a fortune coming to her go to a hell of a lot of trouble to convince everyone they didn't court her for the money. They work themselves into a grave trying to match dollar for dollar. Or, they just turn into spine-less weaklings satisfied to take a handout. Not your Grandfather Will. Right from the start, I guess, he acted like the whole thing was his. I remember him telling me once there wasn't one goddamned thing money was good for except spending. He sure enough did that. When I was about four years old he packed us all up, took along a governess for me, and we went to Europe, traveling around for two years. He'd hire a private car and have it hooked on a train. Off we'd go. I wish I'd been old enough to know what was going on. My mother said it was all she could do to keep him from buying a palace in Italy. She got him home somehow but whenever the humor took him off we'd go again to whatever place took his fancy. I don't ever recall my mother objecting to anything he wanted to do. I guess he was the most exciting thing that ever happened to her and she never got over it." He stood up and reached a hand for Tod. "We ought to be getting back to the hotel. It's been a good afternoon."

Watching the Florida landscape as it unreeled before the train's window Tod experienced an acute sense of disappointment. From the things his mother had said he expected to see bands of naked, howling Seminole Indians beside the tracks, and the drainage creeks swarming with alligators and other fearsome creatures while monkeys capered through the trees. His father in his enthusiasm also had led him to believe Florida would be something out of the adventure books and every minute filled with excitement. To Tod's critical eye the stretch from Jacksonville southward didn't appear to be anything more than a continuation of South Carolina and Georgia. There were the same desolate reaches of heavy broom grass dotted with occasional bootjack palmettos, scrub with heavier stands of pine in the distance. Now and then a mirrored swamp flashed past. Here the cypress, gray as old men and with trailing beards of Spanish moss, reared on spindly roots in the dark waters. Buzzards rested on the withered limbs and now and then he caught a brief glimpse of a white crane feeding in the pools.

It was only when the train rumbled slowly over the bridge at Ormond, crossing the Halifax River to draw up before an enormous hotel with its wide, encircling porches and cupolas, that he was aware of a change. While the train was at a halt he and his father went outside, walking the length of the cars. There was a salty freshness in the air and the unmistakable throaty murmur of the ocean a quarter of a mile or so away. Here the oaks were huge and ancient, the magnolias tall with their leaves of polished green and creamy white blossoms. The gardens were brilliant in their color. They stopped to watch as a horse-drawn streetcar took on some of the hotel's guests for a trip to the beach. Other men and women rode in basketlike chairs pedaled from behind by Negro boys on a bicycle contrivance. On a section of the hotel grounds young ladies and men played croquet. They wore sports clothes suitable for the game. The women were in long white skirts and shirtwaists with sailor collars piped with red and blue. The men were dressed in trousers of white duck, blue coats and stiff straw boaters fastened by a black cord to the lapels of their jackets. Tod stared enviously at the spirited contests. Varnished mallets flashed in the sunlight and there were squeals of elation or dismay as wooden ball cracked upon wooden ball. This wasn't at all the primitive wilderness he had expected but it was, he admitted, different from anything he had seen before.

35　★

"The next stop is Daytona." His father could not hide his impatience as they boarded the train again. "I expect your grandfather will be waiting. We sent him a telegram from Jacksonville. The train is late but it always is. I wish I had asked him to drive up to meet us here. Then we could have taken the carriage back along the beach. That's really something to see. The sand is packed as hard as cement but the dunes are as white and soft as sifted flour. Daytona is about ten miles away and that's quite a drive to make up and back."

Tod noticed that even his mother was displaying signs of excitement. She smoothed nervously at her traveling suit of cocoa-colored light wool, adjusted the hat with its ornament of yellow-spotted bird's wing, tugged gently at her gloves. Her cheeks were flushed and her eyes bright.

Dennis Lathrop patted his wife's knee and winked at Tod as she brushed his hand away, embarrassed by such open familiarity.

"Your mother's behaving like a bride. She's never met my mother or father. You don't have to be afraid, Alice. They are quite civilized. They'll like you and you'll like them. Maybe my father will take a little getting used to. I guess he's what you call an individualist. There just aren't any rules for Will Lathrop. I wonder if he's changed much in ten years. Older, I mean," he amended. "I don't guess anything will ever change him." He seemed to take an honest satisfaction in the notion.

The porter had their bags in the vestibule and the conductor came through the car calling out Daytona as the next stop. Now the train was slowing but there was nothing outside to indicate they were near a town. Beside the tracks there was a wild, massed tangle of vines, trees and bushes with what looked like holly berries on them. The train ground to a halt before a small, mustard-yellow station. Then the porter was helping them down and they stepped to a narrow board platform.

Tod's first impression was of his grandmother. If he had wanted to describe her and knew the word he would have said she was regal. She was tall, stately and with an unassailable dignity. Where her hair peeked out from beneath her hat it was shimmering white.

"Alice, my dear." She embraced her daughter-in-law first and placed a reserved kiss on Alice Lathrop's cheek. "Dennis. How good it is to see you after this long time." Her fingers rested lightly but with affection on her son's arms as he kissed her. "This must be Tod." She gazed at him and her eyes were merry. "Don't squirm so, boy. I'm not going to kiss you." She offered her hand gravely. "It is so nice to see you all. We have been counting the days."

Then everyone seemed to be talking at once. Dennis pumped his father's hand and then hugged his shoulders. He presented Tod as though he were a grown-up.

"Tod. This is your Grandfather Will."

"How do you do, sir?"

"Tod, eh?" The voice was sharp and clear. "I wondered how you were going to get out of Stoddard. It's damn near as bad as Willard. I had many a bloody nose, I can tell you, before I got it changed to Will. You're a fine-looking boy. Manners, too."

Somehow, Tod had expected his grandfather to be a huge man of roaring voice and manner. Instead, he looked up into a suntanned face set with eyes of ice-blue which actually sparkled with glinting lights. He was slender with almost dainty hands and feet. A tiny, spade-shaped beard of grayish-white was carefully groomed at his chin. He wore an immaculate suit of white pongee silk with a curled-brim hat of soft Panama straw tilted slightly on his head. He carried a Malacca stick, tapping it now and then against his boot. Everything about him was perfection, from clothing to manner. When he spoke, his words were incisive but tempered with a modulated note. There was no affectation in any gesture or inflection. He was completely sure of himself and certain of his place in the world. He would be at ease in any company or surroundings.

A Negro man came up, taking off an old felt hat with a deferential bow.

"Mistuh Dennis, suh an' ma'm. Welcome home."

"It's Washington, isn't it?" Dennis smiled and offered his hand.

"Yessuh." The man shook hands proudly. "Ol' Wash don't change much wit th' year. Ef you got th' baggage check Ah'll see about loadin' th' trunks en things en th' waggin en bring 'em raight along to th' house."

Dennis passed him the claim checks. The Negro bobbed his head and left them.

Drawn up at the edge of the station's platform was a handsome barouche with a beautifully matched pair of roans in the harness. A coachman in full livery stood beside the carriage. His gray beaver top hat was sleek with brushing and a cockade of feather in it was a subdued red. He swept the hat off now in a stately bow.

"Welcome home, Mister Dennis, sir, and Madame."

"Hello, Mark." Dennis again offered his hand and it was taken by the Negro with a slightly embarrassed reluctance. "I'm glad to see nothing has changed in the ten years I've been away."

"No, sir." There was barely a trace of accent in the coachman's words. "Everything's the same 'cept, maybe, we're all ten years older."

Dennis assisted his mother and then Alice into the carriage. The two seats faced each other. He waited with Tod to follow his father.

"Can I ride in the wagon, please?" Tod made the plea eagerly.

Will Lathrop touched his goatee. "Well, now," he spoke with thoughtful gravity, "it is obvious you *can* ride in the wagon with Wash and the trunks. The real question is *may* you?"

"Yes, sir." Tod fidgeted unhappily. "That's what I meant. May I ride in the wagon?"

"That's better." The tip of the cane touched lightly at the boy's rear. "Always say what you mean. Be careless with money but not with words. Go on, run for it."

Tod raced back along the platform, down its length to where the trunks were being hauled on a hand truck.

"Mr. Washington," he was breathless, "Grandfather Will said I could—might ride with you."

"Who dat Mistuh Washington?" The big Negro looked around with pretended bewilderment. "Who he?"

"Why . . ." Tod was disconcerted. "Why, he's you."

"Ef hit's me den you bettuh jus' say Wash. Otherwise I don't know who you talk wid. Mistuh Washington." He grinned broadly and his laughter was a rich, throaty sound. "I don' 'collect anyone evuh cahl me Mistuh Washington befoah."

"Why not?" Tod fell in beside the man as the station helper pushed the truck toward an open bed wagon. "It's your name, isn't it?"

"Well . . ." The Negro scratched at his head. "Hit is an' hit ain't. Hit's Washington suah enough but hit ain' Mistuh. You cahl me Wash. We gits along fine, I kin see that. You a good boy."

When the trunks and hand baggage were loaded, Tod climbed up on the flat board seat. Wash picked up the reins and slapped them at the horse's rump. The road was of soft, sandy ruts sprinkled with brown pine needles and the small leaves of oak. It led upward in a long, gentle slope and on either side were lush meadows covered with white and purple violets. They turned right at the top of the ridge. Here the great oaks were so heavy of foliage they almost met in the topmost branches, forming a long, shaded arcade. There were few houses here and Tod began to wonder where the town began.

"Dey cahl dis heah th' ridge wood. Down yondah," he swept a hand to his left, "is the town. Hit's mostly strung out along th' rivah bank. Hit a real pretty rivah. You laik t' fish?"

"I don't know. Sometimes I used to go out with my father on the lake but it was mostly sitting in the boat. I never caught anything."

"Whin I gits th' time an' Mistuh Will give me leave I take you fishin'. You catch plenty. I promise. I heah Mistuh Will say you all goin' to stay heah from now on, maybe."

"I don't know." Tod's fascinated gaze followed two squirrels as they raced up a tree. "No one tells me much."

Wash laughed quietly. "No one don' tell me much eithuh 'cept Wash do dis, Wash do dat. Mistuh Will a fine man though. He gots yahd boys to do most of th' wuk 'roun' th' place en girls en th' house. He use Wash foah special thing laik dis, gittin' trunks en things. I hoped once he'd make me coachman laik dat Mark but I don' guess it evuh happen. Whin he's goin' huntin', though, he always take ol' Wash en leave dat uppity Mark behin'. I guess Ahm about th' bes' huntah heahabouts. Maybe Mistuh Will take you, too."

They were moving down the opposite slope from the ridge now. Here and there a small frame house stood within its grove of oleanders and live oak. The sun was warm and the breeze had the softness of his mother's hand when laid against his cheek. For a moment, through the trees, he caught the glint of light upon the water. Suddenly his heart was bursting with the excitement of everything and he wrapped his arms before him, hugging himself out of sheer delight.

III

NOW was the wonderful time of growing up; the discovery of Tod Lathrop as a person and an awareness of the world, its people and their relation to him and the things he did and thought. Here, on the shore of the broad Halifax River, the days unfolded like brightly colored scenes on a fan as it was opened pleat by pleat.

This was their third year in Florida and he was ten years old. At first, in this new land, he had missed the sharp division of the seasons as he had known them in New York State. There was no autumn with the trees undergoing their annual transformation into pillars of brown, gold-red and yellow leaves. Snow did not fall with the winter. Spring did not come with the breaking of ice in the creeks, the newly awakened rush of small streams unlocked after their months of imprisonment. There were, of course, changes. September and October with their rains of the equinox. November when the great bass ran in huge schools and sharp-toothed gales lashed the ocean into a frothing, roaring terror. It reared and mounted sending balls of spume tumbling along the beach until the wind tore them apart. Then the spring came unobtrusively with mulberries showing as green buds, the jessamine and honeysuckle spending their soft perfume on the air, the chinaberry trees filled with small, hard pellets which made fine ammunition for a slingshot or a catapult fashioned from a flexible splint of bamboo. Then came the long, glorious days of summer with no school and his world lay open for exploration and adventure.

Florida had yet to be discovered. It was regarded by Northerners as a privileged sanctuary for the wealthy who had their small colonies at St. Augustine, Ormond and Palm Beach. The rest of the state passed unnoticed. It lay dark and quietly mysterious with vast stretches of virgin pinelands and cypress swamps and mile upon mile of scrub palmetto covering the incredibly beautiful coast fronting the beach and ocean from Jacksonville to the town of Miami, which seemed to have no real reason for being other than serving as a terminus for Henry Flagler's railroad.

Daytona straggled along the river for no more than half a dozen blocks or so. It started at Volusia Avenue, the northern boundary, and ended, to all purposes, near Orange. It lapped over here with a small drugstore, a grocery and meat market and the Merchants Bank. This, it was generally agreed, was just about as far south as the town's limits would ever extend. The buildings were of frame construction. The one exception was the Merchants Bank. This had been built of native coquina rock—a pinkish-red shell stone quarried down around New Smyrna. There, also, were the miles of oyster-shell mounds built up over thousands of years by the land's earliest inhabitants, the pre-Columbian, prehistoric Indians. In using coquina for building, the bank's founders showed a rare wisdom. Standing out from the weathered storefronts the bright stone of its construction gave people confidence. It seemed proper for a bank to offer this protection for their money.

Beach Street, the little town's principal artery of traffic and trade, followed the river's line. It was paved with crushed oyster shell hauled in wagons from the New Smyrna mounds. When the ruts and holes made it all but impassable, a cart was driven along and Negro men dumped fresh shell into the depressions. These repairs were then hand rolled to smooth them with a heavy iron cylinder filled with water to give it added weight. Often the work was done by convicts in black and white striped prison clothes with a white guard standing nearby, Winchester cradled over one arm. The spectacle of the prisoners laboring was a titillating event, always drawing a crowd of boys and idling men who spent the day watching in the unspoken hope one would try to escape and be shot down by the red-faced deputy warden. It never happened. The laborers seemed happy at their work, singing and chanting in unison, glad to be away from the oppressive heat and swarming mosquitoes of the stockade inland.

The Lathrop home was set in a full block running south from Live Oak Street and bounded by Beach Street on the east and Palmetto Avenue on the west. Gigantic oaks and magnolias filled the tract. Sago palms, with their graceful drooping, were spaced about carefully tended flower beds. Wisteria, honeysuckle and the Cherokee rose grew in colorful profusion and the entire northern section was fenced in by massed oleander of pink and white.

Despite its designation as an avenue, Palmetto was little more than two sandy ruts with a few houses scattered on both sides. There was a whitewashed livery stable on the corner of Live Oak and Palmetto and the establishment provided Tod with hours of diversion. He was fascinated by the glowing forge and sometimes, when he was in a good humor, the blacksmith, Mr. Otis, allowed him to pump the bellows while he hammered and shaped the shoes for the fitting to the animals' hoofs. This was the moment for which Tod waited in excited apprehension: the setting of a red-hot metal shoe on a hoof; the sharp, acrid smell of burning callus, the sizzling sound as they were pressed and then nailed into place. He could never understand why the horse wasn't maddened by pain. Mr. Otis assured him the animal didn't feel a thing.

"It's like when you cut your toenail."

On Saturdays, when there was no school, Tod had certain rounds to make. First, there was the morning's visit to Mr. Otis. From there he went back to the river and walked uptown, balancing himself on the large boulders of coquina serving as a breakwater, leaping with a goatlike agility from stone to stone. At Orange Avenue there was a popcorn and peanut stand. It was really a wagon with its shafts still in place and the man who owned it, a Mr. Shad, came to Daytona each winter and parked his vehicle in the same place. He always arrived on the same date. Peanuts were roasted in a small oven fed by a kerosene burner. The corn whirled and burst into cotton like blossoms in a revolving, wire-meshed basket. He kept an enameled coffeepot filled with melted butter on a warming pan and always added an extra dollop of the golden fluid over Tod's nickel sack of corn.

They had a personal ritual which never varied. Tod would reach up to place his coin on the small counter.

"Good morning, Mr. Shad."

"Good morning, Mr. Lathrop, and what will it be this fine day?"

"A five-cent sack, please."

"You get more than twice as much for a dine. It's a real bargain you ought to take advantage of it."

"I only have a nickel to spare."

"Well, one of these days you'll have a dime. I guess that's the real reason I keep coming back here every winter."

While the corn was being scooped into a paper sack Tod would watch the spinning figure of a clown as it whirled on a pedestal driven by a cord belt attached to the rotating popper.

"How is your horse, Mr. Shad?"

"Well, he's just fine."

"Do you honestly drive him down from Pennsylvania every winter?" Tod had never seen the horse.

Mr. Shad would wink, holding the drooped eyelid for a long time. "Some say I do. Some say I don't. Here's the corn and don't get butter on your shirt. I appreciate your patronage, Mr. Lathrop."

The formalities and purchase concluded, Tod would go back to the seawall. It was harder to walk this way than it would have been on the unpaved path or the small boardwalks fronting some of the stores. But this made the journey far more entertaining. In the clear, shallow water small mullet, whiting, an occasional snapper, fed on the tiny, transparent shrimp. Along the shore hundreds of fiddler crabs played, hunted for food and dove into their holes, alarmed by his shadow. Fiddler crabs made fine bait for the sheepshead which could be caught with a handline around the barnacle-encrusted pilings of a dock. The eating habits of fish always puzzled Tod. Sheepshead liked fiddler crabs. The sea trout would only take a live shrimp. Snappers would strike at a dead shrimp or piece while a mullet wouldn't take anything on a hook. He often wondered how they had arrived at these decisions and preferences.

Near Volusia there was a small pergola, yellow with a red roof, set on the end of a short dock. If it was a real lucky day, John Van would be sitting there. The sight of John Van always sent a shiver of excitement down Tod's back. The man invariably appeared in the same dirty gray suit of roughly woven wool. He was indifferent to the temperature. His hair, uncombed, grew in lank strands to his shoulders. He carried a cane which was the steel rod of an umbrella with the ribs stripped away. When he spoke, and this was rarely, it was in a high, shrill, petulant voice. No one knew how he lived or on what he fed. No one really cared.

Driving uptown in the carriage one day with Grandfather Will, the man had told him a little something about John Van.

"They say," Will Lathrop took off his hat and leaned back against the cushion, gazing up at the sky, "John fornicated with a young colored girl. Do you know what that means?"

"No, sir."

"Well, never mind, you'll learn soon enough. Anyhow, he was a religious man and his conscience bothered him. He had sinned against the Lord. One day he took a knife and castrated himself. They say, although I don't understand how anyone could really know unless he was there, John just laid his private parts out on a tree stump, took a knife and: Whack! Off they came. It's a damned wonder he didn't bleed to death. He said an angel appeared and commanded him to do it. He's been the way he is ever since." Will Lathrop whistled softly. "If there's a moral there I guess it is that you shouldn't carry a pocket knife if you're going to screw a colored girl."

Usually when John appeared on the streets he was followed by a small gang of young boys who dogged his steps and chanted:

"John Van. The nutless man.
John Van the nutless man."

John would cut at them ineffectually with his cane and they would scatter with delighted yells only to re-form and continue their singsong rhyme until they tired of the sport. From this Tod learned what castration meant.

Tod, half fearfully, always spoke to John when he found the man seated in the pergola's shade.

"Good morning, Mr. Van."

Usually John refused to answer. He only stared with sad and vacant eyes. Once in awhile, though, he would wave his cane at Tod, beckoning him to come closer.

"Do you want to hear about my snake, boy? It's part of the terrible affliction the Lord put upon me."

"Yes, sir." Tod never went beyond the pergola's entrance, held back by some nameless fear and the man's wild appearance. "Yes, sir. I sure would." He had been told the story by John many times but it and the exhibition accompanying the tale never ceased to fascinate him.

"You're a good boy. I notice things. You never call after me like the others. So, I'll tell you about my misery and how it come about." The tired eyes took on a fresh, momentary light. "I was out in the backcountry one time. It was a hot day. About as hot as a man can stand it. I'll tell you I was thirsty. I come to this swamp and drank some of the water. Now, this is the real part, there was a little snake, no bigger than a piece of thread. I couldn't even see it when I scooped the water into my hands. I drank it and it stayed in my stomach. All these years it's been there, growing bigger and bigger. I can feel it now. It's beginning to move. It don't like to be talked about. There it goes." His eyes rolled back in his head and his body was convulsed in a spasm. "He thrashing around inside of me. Oh, he's wild today, I can tell you! There he is." The clawlike hands would knot and grasp, kneading at his belly, and then fix themselves, tightening. "I got him. I got him right now by the head." There was exulting triumph in the announcement. "He can't move an inch. I got him pinned down." The panting breath subsided, the insane light in the eyes flickered and died. "He'll be quiet now for awhile. Oh, I tell you! We have some terrible wrestles. Sometimes he throws me. Other times, like just now, I get him." The hands were flat now, the fingers motionless. A pathetic, vapid smile crossed the weathered features. "Now, go along, boy. I don't want to talk anymore." The cane would be raised menacingly and Tod would race away with tingling excitement.

If the pergola was empty Tod usually went inside to lean over and watch the big, blue crabs on the river bottom. With a piece of meat tied to a string you could catch a bucketful of crabs in half an hour. They'd fasten their claws to the meat and just hang there while being pulled from the water. Wash, though, had told him these river crabs were no good. The town's sewage flowed into the river here and they fed on it. The real good eating crabs could be netted down by the inlet where the ocean pushed into the river.

From the pergola Tod would cross Beach Street to his father's office. The door and windows were lettered in black and gold paint.

Dennis Lathrop—attorney at law
Real Estate

This was something Dennis Lathrop had talked over with his father shortly after their arrival. Sitting on the broad front porch overlooking the river, Will Lathrop had listened to his son's plans. He understood his discontent and also his determination to be independent.

"There's not much legal work here now, boy. Most disputes are settled out of court. Maybe in time, when people around here begin to scramble a little harder, snatching at this and that, you'll be able to build up a practice. But right now about the last thing Daytona needs is another lawyer." He studied Dennis. "I can feel something in you, son, a restlessness, discontent. What is it you really want to do?"

"Chop down trees. Level the earth. Change the shape of things." He made the statement unsmilingly.

"Those things make up a pretty strenuous occupation for a lawyer."

Dennis grinned at his father. "I guess I don't mean them literally. But, I look around. I'd like to do things with the land; develop it, have a part in making it grow. It's wide open. There's no limit to what can happen here once things start moving. Right now most persons think of Florida as a private preserve for a privileged few. It isn't so. Or, it won't be. A man with a small farm in Ohio could do better here with the same acreage. When he realizes this there will be one of the great migrations of the century. I want a part of it, the contest." There was no mistaking the enthusiasm.

"You're maybe twenty-five or thirty years ahead of your time, boy," Will Lathrop reflected. "I noticed you put 'Real Estate' on your office door. I suppose you want to trade in it. Right now there's so much vacant land in the state people give it away to their friends in the North so they'll come down and they'll have someone to talk with. There's not much buying and selling." He gave a short laugh, almost of embarrassment. "I own maybe a couple of miles over there on the beach side and damned if I'm sure why I bought it. It's not all in one piece, you understand, but scattered along in tracts all the way to the inlet. It runs in sections and quarter sections right across the peninsula from ocean to river and there isn't a damn thing on it but scrub palmetto, stunted pine and brambles. The taxes don't amount to anything so I just keep it." He lit a cigar and watched the blue smoke spiral upward. "You know something? You ought to have married money the way I did. It's the best way I know how to get it."

"It isn't just the money," Dennis objected.

"Well, it damned well ought to be. Money is a handy thing. I'm always suspicious of someone who says he doesn't care about it."

"Of course I care about it." Dennis was almost angry. His father didn't or wouldn't understand. "But I want to make it in a certain way and that way isn't in the courtroom. This I'm sure of."

"That relieves me some." There was a hint of laughter in Will Lathrop's voice. "Once you have it it's fine to say it doesn't mean anything. People will almost believe you."

Dennis smiled. He knew his father meant exactly what he said. Long ago his mother, Felicia, had half humorously resigned herself to the ebullient irresponsibility of Will Lathrop. Despite a most conservative upbringing she had slowly reached some of the conclusions held by her husband. Money was for spending. It was to have fun with. It made possible a gracious way of life and provided a key for almost everything. Most of her fortune was in sound investments, made by her father. The dividends were more than sufficient for their needs. They lived well. She was happy in her marriage. Will Lathrop was different from any man she had ever known. When he decided to be particularly extravagant—a trip around the world, a shallow-draft houseboat, fitted with every known luxury, with which to cruise up and down the river, the hunting lodge in North Carolina, a stud farm in Kentucky or whatever struck his fancy—they simply sold off some of the holdings to pay for these things. They shared a pleasure in the acquisition and the pride of having something beautiful. The philosophy kept them both young and vital and dismayed the banks and financial advisers.

Shortly after Dennis, Alice and Tod arrived in Daytona, Will Lathrop took his son into his "den." This, Dennis thought, was as weird a room as the imagination of man could conceive. The walls were hung with the most exquisite of Oriental brocades and ornamented with crossed scimitars, antique Saracen swords, knives and

47 ★

shields. Incredibly beautiful Turkish rugs were scattered about the floor and there were rare incense burners of engraved copper inlaid with silver. Instead of chairs there were cushions and divans and Arabian hookahs, the bottlelike pipes with the smoke drawn through water by flexible tubes.

"Isn't this the damnedest place you ever saw?" Will motioned with one hand to indicate the room. "I bought all this stuff when your mother and I were in Constantinople and had it shipped back."

"All it needs are a few harem girls."

"I thought about that," Will admitted. "But, although Felicia is a woman of rare understanding, I had an idea it would upset things. Sit down." He motioned to one of the couches. "I think we ought to have a talk."

"Don't you put on a fez when you're in here?"

"Hell yes." Will opened a cabinet and took out two tasseled caps. He tossed one to Dennis and cocked the other at a rakish angle on his head. Then he went to another cabinet and brought back a bottle of whisky and two glasses. "The only trouble with these divans is you have to learn to drink lying down. Of course, you can sit on the edge but the position is more Occidental than Oriental."

"I'll sit." Dennis accepted the liquor.

"You want to try one of those pipes or a cigar?"

"A cigar. You be the pasha."

"I never really use them. They bubble and gurgle, disturbing my meditations. The Turks manage them. I met a couple of princes in Turkey. They showed me how it was done but maybe their meditations are different from mine. Now," he settled himself with the decanter in easy reach between them, "there is something we ought to have straight between us."

Dennis said nothing, knowing it wasn't expected of him. He watched his father with a bright interest. Will Lathrop turned the glass in delicate fingers.

"I've never held with doing things the hard way, son. I don't believe a wealthy man's children should make their own way simply as a test of character. I have very little character as most persons understand the word. As a result I have been a completely happy man. I have even corrupted your mother to a certain extent. Character, overemphasized, is quite likely to ruin an otherwise good man and

★ 48

pleasant companion. I let you alone while you were in Rochester because I had an idea that was what you wanted. But you're here now of your own choice and things will be different. I want you to take an allowance from Felicia and me; whatever you need to live well. There's that small house down on the corner of Live Oak and Palmetto. I had it built just in case. It's yours. We'll fix it over if you like. You, Alice and Tod move into it. It's better if relatives don't see too much of each other. Your mother and I will deed the property and building over to you. Now," impatiently he waved aside the protest he could see forming in Dennis's mind by the set expression on his face, "don't make an ass of yourself with some nonsensical idea of pride. It's family money and we'll damn well use it as such. This is a small community so if you are concerned about what people might say or think, we'll make a monthly or quarterly deposit to your account in Rochester. You can draw from it and open an account here in the Merchants Bank. So far as anyone knows it's yours. You made it and need help from no one. Does that satisfy you?"

"It's generous of you."

"Generous? Hell, boy. You're my son. I'm proud of you. When things pick up and you no longer need any help we'll cut it off if that's what you'd like. In the meanwhile ride with the current." The eyes brightened. "You know something? At the rate I'm going I may not leave much more than burying money behind when I go so take what you can now."

This had been the arrangement and none of them ever mentioned it again. Dennis had built a small practice but his income from it would not have supported them. In his spare time, and of this he had plenty, he would study the wall map of Florida. It was an extravagant piece of cartography and had been made to order by a firm in New York City. It was in relief and he liked to run his fingers over it, tracing the ridged spine running down the state's center; following the indentations and depressions on both coasts; marking the Keys as they stretched out from south of Miami. He would half close his eyes and try to visualize how Florida would look once its full potentialities were recognized. There was something here for everyone. It need not be a haven for the wealthy but a home for the many. He was stirred by a magnificent conception; made impatient by what he felt certain must happen here, wondering why so few men with capital and pioneer spirit refused to see the opportunity. Two or three northern capitalists were making tentative, probing explorations, guided more by instinct than facts. They sensed what would eventually develop in this all but virgin state. They recognized that the first need was for transportation. The people would come later. A small steamship line was operating on the St. Johns and another on the Indian River between Titusville and Jupiter. Hamilton Disston, who had made a fortune manufacturing saws in Philadelphia, bought four million acres of swamp and overflow land for twenty-five cents an acre. Through this wild territory he began a system of navigable canals which would connect with a railhead at Kissimmee, on Lake Tohopekaliga, and service ports on the Gulf of Mexico. He had even imported side-wheel Mississippi River boats to ply his inland waterways.

Henry Flagler kept pushing his Florida East Coast Railroad farther and farther south. Henry Plant, with his reorganized Savannah, Florida and Western Railroad, was thrusting across the state from Waycross and Jacksonville to Tampa and the Gulf towns. Dennis enviously studied the activities of these men and understood well what they were doing. Plant, for instance, had purchased a state charter for $30,000 with the intention of building a rail line from Kissimmee to Tampa, a distance of seventy-five miles. He was granted 5,000 acres of land along the right of way for every mile of track and in this manner picked up three hundred and seventy-five thousand acres of fertile, heavily timbered grazing and farming property whose potential was almost beyond imagining.

It was the knowledge of these things which so frequently brought Dennis Lathrop to stand dreaming before the map. Here a giant lay sleeping. He wanted to help shake it awake. It had become an obsession. First, though, he wanted to see some of this state himself. It would have to be done a little at a time but he would do it.

One of Tod's way stops on his Saturday ramble was his father's office on the corner of Volusia Avenue. He left the pergola's dock now and crossed Beach Street, pretending to tie his shoe in front of the pool room. This was a place of sinister mystery, or so it seemed. His mother had declared it to be off limits to him. "It is," she said firmly, "a place of low characters and I don't want you loitering around it." Tod tried to fix these "low characters" in his mind but they only seemed to be very ordinary men; the ones he saw almost every day on the streets, driving their wagons into town, working in the stores. Once inside, though, moving through the haze of tobacco smoke, chalking their cues, leaning to make a shot on the green felt tables, they were assumed to achieve a dissolute nature and be filled with iniquity. This, of course, gave the place a fascination and Tod never missed an opportunity to peek in. He yearned for the day when he would be old enough to walk in boldly, select a cue from a rack and set the colored balls clicking. He might even be able to wear the frilled pink or red elastic bands to hold his sleeves and keep the cuffs from becoming soiled.

Reluctantly he straightened up and walked toward his father's office. Despite a few shouts of triumph or a mumbled curse nothing really seemed to happen in the pool room. He was optimistic, though, and never failed to slow his step when passing in the hope that something violent and dramatic would occur.

His father was standing before the big map covering half of one wall. He turned at Tod's entrance and smiled a welcome.

"Watchman, what of the night?"

"All's well, sir. But I'm the day watchman."

This had become a standard greeting when Tod visited on Saturday. Sometimes, when Dennis had nothing to do, he and Tod would have lunch at a small restaurant run by a Greek gentleman by the name of Demos who always gave Tod an extra large slice of lemon pie for dessert.

"Have you covered the waterfront and sought out the pirates?"

"Yes, sir."

"Good." Dennis pulled a chair before the map so Tod could stand on it and have eyes level with his. "I had a talk with your teacher Miss Simms this morning."

"Yes, sir." The reply was dubiously voiced. Tod wondered what he had done now.

"She told me you were the brightest pupil in the class and really should be in a higher grade. She is going to speak to Principal Weaver and have you moved ahead after the Christmas vacation."

Tod supposed this was good and his father pleased but he decided to say nothing. It was better to hear what his father had in mind. Parents could be pretty tricky sometimes.

"I asked her," Dennis Lathrop kept his gaze on the map, "if it would do any harm to take you out of school for, maybe, three weeks before the Christmas holidays. She said no. You are so far ahead of the class it wouldn't make any difference. So," an affectionate hand rested on the boy's shoulder, "how would you like to make a trip with me; a sort of camping, exploring trip? We could start Monday and have a month or so before coming back home for Christmas."

"I'd like it fine." Tod's eyes were shining with excitement. "Would we really camp out, sleeping in a tent at night with a fire and all?"

"Yes, sir. We'd really camp. Just a couple of explorers. I've been thinking about it for a long time. We'd have to go in the winter. The mosquitoes are too bad during the summer. December would be the best month of all. That's why I spoke to Miss Simms. I want you to go with me. It's something we should do together. We'll take that flat bed wagon of Grandfather Will's. Washington will come along and bring his bird dog. We'll shoot quail, rabbits and maybe even a turkey and cook them over the fire. I'll buy you a .22-caliber rifle and you can learn to shoot. We could have a fine time together and see a lot of things I want to look at."

"Will Mother let me go?" Tod was doubtful. The idea was too magnificent to accept.

"Yes. I've talked it over with her. She thinks it would be a fine thing for us both. Now," he put a pencil on the map, "here is where we'd go." He moved the pencil. "Over to DeLand first, then down to Lake Monroe. There's a town there, Sanford. We'll look around and find us a good camping spot on the lake. Then," the pencil moved again, "we'll come across to New Smyrna and then back up to Daytona. If we had the time I'd like to hire a boat and go down Lake Monroe to Lake Harney with Wash following us in the wagon. But," his regret was apparent, "we'd never be able to make it in time. In a lot of places there won't even be a road. Your mother wouldn't forgive us if we weren't home for Christmas. She and the Pope take it pretty seriously."

"When can I get my rifle?" Tod jumped down from the chair. The map, the irregular triangle his father had drawn, such names as De-Land, Sanford, Lake Monroe, meant nothing. The rifle was something real. "Could we get it today?"

Dennis shook his head with mock resignation. "I'm afraid you don't have the proper imagination for an explorer. You should be interested in the things to see, places to discover. Why, we could come across stretches of country where, maybe, no white man ever crossed before."

"Well then, I'll sure need that rifle." Tod was not going to have the opportunity brushed off so casually. "There might even be Indians."

Dennis Lathrop looked at his watch and then snapped the case closed. "It's lunchtime. We'll go home today. Wash was going to pick up some smoked mullet I ordered. If there is anything I like for lunch it's smoked mullet."

Outside, they stood looking at the wide sweep of the river. Pelicans cruised up and down, gulls fought in screaming flight over small fish. The Halifax was actually a lagoon, falling and rising with the ocean's tide as it surged through the inlet some twelve miles to the south. Farther to the north, above Ormond, the Tomoka River emptied into the Halifax and the water there was fresh. Here it was salt. The beach side shore was solidly green with massed oak, bay, cedar and magnolia trees. Save for the Gamble house down by the bridge and one or two widely spaced toward the north, the river frontage was without habitation.

"One of these days that shore over there will be built up. Take my word for it. No one believes me. They all think it is only a place to go for a picnic. The beach is for a summer cottage. Wait until the people from the North discover what is there. Then you'll see the damnedest boom in real estate anyone can imagine."

"We could stop in at Dunn Brothers hardware store on the way home and look at some rifles." Tod made the suggestion casually.

"Yes, I suppose so." Reluctantly Dennis turned away from the river. "I sure hate to see a man with a single-track mind." He ruffled Tod's hair. "Here I'm trying to show you a vision and all you think about is a rifle."

They bought the .22 at Dunn Brothers. It was a single-shot Remington with a bolt action. Tod's hand caressed the blue sheen of the steel. With the rifle Dennis purchased a dozen boxes of ammunition and Mr. Dunn threw in some cardboard targets. Tod gazed enviously at the racked shotguns. One of these days he'd be old enough for those. But now, this rifle was his very own. Mr. Dunn offered to have his initials burned into the stock but Tod was reluctant to let it out of his hands for even a few minutes. The initials could wait.

They walked home together in the warm winter's sunlight. Daytona was a pleasant friendly town of less than two thousand persons. Almost everyone knew everyone else. Most of the stores had corrugated metal overhangs with a bench or two set in the shade. Here the shoppers could rest and gossip. Between the buildings there were many vacant spaces. Here the boardwalks ended and there was only deep sand to walk through until the next building was reached. Ordinarily this would be the finishing half circuit of Tod's weekly inspection tour and he would stop to talk with Mr. Oyama, a Japanese who ran a curio store. This was a place of wonders with incense pots, joss sticks, Oriental fans, silk kimonos and lacquered boxes which fitted into each other growing smaller and smaller as they were taken out until the last was no larger than a fingernail. Sometimes, Mr. Oyama would make him a present of an envelope filled with tiny pieces of wood. When dropped into a saucer filled with water they opened into many-shaped and colored flowers. Mr. Oyama bowed politely and admired Tod's rifle.

A few doors farther down, Mr. Wallace, who also had a souvenir store, stopped them to comment on the .22. Ordinarily, Mr. Wallace was a gruff, unsmiling man and so his interest was all the more gratifying. Mr. Wallace's son, Bob, was in the same grade with Tod and they frequently played and fished together. Bob Wallace occupied a high place of interest because if you were his friend, he would take you back of the store where his father kept a pen filled with live alligators. The few winter tourists who came to the store were always shown the ugly beasts and then Mr. Wallace sold them alligator belts, purses and wallets. The alligators stank but they stimulated business. Mr. Maley, who had a furniture store next to the Wallace shop, was always complaining about the odor. He said it got into the upholstery of his sofas and chairs, even the mattresses and pillows. He was always threatening to sue Mr. Wallace but they were both members of the Elks Lodge and so nothing ever came of the dispute.

The final stop was Shank's ice cream and candy parlor. Mr. Shanks made taffy, molasses, chocolate, peppermint and strawberry. It was poured into large, flat pans and broken into pieces with a wooden mallet. Dennis always brought a pound home on Saturday and when Tod accompanied him, Mr. Shanks threw in a candy corn biscuit as a special bonus.

All in all it was the most wonderful of days in the most wonderful of worlds. The rifle caught the sun's light and threw it back. Tod was quite certain he would never want anything more as long as he lived. Shyly, because he was almost grown now and too old for such things, Tod slipped his hand into his father's, clinging to it with proud confidence. The man glanced down with a faint smile and a little envy. To be ten years of age and with the privilege of being a boy in Florida at this time.

"After lunch and I take a little nap we'll go over to the beach and put up a target against a sand dune. We'll find out just what sort of a shot you are and companion on an exploring trip."

"We could go up to the ridge wood and shoot at squirrels." Tod voiced the suggestion hopefully.

"I never really liked killing for the sake of killing. If you need a squirrel, a rabbit, or even a deer, for food it's different. You think about it."

"Yes, sir."

Tod thought about it but his father would have been surprised at the turn of his thoughts. In Tod's mind he was an unfailing marksman. A frisking squirrel high in an oak tree was fair game. That was what a rifle was for.

IV

THE road wandered like some drunken straggler, seemingly without purpose or destination. It was more trail than highway. Two deep ruts were worn into the grainy soil. They were humped in the middle with clumps of tough wire grass and, now and then, a bouquet of pink phlox, and curled westward from Daytona to the town of DeLand some twenty miles away. In the sandy troughs the flat bed wagon rolled as gently as a boat in a light sea.

Once beyond a small elevation, a hill of coarse, red soil known as Mount Ararat, the flatlands stretched to the horizon, unbroken by a cabin or plot in cultivation. Here was the emptiness, spotted only by clumps of palmetto, islands of pine and brief patches of marsh where the reeds grew tall and brown in color. The uniformity wearied the mind after awhile. But seen through the eyes of a ten-year-old boy it had a bright enchantment, filled with mystery and surprise.

Seated between his father and Wash, Tod experienced the wonder of what seemed to be vast distances. His gaze roved constantly, missing nothing from the high, wheeling buzzards in a cloudless sky, a rabbit bounding in fancied terror, a gopher, the Florida land turtle, ambling unhurriedly across their path, to the flashing scatter of redwing blackbirds disturbed at their feeding by the passing wagon. For the first few miles Washington's hound coursed eagerly from side to side, giving tongue in a hoarse pleasure when it bumblingly flushed out a covey of quail or followed a small animal's scent. Wearied now, it lay panting in the back of the vehicle, its tongue lolling wetly, muzzle between paws, eyes closed.

They had started late. The sun was well past the meridian. In the slanting light the brown scales of the pines took on the color of polished copper and the scrub appeared to have been dusted with a silver powder.

"When you find a good place, Wash"—Dennis pushed an old straw hat down over his eyes to shade them—"we'll pull off and make a camp for the night."

"Yessuh. We find us a stand o' pine an' maybe," he glanced back at the hound, "Ol' Useful theah kin run us down some birds foah suppah. Oah, likely, we could catch us some brim in one of these ponds. Ain' nothin' much bettah than brim fried crisp wid grits en th' side."

"What's a brim?" Tod had never heard the word and wanted to miss nothing.

"It's a small freshwater fish. Bream." Dennis corrected Wash's pronunciation. "Some people call them sunfish. They are good eating. I remember when I used to come home from college Wash and I would come out to the lake around Mount Ararat and catch them."

"Yessuh." Wash accepted the correction amiably. "You ought to learn correct, Mistuh Tod. Bream, laik youah daddy say. Mistuh Will's always tellin' me: Damn hit, Washington, hit's bream not brim. White folks cahl 'em bream. Nigger cahl 'em brim. Same fish, though, en good eatin' no mattuh how they cahl."

This was something else Tod couldn't quite understand. Grandfather Will had been emphatic on the subject after he heard Tod use the word. "Call a colored man a Negro, boy. Not nigger." Yet, he constantly heard Wash and the other servants call each other nigger and no one was offended or made angry. He was puzzled by the contradiction.

"Useful is a funny name for a dog, Wash." He looked up at the big man.

Washington chuckled. "Ah used to cahl 'im Duke but seemed laik everahone else had a dog cahled Duke. Then I discovah he got a lot o' talents. Now, some dog only do one thing. Useful, theah, do lots. He tree a coon foah you. Run a rabbit. Bark at stranguh en th' naight.

57 *

Chase a cow. Come to a point on birds. You want to git rid o' somethin' give hit to Useful. If he can't eat hit he'll bury hit foah you. Yessuh, he gots lots o' talents so I stahted to cahl 'im Useful 'cause that's what he is."

They drove for perhaps an hour more, the horse drawing the light wagon at an easy, rambling pace. The wheels turned without sound in the bed of powdery sand. There were occasional swamps now, rimmed with small, pink flowers and the cypress motionless in the reflecting water.

"I cum ovah heah wit Mistuh Will onct." Wash offered the information as conversation to break the monotony. "Hit good bird country en Mistuh Will used to be a fine man foah shootin'. He don' go out much no moah. Ennyhow, theah convic' camp three oah foah mile up th' road from heah. Th' county rent out the men foah timbuhin' en turpentine tappin', mekkin' road oah whatevah th' white people gots foah them to do. Mistuh Will stop theah while he talk wit warden. Seem laik he wan' some boys to cleah up th' scrub to property he own en th' beach. Ahl them nigger yell en whoop at me, sayin': Hey! You, boy. What th' hell you doin' ridin' aroun' en a fiahn rig laik dat? You come on en heah wit us. Then they laugh laik crazy en' I 'spect they ah. En' th' summahtime this maybe the worst mosquito country theah is. Out heah you don' slap at 'em. They's so thick you kin jus' wipe 'em off youah ahm by th' han'ful. Whooee! I suah wouldn' wan' to be in no chain out heah."

Dennis knew peonage was a common practice in Florida. The County Sheriff and the camp wardens rented out their prisoners to individuals and pocketed the money. Very few persons seemed interested enough to object. He was, though, a little shocked by the knowledge his father was a party to the outrage.

"A nigger from up Georgia way," Wash continued, "tol' me onct that ef a man take a wad of turpentine gum from a blazed tree en chew it th' smell git en theah blood en come out en theah skin. Mosquito don' laik th' smell en stay away."

"Is that true, Father?" Tod was interested in this valuable information.

"I guess if a man from up Georgia says so it must be."

"Well, ennyhow, that's what I heah." Wash was mildly skeptical. "We git mosquito to home durin' th' summah but whin hit come seem laik I nevah have me no turpentine gum. But hit's somethin' to remumbuh ef you evah git caught en a swamp. Hit could save youah life, likely. That theah look laik a good place foah th' naight, Mistuh Dennis." He pointed toward a small knoll ringed with tall, longleaf pine. "Hit dry en we rake up them pine needle foah a mattress undah th' blankit."

They made a camp quickly. Wash led the horse from the shafts and tethered him at the knoll's edge where the grass could be easily cropped within the radius of the rope. They had brought sacked oats for the animal in case they camped where fodder was scarce. In Tod's eyes Wash was the repository of all outdoor wisdom and he followed him as the man went about the work, humming contentedly as he laid out the things they would need for the night. He opened a canvas chair for Dennis, then, with the help of Tod's eager but sometimes clumsy hands, stretched a clothesline between two young pines. A tarpaulin was slanted from this and pegged to the ground to make a lean-to. Then, a short distance away, he set up a similar shelter for himself.

"Whin I git th' time," he spoke to Tod, "I show you how to make a thatch lean-to wit some vine an' scrub palmetto fan. Hit a good thing to know en easy to do onct you got th' knack. Now," he glanced about the small clearing where the brown pine needles made a thick carpet, "we catch us some fiah wood foah th' naight. Then, ef youah daddy say so, we see about them bird foah suppah."

With Wash shouldering the ax and Tod carrying his rifle in case they were attacked by savages or wild beasts they walked through the light brush until they came to a fallen pine. The Negro lopped off small branches first for kindling and then cut into heavier limbs.

"Fatwood pine, make a fahn, fas' fiah," he explained, "but hit don' las' en ain' much good foah cookin' ovah. We fin' us some oak what burn down slow en leave a good bed o' coal. Lay the oak raight en hit burn ahl naight foah you."

"Are there any bears, wildcats, things like that out here?" Tod looked about and held the prized rifle at his chest."

"Some hog, maybe." Wash laughed with sudden pleasure. "Mistuh Will tell me a funny thing about the hog. Some of th' hog run wild, razorback they call 'em. Well, hit seem laik whinevah a man feel laik havin' hissef some pork he go to th' wood en' shoot hissef a razorback. Only," he laid a finger alongside his nose and winked, "they ain' always wild hog but belong to some farmah neahby. So, they drug each oather ento court en one man say 'bout th' oather: Judge, suh, this man shoot my hog. The oather man say: Ah think hit a wild, razorback hog, Judge. How I know hit belong to someone? So, you know what Mistuh Will tell me? He say th' State Legislatuh pass a law en th' law say they ain' no moah such thing as wild, razorback hog. Ahl hog belong to someone en ef you shoot one you kin get drug into court en mek to pay a fine oah go to jail. Jus' laik that they 'bolish ahl wild hog en Florida." He shouted with happy laughter, tickled by the devious workings of the law.

When the wood—pine and oak—was piled in the clearing Wash glanced up at the sky. There were a couple of hours before sunset and in the hush the birds would soon begin to leave their feeding grounds for the nesting places. Long streaks of indigo-colored clouds were beginning to draw themselves out along the western horizon.

"Mistuh Dennis. Ef you laik, we maybe kin git us some bird, dove en quail, foah suppah?"

"All right, Wash." Dennis Lathrop replied absently but remained seated. He had been in deep thought, trying to look far ahead into the years. All of this land, the great, empty spaces. Millions and millions of acres spread untenanted up and down and across the state. It waited for the clearing, the plow, the farmer and builder, the hand of man upon it. In his mind there had slowly grown an idea. It was amorphous, difficult to put together. But as he mused it began to take a vague shape. It was something no one had ever attempted here or, as far as he knew, any other place: a planned community. When the people came. And they would come—of this he was certain—the settlements could be laid out in advance. The communities would not grow in a straggle of nondescript dwellings about and because of some crossroad's store or a railroad junction. They could be predesigned. The concept was so revolutionary, so filled with tremendous possibilities, that Dennis tried to shake it off as a wild fancy. People wanted a freedom of choice. They wanted to build what and where they wanted. But, he wondered, did they? In the North there were hundreds of thousands of elderly persons living on small pensions, interest from investments, annuities or inheritances. If they could be reached. If there was some way to tell them: Here, in Florida, where the sun always shines, snow and winter do not lock you in for long, dreary months. You can have a better home and life on the same, or even less, income. Here is a town. Its streets are laid out, lots staked, plans for your homes ready and free for your selection, lumber and labor for building cheap. Why should you endure the discomforts of the North when down here you can step from your back porch and pick a breakfast orange?

Then, his mind raced on, there were the small, marginal farmers in the New England States, the Midwest, who must contend with drought, fierce, bitter winters and land already tired from too much planting of the same crops. How to reach them? How to convince them life here could be easier and the untilled acres of rich soil in Florida could produce an unbelievable bounty with half the effort? He sighed, wishing he had someone to talk with. This was no wild promoter's dream of quick money but a long-range plan. Perhaps, as his father said, he was twenty-five, even fifty years too early with his ideas. It was unheard of to diagram a community and to sell it from a map. But, and of this he was certain, it could and would be done in time. What he was going to see on this trip was only a miniscule part of the whole. But he would follow this with other explorations until he was familiar with the entire state from the Gulf to the Atlantic, from the Keys to the Georgia line. Half laughing at himself he thought how marvelous it would be to have a balloon and be able to drift up and down and across the peninsula, seeing it unfold below like a gigantic map; marking every stream, river, lake, swamp and inlet. Then he would be able to say: Here we can do this. There we can do that. This can be drained and cultivated. Here is great pasture-land for cattle. There are the enormous stands of timber. We will take it for lumber and reforestrate as the trees are felled. We'll dig canals here and so, people living five, ten or even fifteen miles away will have access to the rivers, lakes, the Gulf of Mexico and the Atlantic. There is nothing man can imagine that can't be accomplished here.

When he had tried to talk with his father, Will Lathrop had been pleasantly tolerant but he was not really interested. There was in him no drive to create. He was completely satisfied with the life and comforts with which he was surrounded. He listened to his son with a mild curiosity, as though he were being told some fanciful and diverting tale. One concession Dennis had been able to extract. His father assured him he would not dispose of the property he owned on the beach across the river from Daytona.

"If you want it, boy, it's yours. I'm damned if I know why I bought it in the first place. Maybe because it was cheap or someone talked me into it. I honestly don't remember. I'll put it in my will for you. As a matter of fact I'd give it to you now outright but then it would be nothing but a drain on you for taxes. Boy, there just isn't anything there but scrub, live oak, slash pine, some stunted cedar and the like. The most anyone will ever do with it is to build a cheap summer cottage on the sand dunes so he can get the ocean breeze. The rest is just waste. Take my word for it. As for building a town on paper and selling it to people from pictures—it's ridiculous. They want a freedom of choice. It's the pioneer spirit."

"I don't believe it. A cabin in the wilderness belongs to another century."

Will Lathrop shook his head. He enjoyed the small argument and this association with his son even though his ideas were fantastic.

"Florida is a place for those with money and leisure; an escape from the discomfort of a Northern winter. Think of it as a seashore resort, nothing more. The interior will never attract a population much beyond what it has now."

"Is it all right if I take a little of your whisky, one of those cigars and tell you, at the same time, you don't know what you're talking about?" Dennis smiled.

"Help yourself." Will gestured toward the decanter and humidor. "Those are the privileges of the wealthy I just spoke about. A drink, a good cigar, a chair on a porch overlooking a private view of the river."

"The people will come." Dennis tasted the rich bourbon. "They'll come here as they went to California only the way is a damn sight easier. They'll come when they learn what Florida has to offer. They'll sell their little stores, their tailoring establishments, bring their carpenters' tools and their plumbers' wrenches. They'll sell their practices in medicine in the small Midwest towns and close their little law offices to reopen them here. The farmers in the Dakotas will find out how much easier it is here and the small cattleman in Montana will discover the vast grazing lands. They'll bring their talents, their skills, their dreams and their families. I only hope I'm around to see it and to have a part in the building. In the meantime," he shook his head resignedly, "I'm not a very successful lawyer, but at least I have a wealthy father."

"I don't think you were ever meant for the law any more than I would have been a really good doctor. We were both victims of a family tradition. I broke it. There's no reason why you shouldn't do the same thing. What you do know of law may stand you in good stead even though you don't practice it. I rarely offer advice but don't attempt to force young Tod into a pattern. Let him decide for himself when the time comes."

"Mistuh Dennis?"

Wash's questioning voice roused him now. He realized he had been sitting there, staring into the distance and seeing it peopled with his imagination.

"Yes, sure, Wash. Get the guns."

Three abreast with Tod in the middle they moved slowly across the knee-high scrub. The dog cast back and forth, all business now.

"I give Useful a talk," Wash confided. "I say we aftah bird not no rabbit, not no nothin' but bird so keep youah min' on what you do."

"I never saw a hound point birds." Dennis watched the eager animal.

"Useful don' know he a houn', Mistuh Dennis. So I don' tell 'im no bettuh. Raight now he think he a bird dog. You jus' watch."

Five minutes later the dog froze on a heavily grassed section. True, he did not come to the classic pose of a pointer but there was no mistaking he had found what he was looking for. The body was rigid, muscles quivering beneath the sleek coat, all four paws planted solidly and the muzzle raised as though he were about to give tongue in a deep-throated bay.

"See what Ah mean, Mistuh Dennis?" Wash could have been no prouder if the animal had just taken a blue ribbon. "He figuah that how he tell us bird theah. Ahl raight, boy." The command was softly whispered.

The hound rose stiffly on his hind legs and then bounced forward.

The action was slightly ludicrous but it served the purpose. The quail came out, one streaking straightaway, the others in a tangent flight. Useful then set up a wild clamor of excitement, running in frenzied circles. To anyone accustomed to shooting over a trained bird dog it was a startling exhibition.

They took a dozen fat quail within an hour. By unspoken agreement Dennis and Wash emphatically declared four of the birds had been winged by Tod and the .22 even though one of them had tracked and shot them.

"Ah tell you, Ah nevah see no one who kin hit birds with no rifle laik Mistuh Tod heah." Wash spoke with admiring awe.

"Did I really get them? Did I?" Tod was anxious to be reassured.

"Well who else?" Wash had the quail on a string. "Me? I was lookin' at oather bird. Youah papa, too. So, hit jus' had to be you. Ahm goin' to mark 'em en cook 'em special foah you."

Back at the camp Tod squatted with Wash beside a drainage creek while the Negro plucked, cleaned and rinsed the quail. Then the man cut and trimmed an oak branch for spitting over the coals. With their feathers stripped away the birds seemed absurdly small and naked.

"We wrop these wit a strip of bankin so th' fat run down en mek 'em crisp like en brown, too. We stick some yam en th' coal to bake en ef youah papa like we fix us some rice wid bean. We gots some of them jarred up guava foah dessert. We eat good dis naight." He made a smacking sound of anticipation with his lips and winked at Tod.

The boy watched everything the Negro did with unflagging interest. The man worked with a minimum of effort and Tod hunkered down beside him, eyes bright with the novelty of everything. Dennis sat to one side of the fire in the canvas-seated camp chair. His legs were stretched comfortably before him. He had fixed himself a toddy of bourbon and hot water and was enjoying the rich flavor and steaming fragrance. Watching Tod and Wash he smiled a little, recognizing the boy's open adoration for the big Negro and his gentleness. The fire was burning down well and the countryside was enveloped in the hazy softness of late afternoon. A light wind moved with quiet restlessness through the high tops of the pines with a faint murmur. Now and then a small shower of the brown needles fell upon his lap. The hound came to lie beside his chair, muzzle flat to the ground and pointed toward the fire's warmth as it rippled toward them. Dennis reached down to scratch behind the responsive ears. This, he thought, is the best of all possible times in the best of all possible worlds. He had never known such a full measure of contentment.

While he was waiting for the fire to reach the proper depth of glowing coals Wash cut a small stack of palmetto fans from the scrub. Now he was showing Tod how a thatch was made, talking as he worked.

"Hit a good thing to know case you evah git caught widout no sheltah. Now, ef youah fixin' you a lean-to you firs' fin' you a couple o' saplin' oah tree what growin' faih close togetah. Ef you kin fin' some vine you lace hit across from tree to tree. Ef you ain' got no vine you got to lay some branches crosswise. Den you staht from de bottom up, laik dis." He had left the spiny stems on the fans and these he thrust into the ground. Then he deftly inserted a fan downward through the upright one so they interlaced. "Jus' keep workin' up en up laik dis. Firs' thing you know you got you a fine, watahproof slant to crawl undah. Well," he amended honestly, "hit watahproof widout you got no real, big storm laik a hurricane, maybe. Foah jus' en easy rain hit as good a sheltah, almos', as a canvas." He stood back and admired his work. "We bes' see about ouah suppah." Wash left Tod to probe about the thatching, exploring the interlocking fans with inquisitive fingers.

Dennis refilled his tin cup with a second toddy, dropping a small lump of brown sugar in the mixture and stirring it with a twig.

The yams they had brought with them were buried deep within the coals, covered with earth so they would bake and not burn. A small pot of rice cooked at one end of the fire and the quail roasted on their spit with the bacon grease dripping off to send small spurts of flame from the glowing oak. Tod squatted beside his father's chair.

"Will we do this again, Father?"

"You can bet your bottom dollar we will." His hand rested on the boy's head. "You and I are going to explore the whole state. We'll see it together. I almost wish we were of an age when we could grow up in it as boys. When I think of all the years I have wasted. So, you can be young for the both of us. I'll see it through your eyes as well as mine."

Tod wasn't quite sure just what this meant but there was a note in his father's voice he had never heard before. More than this, though, he wasn't the familiar parent; the man of authority. It was more like having a big brother; someone to rely upon but who exerted no discipline. A little shyly, almost hoping he would not notice, he leaned against the man's knee. It was the first time he could remember drawing pleasure from the physical contact.

They ate while it was still light although the shadowy curtain of evening was drawing across the world and darkness would come soon. Wash fixed their plates, breaking open the steaming yams and putting a thick slice of butter in the deep gold of the sweet potato. The quail were delicately brown and no larger now than a man's fist.

"You're sure these are the ones I shot?" Tod broke off one of the small legs and bit through the meat to the delicate bone. "You didn't get them mixed up, did you, Wash?"

"I set 'em special en th' fiah en' o' de spit. Can' be no mistake 'bout dat."

Wash then prepared his own plate, heaping it with the rice into which he had mixed some home-cooked beans the house cook had baked for them. Both Tod and his father refused the mixture. The Negro ate it with a hungry relish. When they were finished and the potato skins and little piles of bones burned, Wash rinsed off the tin plates. Then he built up the fire with pine and oak which made a warm, bright wall about them.

All of his life Tod Lathrop was to remember this night although nothing memorable or exciting happened. Wash hummed mutedly to himself, a gentle lament born of the white man's religious hymns. Somehow he made it sound strangely barbaric. There was the hoot of a distant owl. The sad note of a whippoorwill and the answer from a second bird somewhere so far away it could barely be heard. Wash had gathered a stack of pine cones, and now and then he or Tod would toss one into the flames and watch with silent concentration as it caught fire, curling and twisting as it burned. No one said anything for it was as though they were all held in the spell of silence born of companionship out of this hushed and fragrant land.

Later Tod and his father moved in underneath the canvas shelter. Wash had spread a heavy mat of pine needles and drawn a blanket over it to make a bed. Another light robe served to cover them.

"Good night, son." Dennis looked down into the young face. "Sleep well. We'll be up early in the morning."

"Good night, Father."

From where he lay Tod could see a patch of the sky and it was heavily dusted with particles of silver. There was no sound save the occasional cracking of a log as it burned and split open. Tod turned until he was lying on his belly, arms outspread. The perfume of the pine seeped through the blanket. Suddenly, and for no reason he could understand, he pressed his body hard, digging his hands into the ground as though he wanted to merge himself with the earth and become a part of it. In this fashion he went to sleep.

On the western outskirts of DeLand they saw the first orange groves on a large scale. The trees stretched in long, orderly rows and the fruit hung in heavy, golden globes. Dennis talked with everyone they encountered. Few of the farmers were natives of Florida. Most of them had come from Ohio, Illinois and the New England States but a few had migrated from Alabama and Georgia. None regretted the move although they were making only a bare living in most cases. They spoke of the future in practical terms and without optimistic enthusiasm. A man with a small farm or grove was always in contention with the imponderable. Nature could fall upon him with unpredictable savagery. But here in Florida, the contest was more agreeable. The soil was fertile and the climate made it possible to have some sort of crop growing almost the year 'round. Their kids were happy and healthy in the warm sunshine. Their wives reasonably contented and glad to escape the northern winters. It was a good life even though no one got wealthy. Hell. Whoever heard of a wealthy farmer except the big combines?

From DeLand the road, such as it was, wound southward. Here again they encountered the vast stretches of uninhabited country. It was the virgin land, mile upon mile without so much as a cabin to break the unchanging scene. But neither Tod nor his father found it monotonous. Sometimes they sat with Wash on the seat, their eyes searching eagerly; finding excitement in the slow hovering of a hawk and its sudden dive upon a small animal; the majestic soaring of the buzzards as they wheeled high in the sky searching for carrion. Once a small, black bear ambled hurriedly through the thick scrub to disappear in a wooded grove. At other times they abandoned the seat to stretch out on the wagon's flat bed, feeling the sun upon their faces and watching the great, cloudless dome unrolling overhead.

They followed the river as it flowed between Lake George to the north and Lake Monroe to the south and camped each night beside it. Here was the dark mystery of silent movement. The ancient, moss-laden trees were reflected in the unruffled water. An alligator would slide from a bank and disappear until only its ugly snout and crown of head showed. Migrant waterfowl rode upon the sheen of water. Nervous deer came down to drink in the early evening and went bounding off at their approach. Wash had brought three bamboo poles with their other equipment and they fished from the banks for the hungry bass which were later cleaned, rolled in cornmeal and crisply fried for their suppers. Once Dennis brought down two ducks out of a flight which came in just before sunset. They fell into the river far out of reach. Wash did his best to get Useful to retrieve the birds but this was far beyond the hound's comprehension and experience. In exasperation Wash finally picked up the dog and threw him into the water.

"Go git dem bird. You heah me? Git 'em."

Useful swam in a frantic circle for a moment and then came clawing ashore to shake himself dry and cavort about his master as though they had discovered a new and diverting form of entertainment. After this Dennis tried for no more ducks.

"They would have made a fine meal but there's no sense in shooting what we can't get. Useful may be a fine pointer-hound dog but he's not much of a retriever and I have the feeling he won't learn."

"Nossuh, I reckon not," Wash agreed. Then, trying to find an explanation for Useful's stupidity, he brightened. "Hit jus' might be Useful know dey 'gator en dat rivah. No real, smaht dog would go foolin' aroun' 'gators. So maybe he brightah dan we figuah!"

They spent a night in Sanford on the shore of Lake Monroe. It was a thriving community with citrus groves, and celery was emerging as a major crop. Climate and soil here seemed ideally suited for the growing of the vegetable and already Sanford was calling itself "the celery capitol of the South." It could be true, Dennis thought. The cultivation could be extensive once the land was cleared. Dennis equated everything he saw in terms of expansion. He laughed a little to himself. Each vacant acre was an affront to the idea which had become almost an obsession. People would come to Florida. They would come by the hundreds of thousands. It was inevitable. This land of soft beauty, of promised abundance, could not lie untenanted. If people would not discover it for themselves it must be done for them and he, Dennis Lathrop, wanted to be the man to do it. His curiosity was insatiable. He talked with everyone: shopkeepers, the manager of the small hotel, farmers, sharecroppers, men who held vast tracts of pine. What did they think of the future of Sanford, of Florida? Had they ever been to the east coast of the state? How many new families had settled in or around Sanford in the past five years? No one seemed to understand the questions. No one thought about the future in terms of new families, a population increase, the growth and expansion of existing farms, the creation of new ones. Their imagination was bounded by their own small problems and the horizon limited. A few thought this inquisitive stranger a little touched and humored him.

They remained in Sanford for two days. A real bed and a hot bath felt good again or so his father assured Tod. Secretly the boy preferred the woods and Wash's cooking. He could always sleep in a bed or take a hot bath at home.

The way back to Daytona from Sanford led them eastward to Lake Harney. Here they came upon a small cabin back from the shore and an Indian, a Creek, with the odd name of Campbell. He had a wife and five children who crowded about Dennis, Tod and Wash, staring at them with silent, intense curiosity. Campbell had small patches of corn, beans and squash growing and his cabin seemed to be constructed principally of odd pieces of timber laced with thick branches. The inside was dark, airless and filled with an almost over-powering odor of people living in close confinement. The man, Campbell, spoke a halting but unaccented English. They stood outside the hut and after Dennis had offered Campbell a cigar some of the Indian's reserve yielded. He walked with Dennis and Tod beside the wagon as Wash drove and showed them a clean, white, sandy stretch of beach at the lake's edge where they could camp. They passed a grove of some two hundred or so orange trees, neatly tended but still too young to bear fruit. Campbell told Dennis he worked for a man by the name of Herndon who lived, he swept his hand vaguely toward the north, somewhere up there and only came down once or twice a year. He hunted, fished a little and looked the place over. There was a small white cottage at the grove's end where he stayed.

Campbell watched with critical interest as Wash set up the camp. Not many persons came this way, he said. He and his family lived mostly off the land. There were fish in the lake, birds and wild turkeys within easy walking distance. The few things they had to buy —meal, lard, flour, sugar and salt—were brought to them once a month from a store in Titusville through an arrangement made by Mr. Herndon. In addition to the grove they also had some cattle. He said this with an oddly half-baffled expression. Mr. Herndon was fooling around with some sort of an idea on an island at one end of the lake. No one had ever seen any cattle like these before around here and Campbell said he didn't know where they came from. In the beginning there was a bull and two cows but Mr. Herndon had brought in some regular Florida stock to breed with the bull.

"Nothin' bother them cattle. No tick. No worm. No sickness an' they eat anythin'." He paused and stared at the sky. "Goddamnedest cattle you ever see an' mean, too." He said this a little proudly.

Dennis's curiosity and interest were immediate. Whatever was new or unusual here in Florida occupied his full attention. He brought out what remained of the bourbon and shared a drink with Campbell. The Indian accepted gravely but his eyes widened with pleasure as he tasted the full, rich body of the whisky. They had a second drink and emptied the bottle. Mellowed by this, Campbell offered to take Dennis and Tod over to the island so they could see the cattle for themselves. He wasn't sure Mr. Herndon would like it, but then, Mr. Herndon wasn't here.

Campbell rowed his flat-bottomed boat across a narrow arm of the lake to the island and they walked inland. Grazing on the tough grass were scattered cattle such as Dennis had never seen before. They were long of horn and with a hump on their backs. Vaguely he recalled a book on the Far East in his father's library. In it were pictures, drawings. He remembered a street scene through which the cattle roamed. They were, he thought, native to India and were called Brahma or Brahman. The sight of them here, in this backwoods district of Florida, stirred him as nothing else had on the trip. Here was the sort of thing Florida needed. It was new and exciting in concept. A man with the money, vision and an inquiring mind was experimenting in this isolated section of the state. If, and Dennis's mind raced ahead, this Brahma strain could infuse a vitality and toughness, an immunity to the usual diseases of cattle, then the vast plains of southern Florida might be opened up as a beef-producing area which, except for size, could offer rivalry to Texas and its great ranches. He could barely control his enthusiasm. He walked around the herd, studying the animals and wishing he knew more about cattle. He wondered what manner of man this Herndon was.

Campbell shook his head in answer to a question. He didn't even know Mr. Herndon's first name. He was paid twenty-five dollars a month just to live on the place, weed around the orange trees, spray them now and then for pests, keep an eye on the cattle and strangers off the property. His money came to the post office in Titusville every three months. That was all he knew. Mr. Herndon usually came down late in January or early February and stayed for two or three weeks. Sometimes he brought a cattle doctor with him who inspected the increasing herd. Then they went away and he didn't see or hear from Mr. Herndon for another year.

Long after they had finished supper Dennis sat on a fallen tree, smoking and mulling over what this Herndon was doing. He talked aloud, half speaking to Tod because he needed someone to listen. Here was something to stimulate the imagination. Florida beef had always been tough and stringy. This was the beginning of an entirely new breed. It could be immune to the ailments of most cattle. In time Florida could supply the South with beef of high quality. He determined to learn what he could from the books available. He had no intention of going into the cattle business himself but what affected Florida also, now, touched Dennis Lathrop. Here was his destiny. Of this he was convinced.

On the way home they halted overnight at New Smyrna and the next day visited the thick-walled ruins and cumbersome machinery of the old sugar mills. Dennis told Tod what he knew about the Minorcan colony brought here by Dr. Andrew Turnbull. How he worked them as slaves until they revolted and took the long walk, some one hundred miles, to ask protection of the Spanish at St. Augustine. Here was a dark reminder of the past.

Christmas was in the air. They followed the barely defined road as it twisted and curved with the rivershore. On a point near Rose Bay they found a small grove of cedar and Wash selected and cut a thick, full-branched tree to take home with them. They gathered great bunches of waxy mistletoe from the oaks and found holly bushes and a shrub Wash called Christmas berries hung with small, scarlet globes. The wagon was piled high with festive greenery.

> "Deck the halls with boughs of holly
> Fa La La La La La La La La
> 'Tis the season to be jolly."

Dennis caroled at the top of his voice and Tod laughed secretly to himself thinking he had never known how much fun it was to be with his father before this adventure. They had talked as never before; seen and done things together which a year ago wouldn't have seemed possible. And, although he didn't understand fully what his father was talking about, some of the man's enthusiasm had communicated itself. The days and nights in the woods, along the roads, the rivers and lakes had given him a feeling for the land. It was something he couldn't have explained and didn't quite understand himself. But it was a personal kinship as though he belonged to the pines, the scrub, the water, the earth, and they to him.

"Will we make another trip together?"

"You and I are going to cover every acre in Florida before we're through. The law profession be damned. I'm off on a new path. I don't know where it leads but I'll follow it. When school is over," he lit one of the two remaining cigars he had brought, "we'll take a train from Jacksonville to Tampa and have a look at the Gulf of Mexico and see what's over there. It will be hot as hell. I can't take you out of school every winter. When we get through with the west coast we'll go to Palm Beach and Miami and find out what's happening."

"Maybe Mother won't let me go." Tod was doubtful.

Dennis winked. "When summer comes it would be a good idea for your mother to get away from the heat and mosquitoes. Probably she'd like to go to the North Carolina mountains with your grandfather and grandmother. I'll suggest it. You and I will 'bache' it along with Wash here and just go off whenever we feel like it."

"Yessuh," Wash beamed, "I figuah, maybe, you fo'gettin' ol' Wash heah. I suah like to mek dem trip wid you an' young Mistuh Tod. We had us a good time, Mistuh Dennis. We suah had us a good time."

Wash slapped the reins over the horse's rump and the animal, which had been poking along lazily, lifted her head and broke into an easy trot.

* V * *

IT was the year of 1910 and an undercurrent of excitement ran through the country as men probed farther into space and beneath the earth. The Pennsylvania Railroad sent its first trains through tunnels underneath the Hudson River. Glenn Curtiss flew the 137 miles from Albany to New York City in 2 hours and 32 minutes and Walter Wellman launched his dirigible at Atlantic City for a flight to Europe. It covered 1,008 miles before going down in the sea. Crew and passengers were rescued by the steamer *Trent*.

Across what was known as Spanish Creek, running parallel to Bay Street, the small frame schoolhouse, serving the town for a generation, was replaced by a large brick structure. On this pleasant spring night its first high school class was being graduated. Parents, relief on their faces, accompanied sons and daughters out of the building. The youngsters, with self-conscious pride, clutched their ribbon-tied diplomas and tried to pretend the event was unimportant. But they winked at each other in passing and their expressions were of relief that they had finally made it.

Tod, with his father, mother, Grandfather Will and Grandmother Felicia, stood in a group on the steps saying their good nights to friends and neighbors, offering congratulations to the graduates. The town was still small enough to enable everyone to know almost everyone else. The Reverend Rutter, whose church was just across the street, stopped with his son Joe and daughter Cleo to shake hands.

The minister never really gave up the earnest hope for Will Lathrop's conversion but his tentative approaches were met with an argumentative agnosticism. Will Lathrop actually enjoyed the exchanges. He admired Dr. Rutter for his single-minded purpose and there was a friendship between the families. Tod glanced covertly at Cleo. He thought she was the most beautiful girl he had ever seen with her quick smile, clear complexion and long, blond curls. He and Joe were at a state of guarded companionship. A few years before, Tod had asked his father about the mysterious business of babies. How and where they came from. Dennis's answer had been forthright and explicit. Tod had been fascinated and a little startled by the information. Thereafter, at the dinner table or when they were together in the living room or on the porch, he would allow his gaze to rove between his father and mother with concealed astonishment. It seemed like such an undignified thing to do. He simply couldn't reconcile his mother with the act. One day he and Joe had been sitting beside the canal, watching the dark flow of water and tossing in an occasional twig to see it float away. Tod had shared his newly acquired knowledge and the two had come close to a tumbling fight over the subject.

"Your mother and father may do that." Joe had been flushed and indignant. "But mine don't. I know they don't." He was mortified and angry.

Tod had shrugged and let the matter drop. Surely his father must know what he was talking about. Now he and Joe were older, high school graduates, but Tod always wondered if his friend still believed a stork brought babies. They never discussed the subject. Joe thought he would follow his father in the Church. Tod was not quite so certain of his future. As he had promised, Dennis had taken his son on one trip after another until, as he was fond of saying, they had covered every "damn, square inch" of Florida. He had made the explorations exciting by his enthusiasm and this Tod was beginning to share.

"When you get back from college," Dennis had said, "we'll open up this state like a can of beans. Maybe you ought to go to the Harvard School of Business. I don't know what they teach but it sounds impressive."

Tod still hadn't made up his mind but he knew this was his home, his state. It never occurred to him he would seek a life outside it.

Parked now in front of the school was Will Lathrop's new automobile. It was a thing of shining splendor with polished brass headlights, slick, curving mudguards, a horn which was sounded by squeezing a rubber bulb, and wheels with wooden spokes of bright yellow. Behind the car was the family barouche with the coachman Mark sitting on the box with proud disdain and a scornful eye. Even Will Lathrop had to admit the automobile was an unpredictable conveyance. So, he always had Mark follow them with the carriage. Adding to the indignity the task of cranking the automobile's engine had been delegated to the Negro. This job he performed with something close to a sullen defiance. He would thrust at the crank as though he hoped to tear the engine from its bed. Then, after tentative explosions and backfiring, when the thing finally began to run, Mark would go back to his empty carriage and follow in the car's noisy path.

When he drove the car Will Lathrop attired himself in a linen duster, visored cap, gauntlets and goggles. In this weird costume he would settle himself behind the wheel with the air of a man about to take a trip to the moon. He would adjust the spark and throttle levers and wait for Mark to crank up. Then he would glance back to see that the ladies had veils securely tied over their hats to hold them down, and nod with happy satisfaction. With everyone in the proper state of apprehension there would be a clashing of gears under full throttle and they would go rocketing down the uneven streets, bouncing over holes, slewing in the ruts. His passengers in silent terror clutched at each other and the metal handholds to keep from being pitched out into the road. Tod was usually given the place of honor beside his grandfather as he crouched over the wheel with a smile of demoniacal pleasure on his face. Tod was delighted by his grandfather's recklessness and his airy indifference to the town marshal's repeated threats to arrest Will Lathrop if he didn't drive slower and stop throwing Beach Street into a panic everytime he came uptown.

"How would you like to take a spin along the beach?" Will turned and shouted the invitation to the family. "There's a fine moon out. Nothing like a spin in the moonlight."

To Tod's disappointment his grandmother shook her head vigorously. "Please, Will. Let's just go home. We're all tired from the school ceremonies. Can't we go home, Will?" This plaintively.

"Really, it's bad enough driving with you in the daytime."

"All right." Lathrop was plainly disappointed. "After all, I only bought this thing for your pleasure." He shifted through the gears and they exploded off down Palmetto Avenue. He made a screeching turn at Magnolia toward Beach Street, straightened out, but for a frightening second the car was tilted on two wheels. Will slapped Tod's knee exuberantly. "Tomorrow you and I will go over to the beach. I'll teach you how to drive. These are the coming things, make no mistake about it. Keep your eye on me and see how it's done." They roared into the intersection of Beach Street and Magnolia Avenue, barely escaping plowing through Peck's dry goods store on the corner. "There's nothing to it, boy!" Will yelled. "Just a firm hand on the wheel. Nothing to it at all. Don't plan anything else. We'll go to the beach in the morning."

A trip to the beach with Grandfather Will was more than just an exciting and unpredictable ride. There was a new bridge now across the river at Orange Avenue. Nothing made Will Lathrop happier than to drive over it at full speed, setting the planking to a shivering rumble. This ominous sound always brought the drawbridge keeper running from his little house to see if the entire span was falling apart. Will would wave nonchalantly, cigar clamped between his teeth, driving with one hand while the bridge attendant swore wildly at him for not stopping to pay the fifteen-cent toll required of all vehicles. This, Will Lathrop delegated to Mark following in the carriage. He always gave him the toll money in advance. There was an open feud between Mr. Pellicier, the bridgekeeper, and Lathrop. Will was always put into an exceptionally good humor by the spectacle of the man's screaming frustration as he went roaring past. They plotted and schemed to outwit each other. Sometimes Mr. Pellicier would hear or see Will Lathrop as he started across from Orange Avenue. When this happened he would hastily put down the wooden barriers, rush to the crank and run in a circle with it, opening the drawbridge so Lathrop would have to come to a shuddering halt or crash through the gates and into the river. Then, with the car at a standstill and from his place of security on the open draw, Mr. Pellicier would politely inquire about Mr. Lathrop's health and that of his family, naming each one with solicitous deliberation. He would add a comment on the weather and a prediction for the future. Will Lathrop's reaction never failed to delight Tod. His grandfather would stand up, take off his goggles and shout his anger.

"God damn it, Pellicier, close that drawbridge. You know damn well there isn't a boat in sight."

"Now, I was sure I heard one blow a horn, Mr. Lathrop." Pellicier with bland innocence would shade his eyes and look southward toward Mosquito Inlet, then turn and stare northward. "I just would have sworn there was a boat what wanted to come through. You know it's my job to open the bridge when a boat comes up or down. It's in the franchise."

"There isn't a boat in sight. You know it. I know it. You're a sly son of a bitch, Mr. Pellicier. That's what you are. A sly, conniving son of a bitch."

"Oh! I guess you don't really mean that, Mr. Lathrop." Pellicier's refusal to take offense only infuriated Will Lathrop. "You going to pay your toll today, Mr. Lathrop? Each vehicle has to pay its toll."

"God damn it. You know my coachman always pays it."

Pellicier would shake his head regretfully. "It ain't according to regulations, Mr. Lathrop. The rule says each vehicle must pay its own toll. Now, if you'll just get your fifteen cents ready I'll close the bridge and you and that fine boy there can be on your way in a jiffy. I must have been mistaken about a boat wanting to pass."

"One of these days I'm going to smash right through those gates." Will, defeated, would fumble for the change.

The victorious Mr. Pellicier would nod a solemn agreement. "I expect you will. A man of temper is likely to do anything. But I'll tell you one thing. When you do, you and your goddamned automobile are surer than hell going to be in twenty feet of river."

"Then I'll get a new one and run it through your house. How would you like that?"

Mr. Pellicier would refuse to become a party to such an absurdity. With a painful slowness, pretending the big crank was far too heavy for one man to turn, he would take a full ten minutes swinging the draw into place. At a point where it was not yet fully closed but the opening short enough to enable him to leap over Mr. Pellicier would come and collect the toll from Lathrop. Then he would go back, turn the draw into place, lock it, lift the barriers and genially wave Lathrop on.

Muttering all manner of curses and threats to himself Lathrop would drive with more than his usual lack of caution. He would take the curve past the Gamble house at full speed, roar through the cut between the high dunes which was Silver Beach Avenue and down upon the beach itself with the sand flying and the car on the verge of overturning.

"When you get a son of a bitch like that you just don't know what to do with him."

"No, sir," Tod would agree. "I guess not. A son of a bitch is always a son of a bitch and there's nothing anyone can do about it."

This would always restore Will Lathrop's good humor. He would grin and sometimes laugh and wink at his grandson.

"He's tricky, that Pellicier. I'll say that for him. But he doesn't always catch me the way he did today. I sneak up on him sometimes. It spoils his whole morning, and afternoon also."

The beach was hard packed and glistening, backed up by dunes of incredibly white sand, soft and powdery. It stretched some twelve miles southward to Mosquito Inlet and its lighthouse of mellowed red brick. To the north it extended eight or ten miles and then, for some reason, the surface became soft and liberally sprinkled with particles of red shell. But from Ormond to the inlet there was an unbroken driving surface of about twenty miles. Earlier in the year a racing driver, Barney Oldfield, broke the world's speed record on the strand by driving a mile in twenty-seven and two-thirds seconds. The scrub was an unbroken tangle, so heavy it seemed as though a man might walk upon it. It filled the space between ocean and river and ran all the way to the inlet. Every time Will Lathrop looked at it he chuckled. Dennis just couldn't see the scrub. He stared at it and imagined it cleared and filled with homes.

Whenever Will took his grandson to the beach he would regard the scrubland with unconcealed amusement. Who in hell would ever tackle this?

"Your father," he was fond of ruminating on his son's eccentricity, "doesn't see what you and I look at, Tod. That's just one hell of a lot of palmetto scrub. Dennis has a different pair of eyes. He imagines houses and hotels from the pier to the inlet and the whole peninsula settled from ocean to river. Where the hell are all the people coming from? How are they going to make a living after they get here? You know?" Reluctantly he would reduce the car's speed so he could safely divide his attention between the machine and his favorite monologue. "When I ask the question he says the people will come and when they come they will create the jobs to sustain them. He is always after me to invest in more and more property. He even has his eye on a stretch along the river down near the inlet. He insists that one of these days or years someone will build a hotel there or even a private fishing club with docks and mooring facilities for boats. There will be cottages on the grounds for the northern sportsmen who can fish the river or take their craft outside through the inlet for deep-sea angling. You know something? I'm almost tempted to buy it just to see him sweat. Why, hell, boy, you and I know there isn't even any way to get to it; no approach from the beach, no road and there never will be."

"A road could be built, couldn't it, Grandfather? I mean it doesn't have to stay this way forever."

Will Lathrop regarded his grandson with surprise. Ordinarily the boy listened without comment.

"Don't tell me you are beginning to believe it, also?"

"I don't know, sir." Tod had been embarrassed. "But, he could be right. I guess everyone thought Mr. Flagler was crazy when he built his railroad down here."

"Well. He was." Will refused to concede anything.

This morning, after they had plowed their way through the deep ruts of soft sand to the solid surface, he brought the car to a skidding halt, exchanged places with Tod and explained the workings of the clutch, the gear shift, the hand and foot brakes, the spark and throttle levers. Tod's first attempt at a start caused the car to leap and almost rear. The engine died.

"You let the clutch in too fast, boy. Ease it slowly." He stood up and called to the long-suffering Mark, who sat in lonely grandeur on the box of the barouche behind them. "Come here and turn her over." Then he reassured the nervous Tod. "Don't worry. I had the same trouble at first." This was a rare concession. "I used to go off like a cowboy on a bucking bronco. It just takes a little practice." He settled back, cigar in mouth, leaning against the cushioned leather, leaving the entire operation to his grandson.

After a few experimental starts and stops Tod gained some confidence. It wasn't really difficult; just a matter of controlling the pressure of foot on clutch pedal. They drove for a couple of miles south and then Will told Tod to make a turn.

"There's plenty of room. Just guide it around with the wheel. The big mistake in driving one of these things at first is overcontrol. Ease the steering wheel around sort of feeling as you go. Now, I know what I'm doing every minute. Sometimes, maybe, I take a corner a little too fast. But all that really happens is your grandmother gets a touch of nervous indigestion. I don't imagine women will ever be able to handle an automobile. They're not temperamentally suited for machines. You're doing fine for the first time."

Tod glowed beneath the compliment and did his best to assume a casual attitude. But the white showed on his knuckles as he gripped the wheel and his eyes were set in a tensed stare as he surveyed the empty beach ahead.

The small community on the beach side had shown little change over the years but what expansion occurred was toward the east and ocean front rather than along the river where the first few settlers had gathered with a group of small homes, a church, grocery store and the post office, a frame building, on the corner of what was known as Halifax Avenue and Main Street. Usually the hub of any village, the post office was all but isolated now as the sparse population increased slowly but most certainly was moving toward the beach. This convinced Dennis Lathrop more than anything else that his predictions for the future were accurate. The coastal areas would feel the first waves of the immigration he was certain must come. They would seek out the beaches, the ocean, the cool breeze. Later they would turn to the river fronts from Daytona to Miami. After that the interior sections of the state would open up for farms, ranches, large orange groves with towns and developments to supply their needs.

Relaxing now as Tod drove northward, Will Lathrop speculated idly on his son's arguments. He could be right. But Will wasn't interested in making money or seeing Florida grow. He liked it the way it was. However, he loved his son, admired and respected him; recognized the drive possessing Dennis Lathrop. His enthusiasm, Will understood, didn't spring from the hope of making himself wealthy and independent. He would even admit, at times, his conception was years away and he might not see it in his lifetime. Despite this gloomy and disappointed admission he remained a builder, a creator and an architect for the future at heart. He found his life's excitement and interest in these things. So, Will mused, why not let him have them? Most of Felicia's considerable fortune was intact. Oh—he laughed to himself—he had nibbled at it, taking some chunks out of the pie. They had done this together and in accord. She was an understanding woman. Or at least she was after all these years of marriage to Will Lathrop. Money, she now agreed with him, wasn't something to be hoarded but bright coins to be tossed into the air for the pleasure of watching them glitter.

"You know? I'm going to do it." He spoke abruptly and without any preliminary explanation.

"What, Grandfather," Tod kept his attention on the length of beach, "what are you going to do?"

"I'm going to let your father have his fun. We'll buy the property on the river near the inlet just for the hell of it. If Dennis wants to sit on the scrub and hatch it out he can do it. You know? He could be right. I won't see it happen and maybe he won't either. So, it may all drop in your lap someday." He examined his cigar and threw it away. "Now that you've been graduated from high school, what are your plans? Are you going on to college?"

"Mother and father want me to."

"Well, boy, take my advice and don't learn anything practical; something that will put you to work. If I had it to do over again I'd devote myself to acquiring an education; something of philosophy, anthropology, art, music, languages, literature, history. Do this and look around, find yourself a wealthy girl to marry. Then you'll be in a position to enjoy what you have learned. That's the real pleasure of knowledge—to be able to know what you're seeing or hearing and why. Every day is a fresh page in a new book."

Tod smiled. He was certain his grandfather meant exactly what he said.

"I expect I'll have to make a living. Maybe there won't be any wealthy girls around when I'm ready. Right now I haven't any idea what I want to be or do."

"Well then," Will Lathrop was pleased, "you are the very best material to work on for what I would consider to be a cultivated gentleman. Go to college. When you finish I'll send you to Europe for a couple of years. Travel. See Italy, France, Spain, Germany. There's not much in England but moldy history and a closed mind. On the Continent you get an understanding of wines, good food, the manners and habits of a different world. You'll come back home and be easy with anyone from a hod carrier to the Prince of Wales."

"I imagine Father wants me to have a profession."

"Don't you do it unless you really want to. Dennis damned near ruined his life, practicing law when he had no sincere interest in it. He saved himself just in time and was lucky. To tell you the truth, and I rarely admit this, I wasn't much of a doctor and never would have been. It was a good thing your grandmother came along when she did or I'd probably be in jail this very minute for malpractice, ignorance and indifference. Don't let yourself be forced into anything. You go after what I would call a well-rounded education and take the future as it comes. If you should turn out to be a day laborer, which isn't likely, you would have the pleasure of an active and inquisitive mind. It can be a storehouse of great riches from which you can draw sustenance when everything else has failed. You had better let me take the wheel now."

Tod brought the car to a halt, dropped to the ground and went around the car to move into his grandfather's place. Ahead, crossing the beach with wide openings between the supporting pillars, was Keating's pier. At the shore end it was attached to a large building known as Keating's Casino. Its lower floor was a series of bathhouses where visitors to the beach could change into bathing suits for a frolic in the surf. The top floor, a large rectangular room with a fireplace in one corner, offered fishing tackle for rent, lines, hooks, candy, cigars, cigarettes and soda pop for sale. Captain Tom Keating lived with his family in one of the few imposing houses. He always wore a nautical cap but no one was ever certain whether he was really a sea captain or the title self-bestowed. His operation of the casino was often erratic and unpredictable. One year he would turn it into a dance hall where an orchestra, piano, drum and violin played on Saturday nights. The following year he might decide that what the town needed was a bowling alley. The dance floor would vanish and the nights would be filled with the rolling thunder of balls and flying pins. Twelve months later Captain Tom would come to the conclusion the new moving pictures were the thing. Out would go the bowling alleys. Folding chairs would be set up, a screen erected and the projector mounted on a stand behind the audience. The pictures were in single reels, usually without much of a story—pie-in-the-face comedies. But the novelty of seeing horses, trains rushing at full speed, street scenes of the traffic in New York City, mounted Indians and cowboys chasing each other, was enough to bring the people in to exclaim in delighted wonder.

At the conclusion of the performance Captain Keating would take a position before the screen and announce in a hearty, booming voice, "And tomorrow night we'll give a double show."

This simply meant that the next evening there would be two or three more reels of film shown. The idea, though, quickened the pulses. Here, certainly, was a bargain and it brought the residents back to the casino the following night, for there was nothing else to do.

Will Lathrop narrowly missed one of the pier's pilings as he drove between them but nothing in his expression indicated he had barely avoided an accident. The fresh cigar was tilted at a cocky angle as he slid the transmission lever into low gear. With a roar and spinning of wheels the car swayed and skidded through the soft sand until they reached the shell-paved surface of the road.

"One of these days," he shouted above the racket, "they're going to have to do something about these beach approaches. Automobiles are here to stay no matter what people think. In a few years the horse and carriage will be a novelty and the blacksmith a mechanic. Of course, they make a noise and stink some but a man either adjusts himself to such things or improves them. The automobile is here and there will have to be roads built on which to travel. It wouldn't surprise me a bit if, say ten years from now, we won't be able to drive all the way to Jacksonville."

Tod wished his grandfather wouldn't talk so much when he drove. They all but took the rear wheels off a wagon as it came down the slope at the corner of Main Street and Ocean Avenue. There were a few cottages on the ridge of Ocean Avenue overlooking the sea, and three hotels, the Breakers, the Daytona Beach Hotel and the Seaside Inn. A block down on Main Street was a massive and ugly structure of gray cement blocks appropriately named the Greystone Hotel. Their guests were all elderly persons who came to Florida in the winter and stayed until late in the spring.

"You see what I mean, boy?" Will waved a hand at the broad porch of the Seaside Inn. "They are old people, retired. You don't see any young people there because the young ones are busy scratching for a living up North. That's why your father is wrong about this thing. There is no way for the young ones to make a living down here. A few of the middle wealthy come and stay up in Seabreeze at the Clarendon or the Colonnades. The real wealthy stop off at St. Augustine or go on down to Palm Beach, which is sort of their Newport in Florida. It takes youth and money to build a thriving economy. By the time the young have the money they are too old to have the drive."

"I guess so, Grandfather."

Tod didn't really care. It was a wonderful thing to grow up here. Dennis Lathrop had built a small summer cottage far down on Ocean Avenue. It had become an accepted part of the household routine for Alice to go with Will and Felicia to North Carolina during the hot, mosquito-filled months of July, August and half of September. Tod and Dennis then moved to the beach, with Wash coming over in the wagon each morning to clean up, make the beds, wash the dishes and do whatever small chores were left to him. They had a fine, carefree life, father and son, in the summer.

First, in the morning, a race down and over the high dunes, across the beach and into the ocean for a swim. Then back at the cottage with Wash cooking bacon and eggs or some fresh fish dropped off by Bunk Ohler who seined the ocean every night and sold his catch from door to door. Bunk always picked out half a dozen or so hand-sized pompano for Dennis. Only an hour or so out of the water they were, when rolled in corn meal and fried in deep fat, the sweetest and most delicate of all fish. After breakfast Wash would clean the kitchen, make the beds and tie up the mosquito nets under which they had to sleep even over here. The prevailing summer winds were from the west and it brought the pests which swarmed over the mainland from the ditches, swamps, stagnant ponds and pools and made the nights and afternoons all but unbearable. Then, if Dennis didn't have to be in court or had appointments at the office they would take the wagon and the three of them spent the day fishing down at the inlet; lying around in the sun stripped to the waist; scoop-netting a couple of buckets full of the fine blue crabs. Wash later cooked and picked them and with surprising skill made a deviled crab mixture which was packed back into the shells and baked in a portable tin oven atop the kerosene stove. In the evenings they ate and read, sometimes by the light of a kerosene lamp. It was a fat, nickel-plated affair with a white, opaque glass shade and called a Rayo. Years later Stoddard Lathrop would recall the lamp, its name, and wonder why it should stick in his mind.

There was no traffic on Main Street, which had nothing but the name to give it importance. Will clashed through his gears and went racing down it. Once off the street, on both sides, there was nothing but scrub. There was a Mr. Branch who had a livery stable just off the corner of what was known as Coates Street and he waved as they passed. Tod and Mr. Branch were friends and the man let Tod exercise the horses by taking them down to the beach and trotting them through the shallow waves. He rode bareback, for these were carriage rental animals and Mr. Branch had no saddles.

"If I were you and going to college"—Will Lathrop always plunged into a new subject from an oral tangent, the subject seeming to have nothing at all to do with what he had said a moment before—"I'd go to Princeton. When I was in school they called Princeton a snob college. Maybe it is. But let me tell you that isn't such a damn bad thing. There's no reason for a democracy, which we claim to have but don't, to operate on the level of the lowest common denominator. To a pool hall bum a man who speaks grammatically, takes a bath every day and changes his underwear and clothing, eats with a fork instead of a knife, is a snob. In his mind there's no room for good manners, courtesy and gentility, the humanities which make life bearable for a man of breeding. If he reads at all it is the sports section of the newspaper. His idea of art is the picture of a naked girl on a couch; the kind they hang above the bar in a saloon. You have to start out right away believing, knowing, you are different and better. You are those things by education, breeding and association. I don't care much for the British. Their minds are insular. But, by God, they keep things in order. Yes, sir. I'd think about Princeton if I were you. You'll have to take entrance examinations, I expect. The high school here is hardly an accredited institution but your father tells me you're smart. Most of the Princeton boys come from eastern preparatory schools. You, coming from a public school, will be regarded as something of a maverick. You'd better learn to handle such a situation right away. Princeton will polish and refine you. Take my advice."

"I'll think about it, Grandfather."

There was a small cemetery on the corner of Main Street and Peninsula Drive. Will slowed down, glanced back to see if Mark was still following them with the carriage.

"I think we'll go across the river here at the North Bridge. That'll keep that son of a bitch Pellicier down at the South Bridge jumping and nervous all day trying to catch us as we come over. He probably won't even take time out to eat his lunch for fear I'll get past him again." The idea pleased him and he speeded up.

As they rattled over the first few yards of planking Tod glanced out of the corner of his eye at his grandfather. A slow smile began to play around his mouth and finally broke into an open grin.

"You know, Grandfather." He spoke slowly and without impertinence. The words sprang from affection and admiration. "I think you're something of a son of a bitch yourself, aren't you?"

Will Lathrop threw back his head and roared with laughter until tears filled his eyes. "I guess," he shouted, "that's about the finest thing you ever said to me, boy."

He chuckled his pleasure and they almost dove into the guard railing, off the bridge and into the river before he recovered sufficiently to give his attention to the car.

* VI * *

IN the Biltmore Hotel's high-ceilinged dining room with its heavy crystal chandeliers, maroon drapes and paneling of fine wood, Dennis and Tod had finished breakfast and were talking idly over their coffee. A copy of the New York *Tribune* was folded at one side of the table. The headline leaped from its front page.

The Archduke Franz Ferdinand, heir to the throne of Austria-Hungary, had been assassinated with his wife, the Duchess of Hohenberg, at a place called Sarajevo by a Bosnian student.

"I don't know what makes everyone think it is so important." Dennis snipped off the end of a cigar, lit a match and held it across for Tod's cigarette, then put the flame to the cigar. "Assassination in the Balkans is pretty commonplace and there is always ferment in middle Europe. It's been going on for centuries."

"It will make a fine excuse." Tod sipped at his coffee and enjoyed the morning's first smoke. "Germany has been looking for one and for trouble. The drive to the East, they call it." He smiled suddenly. "Pol. Science 11." The amusement faded. "The first thing you know there will be ultimatums being handed back and forth. Austria to Serbia. Then Russia will get into it. Germany has to follow. When that happens France, Great Britain, Italy and maybe, before it ends, the United States. It could really be a world war. But," there was a glint in his eyes, "we've a good man in the White House. A Princeton man."

Dennis whistled a low note of mocking admiration but he could not conceal the pride he felt in this handsome, self-assured young man who was his son. Tod had grown tall and when they walked through the lobby it had been shoulder to shoulder. Athletics had filled him out, giving him an easy, graceful stride, and a manner of holding himself. He had played Varsity tennis, baseball and had a place on Princeton's swimming team. More than anything else, though, the four years at the university had polished and refined him. He had poise and a quiet dignity beyond his age. There was a charm, indefinable but engaging, although beneath it Dennis recognized a will, a lithic quality. It was determined rather than hard. In the years to come, he thought, he will not be easily swayed by what anyone says or thinks. Tod would go his own way and make his own decisions.

"Your grandfather and grandmother are in Germany. I wish they would come home if there is going to be trouble in Europe."

"I had a letter from Grandfather Will last week." Tod's eyes lighted. "He and Grandmother were in Baden-Baden. He wrote he was taking the cure but didn't know what the hell it was supposed to do for him since he felt fine. He wrote he hadn't forgotten he promised me two years in Europe after graduation and wanted to know if I cared to join them for awhile before starting off on my own."

"You're not going?"

Tod shrugged. "I guess not." He put out his cigarette. "A Europe at war doesn't sound particularly attractive. And if it goes all out, as it could, I may get there in a uniform. That isn't exactly the way I had planned the Grand Tour."

Dennis was silent, thoughtful, for a moment. Although Tod had come home each summer vacation, arranging his time so he could stop off at Asheville to see his mother, grandfather and grandmother in their North Carolina retreat, Dennis had the uncomfortable feeling they would have to get to know each other all over again, meeting on an adult plane. The change in Tod had been so subtle he had been unaware of it through the short summer months. Now he was confronted by a maturity he hadn't prepared himself to accept.

"What are your plans?"

Tod looked up, surprised. "Why, I thought we'd do what we have always done—spend the summer together on the beach. But," he paused, "I don't suppose Mother will want to go to North Carolina by herself. Will you go with her?"

"We really haven't talked about it. I expected your grandfather to be back for your graduation and things would go on as they have for years. Now," he was actually puzzled, "I'm damned if I know. I suppose I should have talked it over with Alice. It simply didn't occur to me. I haven't any idea what she'll want to do."

"Suppose we go and ask?"

Dennis signed the check and they walked through the lobby toward the elevators. For a moment Tod halted and gazed up at the large clock. A smile grew behind his eyes.

"It may not look it"—he spoke to Dennis with a dry amusement—"but I have an idea that clock has timed the deflowering of many and many a virgin. It, here, has been a meeting place for the men from Princeton and that other college, whatever its name is, up in New Haven and their dates. I'll meet you under the clock. It was all anyone had to say. Everyone understood it meant the clock in the lobby of the Biltmore."

"Things don't really change much. When I was at Columbia we'd say: I'll meet you on the steps. Everyone knew this meant the library steps."

Moving toward the elevator they made a striking pair. The resemblance was unmistakable but Dennis could well have been the elder brother. There was an aura of vitality, of controlled energy and suppressed excitement about them. Suddenly, and he couldn't have explained why, Tod put an arm over his father's shoulders and they walked the remaining distance in this manner without a trace of self-consciousness.

Alice Lathrop had had breakfast in her room. She was dressed now, waiting for husband and son. At the window she looked down upon the ever changing scene in the city's streets and assured herself she most certainly wouldn't want to live here again. Once it had been exciting and wonderful. Now it was only overcrowded, dirty and noisy.

She turned as Dennis and Tod entered the suite's living room and thought, as she always did, how handsome her son was, marveling she had given him life and birth. Little Tod. Toddy. How stubbornly he rebelled against the affectionate diminutive. It was difficult to remember what he had looked like as an infant and small boy before turning into this man of quiet charm, of dignity, of sudden laughter and purpose. He was a man. At twenty-one he was certainly no longer a boy but then he wasn't exactly a man either. My son. My son. She said the words tenderly to herself. How much you will have to learn. How good life has been to you this far. How simple and easy.

"Well," her smile broke upon both of them, "will you forgive me for being lazy and having breakfast here?"

She went to Dennis and lifted her face for his kiss. Then turned for Tod, who pressed his cheek against hers and held it there for a long moment.

"Maybe," Dennis spoke gravely, "it's just as well you didn't come along. Tod and I have a problem. With Father and Mother in Europe you certainly won't want to go to North Carolina this summer alone. We don't know what to do with you."

"I see." She assumed a thoughtful air. "Of course the two of you could spend a summer away from your beloved beach and go with me. Then again I suppose you could hang me in a closet somewhere, scatter a few mothballs around and take me out in the fall." She linked her arm with Dennis's. "But, if you'd really like to know what I want to do I'll tell you. I'd like to spend the summer with you at the beach cottage."

"We've never had any women around." Dennis was dubious.

"You could probably get used to me. I could scrub the floors, do the washing, paint the cottage; any odd jobs you can think of to keep me occupied while you two fish and lie around in the sun. I promise not to get in the way. I'll even have my meals on the back porch."

Dennis winked at Tod. "The cottage does need painting." He was thoughtful.

"And," Tod added, "Wash isn't much for scrubbing the floors. He sweeps but that's about all."

"You wouldn't expect any salary?" Dennis was suspicious and skeptical.

"Just board and room and a pat on the head now and then."

"No more shopping to do?" Dennis asked.

"No."

"Tod? Things to do, girls or friends you want to see?"

Tod shook his head. "The bright college years are behind me. I don't expect I'll ever be much for class reunions; the perennial collegian. I've kissed my girl good-bye and made an indecent proposal which she rejected." He winked at his mother.

"Well." Dennis was brisk. "What are we waiting aound in this Yankee territory for?"

He went to the telephone, told the porter's desk the accommodations needed; waited a moment and then nodded.

"Good. A bedroom and a lower. Lathrop." He hung up. "The porter thinks he can get us out tonight. I have a couple of things I want to do. Then, suppose we have a bang-up lunch and kill the afternoon with a matinee at the Palace?"

"You're quite sure I won't be in the way?" Alice was meek.

"If you are we can shift you to another cottage." He put his arm around her and spoke to Tod. "I didn't write you but after you were home for the Christmas holidays I built four cottages on those vacant lots below the Breakers. Things are happening at Daytona Beach but not just the way I expected. Maybe you noticed. We are getting a summer crowd; people from the interior coming to escape the heat; vacationists from Georgia and Alabama. The town may turn out to be a bigger summer resort than it is a winter one. With the roads being improved all the time they are using their automobiles. I have an idea for something new. It's never been tried. I've talked it over with Conrad at the Merchants Bank. He's a little skeptical because no one has come up with anything like it before. I think, maybe, he'll come around though and let us have the money." He halted, almost surprised by what he had said. "I guess I'm taking a lot for granted. I said us. It's possible you have plans of your own."

"No." Tod was serious. "I took Grandfather Will's advice. He told me not to major in anything of a practical value. I didn't. So," his smile was engaging, "I imagine I come under the heading of unskilled labor. If you can use a hand I'm available."

"Lathrop and Lathrop." Dennis tested the words. "I think I like that better than Lathrop & Son." He extended his hand. "Welcome to the firm. I still practice a little law and this may be handy in keeping us out of jail when we really begin to manipulate. We'll talk it over on the train."

The ominous thunder of men, arms and the great machinery of war began to roll over the world. The German Kaiser announced to Austria it could count on "the full support of Germany." Russia began to mobilize. England ordered the first fleet to Scapa Flow. In a note to France, Germany asked what that country would do in the event of war between Germany and Russia. France replied it would do "what her interests demanded." Great Britain assured France of the assistance of the British Fleet, and the Germans began their invasion of France near Longwy and the war was on. Almost daily, as one European country after another became involved, the United States announced her intention of remaining neutral. Germany declared war on neutral Belgium and drove a spearhead at Liège. This was the war which could not happen because men had been forced to learn armed conflict settled nothing. Yet, once set in motion by the fanaticism of a young student who pointed a gun and pulled the trigger, nothing could halt the ponderous tramping of the monster.

During the following two years a deadly ferment bubbled with a sinister persistency in the United States. There was an uneasy feeling of apprehension. Trivial incidents were exaggerated out of all proportion to their real importance. Almost daily President Wilson appealed for sensible arbitration and was ignored. Unrest plagued the United States. A steelworkers' strike in Youngstown, Ohio, turned into a riot with the men senselessly looting the town's business section. Great Britain and the United States were dangerously near an open breach when this country insisted it needed knitting needles of German manufacture for the operation of its mills. Mexico began to display an inexplicable truculence. American Marines, landing at a wharf at Tampico for supplies, were arrested but later released. Rear Admiral Mayo demanded an apology in the form of a salute to the American flag. In a childish exhibition of petulance on both sides, Mexico said it would salute the American flag if the United States would salute the Mexican flag. Fourteen battleships were ordered to Mexican waters and Vera Cruz was occupied by American Marines who seized the customhouse there. Labor strikes and riots began to be commonplace. "General" Coxey marched on Washington for the second time with an army of unemployed. A federal grand jury indicted Captain Franz von Papen and Captain Hans Taucher on a charge of conspiracy to destroy the Welland Canal. *The Fatherland,* issued by German-Americans, began publication in New York, and German-American social clubs were organized in cities and towns across the nation. It took a long time for the Government and the people to recognize and admit they were propaganda fronts set up to keep the United States neutral. Germany was planning well in advance for what she knew must eventually happen: America's entry into the war. The U.S.S. *Tennessee* sailed for Europe with $6,000,000 in gold for assistance to the Americans stranded there.

In Berlin, Will Lathrop vocally expressed his indignation over what was happening and made no effort to hide his displeasure. He berated the harassed manager of the hotel, the American Embassy, the hotel porter for the disrupted railroad schedules. Germany he was fond of but the Germans were bullet-headed, thick-necked fools who were alternately arrogant or whining. In return he was told by his German friends, dangerously close to losing their patience with him, that Germany didn't want a war. It was forced upon them. There was a worldwide plot. *Einkreisung.* Encirclement. A perfidious movement by France, Russia and England to isolate Germany and prevent the fulfillment of her destiny. An attaché from the Embassy quietly suggested that Mr. Lathrop make arrangements to leave Germany. In anger and disgust Will had his German valet and Felicia's maid pack their things. He paid the couple off with a bonus, then he and Felicia went to Holland, found passage on a small ship out of Rotterdam to Southampton. From there they were able to book accommodations on the *Lusitania* out of Liverpool for New York. The liner had already raised protests from the German Government because she flew the American flag when passing through the submarine-patrolled waters off the British coast.

In Florida the war's echoes were barely heard, but small propaganda forces were making themselves felt. In an all but empty block on Beach Street between Bay and Third Avenue a large, sprawling structure of the bright, golden coquina rock was erected by a German named Kreitzburg. The central portion was devoted to a roller skating rink which immediately became popular. An arcade leading to it housed small novelty and candy stores and a tailoring establishment. On the second floor the newly formed German-American Club counted among its members most of the town's male population. Here they gathered weekly to drink beer, imported in kegs from Jacksonville, and sing. *"Ist das nicht eine Schnitzelbank? Ja, das ist eine Schnitzelbank."* Between the singing and the steins of good beer speakers took a few minutes to explain Germany's unhappiness over what had occurred in Europe. She was the victim of rapacious nations who were determined to reduce her to a second-rate power. The lectures were well received and everyone agreed Germany was an innocent, peace-loving nation which only wanted to be let alone.

During the first years of the European war Daytona grew slowly and seemingly without plan. Small business establishments sprang up in unlikely places. A Chinese opened a laundry near what was called First Street. Gene Johnson and his brother had a bicycle and fishing tackle store near the North Bridge. Far to the south of the town's limits, around Bethune Point, McDonald had a small boatyard. In the center of what most persons thought must be the business district, Commodore Burgoyne had his home and yard, enclosed by a coquina wall. The residence occupied a full block from Volusia to Bay on Beach Street and Volusia to Bay on Palmetto Avenue. The Commodore's boathouse was an enormous structure a hundred or more feet high with cupolas and towers. Here the Commodore kept his yacht, taking it out and down the river through a channel he had dug for his private use. No one seemed to know which direction the commercial and residential movement would take. The only area which seemed established and permanent was the Negro section west of the railroad tracks. Here, in two communities, Midway and Newtown, the colored population lived in a miserable collection of shacks with outdoor toilets and water drawn from a few sulphur water wells and carried in buckets to the hovels. The town drew upon the colored men and women for its servants and laborers.

There were more automobiles in the town now but many professional and business men rode bicycles to their offices and stores. Transportation between the mainland and peninsula was provided by "jitneys," Model T Fords which took passengers on an irregular schedule across the river for a nickel. A small launch, the *Yankee Doodle,* served as a ferry and operated from a dock at the Main Street bridge to its mooring place at the foot of Volusia Avenue.

Most of the passengers rode to the ferry on their bicycles and these were loaded on the ferry and the residents pedaled along Beach Street from store to store, doing their shopping.

This state of uncertain growth extended along the entire east coast of Florida. Cocoa, Titusville, Fort Lauderdale, Eau Gallie, Fort Pierce, drowsed in the sun. No Chambers of Commerce prodded the residents for development. Tourists in these places were few and a livelihood was drawn principally from the citrus groves along the Indian River or small truck farms. Only Palm Beach had a substantial air of permanency about it and Miami was gradually emerging with a plan of development.

In this winter of 1916 the tourists were few and late in coming south. In the North small plants and factories, stimulated by the war in Europe, were expanding. The conflict was closer here. The threat was in the air, particularly along the Eastern Seaboard. Although the nation was technically neutral American ships were carrying supplies to the nations allied against the Central Powers. Germany, after repeated and unsuccessful protests, began its submarine warfare. The submarine *Deutschland* surfaced and entered the harbor at Norfolk, Virginia, with a cargo of dyestuffs badly needed by American mills. The United States blandly told England that the *Deutschland* was "an unarmed merchant vessel." Great Britain retaliated by publishing a blacklist of eighty-two American firms, owned by Germans, and dealing with them was forbidden under a Trading With the Enemy Act. The New York Stock Exchange transacted a record sales in one day of $2,192,300, and the German submarine, *U-53,* entered the harbor at Newport, Rhode Island, took on fuel and supplies and then left to sink eleven merchant vessels off Nantucket Island. Thirty-one persons were killed at the Du Pont Powder Plant, near Wilmington, Delaware, by an explosion believed to have been triggered by German agents. Henry Ford chartered a ship, the *Oscar II,* and sailed with a party for Europe on a peace mission designed to halt the war. Factories were working overtime, business boomed and those men who had been in the habit of taking their families to Florida for the winter stayed at their desks.

Dennis Lathrop glumly admitted that his dream of a population boom in Florida, the great migration from the North and Middle West, would now be years behind the schedule he had set up in his mind.

There was little activity along the coasts. The interior of the state was still sparsely populated and there were vast stretches of untenanted land waiting for the plow, the sowing, the herds of cattle he had envisioned. Despite his lack of interest his law practice had grown and he traveled almost constantly back and forth between Daytona and the county seat in DeLand. He had moved the family from the small house on Live Oak to a home on the beach. Will Lathrop stubbornly remained in his river front home on the mainland. He refused to admit the peninsula was more than a refuge for the riffraff. Growing older he had become contentious. He blamed the Germans for the world's disruption, denounced the German-American Club as a nest for spies and told everyone who would listen that a little German barber, Karl Ender, who had his shop on the beach side across the street from the Seaside Inn, was a German agent who would probably blow up the town. The only person he seemed to be on cordial terms with was his grandson Tod. He had bought himself a new Pierce-Arrow and delighted in driving it at full speed down the beach while Tod shut his eyes and offered up a small, silent prayer. After such an excursion they would go back to the homestead and drink some of the old gentleman's fine bourbon.

"I'm not finished yet," he told Tod. "Anytime you want anything you come to me and we'll talk about it. You're a fine young man and damned good company. We'll go shooting together one of these days if I can find that black son of a bitch Wash. The only time I see him is on paydays."

Over the dinner table one evening at the beach house Tod showed Dennis and his mother a letter from a Princeton classmate. He and three others were leaving for Canada to enlist in an infantry regiment, the Princess Pat.

"You're not thinking of doing anything foolish?" Alice pleaded with her eyes. "I mean, enlisting. After all it isn't our war. It isn't any of our business."

"No, Mother." Tod shook his head and smiled his reassurance. "It probably will be our business soon enough. I can wait until then."

"Well, thank God for that. I mean," she stammered her relief, "I'm glad you don't feel compelled to go off just because some of the boys from your class are."

"They're hardly boys, Mother." Tod reached over the table and placed his hand on hers. "Anyhow, I have plans of my own. Maybe I'll stay at home and be a war profiteer."

Dennis studied his son. For some time now he had been aware of his restless discontent. There was a deceptive quality about Tod Lathrop and Dennis had never been quite certain whether it was assumed or natural. Outwardly he appeared to be a man of charming indolence with a quick smile and a dry humor. He made friends without effort. Everyone responded to an indefinable magnetism. He was popular, invited to all the small social affairs, dated the town's prettiest girls but with a casualness which left most of them in a state of exasperated bewilderment. Yet, Dennis sensed an energy, a drive, which was demanding release. It was gathering in him like pressure in a steam boiler.

"What would you really like to do, Tod?"

"I'm not sure, Father." Tod wasn't evasive. It was an honest reply. "But," he continued, "it has to be something on my own. I wonder," and the question seemed to be directed to himself, "if I can borrow some money from Grandfather Will?"

"I'm not certain just how much money your grandfather has left. For years he has been spreading it around with a generous hand. How much do you want? What do you have in mind?"

Tod ignored the second question. "A few thousand at first; more later." He was thoughtful and silent for a moment. "Let's face it. Since I finished school and came home I haven't been much more than a renting agent for those cottages you built over here. It isn't enough. So, I'm going to start something on my own. Do you mind if I take the car, run over and have a talk with Grandfather Will?"

Dennis concealed his disappointment. Whatever it was Tod wanted to do he would have liked to discuss it with him. He was reluctant to break the close father and son relationship.

"Of course. The keys are on the desk in the living room. I had hoped we could work out something together. You know the plans I have. God knows," he smiled ruefully, "I have talked about them enough."

Tod shook his head. "There isn't going to be any real development in Florida until after the war is over. No one can predict when that will be. You, the family, are loaded down with real estate. You

★ 98

bought some property and took options on more. Grandfather Will owns those large river-to-ocean tracts between here and Mosquito Inlet. Not an acre of it means a thing now other than a drain for taxes. Oh"—he could see the objection forming—"in time yes." He smiled warmly. "I'm your disciple. I believe . . . I believe," he intoned in hollow tones. "I expect in time we'll wrap up Florida and tie it with a bright ribbon. In the meanwhile I have an idea of my own." He arose, bent to kiss his mother and nodded to Dennis.

After Tod had left, Dennis finished his coffee in silence. In his heart he knew Tod was right. Nothing was going to happen in Florida now; certainly nothing on the scale he had once imagined.

"He's right, you know." He spoke without looking at Alice. "I'm not so stubborn I won't admit a mistake in timing. I wish he would tell me what he has in mind."

"You must let him go, Dennis." Alice was quietly firm. "I know how difficult it is to remember, sometimes, he's a man and with a mind and will of his own. Don't imagine for a moment," her hands reached out for her husband's, "I don't, also, regret the passing of a small boy. I miss what he was but am proud of what he has become."

"Father once said I was fifty years ahead of my time." Dennis linked his fingers with hers. "Maybe it's true. But," he defended himself, "this damned war has thrown things out of gear. I know I'm right. The years will prove it even though I'm six feet underground when it happens. But," he grinned, "I won't get much satisfaction out of it with a granite slab pinning me down. I'd like to be around to say: I told you so."

"I think you'll look better in Vermont marble, dear. Whenever you growl I know you're all right. You are impatient and always have been. Don't be surprised to discover the trait in your son. Now," she stood up, "let's have our coffee on the porch with a little brandy. I'm getting addicted to the evening tipple. Do you know," they walked arm in arm from the dining room, "sometimes I think Tod is more like your father than he is you? It isn't too apparent yet but I suspect him of being in the grand manner, the ducal gesture."

Tod drove down the beach, turning at the approach to the South Bridge. Settled on the dunes was a little, frame, three-sided structure with its front open to the ocean. Benches lined the roof's overhang. A small sign, neatly lettered, invited the weary traveler to: REST

AND BE THANKFUL. He had no idea who had built the shelter but, and he laughed to himself, the purpose it generally served could hardly be what the donor had in mind. The benches, after dark, were used mainly as hard couches of assignation for the town's boys and girls who went about the business of lovemaking, indifferent to the presence of others. After all, the boards were neater than the loose sand and there was some false illusion of privacy; particularly if a couple was lucky enough to get the topmost bench, back in the shadows.

Mr. Pellicier, bent a little with rheumatism, still held his job as keeper of the drawbridge but he no longer had to walk about with the heavy crank to open it. A gasoline motor now did the work, swinging the span around whenever a river craft blew its horn for passage. Toll fees had been fixed on a yearly basis for the permanent residents, and the owners of automobiles were given a metal tag to be affixed to the radiator. Will Lathrop had not mellowed with time. He still maintained his feud with Pellicier. Actually, the two old men enjoyed it and always had although neither would ever have admitted to such a weakness. Lathrop refused to put the tag on his car.

"I'm busy," he told Pellicier. "My servants are busy. If you want that damn tag on the radiator you're welcome to come over to my place any time and put it on yourself."

"It's not my job to put it on, Mr. Lathrop, and you know damn well it isn't." Pellicier wasn't intimidated by Lathrop's fierce scowling and angry tone. These tilts provided just about his only diversion. "Now, if you don't put it on I'm going to stop you every time you come across and make you show it to me so you had better have it on your person at all times. Another thing. If you try to run past I'll take a shotgun and blow out a tire before you can reach the draw." He actually smirked.

"Well, by God!" Will Lathrop roared. "You just do that. Stop me and ask to see the tag. I'll show it to you but I'm damned if I will put it on my car."

That was the way things were now. Mr. Pellicier would stand in the middle of the bridge whenever he was lucky enough to see Will Lathrop approaching and wave him to a halt. If he didn't catch sight of him Will would stop of his own accord.

"Pellicier," he would shout, "come out here and look at my tag." He would then fumble through all of his pockets, pretending he couldn't find the metal disk. Mr. Pellicier would wait patiently. "It's right here someplace," Lathrop would mumble. "I'll locate it in a minute."

Now, though, Mr. Pellicier had struck upon a new gambit. He would sit in his cushioned rocking chair in the shade of the draw-bridge house. When Will Lathrop came to a quivering halt, prepared for the ritual, Mr. Pellicier would smile and with an indolent wave of his hand signal him on.

"I know you have paid for your pass, Mr. Lathrop." His manner was bland, friendly, a smile creasing his weathered face. "It's all right. Just go on."

This attitude of calm acceptance infuriated Will Lathrop beyond all measuring. Pellicier was sneaky, changing the rules of the game. It robbed the encounter of all sport.

"Oh! No you don't!" He had yelled his exasperation the first time it happened. "You just get off your ass and come out here to look at my tag. That's what you're being paid for." He started the search, his hands darting in and out of his pockets.

"It's all right, Mr. Lathrop." Pellicier rocked contentedly, gazing happily at the sky. "Cross on over. I don't need to see the tag. I know you have one."

"You'd better come and see or, by God, I'll report you to the bridge commissioners as being derelict in your duty. How do you know I bought a pass? Maybe I just didn't do it this year."

"Oh!" Mr. Pellicier was unimpressed. "I get a list from the county. The commissioners know all about you, Mr. Lathrop. I guess just about everyone in the county knows what a bastard you are." There was no rancor in the statement. It was made with an almost admiring benevolence. "Now, just drive on and don't hold up the other people who want to cross." He would pick up a newspaper and pretend to read.

Will Lathrop would sit in his car staring straight ahead, his mouth fixed in a stony expression. Mr. Pellicier would turn a page of the paper, bending to read the print through his rimless glasses. His chair would rock slowly back and forth. This silent contest would last as much as five or ten minutes, neither man willing to yield. Some-

times, however, traffic would begin to pile up behind Lathrop's im-
mobile car. There would be the impatient bleating of horns and the
rasping snarl of the new Klaxons. When this happened Mr. Pellicier
was forced to admit a temporary defeat. Reluctantly he would leave
his chair, waiting while Lathrop made a search of his clothing with a
triumphant snicker which Pellicier ignored. Will would eventually
produce the tag, Pellicier would inspect it gravely and nod. Word-
lessly they would concede the day's victory belonged to Will Lathrop.
But if there was no traffic, Pellicier would simply outwait his adver-
sary. He would even leave his chair and go inside while Lathrop sat
in his car, alone and unattended. Finally he would drive off van-
quished and it would take an hour or more of furious driving on
the beach to restore Will Lathrop's sense of humor.

Crossing the bridge now Tod waved at Mr. Pellicier and the man
returned the salute. He liked young Lathrop and had known him
ever since he was a youngster in knickerbockers and used to come
and fish from the bridge. Everyone in town, he thought, liked Tod.
It was a miracle, Mr. Pellicier admitted, he could have grown from
the seed of such an outright bastard as his grandfather. He smiled
with a gentle humor. All of these years the two of them had been at
this nonsense. In his secret thoughts Pellicier had an idea that when
Will Lathrop died something would also go out of his life. He'd give
up the job as bridge tender and retire on a small pension. There just
wouldn't be any fun in the position without Will Lathrop around. He
wondered if maybe the old bastard felt the same way.

VII

THE house at the corner of Live Oak and Beach Street had grown old with the same grace as its owner. The years seemed to have brushed it lightly. The great oaks stood firm and deeply rooted, spreading their heavy branches over the yard. The sago palms set fifty years ago made a delicate cascade of their long fronds. Poinsettia and hibiscus were vivid splashes of color. Honeysuckle grew in profusion, climbing the sides of the house, and the Cherokee rose twined and embraced the pickets of an enclosing fence.

When Will Lathrop planned the house he avoided the architectural monstrosities of the period. The lines were clean. A broad porch fronted upon the river. Inside, the rooms were high-ceilinged and spacious, filled with light and with perfume from the shrubs and flowers.

Tod drove in through the Live Oak entrance and parked on the graveled stretch of crushed marle. Wash, whose only job now was to keep the Pierce-Arrow waxed and shining, came from the garage. Farther down Live Oak a second driveway led to the stables. The barouche, a jaunting cart and a surrey were rarely used now. Mark and a groom kept the vehicles in a state of sparkling varnish and the horses were as carefully curried and tended as though they were show animals. Felicia, who disliked and distrusted automobiles, used the carriage now and then when she had a little shopping to do or made a social call upon a friend. Other than this they served no purpose. Will kept them because of Felicia and out of a sentimental affection to which he would not admit.

"Good evenin', suh, Mistuh Tod." Wash's hair was tightly curled silver but he did not bend with time. He stood as proudly erect as ever; a powerful and gentle man of deep loyalty. The Lathrops had always been his people. "Mistuh Will an' Missus Lathrop will be right glad to see you, suh. You ain' bin ovah en some time." He shook his head unhappily. "Things suah change. Seem laik no one have time to do like what we uster—fishin', huntin', crabbin' at the inlet."

"We'll get around to it again, Wash. You're right though. Someone's stepping on the gas and we're all going faster than we should."

Will Lathrop was in the living room reading the Jacksonville *Times-Union* and the local paper published by Fitzgerald, the *News*. He smiled his pleasure as Tod entered and rose from the chair with his usual courtesy.

"I'm glad to see you, boy. Indeed I am." They shook hands. "I've been sitting here wondering if I would have to drink by myself. A little whisky after dinner always settles my stomach. How are Dennis and your mother?"

"They're fine, Grandfather Will. Where's Grandmother?"

"In her room, boy. She's not feeling well. Nothing serious. Just a touch of la grippe. I guess that's what it is. She won't have a doctor. What brings you across the river? Never mind." He didn't give Tod a chance to reply. "Let's go and have that drink."

The room he once referred to as his "den" had undergone some startling alterations over the years, depending upon his mood. The Turkish-Egyptian décor with its divans, Oriental rugs, water pipes, damask hangings, crossed scimitars and incense pots on low inlaid tables had vanished. For a time it became a galleon's cabin with leaded windows, lamps on gimbals, charts, telescopes and sextants with grog served from a keg. There followed a Western period with bearskin rugs, old Winchester rifles on the walls, Remington prints, saddles and tack spread about with hairy chaps draped over benches. This was followed by a German influence. It was a *bierstube* with casks set into the wall, heavy mugs, Prussian helmets and dueling swords. However, he became angry with the Germans, blaming them for the world's troubles. Now it was Mexican in character. Fine, hand-woven sarapes hung on the walls, brightly hued rugs of rough texture covered the floor. There were bullfight posters, pre-Columbian figures on the mantel and the chairs were of handcrafted leather.

Will set out a bottle of tequilla, sliced a lime and poured salt into a saucer.

"This is just for atmosphere. I can't abide the smell myself." He opened a cabinet and brought bourbon and a carafe of water with small glasses. "Bourbon is the stuff. Help yourself."

He waited until Tod had poured a small drink and nodded his approval when his grandson sipped it without water.

"I always put water out with good bourbon. Just to see what my guest will do. It is an unfailing test of character. When a man doesn't dilute fine whisky you can trust him. You know," he raised his glass, "we ought to see more of each other, boy."

Tod took one of the velvet cushioned, brass nail studded, straight-backed chairs. He held the whisky glass in both hands at his open knees and studied his grandfather with affectionate amusement. It was impossible not to admire him. People might not like Will Lathrop but they had to respect him.

"I know, Grandfather. I've been trying to set myself on the path I want to travel. It's been a little confusing. As Wash said when I came in: We don't seem to have the time we used to have. Everything's moving so fast."

"Hell, boy, I gave you the best advice. Marry a wealthy girl. Money and the leisure to enjoy it make the finest of all lives."

Tod smiled. "I'm not sure I want to do it that way."

"Suit yourself." The old man finished his whisky and reached for the bottle. "I'm thinking about buying a boat. Not a big, damned schooner like the one the Commodore has but a launch. We could run down to the inlet in an hour for fishing or even go outside when the ocean is smoothed out under a west wind. Boy," his eyes were kindled with a sudden fire, "speaking of the inlet did I ever tell you about the whales and the time Daytona almost became the New Bedford of Florida?"

"No, sir." Tod lit a cigarette and leaned back. "I don't think you did."

"Well," Will Lathrop half closed his eyes and an impish grin played about his mouth, "it happened, I guess, about a year or so before you, Dennis and your mother came to Daytona. Eight or ten fair-sized whales got into the shallows down around the inlet and when the tide went out there they were, high, dry and stranded. "Well." He stood up and began to pace about the room. When he told a story he was a natural, unaffected actor, dropping unconsciously into the manner and the colloquial speech of his characters. "Someone, a fisherman, I guess, brought the word up to Daytona. At first the folks didn't think much about it. A few said they might go down and take a look out of curiosity. None of them had ever seen a whale. Then somehow, and this I heard later, the news was passed around in Claude Pascal's pool room over on the beach side. There's a fellow," he leaned across a table to demonstrate, "just about to put a three ball in the corner pocket. He stops all of a sudden and looks up and lets out a yell. 'By God,' he says, 'my wife pays fifty cents for a little bottle of whale oil she uses on her sewing machine. The way I heard about the stuff is they melt down the blubber and get the oil.' This starts things off. Another fellow said he remembered reading about some stuff called amber grease, meaning ambergris naturally. He said it was in a whale's head and was used to make perfume and was worth maybe two or three thousand dollars a pound. 'My God, boys,' " Will put down the imaginary cue and began waving his arms. " 'There's maybe a million dollars' worth of stuff lyin' around down there at the inlet an' no one's doin' anything about it.' "

Will pushed the bottle toward Tod and waited until his grandson had poured another drink.

"Now, there's no way of knowing," he continued with a dreamy expression on his face, "just how the rumor spread but by the middle of the morning the whole town, here on the mainland and over on the peninsula, goes crazy. They loaded themselves into wagons, sailboats, rowboats, anything that would float. Some even got out their bicycles. The women packed up baskets of food for there was no telling how long this thing would take. It was like a gold rush. The men had saws, cane knives, kitchen knives, axes, hatchets; anything that would cut. The women snatched up the children and the men, knowin' the labor ahead, all brought along a gallon jug of whisky Tom Mears used to make up near the Tomoka River where he had a still. Then just about the entire population started off for the inlet. They were streaming down the beach and on the river. The men had already taken a few belts from the jugs so everyone was in a high good humor and tellin' each other what they were going to do with the money."

He whistled softly at the memory and took a sip of his bourbon.

"I was some curious about the thing myself so I had Mark bring around the carriage and we started down. Well, boy, you've never seen anything like it. There they were, the whole damn town. The men were sawing, slicing, hacking and cutting away at those whales. When I got there they were hip deep in guts, slime, blood and blubber. Some of them had crosscut saws and they were working on the heads, hunting for the amber grease. Up on the dunes and out of the way the women were laying out food like it was a picnic. The men would stop every now and then to take a pull from their jugs. The children were climbing all over the whales, they'd slip and slide down into the mess and come up screaming and covered with blood. Pieces of meat and blubber were lying all over the place and, what with the blood on everyone, it looked like a goddamned Indian massacre. The more the men hacked and sawed the more they drank and in a little while they were reeling around, swinging their axes, stabbing with their knives, and Joe Benton cut his goddamned foot off thinking it was a piece of whale. They ran out of whisky and a couple of fellows volunteered to take a boat over to New Smyrna and get more if the others would promise to save them their share of the treasure. What with a dozen or more gallon jugs to keep their spirits up, by sundown they could barely stand. Some lay down and went to sleep right in the guts that were strewn about. Others kept slicing and sawing. They were all going to be rich. No one in the whole town would ever have to work again."

Will lit a cigar, savored the Havana leaf and poured himself another tot of whisky.

"Now they had the whales cut up. The whole point around the inlet was covered with big slabs and pieces. The children were crying. The women were tired and wanted to go home. Their husbands cuffed them around some until they screamed louder or shut up. Then, all of a sudden, as though the same thought hit them all at the same time, they stopped working and just stood there looking at each other. They didn't know what to do with the stuff. There it was. Finally someone said they had to try out the blubber, melt it down so they could get the whale oil. They were blood from head to foot, stupefied with all the whisky, worn out from chopping. No one knew how blubber was tried out but one fellow said it was just like cooking bacon only more so. They would have to have fires and some big iron kettles, but where the hell were they going to find any big iron kettles? No one had an answer for this one. A couple of women had brought along coffeepots to make a brew for lunch but they all agreed it would take a thousand years or more to try out all that blubber in coffeepots. They hunted through the sawed-open heads for amber grease but no one had any idea what it was supposed to look like. So, they threw down their axes, hatchets and saws and sat on the beach to finish up the liquor. Then they went to sleep. It was hard to tell what was whale meat and what were men. Sometime during the evening the women got them up, back into their boats and wagons. The ones who had come on bicycles sure as hell weren't in any shape to pedal twelve miles back home so they crawled up into the soft dunes and went to sleep. Right then and there the big boom in whale oil and ambergris collapsed. But," he waited until Tod's laughter subsided, "that wasn't the end of it. The tide didn't wash away the blubber, meat and bones. The stuff and the carcasses stayed there. I don't need to tell you what it began to smell like after a couple of days in the sun. The men who tended the lighthouse wrote to Washington. The Mayor of New Smyrna got in touch with the Governor but nothing was done. For a month or more, every time there was a wind from the south that stink would come floating up to Daytona. It got into your hair, your clothes, the houses. The whole town puked. Thomas Oyama sold out his entire stock of incense sticks the first day. Finally, when we couldn't stand it any longer, Commodore Burgoyne, Conrad at the bank, Fred Niver, Henry Titus, myself and some others put up some money. We hired a barge and a towboat along with some Negro men and had the stuff shoveled up and carried out to sea where it was dumped. You look around, though, and you will still see some of the whale bones in the yards over on the beach. People brought them up as souvenirs and made planters out of them."

He leaned back in a chair and began to laugh now that the story was ended. Reaching for the bourbon he offered it to Tod and then took some for himself.

"For a year or more whenever a woman would get real mad at her husband she'd cup her hands to her mouth and yell: 'Thar she blows.' I tell you that sent the men off with their tails between their legs and a silly look on their faces."

"Is that really true or did you make it up?" Tod was still chuckling.

"Boy, you just don't make up such a story. It has to happen. Anyhow, there are those whale bones in the yards to prove it." He shook his head, eyes bright with merriment at the recollection of a frantic day. "Now, I have an idea there's something on your mind. Want to tell me about it? Girl trouble?"

"No." Tod had an idea the old gentleman would have been delighted if he were unhappily involved with a girl. It would lend a little spice to things. "No. I want to borrow some money, quite a bit."

Will Lathrop nodded approvingly. "When you borrow borrow big. Never trust a man who says he needs a few hundred to tide him over for a little while. When you get to the point of being pressed for a few hundred the chances are you really need a hell of a lot more."

"I want to buy some trucks; big ones, as large as they are making. To start with I'll need at least four. I'm going into business."

"Trucks." Will Lathrop tested the word. "Trucks are used to haul things from one place to another. So, I imagine you intend to do that. To tell you the truth I'm a little surprised. It seems an unlikely occupation for you."

Tod merely nodded. He understood his grandfather well enough to know he liked to pursue his thoughts in his own way and arrive at certain conclusions.

"Offhand I'd say the hauling business here in Daytona is limited and pretty well tied up by old man Ridgeway."

"I'm not thinking about local trucking. I'm going after some of the business the railroad handles. Or, to be more exact, what it can't take care of. Suppose you want to ship something from Daytona to DeLand. Do you know what happens?" He didn't wait for the answer. "The Florida East Coast Railroad takes it up to East Palatka. Then the Seaboard carries it to Palatka where it is transferred to another boxcar and routed to DeLand. A truck can haul it direct from here to DeLand faster and cheaper. That's only one example of the short, intrastate transportation. I could name a dozen more. Sanford. Ocala. Orlando. From a dozen points the shipping is involved because there are no direct routes. New and better roads are being built. Jacksonville, with the new brick road connecting it with Daytona, is already within the radius I have in mind. I want," he halted and amended what he had been about to say, "I'm going to set up a truck and maybe even a bus service which will eventually cover Florida. I've been studying this thing for some time. I have the figures. Trucks can carry produce from small communities to the railheads. They can haul the groceries the stores here buy from Jacksonville wholesalers faster and cheaper than the F.E.C. Furniture, small machinery, odd lots of merchandise, can all be hauled by truck. I have comparative rates and costs. From here I fan out to the north as far as Jacksonville with Ormond, Bunnell, St. Augustine, Bayard, to draw business from. Westward the towns I have already mentioned can be tapped. To the south my trucks can run on regular and irregular schedules to service New Smyrna, Titusville, Eau Gallie, Fort Pierce, Palm Beach and, eventually, Miami. As the state grows, small towns will spring up between these places. The potential is there. It may take some years but one of these days it will be commonplace for a truck to load in New York and take its cargo across the continent to California. The automobile manufacturers, the owners of cars, will demand more and better highways. What I start now can move from intrastate to interstate commerce. If you want to see the figures I have put together I'll bring them over."

Will Lathrop regarded his grandson with an expression of troubled sorrow. "Son," he spoke slowly, "you're making me very unhappy. I had great hopes for you; looking forward to the pleasure of your company in the years to come. You see, I've given Dennis up. Not that I ever really regarded his future with optimism. In a way I'm, also, a failure. I started too late to do the job right. But," he shook his head dolefully, "I expected you to turn out better. I said to myself, There he is. Stoddard Lathrop, a product of a fine eastern university who didn't learn one damn thing of value—practical value, that is. He's good-looking, polished, plays a fair game of tennis. This being one of the things he picked up after four years at Princeton along with fingering a few tunes on a mandolin. He speaks reasonably good French, knows a little about wines, brandy, art and music.

Beyond this, though, he can't do a single thing which would help him make a living. In you I thought we had the potential for a graceful dilettant who would worm Felicia's money out of me; spend it in well-bred carousing, wenching and gambling. I said, Here's a young man who will knock up all the eligible debutantes, cause mothers to weep and fathers to rage, and be indifferent to the law's pounding on the door. He will pass through life with the light indifference of a sun-shot breeze. Instead," he sighed, "it looks as though you have failed me and determined to be a solid citizen, a man of business and affairs who will probably amass a million dollars or more through work. Now, boy," he took another drink to assuage the pain of his discovery, "just what in hell are you going to do after you make a lot of money? I'll tell you." He thrust an accusing finger at Tod. "You'll want to go on making more. Oh, I've seen it in other men! It's something like the hives. In the beginning there's only a little itch here or there. You scratch it. Then it begins to itch in another place. First thing you know you're scratching all over. You can't stop. There isn't time for anything else. Take my advice. Don't scratch this first time. It will only spread the rash. Let it itch for a little while and it'll go away and never come back. Then you can be a contented man. Do you think fellows like Rockefeller, Morgan, Gary, Vanderbilt, Astor, Carnegie and the others have any fun? Hell no they don't. They wake up every morning with the itch, scratching and conniving how to make another million. Boy," there was a suggestion of a tremor in his voice, "is that the sort of life you want? Is this all I've been able to teach you? If so I just can't help but feel I've failed somehow." He swallowed his whisky in a single gulp and wiped at his eyes with a fine linen handkerchief.

Tod had listened solemnly to his grandfather, fighting the laughter which threatened to explode with each dirgelike sentence. The hell of it is, he thought, I'm not sure he doesn't mean exactly what he's saying.

"I'm sorry, Grandfather Will." He was contrite and humble. "I expect I've failed you. But," he offered this as a hopeful explanation, "a black sheep turns up every now and then in the best of flocks. All its loved ones can do is turn a brave face to the world and pretend it isn't there."

The old man nodded. "You're probably right. It isn't your fault.

I'll try and keep it in mind and be tolerant. But," he was defeated, "an opportunity such as you had doesn't come along every day. Trucks. Buses." He somehow managed to make the words obscene and revolting. "As you say, nature is far from perfect. She makes a mistake every now and then. This thing which has touched you must come from the Stoddard side of the family. There is no other honest explanation." He selected a cigar after offering the humidor to Tod, who shook his head in refusal. "About this loan. Suppose you meet me at the bank in the morning about eleven o'clock." He smiled with rare pleasure. "Conrad and Fred Niver don't consider me much of a personal risk so I'll have Felicia sign over some stock as security. I tell you, boy. There's an understanding and appreciative woman." The praise seemed to cheer him up. "She realized from the start what she had in me and was grateful. We've never had a word of misunderstanding from the day I gave up my alleged practice of medicine and began living off of her money. You can't imagine the fun she's had. And to think she almost married the son of a wholesale butcher in Cincinnati. I saved her just a few steps from the altar and she's always willingly acknowledged the debt with generosity and tenderness."

They walked from the room, down the long hall, out across the porch and along the path through the yard. The evening was warm and fragrant with a southwest wind. In the air there was the almost cloying perfume of magnolia and oleander. The long, gray beards of Spanish moss in the great oaks flew out as though from old men running. Up the river a couple of blocks a few lights from the Yacht Club fluttered on the water. A quarter-moon rode the sky. Over everything there was the deep, muted thunder of the ocean as it washed upon the hard sands of the distant beach.

The old man halted, listened, sniffed at the air like an animal whose senses have been alerted.

"If I was your age I'd be wound up with some girl in bed or the back seat of an automobile on a night like this instead of talking about money and trucks." He turned abruptly to face Tod. "There isn't anything wrong with you, is there, boy? I mean you have everything a man needs to be normal? You're not one of those lacy-dacy boys who don't like girls? I've seen a lot of them in Europe, mincing around, holding hands with each other. God knows you've slid far enough as it is. I'd hate to see something like that turn up in you."

"No, sir." Tod was gravely respectful. "My feeling about girls is normal. So was everything else the last time I looked."

"Well, that's something." Will Lathrop was relieved. "You keep them that way. Maybe, in time, I'll be able to forgive and forget this other thing."

He stood by the side of the marl driveway and watched as Tod backed toward the open gates. He lifted a hand in a salute of good-bye and then shouted. His voice was clear over the motor's sound.

"How much money do you intend borrowing?"

"About twenty-five thousand." Tod yelled the answer triumphantly.

"Well. That's all right. I wouldn't want to bother Conrad for any little five or ten. Twenty-five thousand." He took a certain pleasure in the amount. "That will give him something to fret over. The stock market might crash and Felicia's collateral wouldn't be worth a damn. He'll have to think about that and worrying is about all the pleasure a banker gets out of life."

Drink in hand Tod stood at one of the windows of his room in the Seminole Hotel, in Jacksonville, and looked out over the city. There was a thoughtful frown on his face and he swallowed some of the whisky without actually tasting it. Scattered on a desk and over some chairs were folders and brochures supplied by the few dealers in automobiles, tractors and trucks who had offices and showrooms he had visited.

Supine on a bed, legs spraddled apart, clad in the sacklike BVD underwear, taking what breeze he could from the slowly revolving ceiling fan, Willie Estes dug a finger at his navel and with a slit-eyed cunning studied Stoddard Lathrop's back. Willie was a softly fat, gross and almost oval-shaped man who sweated profusely. His complexion was moistly pink and the face never showed more than the lightest down of a beard. Always he seemed a little dirty, even after a bath. He was all but illiterate, incredibly and senselessly foul of speech and mind; a man who equated courtesy with subservience. He was swaggeringly contemptuous of those he considered to be his inferiors; craftily obsequious in the presence of his superiors. He was possessed of an unreasoning hatred of all *niggers* and even spoke the word with a vicious lash of his tongue. The bastard son of a Georgia sharecropper, he had been shunted off by a slatternly mother to an aunt in Florida at the age of three. Through the easy democracy of the public school system he had passed through the first seven grades in the same classes with Tod Lathrop. So they had known each other for years without actually having any social contact beyond the schoolyard on Bay Street. Willie was mean, dishonest and avaricious. He would fawn, crawl upon his belly or fight with a savage disregard for the consequences to gain something he wanted.

Tod could feel the man's eyes upon him. The very fact that Willie was lying on the bed instead of going into his own and adjoining room annoyed him. He was also angered by the association. But, he had reasoned, in business it would always be necessary to adjust one's self to an arrangement having no relation to friendship, intimacy or even respect. He needed Willie and Willie, with a feral instinct, knew this. So he endured Willie and steeled himself against the man's vulgarity.

Willie Estes had the flair of a genius with machinery. It was a strange, inexplicable talent. In him there was an almost mystical feeling and touch for an engine. He could take a seemingly useless pile of junk—cylinders, block, rods, pistons, clogged fuel lines and carburetor—and fit them together so they would operate as a whole. Given the education, the training, he would have developed into a skilled designer of internal combustion engines. He did seemingly impossible jobs with the ease of a child piling one cube upon another. As it was he had become the acknowledged master mechanic of Daytona's one garage servicing the town's growing number of automobiles. The townspeople often said Willie knew more about cars and engines than the manufacturers themselves. It was this which had brought Stoddard Lathrop and Willie Estes together.

For what he planned, Tod would eventually require the technical knowledge of a Willie Estes, and Willie sensed he could use Tod Lathrop. This was an understanding unadmitted between them. Each followed it in his own way. Both were satisfied to pretend it didn't exist. Tod carefully avoided any suggestion of an employer-employee relationship. He called Willie Willie as he always had when they were youngsters. He even endured Willie's reference to him as Toddy-boy in a tone suggesting a genial companionship and equality. Once, early in their association, he had fired angrily.

"For Christ's sake, Willie, stop calling me Toddy-boy! Call me Tod. Stoddard. Lathrop; any damn thing you like except Toddy-boy. It makes me want to puke."

"Well, sure, Toddy-boy. Tod, I mean." This was added quickly and with sly innocence. "I never knew it bothered you. It comes natural, somehow, we knowin' each other all these years like we done. 'Course," he continued with a mild tone of injury, "we was never really close; playin' together like you done with the other kids an' me comin' to your birthday parties to the big house of your grandfather. I don't hold no grudge. It ain't no fault of yourn my folks was poor an' yours rich. I'll try an' remembuh you don't like Toddy-boy." Willie's accent defied an oral translation. It was something to which the ear became accustomed.

With the loan from the Merchants Bank secured, Tod had sought out Willie. Dennis had recently purchased a Cadillac touring car and Tod used it until he could get one of his own. He had ordered a Buick roadster with a folding top, long, shining brass steering column, gear shift lever and hand brake. It was a sport car of bright red and the top had detachable, isinglass curtains which could be snapped on when it rained. He drove to Holland's garage with the Cadillac and a vague explanation of something being wrong with its engine. Willie listened to the motor for a minute and then motioned to Tod to shut it off.

"There ain't nothin' wrong. Maybe you just don't set the spark right. You got to feel for how it needs while you're drivin'. Sometimes you need more spark. Sometimes you gotta have less; like when you're plowin' through sand an' she begins to knock some you gotta cut down on the spark." He wiped his hands on a ball of greasy waste and peered quizzically at Tod. "What the hell's really on your mind, Toddy-boy?"

"I want to talk with you. I thought maybe, when you're through, we could go up to Clifton's and have a drink."

"Well, now, ain't this somethin'?" Willie managed a tone and expression of pleased astonishment which at the same time conveyed derision. "I never figured a Lathrop an' an Estes would be settin' down together over a drink."

"Stop talking like a goddamned fool." Tod was angry. "We never had a drink together because there wasn't a reason for one. I have a proposition to make if you want to listen. If not say so and take that silly smirk off your face."

"Oh, I'll listen if it's only the time of day you want to pass. You gotta agree, though, the offer of a sociable drink sounds funny comin' from you to me." There was a venom here. "I'll listen with both ears but whatever it is don't figure to give me the dirty end of the stick." He glanced around. "I'll just get out of these overalls. Old man Holland ain't likely to come down this late in the day. I'll close the shop."

They drove up to a section of the river shore near Ormond. Florida had local option and Daytona had voted itself dry. Those who wanted whisky, beer or wine could have it shipped down from Jacksonville. Most of the residents, though, bought the illegal moonshine. Clifton had a shack built out on the end of a dock and sold a good, aged corn whisky by the bottle or glass.

At a small table by a window overlooking the placid river they had a drink and Tod explained what he had in mind while Willie listened.

"I'm going to buy four trucks to start with. Later I'll add to them. I've talked to people at the county seat and can get a bus franchise from here to DeLand, Sanford, back by way of New Smyrna to Daytona. I'll operate on a regular schedule even if I lose money at first. With a little pushing and influence I can probably tie up a long-term franchise for local bus service between Daytona and the peninsula to take in Seabreeze. The jitneys are driving the ferry out of business. A couple of good buses on schedules will run the independent jitneys off the streets."

"Where do I come in?" Willie squinted at Tod.

"The financing, the business, the political angles I can take care of. What I don't know I'll damn soon learn or go bankrupt. But I don't know anything about mechanical maintenance. Trucks and buses are sure as hell going to break down. I'm going to have to

★ 116

have a shop for repairs and someone to run it. How would you like to come in with me?"

"You mean like a partner?" Willie appeared sleepy-eyed but the pose was deceptive. "Like Lathrop and Estes?"

Tod thought quickly. It had to be settled between them now and without question. There was a danger, a latent menace, in Willie Estes. Intuitively he was aware of this. Willie was the hungry dog set to watch the meat market. Yet, at this moment he had to be careful with his answer. He must be firm without giving offense to a stupid vanity.

"No." He didn't emphasize the word. "I don't mean like partners. I'm putting up all the capital, taking the risk. It's my truck line. My bus route."

"Well, then, hell." Willie yawned. "If it's just a job I already got one." He lit a cigarette and stared at the ceiling.

"This can be a better job." Tod didn't want to be maneuvered into urging Willie to take something. He wanted the man because he felt instinctively he was the best for the job. "I'm going to form a company, a corporation. It will pay you a better salary than you are getting now. As things work out as I expect they will the work of maintaining a fleet of trucks and buses will expand. You will have to train mechanics to work under your direction." He was aware of a change in Willie's truculant attitude. The idea of men working at his orders was irresistible. "Also," Tod continued, "as we grow you can buy into some of the corporation out of your salary. You'll have an interest. But," he was cold, firm and unmistakably adamant now, "Stoddard Lathrop is the head of the company, the president and controlling shareholder. Willie Estes is Superintendent of Maintenance with an interest in the profits. You don't have anything to lose and a hell of a lot to gain."

Willie grinned. "You got a real need of me, ain't you, Toddy-boy? There ain't nobody between Miami and Jacksonville who knows automobiles an' engines like Willie Estes. Your trucks break down like you say. Who the hell's goin' to get them runnin' again but Willie?"

"All right. Let's say I need you." It was a statement of fact and nothing more. "You're here, on the spot. You're the best there is I know of. But, if I have to, I'll pay for a factory-trained mechanic to come down and take over the maintenance end. So," he was icy, "don't get the idea I'm going to let you shove it up me, Willie." He pushed back his chair.

"Sit down. Sit down. Don't get your behind in a sling." Willie was almost jovial. "Willie Estes. Mr. Willie Estes, Superintendent of Maintenance." He spoke the words with a dreamy reflective pleasure. "It'll sure do me good to tell old man Holland to kiss my ass. I been wantin' to for a long time." He regarded Tod for a second. "Pull your chair back. Let's have another drink. Maybe we can get together. Only," his voice rasped, "I'm goin' to have a lawyer to draw up a legal paper so's every minute of the day or night I'll know how we stand. Because, Toddy-boy," he leaned forward, lips slightly parted, teeth showing, "you ain't goin' to shove it up me neither."

In such a fashion had this unlikely relationship been formed. Tod was alternately fascinated and repelled by Willie Estes. There was no limit to his vulgarity. It embarrassed Tod when they were alone together. In the company of others he cringed at Willie's display of arrogance. One of the first things Willie wanted to know was what Tod intended to call his proposed truck and bus service.

"I was thinking of something like The Citrus Belt Line. We'll be taking in a lot of grove territory."

"Don't think no more." Willie had rubbed his hands delightedly. "That there's it. You hit it right on the head." For a moment his admiration for Tod's ingenuity overcame his almost perpetual air of suspicion.

He had printed cards now.

WILLIE ESTES, Esq.

Maintenance Superintendent

The Citrus Belt Line

These he distributed among his acquaintances and here, in Jacksonville, handed them to bellboys, waiters, salesmen and cigar counter clerks. He always carried a small deck held together with a rubber band.

Against his boorishness, his clownish extravagance of dress and manner, a tongue which clattered an idiot's preoccupation with filth, was the devotion with which he approached anything mechanical. In this he was a different man. They had visited the showrooms of every automotive dealer in the city. Reo. Autocar. White. Dodge. G.M.C. It wasn't enough for Willie simply to look at a truck. He had brought with him a suit of mechanic's coveralls. Drawing this on he crawled beneath the vehicles, inspecting every inch of them from differential to steering knuckle. He tested springs, driving shafts, took off wheels to look at the axle mounting. Removed the plates from transmission boxes and studied the gears. He had the motors started and listened to them as a physician might take a stethoscope and search for a heart murmur. He was contemptuous of the salesmen and agency managers, waving them away when they tried to elaborate on the excellence of their product.

"You wouldn't know your ass from a universal joint. Leave me alone."

He had driven each truck and bus, testing them in all gears and speeds, and made no comment when they returned to the showroom. He wouldn't even let Tod know what he thought.

Now, from his place on the bed, he belched and expelled gas with the sound of tearing cloth.

"The White. We buy the White, Tod. The truck and the bus. There ain't no question."

Tod turned from the window. This was the first opinion Willie had given during the three days they had been in Jacksonville.

"We'll take the White truck, the big, open, flatbed ones. Same goes for the buses."

"Those open trucks?" Tod was surprised. They had looked at a G.M.C. truck with a special paneled body. "What happens to the load if you run into a rainstorm?"

"Christ's sake!" Willie was as impatient as though he were being forced to explain something to a stupid child. "We cover 'em up. Here."

Reluctantly he rolled from the bed, took a pencil from a row clipped to the outside pocket of his coat where it was draped over a chair. Going to the desk he swept off the literature and laid out a sheet of the hotel's stationery. With the pencil he drew an inverted U.

"We get a blacksmith to make us three iron ribs like this an' bolt 'em to the sides. Then we stretch some goddamned waterproof canvas over them like a tent with a flap in back. Lash the canvas down an' it don't make no difference what the weather is. If them stupid bastards at the factory weren't so stupid they'd have figured something like this out themselves. That panel body'll shake itself to pieces in a month over the roads we got now." He tossed the sketch into a wastepaper basket.

Here, again, Tod realized, was the reason for his ambivalence. Willie was able to go to the core of a problem and make it seem preposterously simple. This was the man he needed and to have him he must endure everything else about him which was offensive.

Willie scratched at himself, hunting beneath the loose underwear with the rapidity of a monkey's paw. He squinted at Tod and a curious smile hovered for a moment about his heavy lips.

"You don't like me for a damn, do you?" He didn't give Tod a chance to reply. "Well. You pain me some in the ass too. But, you got what I need an' I got what you have to have. So, we'll get along without no pretendin'." He went to the telephone. "This here is Mr. Estes." He spoke to the operator. "Send me up a nigger." He hung the receiver back. "I'm goin' to get me a whore or two." He pronounced the word as "hoor." "Then I'm goin' to drink some liquor. You go ahead an' give them White people the order for the trucks."

The next afternoon, with Willie red-eyed and still a little drunk asleep in the back seat, Tod drove the one hundred and ten miles back to Daytona. The new brick road, barely wide enough for two cars to pass on, was already coming apart. There were dips and depressions which wrenched savagely at the springs. In some places the bricks were up-ended, tossed into this position by the passing wheels. In a couple of years the highway would disintegrate entirely. On a sudden impulse he pulled off to one side, went to the center of the road and with nothing more than his fingers lifted one of the bricks. Below there was nothing but sand and a thin coating of tar or asphalt. The contractor hadn't even made a pretense of laying a foundation. He pressed the stone back with his foot. Someone's pocket had been well lined with this job and there must be a trail of the graft leading all the way to Tallahassee. He'd make a trip to the

Capitol sometime and nose around the records. It might come in handy someday to know who the grafters were. If they could be used once they could be manipulated again and the Citrus Belt Bus and Trucking Line was going to manipulate.

* VIII * *

T HE old warehouse on Orange Avenue near Palmetto
had been untenanted for so long most persons couldn't remember why or when it had been built. Over the years it took on a scab-
rous appearance of neglect and the sides were covered with the crude
scrawlings of small boys.

Now it gleamed with fresh paint. Broken windowpanes were replaced. The cavernlike interior was bright with huge electric lights
which shone upon the four heavy-duty White trucks. Over the double
doors at the entrance was suspended a sign. On a vivid, orange-
colored disk were the words:

THE CITRUS BELT LINE
Local and Long Distance Hauling.

At each corner at the front of the building were two offices identi-
cally furnished. Lettered on the door of one was the simple legend:
GENERAL OFFICE. The other was identified as MAINTENANCE DE-
PARTMENT—*Willie Estes, Sup't.*

Tod, with a weary resignation, consented to this appeasement of
Willie's aggressive vanity.

"I don't know what the hell you're going to do with an office. Most
of the time you'll be in the shop."

"Well, when I'm not in the shop I'm goin' to sit in an office. That's what I'm goin' to do." Willie had been adamant. "I'm goin' to have me a desk to put my feet up on an', when we get goin' real good, I may even hire a blond secretary to pinch on the behind when I feel like it."

Sometimes Tod wondered whether Willie was worth the minor irritations. Certainly there were other mechanics who could be brought in but none, he admitted, with Willie's dedication to the proper functioning of a motor or vehicle.

"All right, Willie. I don't care what you pinch or what you sit on just as long as those trucks are kept running."

"You do your job. I'll do mine."

So, Tod had ordered Maley's Furniture Store to fit the offices, desk for desk, chair for chair. Then he had gone out to find the business the new firm must have. In the beginning he was treated with an attitude of good-humored tolerance. Will Lathrop was an eccentric but one of the town's first citizens and the family wealth exaggerated in the minds of most persons. That Tod Lathrop was seriously going into the trucking business was accepted as something of a joke. Tod, though, stubbornly fought this notion. He was affable but filled with a purpose. He had figures and answers for the questions and skeptical humor. He knew what his trucks could do and was determined to prove it.

The first contract came from Webster, who ran a grocery store over on the beach at the corner of Main Street and Peninsula Drive. All of the store's orders were made through salesmen working out of the wholesale firms in Jacksonville. The merchandise was then shipped down on the Florida East Coast Railroad.

"We can do it cheaper for you, Mr. Webster." Tod had laid a typewritten list of figures on the counter. "Right now you have two charges. One is, maybe, hidden but it is there—the freight charge from Jacksonville to Daytona by the wholesaler. Then you have to pay to have the goods picked up at the freight depot across the river and brought to the store. We'll deliver to your back door and it is all one job. It will cut a third of your costs."

"I don't know, Tod." Webster hesitated. "There's something solid, reliable about a railroad. I mean, you know it's going to stay on the tracks. Suppose your truck goes into a ditch?"

"My trucks won't go into a ditch and my insurance will cover any loss. My schedule will be as tight and reliable as the railroad. This thing is going to work, Mr. Webster." He fought against betraying any eagerness. "It's going to work because I'm going to make it work."

He wore the grocer down finally and Webster gave him his first consignment, a full load of cased canned goods and assorted staples. McDonald's Meat Market, on the mainland just south of Orange Avenue, was the line's second client. Then Hankins, the druggist, gave the firm a pickup from one of the wholesale pharmaceutical houses in Jacksonville. Here and there, as the deliveries were made promptly and without damage, the new enterprise picked up business. There was, Tod realized, an untapped field he would be unable to touch; certainly not in the foreseeable future. These were the orders by local merchants from firms in New Jersey, New York, Atlanta, Georgia, and Pennsylvania who shipped by direct rail, point to point, in freight or express cars which were not unloaded in Jacksonville. Maley, of the furniture store, had stated his case.

"I'd give you all my business, Tod. When I buy in Jacksonville you can haul it. Your rates are better than I can get from the F.E.C. But," he shook his head, "it doesn't make sense when I order from a factory in, say, Trenton, New Jersey, to have it taken out of the cars in Jacksonville when they're going to come right through Daytona on the way to Miami. I'd like to see you make a success of this. I honestly didn't think you had the guts to dig in this way. Whenever one local business prospers everyone in town benefits a little."

Tod understood the logic of Maley's argument. He didn't press his case. Most of the persons who had given him consignments were old acquaintances if not friends.

"One of these days," he told Maley, "you'll see the Citrus Belt Line with trucks three times the size of what we have now. We'll haul direct from Atlanta and Trenton, New York and Philadelphia to Florida. I'll even have refrigerated trucks that can make long runs with perishable foodstuffs—oranges, pineapples, alligator pears, tomatoes."

"Sure, Tod." Maley had clapped him good-naturedly on the back. "And about that time these airplanes will be carrying freight, too."

"Don't be too sure that won't happen, also." Tod grinned at the fancy.

He worked constantly at the job set for himself. His approach was not one of hat in hand. He was convinced of the service he had to offer and could prove it. All he had to do was get a prospective client to listen, and since there was plenty of time in Daytona and most of the merchants had known Tod Lathrop since he was a youngster, he found talking with them easy.

He was rarely at home these days, traveling constantly to the towns south along the coast; Titusville, Cocoa, Fort Pierce. Sometimes he rode one of his trucks. Always he managed to pick up a little business. It wasn't much but he was establishing himself. The Citrus Belt Line was proving out. He was convinced by now that sooner or later offices must be opened in Jacksonville. A great amount of freight was brought into the city by the Clyde Line, operating its ships out of New York with ports of call including Charleston and Savannah. From the docks these goods must be transferred to points inland. The most direct method was by truck but the roads were far from ideal. The drive from Jacksonville to Tallahassee was little short of an adventure. In many places the highways were wagon trails, tracks in the sand across uninhabited pine flats.

His drivers were a constant problem. They were, in the beginning, local boys with no experience beyond a Model T Ford. They drove with a wild abandon and a complete disregard for the equipment. They came in with broken springs and axles, motors pounding because they neglected to check the oil or water in the radiators. The schedules were sometimes disrupted because they ran out of gasoline and sat by the road until someone gave them a lift to a gasoline pump. Willie put an end to this by having five-gallon cans of fuel bracketed to the trucks' running boards. This was to be tapped only in an emergency.

"You think you're a lot of goddamned cowboys." Where his beloved equipment was concerned Willie shed his attitude of lazy, scornful indifference. He raged at the drivers with a startling fury. "You come in here with burnt-out bearings because you were too busy with some little whore in Jacksonville to check a grease job. You break springs because you think you're Barney Oldfield." He had picked up a heavy wrench. "I'll tell you this," he screamed. "The next time you bring in one of my trucks torn apart I'll use this on your goddamned knot heads."

Little by little, though, Tod was able to replace the young and indifferent drivers with older men who had families and responsibilities and who took their jobs seriously and not as some road race. Even so there were still problems. He knew there were irregularities which, if discovered, could seriously affect his insurance premiums. The drivers would, by prearrangement, pick up a passenger or two in Ormond or Bunnell and transport them to St. Augustine or Jacksonville for much less than the train fare. It was a small dishonesty which put a few extra dollars in their pockets. By checking mileage he knew there was cheating and collusion when the men bought and signed for oil or gasoline at way stops. They presented bills for emergency repairs which were fraudulent. These things disturbed him beyond the matter of operating costs. He wanted a good and efficient organization with men who took a pride in their work and the reliability of the Citrus Belt Line. This was a problem, for most of them saw nothing beyond the job and the weekly paycheck. He instituted a monthly bonus award for the driver with the lowest operation and maintenance record. He had a uniform designed for the drivers and helpers—gray trousers and a pullover blouse of the same material with the orange-colored disk insignia to replace the nondescript work clothes. Their smartened appearance seemed to give the men a certain *esprit de corps* he was desperately seeking.

The war in Europe was but a distant rolling here on Florida's east coast. The people read about it in their newspapers but few seemed to realize how close was the monstrous thunder of war and how relentlessly the storm's tide moved toward the American shore.

For over a year there had been provocative acts on both sides. The United States, while asserting its neutrality, was undeniably favoring the Allies in the shipment of war matériel. There was little question as to where the sympathy lay. Germany retaliated as best she could. The cruiser *Prinz Eitel Freidrich* put into Newport News, Virginia, and admitted sinking the *William P. Frye,* an American ship bound for England. The German Ambassador, in Washington, publicly warned Americans not to take passage on the Cunard liner, *Lusitania.* This was ignored and six days later the vessel was torpedoed and sunk with the loss of over a thousand lives, one hundred and fourteen of them Americans. During this same period the United States was embroiled in Mexico where the bandit, Villa, was raiding along the border. Eighteen American mining officials and employees had been taken from a train at Santa Ysabel and shot. Villistas had crossed the frontier into New Mexico, raided the little town of Columbus and killed seventeen Americans. Brigadier General John J. Pershing with 6,000 troops went into Mexico in pursuit of Villa. President Carranza demanded the withdrawal of American soldiers from Mexico and Pancho Villa raided and looted the towns of Glen Springs and Boquillas, Texas. Most Americans, save the men doing the fighting, looked upon the Mexico trouble as a Western comic opera. More and more the attention was being focused on Germany. In San Francisco the German Consul General and four aides were found guilty of conspiracy to blow up shipments of munitions for the Allies. Ambassador von Bersdorff was discovered to have asked his Foreign Office for $50,000 to influence Congress to prevent the United States from entering the war and a wireless message was intercepted and decoded revealing that the German Government was negotiating with Mexico. In the event of war with the United States and as a reward for its assistance, Germany promised Mexico the return of its lost territory in Arizona, Texas and New Mexico. The German Government finally announced unrestricted submarine warfare and President Wilson answered by declaring American ships would be armed and supplied with naval gunners. The Government called out units of the National Guard in nine eastern states for "police work" and the American ship *Aztec* was torpedoed and sunk without warning. On April 6, 1917, the President, by proclamation, declared the United States at war with Germany.

On a blackboard before the *Daily News* office, on Beach Street, the news that the country was at war was chalked in heavy, white letters. The paper came out with an early afternoon edition reaffirming the fact. No one in town quite believed it. Despite mounting tensions Europe seemed so far away. It was none of our business. What had we to do with Europe?

Over dinner, at the house on the beach, Dennis, Tod and Alice soberly talked over what had happened and of the future. Tod was rarely home these days for he traveled constantly and had not seen his parents for almost two weeks.

"I suppose you'll go, Tod?" Dennis regarded his son with unhappy eyes. "That is the way it will be."

"Oh, no, Dennis!" Alice protested quickly. "We have a regular army, haven't we? I mean, there are trained men, the National Guard, professional soldiers. Surely they don't need Tod."

"They'll need a million Tods before it's over, Mother." He reached for her hand and forced a comforting smile.

"Not right away, Tod," she pleaded. "Wait and see what happens. You're so young." She said this with a wistful helplessness, knowing it wasn't true. He was a man and must take a man's responsibilities.

"I promise." He tried to make a joke of it. "I won't be first in line at the recruiting office tomorrow."

Later he and Dennis stood outside on the porch. The ocean rolled with its hushed cadence and, as sometimes happened, the water held a peculiar phosphorescence making of each breaker a curling, brilliant streak.

"You'll do what you have to do, Tod." Dennis spoke without looking at his son. "So, I won't offer an opinion."

"There really isn't much choice, is there? I don't think this is something we can handle with the regular army and National Guard. There will be a draft. Do you know," he sounded embarrassed as though angry with himself, "right now my view of the whole thing is pretty narrow and personal. I'm thinking of what will happen to the Citrus Belt Line. Maybe it will be considered essential. Most of the railroads' cars will eventually be tied up. Damn it. I was just getting things moving. That's pretty cheap, isn't it?" He didn't look at his father. "Men are getting their guts blown out and I'm worrying about four trucks and a possible bus line. The country's going to be involved in the world's greatest war and all I can think of is whether I can hold my drivers, the gasoline and mechanics to keep things rolling." He sat on the porch railing and stared at the sea.

"I wouldn't feel guilty about it." Dennis spoke with quiet reflection. "There must be a million or more men who are having the same thoughts this night. They are saying, What's going to happen to my job while I'm away? If I get back will it still be there? Will I have a chance to finish college? Who is going to look after the little business I started? If and when they start taking the married men who will take care of my wife and children? They are asking themselves how and why we are tangled in a European war which seemed none of our affair. Those are not unnatural or selfish concerns, Tod. They are human. Only a clod is able to accept today without a thought for tomorrow."

"Thanks for the rationalization." Tod swung off the railing. "I think I'll take a little walk. Want to come along?"

"I'd like to. Wait until I tell Alice." He went to the door.

Tod stood, gazing up at the star-shot sky, and found himself remembering a night, years back, when Halley's comet appeared and showed itself with a long, silver streak as though someone had taken a brush and drawn it against the great dome of space. He heard his father's step and turned.

"When was Halley's comet up there?"

"I'm not sure." Dennis fell in beside him and they began walking toward the dunes. "1906—'07—'08. Sometime around there. We were here, in Florida."

"I suddenly found myself thinking about it and wondering if I would ever see it again. It comes around every eighty or so years, doesn't it?"

"I think so. Eighty. Eighty-five."

They walked down, up and over the high dunes. There was a series of five of the powdery hills as though the ocean's waves had frozen there centuries ago, leaving their impression. Morning glories and brown sea oats covered the crests and the vines wound through the depressions in a purple tangle.

"I was talking to old man Stringer. He must be ninety-five." Dennis lit his pipe. "He told me when he was a boy these sand dunes were seven in number. Over the years two have been washed away."

"Old men have faulty memories." Tod wasn't impressed.

"No. I think maybe he is right. I've noticed in the seventeen or so years we have lived here, each equinox the storms take a little higher bite out of these dunes. Someday there may be only one left as a bulwark against the tide."

"They'll shore it up with concrete, palmetto pilings." Tod put an arm about his father's shoulder. "We're not talking about what is really on our minds, are we? It's just as well. All of a sudden I find myself recalling the most irrelevant things. A day when you, Wash and I went down to Rose Bay. Wash brought along an oyster rake. We built a low fire and roasted the oysters over the coals. I think we must have eaten a peck or more apiece. Nothing ever tasted so good. The day when we were over fishing on the St. Johns and left the fish on a sack up the bank and wild pigs carried them off. I wanted to kill those pigs for doing what came naturally. We've had fun together. There's never been any strain."

They were on the hard beach now and the footing was easier. In the half light of the stars they could see the sand crabs racing and diving into their holes.

"Do you know what sand crabs eat?" Tod asked abruptly.

"No."

"Neither do I. I've spent most of my life here and watched them run but I've never seen them eating anything."

Twelve miles to the south the lighthouse at Mosquito Inlet showed its steady beam.

"There's a petition out," Dennis spoke casually, "to change the name of Mosquito Inlet to Ponce de Leon Inlet. Someone has an idea the word mosquito makes it sound unattractive to tourists."

"Ponce de Leon must have had a fast horse. He certainly got around Florida. There must be fifty springs over the state called De Leon. When I decide what I'm going to do I'll just do it without saying anything to you, Mother or anyone. You understand?"

"I had an idea you'd do it that way."

"Don't let them change things too much while I'm away. When I come back I'd like it still to be home."

"I'll keep it for you, Tod. When it's changed we'll help do it together. I've never given up the idea. I still believe as I always have. This is a tremendous state. People will find out about it one of these days. But," he half smiled, "I've discovered I can't force things."

"Should we go back now?" Tod halted. "I think we've said what needed to be spoken between us. I just wanted you to know."

"We've always understood each other pretty well, son. That's been the best part of it."

They turned and retraced their steps toward the house, where the lights were warmly yellow against the night.

Daily now the young men were leaving and as the familiar faces disappeared from behind the counters, the soda fountains, pool hall, the group always gathered in front of Peter Paul's drugstore on the corner, there was a feeling of emptiness in the town. This was followed by an odd tension and suspicion. The German-American Club was closed and few would admit ever having been members. Those with names indicating German extraction became suspect. Each day brought a new rumor. Strange lights had been seen at night on the darkness of the ocean. A submarine had surfaced near the inlet. Bunk Ohler, who continued his nocturnal seining, told everyone that when he put his ear to the water he could hear the unmistakable dot and dash of Morse code.

A Home Guard was recruited and those too old or too young to enlist or be drafted were put into ill-fitting O.D.'s of scratchy wool, issued rifles without ammunition and put to drilling on City Island, which lay just off Beach Street and was connected by a walkway with the South Bridge. They marched with set faces and walked a lonely tour on the beach at night with empty rifles in case the Germans attempted a landing. It was rumored that Colonel Bullard was the head of a secret, antisabotage service in the Government and two boys who were playing with flashlights on the beach one night were captured by the Home Guard and taken to the Colonel's home to be lectured sternly. This was no time for horseplay.

At Jacksonville a quartermaster depot, Camp Jackson, was activated and over in the interior, near Arcadia, Dorr and Carlstrom fields were training pilots with a weird assortment of Curtis Jennies, a few Standards with the Hispano-Suiza motors and some DeHavilands, sent over by the British Government. They made practice flights to the beach and their planes were protected by units of the Home Guard. In Washington, Theodore Roosevelt demanded that Secretary of War Baker permit him to raise an infantry division under his command and take it to France. Teddy had an idea the whole thing was just another San Juan Hill. A Shipping Board was organized and placed under the direction of Charles Schwab. A French War Commission, headed by Marshal Joffre, arrived at Hampton Roads, Virginia. He wanted money and privately expressed the opinion American troops were incapable of operating as a unit but must be integrated into French and British forces where they would have the benefit of experienced leadership. Since the French and British were taking a hell of a beating at this time the Marshal's argument was doubtfully received. The United States began tapping the till. $200,000,000 was loaned to Great Britain, $100,000,000 to Italy,

$100,000,000 to France and $100,000,000 to Russia. Over ten and one half million men registered for the draft and twenty-five firms in Chicago were indicted for an attempt to monopolize interstate trade in butter and eggs. Already the old game of who could get the mostest fustest had started. The Liberty motor for airplanes was designed by a group of prominent engineers, and flour, meats, fats, coal, fuel oils, gasoline, iron and rubber went under Government controls. Liberty Bond drives were under way and posters, with Uncle Sam pointing an accusing finger, appeared. The word "slacker" began to be heard, and young men still in civilian dress were sometimes spat at, reviled and attacked by boozy new recruits.

Tod sat in the office of the Citrus Belt Line with Willie Estes. There was a bottle of bourbon on the desk between them.

"You're a goddamned fool." Willie made the statement with a malicious satisfaction.

"I have an idea you're right," Tod agreed. "But I don't seem to be able to do anything about it."

"I got everything goin' for me." Willie was complacent. He reached for the whisky. "Flat feet, gas on my stomick, a hernia an' piles. To be sure there ain't any slip, I'm goin' to marry Francie Booker sometime next week. I'll knock her up fast so's I'll have me some dependents."

"Francie's a lucky girl." Tod expressed the opinion drily. "I'll have to congratulate her." He stood, walked to the window. "Do you think you'll ever recover from being an all-out bastard?"

"I ain't workin' at it." Willie refused to take offense. He squinted at Tod. "You ain't got much choice, have you, Toddy-boy?" The grin broadened as Tod turned. "I know what's worryin' you. It's leave me in charge or close down the line. That's about it, ain't it?"

Tod stared at him, started to speak and changed his mind.

"Then again," Willie continued, "there'll be a lot of good openings for a man like me. The Government's goin' to need trucks, ambulances, staff cars. I can probably have a top job with Studebaker, White, G.M.C., Ford. Take my pick. So if I should stay here an' keep things goin', it ought to be made worth my while."

"What do you want, Willie?"

Estes pursed his lips into a rosette and blew softly. It was almost possible to see his mind working. The eyes glinted as he figured just how much of an edge he had at the moment.

"Twenty-five percent." He was probing for a reaction. "Twenty-five percent of what we got goin' now an' whatever happens later. I mean, if the line grows an' branches out I still hold a quarter interest no matter how big we get. After all, gettin' married, havin' responsibilities, I gotta have security." The whine was in his voice even though there was no need for it.

Tod nodded an assent. He had expected the man to demand more. Willie instantly sensed this and his face drew into a pout of disappointment. He'd been crazy to settle for twenty-five percent. He might have held out for half.

"I wouldn't have given it to you, Willie." Tod was mildly amused.

"What?" The question expressed a child's innocence. "What wouldn't you have given me?"

"Whatever it was you were thinking of. Sometimes I can see the wheels working in your head. A moment ago they were tuned up to about half of the Citrus Belt Line. You were wondering why you hadn't asked for it."

Willie chuckled. "I don't like you for hell, Toddy-boy, but you're smart. I gotta say that. Now, we'll get us a lawyer, not your father neither, an' have the papers drawn up. Then you can go off with your popgun an' play soldier."

Tod nodded. "That's all right with me." He paused. "Do you know what I'm going to do, Willie?" He made the question a pleasant, friendly inquiry. "The next time you call me Toddy-boy I'm going to boot your ass from here to Beach Street—piles, hernia, flat feet and all."

"I keep forgettin' you don't like it." Willie was hypocritically meek.

"Also," Tod ignored the sarcasm, "while I'm away I'm going to put in an accountant to watch every penny. I'm going to make an honest man out of you for awhile, at least. And, Willie, I consider that to be in the nature of a small miracle. I think you'd even steal from yourself out of habit. Now," he returned to his chair behind the desk, "do you know what's going on in Jacksonville?"

"How the hell would I know? I never get out of the shop." Willie was injured.

"Well, I'll tell you. There are possibly twenty-five or thirty thousand men at Camp Jackson. When they get leave there's no place for them to go but into town about fifteen miles away. Every afternoon and evening there are ten thousand or so troops trying to get transportation. There are a few taxicabs but no fixed rate, nothing the men can depend upon. I can make a deal with the Commanding Officer and the city for the exclusive right to operate a regular service from Camp Jackson to Ortega and Jacksonville. We charge fifty cents each way. I've talked it over with Don Fairfield, at the Atlantic Bank up there. They'll give me the financing."

"What are you going to use?" Willie was interested but skeptical. "I hear the Army has tied up production of trucks an' buses."

"I can get fifteen Studebaker touring cars in Jacksonville right now and five more in Atlanta. With the jump seats we can carry seven men, not including the driver. That's seven dollars a round trip and the cars will be on the road eighteen hours a day. For drivers we'll have to use men above or below the draft age but that's no problem. The real problem will be maintenance. Do you think you can handle it, put a good man in or divide your time between here and there?"

"I ought to get some sort of a bonus." The objection was automatic.

"You have twenty-five percent. Now listen, Willie." Tod was suddenly and dangerously emphatic. "You'll do this job and do it right or I'll bring someone in who will. He may not be as good a mechanic as you are but I can at least go away knowing he won't steal the horse and the barn door also."

"Oh, I'll do it." Willie was sullen. "But it does seem like I ought to get more for double work. How is Francie goin' to feel, after we're married, if I have to go runnin' off to Jacksonville every week or so?"

"Offhand I'd think she'll be delighted."

"You're a nasty son of a bitch, ain't you?"

"It's the company I keep, Willie. Some of you rubs off on me." His manner changed to one of brusque determination. "Now, you bring in any lawyer you want. Tomorrow we'll sit down and draw up an agreement. Then I'm going to Jacksonville and set up a deal to buy those cars, tie the franchise together and get some drivers. I don't know how long we can keep the trucks operating on the routes we have. But I'm pretty sure if gasoline and oil, tires and parts are rationed we can get an essential allowance from the Government. I'll find a good man to put in charge of the office there and rent garage space. After that it's going to be up to you."

"You really goin' to enlist?" Willie was honestly puzzled. "Even though you probably wouldn't have to. What for?"

"To keep the world safe for the Willie Estes."

"I hope you get your ass blowed off." Willie turned and walked away.

Tod told only his father and grandfather of his intention to enlist. "I don't want any tearful good-byes, no wailing at the bar or wherever they do it."

"It seems to me you're in one hell of a hurry," Will Lathrop grumbled. "Wars always wait for the good men."

"I've tried to talk myself out of it," Tod admitted ruefully. "Somehow it isn't convincing. If you ask me why I think I ought to go now I honestly couldn't tell you. I feel an obligation. That's about as close as I can come to the reason."

So, in this year of 1917, Stoddard Lathrop finished up his business in Jacksonville, stayed around long enough to see his fleet of passenger cars working, operating efficiently and providing the much needed transportation between Camp Jackson and the city. Then he walked into a recruiting station on Forsythe Street and enlisted. He was shipped first to Fort Oglethorpe, in Georgia. From there he went to the Officers' Candidate School and four months later went to France as a second lieutenant of the 101st Infantry in the 26th Division.

IX

Now, in this small town on Florida's coast, the service flags with their single, and sometimes double, stars were hung in the windows. As the year dragged on, marked by the weary slogging of millions of feet half a world away, the white emblems were replaced here and there with gold and an air of mourning hung over small homes and yards.

In the evenings families would gather to study the battle maps of France while someone read aloud from the Associated Press dispatches in the *News*. Tongues struggled with unfamiliar names. St. Nazaire. Verdun. Montdidier. Château-Thierry. Armentiers. Toul. Daily there were reports of American ships torpedoed and sunk, of men locked in bloody struggle, and the casualty lists which had only been figures now became personal. Joe Brooks. Tom Charlton. Cass White. Marcus Levy. How had it come about that they should have died upon a muddy field or gone down with a ship on a wintry sea? There were scandals, also, of profiteers, shoddy uniforms, faulty construction of barracks, ammunition which would not fire, field-pieces exploding, combines of men and firms who cornered huge quantities of butter, eggs, meats and sugar to be sold under the counter at exorbitant prices, airplanes nicknamed "flying coffins," waste and irregularities in shipyard contracts and strikes in vital industries. With a zeal which might have been put to better use the Navy Department prohibited the sale of liquor within five miles of any naval training station and so those who had whisky to sell moved out five miles and one yard. Day laborers and shipyard workers wore silk shirts. Draft dodger crept into the vocabulary. The Government hunted for Grover Cleveland Bergdoll, son of a wealthy Philadelphia family, who had either fled the country or gone into hiding to escape induction into the Army. Jack Dempsey, who had been a public idol, was mentioned now with contempt. "If he's such a hell of a fighter why isn't he in the trenches instead of drawing down big money in a shipyard?"

"K-K-K-Katy." "Oh! How I Hate To Get Up In the Morning." "There's a Long, Long Trail a-Winding." "He's a Yankee Doodle Dandy." "Mademoiselle from Armentiers"—who had big ears among other physical attributes. From Tin Pan Alley the songs came and were sung from vaudeville stages or blared from the flowerlike horns of the Victrola. The country rocked with laughter over the letters of a buck private to his girl: "Deer Mable." Sauerkraut became Liberty Cabbage. German pot roast was Yankee pot roast on the restaurant menus. The word frankfurter disappeared and the sausage called a hot dog. The Kaiser was cartooned as a spike-helmeted dachshund with an upturned mustache chased by an English bulldog, a French poodle and a smooth-haired terrier since there was no distinctive American breed. There were meatless days and wheatless days. The Railroad Administration placed an embargo on all freight other than food, fuel and munitions on the three great eastern railroads. Automobiles remained in their garages on Sundays as the public responded to a request for the conservation of gasoline, and an influenza epidemic of frightening proportions raged over the country, sweeping through army camps and the civilian population with a deadly effect.

"Out of the trenches by Christmas." It was a popular slogan but no one really believed it; especially the men on the European western front. Christmas came and in many churches the congregations sang: "Say a Prayer For the Boys Over There" instead of the customary closing hymn.

Save for those homes from which the young men had gone, the war seemed strangely remote to most of those who lived in Daytona and other communities along the sweeping ocean front. There was the ocean and across it in a northeasterly direction was Europe and the fighting. But here no wreckage of torpedoed ships washed ashore; no bodies drifted with the tide. There was no industry of importance although the Home Guard stood watch on the dunes and were posted about the Power and Light Company on Volusia Avenue near the railroad tracks just in case a German spy decided it was a prime target. The tourists were few and most of the hotels had cut their staffs to half the usual number.

Spring and summer came and the beach was crowded with youngsters, men and women of middle age, and the very old who escaped the enervating heat of Florida's interior towns and rented cottages on the ocean front. Then September crept upon the peninsula and hard upon it October with the first of the equinoctial storms whipping down the coast. In this second year of America's participation in the war the great shift in the tide of battle began to show itself in the reports of correspondents, the movements of armies, the straggling lines of the fronts as they were diagramed in the newspapers. There was a feeling of victory in the air. The facts were unpublished but somehow, they filtered through the screen of secret diplomacy. Germany and Austria-Hungary were communicating the first, tentative suggestions of peace but wanted it called an armistice and not surrender. President Wilson's reply was icy, promising no more than "justice even to those to whom we do not wish to be just." Then, just to demonstrate that even a world war wasn't big enough to interfere with the fine old American game of politics, Henry Cabot Lodge and other Republicans subscribed to an open letter accusing Wilson of using "the war as a party asset."

The tremendous machinery of destruction which had been set in motion at Sarajevo slowly ground to a halt. General Foch met with a German delegation in the Compiègne Forest near Rethondes. But even while the negotiations were under way the American troops took Manheulles, Moranville and Abacourt. The British battleship *Britannica* was sunk by a submarine in the Atlantic off Gibraltar. The Belgians reoccupied Ghent and the Kaiser, with the Crown Prince, fled to Holland for sanctuary.

It was over. The world paused to survey the carnage and count the terrible cost even as the Allied armies began their march into Germany. Over three hundred and thirty-one billion dollars. Almost ten million dead. Twenty-five million wounded and roughly six million missing or held prisoners.

Out of uniform Tod Lathrop stood in the vestibule of the Pullman car and watched the flat palm and pine-dotted landscape flash past. He was held by a tense excitement brought about by the sheer pleasure of being home again. In a few minutes the train would cross the bridge at the Tomoka River and this particular site was deeply rooted in his memory and affection. Always at Christmastime he and four close friends had taken a week of the annual vacation for a camping trip here. On the high coquina bank above the darkly winding stream they had built their thatched lean-tos, cut pine boughs over which blankets could be spread. They fished and talked, hunted for quail and doves. He smiled a little thinking of the hunting. Smokeless powder shells for their handed-down shotguns cost seventy-five cents a box in those days. The black powder ones were only fifty cents a box. So, they always bought the less expensive. After a shot at a winging bird it sometimes took two minutes or so before the screen of heavy, black smoke would clear. They would have to search for the dove or quail, since no one could mark the fall through the smoke. Where were they now, these companions of his youth? Stanley Strother. Dick Niven. Jake Odum. Fred Langworthy. Donald McDonald. Bill Freeman.

The train roared across the bridge and he had but the most fleeting glance at the river. It flowed as it had for centuries, draining from the swamps and lakes of the interior. How often had he sat by a fire at night and listened to the insane laughter of a loon in the brown marsh or heard the heavy grunt of an alligator. How young they had all been. Time was without meaning.

The train halted briefly at Ormond, for it no longer crossed the river to the sprawling hotel. Now there was only the brief run of seven or eight miles to Daytona. The porter brought his bag. When they stopped at Daytona, Tod dropped down to the wooden platform and stood looking about. A tiny smile of pleasure crinkled about his eyes. Here, at least, nothing had changed. The station was the same, ugly mustard-yellow color Mr. Flagler seemed to prefer above all others. A couple of worn taxicabs, their drivers leaning against the dented fenders, were parked in the driveway. Harley Davis wheeled the Railway Express truck from the mail and baggage cars. He glanced at Tod without recognition, moved on a few steps and then turned suddenly, coming back with hand extended.

"By God! I didn't know who you were at first." He shook Tod's hand. "All of you boys look different, somehow."

"It ages you a little, Mr. Davis, to have someone shooting at you." He grinned. "Gets on your nerves after awhile."

Davis regarded him with admiration. "I remember you and the other kids, hanging around the tracks here, hooking a ride on a freight train, damn near busting your asses jumpin' off when it got goin' good." He looked up and down the narrow platform. "Where's your family?"

"I didn't let them know I was coming."

"They'll be some surprised, I bet." He paused. "You kind of got to be a hero or somethin', didn't you? It was in the *News* how you got a couple of decorations an' they made you a captain. Is it true you got to let a Frenchman kiss you when he pins a medal on?"

"You know how the song goes. 'The French they are a funny race.' " Tod picked up his bag.

"Well. Glad to see you home. The town ain't changed much." He went back to his truck.

Tod handed his bag to one of the taxi drivers. "I want to go over to the beach but go down to Orange Avenue and across the South Bridge."

The man nodded and they rattled off up the incline of Volusia. Several houses had been built where there once had been only a violet-carpeted meadow. At the top of the slope what used to be called "the ridge wood" was now Ridgewood Avenue. Tod half closed his eyes and tried to remember how it had looked years ago. Now there were fine homes widely spaced with broad lawns shaded by the tremendous oaks and spreading magnolias.

"Visitin' here?" The driver spoke without turning.

"No. It's my home." Tod leaned against the worn upholstery and lit a cigarette.

"I been here a couple of years. Come from Valdosta. It's a real, nice town. Everybody's sayin' there's goin' to be a big boom in Florida now the war's over an' all."

"I've heard that for years. I guess maybe one of these days it will happen."

"A war makes people restless. Take me, for instance, I didn't have no real cause to leave Valdosta. Just took up an' left. A lot of others might feel the same way but then, they could go almost any place. It wouldn't have to be Florida." He turned from Ridgewood onto Orange Avenue.

Between Beach Street and Palmetto Avenue Tod sat up with a jerk and stared incredulously. Where the Citrus Belt Line's shop, garage and office had been a new motion picture theatre stood.

"Slow up a minute. Pull in here." He leaned from the window. "There used to be a truck line here. What happened to it?"

"Oh, you mean the Citrus Belt Line. They had to move. Mayor Titus built this theatre. Named it after his daughter Vivian. The truck line's got a place up near the North Bridge on Fairview. It did real well durin' the war."

"No one wrote me anything about it." Tod snapped his cigarette away.

"What's that?" The taxi driver was mystified.

"Never mind." Tod relaxed. "Let's go on across the river."

He was puzzled. No one had written him about the move but then, perhaps someone had. In the confusion of great movement the mail delivery to the troops had been astonishingly good but letters were lost. It wasn't really important. For a moment he was tempted to have the taxi driver take him up to Fairview, then decided it could wait. He wanted to see his father and mother and then, of course, Grandfather Will. Grandmother Felicia had been among the first victims of the influenza epidemic and had been dead a year or so.

He wondered about Willie Estes. To have kept the line operating at all was something of a miracle. The trucks must have taken an awful beating. Replacements and even parts would have been almost impossible to get. His mind was working far ahead into the future and it amazed him a little to discover how effortlessly he was making the transition back to civilian life. He knew the transportation service between Jacksonville and Camp Jackson had turned in a large profit. With the Government's assistance the fleet of Studebaker touring cars had been augmented. Now the Citrus Belt Line had some twenty-five cars to get rid of, for Camp Jackson would be deactivated as quickly as possible. Well, he thought, there would be a ready market for almost any sort of an automobile and, he laughed softly, by now those Studebakers were just that—almost any sort of a car. It was odd, he reflected, the sense of urgency he felt. There was so much he wanted to do. He was impatient. The war had accelerated the design of heavier and larger trucks. When he had first landed at St.-Nazaire most of the European military equipment had been horse drawn. At the war's end it was all mechanized. The Army would have thousands of new, surplus vehicles on its hands along with tires and parts. With a little manipulating he'd be able to pick up new and better equipment for a fraction of its cost. Beyond this, though, the war had taught the manufacturers much about the production of tough, long-range vehicles. The idea of a truck fleet operating between New York and Florida was no longer fanciful. He knew it could be done and he was going to do it. But, and the idea occurred to him without any preliminary meditation, long distance trucking didn't have to be done by a single, self-contained unit. Suppose, just suppose the motive power, an engine and driver's cab mounted on four wheels, could be made? To this could be coupled a lightweight van, sort of a highway box car. Why! He snapped upright. It wouldn't have to stop there. Two vans could be hooked together as cars were attached to a locomotive. Given sufficient power, a real, heavy-duty engine—and this was certain to come—a train could be put on the road. Its route unrestricted by rails. It could go anywhere, any time, with an incredible freedom of movement. The notion stimulated him to the point where he felt as though he had taken a couple of drinks. It was something to think about; to talk over with a designer and an automotive engineer. He knew what he wanted. An outfit like G.M.C. could make it once someone convinced the top men it was practical. He thought about Willie. Willie Estes. He didn't like the son of a bitch but Willie would understand what he was driving at. Maybe there were bugs in it. If there were, Willie would spot them. Right now the real problem was an engine with sufficient power. No one was making them. Tomorrow, first thing, he would sit down with Willie and they would examine this notion which seemed wild only because it was new. He leaned back again and relaxed. For the first time since his discharge he experienced the satisfaction of a purpose; something at which he could drive. It had only been half confessed but out of uniform he had felt alien in a civilian world. He was no longer a stranger.

It was Sunday and there were few persons on the streets at this hour. They came to the corner of Beach Street and he looked across at the handsome public center Commodore Burgoyne had donated to the town. There was a park along the river front now with beds of flowers, well-tended palms and an esplanade. A concrete seawall had replaced the old, indiscriminate piling of coquina boulders once serving as a breakwater. He smiled reminiscently, remembering how he, as a boy, used to balance himself on the rough stones on his way uptown. Also, then, the community's jailhouse had been a small frame structure of one cell, attached to the bridge by a short dock. It was a moment of fine excitement to stand on tiptoe and peer through the barred window at a lonely and unhappy Negro who had been locked up for being drunk and beating his wife. He couldn't recall the jail ever having a white man as a prisoner.

As they started across the bridge he thought of his grandfather and old man Pellicier, wondering if they were still at it. Then he remembered the bridges were free. There was no longer a toll to pay. This must have taken some of the zest for life out of Grandfather Will. He studied the opposite shore. A few, new homes were half concealed within the deep foliage and old trees. But, for the most part, the beach side river front was much as it had been twenty-five years ago. He wondered a little about his father and the dream he had clung to of a huge migration to Florida. It just hadn't happened. Idly he recalled what the taxi driver had said. A war made people restless. It was true. He could feel the confined energy in himself. It was a time for movement, for change after the regimentation and restrictions. It could still happen. He hoped so for his father's sake for he was aware of and understood Dennis Lathrop's disappointment. He had been forced to content himself with the practice of law after all and was unhappy with it. The vision was unrealized. Oddly enough, and of this he was quite certain, Dennis Lathrop had looked into the future without any real thought of personal gain. His was the unquenchable zeal of a missionary. If it were possible he would have stumped the country saying: Here is the promised land. Come and see for yourselves.

Off the bridge and around the deeply shaded curve where the Gamble house stood within a grove of gray oaks behind its low wall of coquina the driver slowed down and glanced back.

"You want to go to the beach?"

"No, I don't imagine it's changed much. Take Peninsula Drive to Main Street."

Until now he hadn't fully realized how deeply rooted his emotions for home and all the familiar things were. A contentment he had never known before filled him. It seemed as though each mile of this road held some special memory. It was paved now with an asphalt surface but he could remember it with the oyster-shell white. There, at the Hoskins' house, he used to slip in over the fence and fill his blouse with tangerines from the small grove. Along this same stretch he had ridden his first bicycle. He laughed suddenly thinking of one of his closest friends—Clinton Campbell. Clint didn't know how to ride. Gene Johnson had given them an old seat and they had fastened it to the crossbar. On this Clint would sit and pedal while Tod, on the regular seat, would steer and balance, legs dangling with Clint doing all the work. They covered a lot of ground in this fashion until it dawned on Clint he was being had. He wasn't sure now whether Clint ever did learn to ride by himself. The Campbells lived farther up, near Harvey Street, and Tod recalled Mr. Campbell as a fearsome-appearing man with the long, black mustache of a Sicilian bandit. Actually he was a quiet and gentle man who regarded his son's and Tod's minor depredations with an expressionless tolerance. Of all the things about the Campbells which remained most vividly in Tod's mind was the fact that they put catsup in oyster stew. What odd things a man stored up within himself. Why should catsup in oyster stew be something to remember?

The tracks of an ill-fated streetcar line were still visible along Peninsula Drive from what was now called the Broadway Bridge. The venture had been a financial disaster for someone although it must have seemed practical at the time. The tracks started at Orange Avenue and Beach Street across the river, ran north to what was then known as the Concrete Bridge, up Peninsula Drive to Main Street and Atlantic Avenue and along Atlantic through Seabreeze and just short of Ormond. The cars were driven by storage batteries and the newly recruited motormen were local youths who rocked along at top speed, clanging the warning bells from one end of the line to the other. You could hear the brazen clamor all over town. Few persons in Daytona had ever ridden on a streetcar. It was an exciting and novel experience. For the first few months the cars operated at capacity and the promoters must have thought they had a gold mine. Entire families would take the trip across the river and back as an adventure. But, the novelty soon wore off. Residents along Atlantic Avenue and Peninsula Drive complained of the constant, strident bell ringing. The townspeople went back to their bicycles and the jitneys. Finally the line shut down its operation and it was never revived. The tracks remained, rusting monuments to its failure.

The driver called back over his shoulder, "You been in the Army?"

"Yes."

"If this is your home you must have known a fellow by the name of Irving Ballough?"

"Yes. What about him?" Tod vaguely recalled that Irving had gone to Canada and enlisted in its Air Corps.

"He was one of them aviators. He flew back down here right after the armistice. He's got one of them airplanes on the beach now. Carries passengers for five dollars a ride. Making a big go of it. Got a thing painted on the rudder. It says: 'We Furnish the Wreath.' Gets a big laugh from the tourists. They do say," and the voice was lowered to a confidential note, "whenever he gets a pretty girl for a passenger he has some temporary engine trouble way down the beach, across the inlet where nobody lives, and has to land for awhile." He smacked his lips and cackled over this spicy tidbit of gossip. "That's one hell of a way to get it, ain't it?"

"As good a way as any, I guess." Tod smiled. "But you've got to give him credit. It must be pretty hard to do in an airplane cockpit."

"Hell. There's the beach, ain't there?" The driver thought he must have a real stupid passenger if he couldn't figure that out. "All the soft sand an' nobody around to watch."

"Then," Tod was gravely critical, "I don't see how there can be any fun in it."

The man grunted and gave his attention to the road. A smart aleck. They all were; comin' back from the war, knowin' everything.

As they turned up Ocean Avenue Tod looked back at the Seaside Inn. The hotel seemed to defy time. Nothing about it had changed in a quarter of a century. He was willing to bet the original wicker rocking chairs were still on the porch facing the ocean and the same Negroes were porters and bellboys. When he had been a youngster the hotel had a horse-drawn carryall which met the trains. They were probably still using it.

"Womens' Service Club put up that monument there." The driver pointed to a concrete pillar with a bronze tablet.

"Stop a minute."

He left the cab parked at the curb and crossed the street. The names, in alphabetical order, were in relief against the bronze plaque. It surprised him to discover how heavily the war had drawn upon this small community's youth. All of the names were familiar. They were those of boys he had gone to school with or known casually. He stood in the small plazalike square with its flagpole and simple tablet. Some of the names were followed by a star to mark those who had been killed upon the battlefields of France or gone down with a ship at sea. He turned away and went back to the waiting taxi.

"It's the first house the other side of Harvey."

"Oh!" There was a new respect in the manner and tone. "That'd be the Lathrop place. I know it. You the Lathrop boy? There was stuff in the paper about you."

"I was the Lathrop boy." Tod half smiled.

"Yeah. I guess so. Everyone grew up in a hurry."

Now that he was almost home Tod began to dread the first few minutes. His mother would cry, of course, and explain tearfully she was only crying because she was happy. His father would thump him on the back and then embrace him with silent affection. Later, he knew, they would talk over a drink and there would be a constraint none of them could have explained. His father would toss off a casual question. How was it? Sooner or later everyone asked this and he had yet to find an answer. How could you tell anyone how it was?

He paid the driver, stood for a moment on the sidewalk, picked up his bag and started up the steps.

Tod sat in the new offices of the Citrus Belt Line, listening to and watching Willie Estes with mounting amazement. The man, in appearance, had changed little but there was a subtle difference in speech and manner. The snarling truculence, the surly and sometimes hypocritical whining attitude of self-deprecation had been lost.

He carried himself with an air of jaunty confidence which Tod didn't find offensive. His speech was liberally sprinkled with senseless obscenities but he uttered the words without emphasis and as though they had no real meaning.

They had spent the morning going over the inventory and the books with Harry Stilings, the accountant. The trucking line, due to restricted railway service, was operating at capacity and the cars, shuttling troops from Camp Jackson to Jacksonville, had turned in a large profit. The note at the Merchants Bank had been reduced and there were funds available to liquidate part of the loan from the Atlantic Bank in Jacksonville. The ventures had paid off far beyond Tod's expectations.

"You're in real good shape, Mr. Lathrop." Stilings, a quiet man well past middle age, packed his pipe, leaning back in his chair. He had never called Tod anything but Tod before. "But you sure as hell need new equipment. From here on repairs are going to eat too heavily into your returns. Another thing. You ought to open small offices in DeLand, Orlando, Sanford and some of the other towns on the routes. There has to be some way to control your drivers. Right now there is no way to check on them. They pick up a small load in DeLand, say, carry it along with the other cargo to Sanford. There is no counter protection and they put the hauling charge in their pockets. I don't have any proof but I know it's happening. There has to be a method of receipts and bills of lading so the home office knows what has been handled."

Tod nodded. "You figure out the operation, Mr. Stilings, and we'll locate office space. I'm going to set up a bus line just as soon as we can. The two can work in together."

After Stilings left, Tod and Willie were alone.

"He," Willie motioned toward Stilings in the other office, "is sure as hell right. If we don't get some truck replacements we'll be haulin' stuff in wheelbarrows. Every time I send one out I ain't sure it'll come back."

Tod told him what he had in mind—the surplus army trucks which would be dumped on the market.

"They're bigger and heavier than anything we have. Congress is hollering for complete demobilization and the liquidation of all the stockpiles. We can pick up a new fleet at a fraction of the original cost." He studied Willie. "The Army didn't get around to you after all, did it?"

Willie laughed. "I had to register for the draft like everyone else. They even gave me a physical. The Doc just shook his head. 'Estes,' he said, 'when they get around to takin' you the Germans will be marchin' down Beach Street.' Hell. They wouldn't even take me in the Home Guard. I didn't have to marry Francie after all."

"You did get married, though."

"Well," Willie was a little sheepish, "I tried everything else with her but Francie wasn't puttin' out 'less she had the ring an' book. So," he shrugged helplessly, "we had a church wedding an' everything. Maybe you'll come up to the house some night for supper?" He tried to make the invitation sound casual.

"What the hell's happened to you, Willie?" Tod asked the question with an honest curiosity. "You may be the same son of a bitch you always were but it doesn't show through the way it did. It surprises me a little."

Willie turned away and stood for a moment staring out at the bright sheen of the river. Then he swung about and met Tod's gaze.

"No one else's said what you just did but I can sort of feel it in the way they act. Maybe it's because I got somethin' for the first time in my life. I guess so. I mean, I'm not just someone's grease monkey, crawlin' under an' over cars in dirty overalls. It makes a difference. I ain't good at explainin'. I hated your guts, you an' some others in this town, because you had it all, the best. When you left I said to myself, I'm goin' to cheat that bastard out of everything I can. I'm goin' to scheme him right out of this truck line so's when he comes back he won't have nothin'. Then, I don't know . . ." He spread his hands with a helpless gesture. "I got so damn busy I didn't have no time for shovin' it up you. When I did it come to me I was a quarter owner in a business that might grow big. It give me somethin' I never had before. Confidence, pride, I don't know what you call it." He laughed suddenly. "Stilings is right about them truck drivers. I know they been knockin' down on us because I would have done the same thing myself. I never did write you no letters so you don't know. But, them boys we had drivin' for us in Jacksonville tried the same thing. You know how I found out?"

Tod shook his head, keeping his face expressionless to hide the amusement.

"Well," Willie pushed aside an ashtray and sat on the desk, "one night I asked myself, Willie, if you was drivin' one of them cars for the company an' wanted to shaft it good, pickin' up some extra money for yourself, how would you do it? Like you know, we charged fifty cents a person from the Camp into Jacksonville. But," and he whistled a note of grudging admiration, "there's that there midpoint at Ortega where they had a dance pavillion, swimmin' pool an' a stand for soft drinks, near beer an' some bootleg whisky. Some of the soldiers stopped off there an' the fare from the Camp to Ortega was twenty-five cents. So," he was pleased with his cunning, "I said to myself if I was drivin' I would mark about every three soldiers out of a load as havin' only gone as far as Ortega. That would'a left me with a seventy-five-cent knockdown on every trip. With twenty-five cars operatin' like we had an' all the drivers doin' the same thing we'd have had a big hole in our pockets. The way things was set up, nobody could prove them soldiers didn't get off at Ortega. So I hired us some spotters to hang around Ortega. They'd make a note of every one of our cars that passed an' them that stopped to see how many, if any, got off there. Then I had them reports checked against the drivers' slips. I sure as hell plugged it up in a hurry. I put a couple of them drivers in jail as an example. An', I want to tell you, the traffic just to Ortega dropped off in a hurry. You see"—he bit the end off a fat cigar—"you bein' honest would never have thought of that. Me, bein' a son of a bitch at heart, just knew there had to be some thievin' goin' on. I knew where to look for it. So maybe if I've changed some like you say we ought to hire us another dishonest bastard to keep a check on things. It ain't goin' to do to have two honest men in the company. They'll steal us right out of business."

Tod began to laugh. Willie was right. It probably never would have occurred to him to investigate the drivers.

"I don't know, Willie." He was still smiling. "We hire one thief and then we'll have to put in another to watch him. The first thing you know we'll have sort of a conveyer belt of dishonesty and won't know how to stop it."

"I guess maybe you're right. Anyhow," Willie was cheerfully

agreeable, "I probably ain't changed too much. I still can sniff out the rat holes because if I was workin' for someone else I'd be lookin' for one to hide in myself. So, we ain't got no real worry."

Idly, Tod began to mark lines on a pad. When he finished there was a crude sketch of a four-wheeled cab with two trailer trucks attached to it. He pushed the paper across to Willie.

"I had an idea sooner or later we might come to something like this. What do you think of it? Will it work?"

Willie studied the rough drawing and then nodded slowly. He looked up at Tod with surprise.

"It's one hell of an idea. How come you to figure this out?"

"I remembered trucks hauling caissons once through the mud. Another time, where it was real bad and the truck wheels just skidded, they used a tank and hooked three fieldpieces together with chains. The tank snaked them out and hauled them into place. I guess it stuck in my mind. Later I began to ask myself why something like it couldn't be done with trucks."

"Nobody's buildin' anything like that." Willie was impressed. "The truck trailers would have to be made out of lightweight metal. Aluminum would be too expensive. Maybe they'll find a way to make it cheaper and in quantity. When they do you can bet someone will come up with what you have in mind. Why, hell," a note of excitement crept into his voice, "think what you could do with a rig like that. It's like a goddamned freight train on the road—an express train."

"Well," Tod tossed the pencil aside, "it's something to think about. Now," he stood up, "I want to talk with Conrad at the bank. We're going to expand with the bus line, intrastate, and a city line in addition to the truck fleet. We'll have to get financing. Our record is good so I don't think there will be any trouble about money. Then I want to run up to Jacksonville and see what I can find out about surplus trucks. I may even go to Washington and have a talk with our Congressmen. I know the stuff is standing somewhere out in the open rusting away. If the Government doesn't sell now it will be junk." He put out his hand and suddenly realized this was the first time he had ever made this gesture toward Willie Estes. "I'll keep in touch."

"I don't recollect we ever shook hands before." There was no malice in the statement. Neither was there any small suggestion of triumph. "Maybe we're goin' to get along after all."

"We're going to ride the tail of a sky rocket, Willie. Hold on to your hat. The Citrus Belt Line is about to take off."

From the office Willie watched as Tod slid in behind the wheel of his car. The Buick roadster was only a couple of years old but already it looked out of fashion. He felt a warm satisfaction. The son of a bitch might be right and the Citrus Belt Line a sky rocket for sure. Anyhow, he was on for the ride and there was no getting off. Hell! He didn't want to get off. It was part his sky rocket, wasn't it?

X

No one was ever certain just when, how, or even why it happened. For almost three years after the end of the war Florida was lightly washed by a sluggish tide of migration from the northern and Midwest states. The newcomers, though, scattered themselves so widely over the peninsula their number was barely noted.

The nation was in a period of readjustment. Odd, and sometimes ridiculous, events occurred throughout the country. American troops were busy along the Texas-Mexico border chasing bandits and cattle rustlers whose activities seemed better suited to a motion picture scenario than the serious attention of the Army. A person or persons unknown but, apparently, dissatisfied with the postal service sent bombs through the mail to Postmaster General Burleson. Jack Dempsey won the heavyweight boxing title from Jess Willard at Toledo, Ohio, and everyone decided to forget the new hero had been called a draft dodger for working in a shipyard instead of slugging it out in the trenches. Prohibition under the XVIII Amendment became national and everyone who had a friend who was a physician began telephoning for a prescription which would allow him to buy a pint of bonded whisky at the drugstore. Wholesale combines which had collected and hoarded vast quantities of food in anticipation of huge profits from a desperate public during a long war now blandly offered to sell their stocks at a reduced price to the Government. The millionaire draft evader Grover Cleveland Bergdoll, who had eluded his pursuers successfully for three years, was finally captured. To the embarrassment of all concerned, save, perhaps, Mr. Bergdoll, he escaped from his guards when the automobile transporting him broke down on the streets of Philadelphia. A man by the name of Charles Ponzi, in Boston, mesmerized thousands of persons into believing he could make them wealthy overnight. The only one to profit was Mr. Ponzi and his affluence was temporary. He was indicted on eighty-six counts of using the mails to defraud after his investors had been swindled out of some thirty-five million dollars. The chicanery, however, resulted in a new verb, "to ponzi." After a few months of prohibition, the Government appeared to be completely astonished by the law's failure. Persons of low character were smuggling spirits into the country. A supplementary law was passed. Hereafter ships were forbidden to bring intoxicating liquors within three miles of the shores of the United States. What happened? Hundreds of vessels cruised up and down the coast just outside the three-mile limit along what was known as "Rum Row." Fast, motor-driven boats would take on their illicit cargo from the mother craft and deliver it to the waiting bootleggers on the shore from Maine to Florida. This amazed and chagrined the zealots of "the noble experiment." Again the vocabulary was enriched. Prohibitionists coined a word of opprobrium calculated to shame the most hardened tippler. He was called a "scofflaw." It is disheartening to report that no one seemed at all humiliated by the designation. Bill McCoy and his brother, who owned a small boatyard at Daytona, put their schooner, *The Tomoka,* to cruising Rum Row. The McCoy boys were scrupulous in their dealings. Unlike many they never diluted or adulterated their whisky, brandy, gin or rum. It was delivered to the rumrunners sealed and uncut as it had come from the distillers' warehouses. So honest was their merchandise that anything good came to be known as "the McCoy." Later, and with unnecessary redundancy, this was expanded to "the real McCoy." In New York two prohibition agents, Izzy and Moe, became famous for their innumerable disguises through which they attempted to entrap speakeasy proprietors. They knocked on the doors dressed as Salvation Army lassies, as nuns asking for a donation to charity, rabbis and priests, meter readers, employees of the Department of Sanitation, and even as cops looking for a little graft. Eventually a vaudeville team, known as Izzy and Moe, appeared on the stages and the pair was laughed out of existence.

The nation embarked on an era of wonderful nonsense coupled with unbridled lawlessness. Silver pocket flasks became as necessary to the well-dressed man as his trousers. Debutantes carried them in their purses and deposited them with the maids along with their bras and girdles when they went to a dance. Rival gangs shot each other down with machine guns on city streets and, after awhile, this was accepted as not at all unusual although perhaps slightly dangerous for the innocent bystanders.

And now a strange, inexplicable and almost electric current began to run through Florida. In Miami George Merrick, son of a clergyman, had inherited almost 200 acres. His father had bought the land for $1,000. Merrick, with scanty funds, took an option on 3,000 additional acres just outside the unimportant town of Miami. He was a man of imagination, tremendous energy and a persuasive tongue. What he had in mind was a community built upon a scale of lavishness undreamed of in the state. He had sales literature prepared, colored brochures run off replete with sunlit scenes, golden oranges festooning trees of brilliant green, beaches of the whitest sand, Biscayne Bay and an ocean of emerald hue. There were coconut trees, massed bougainvillaea, flame vine of scarlet intensity, lawns of incredible lushness. He pictured a community of unrivaled beauty. Drawing heavily upon the French and Italian Rivieras the homes were all to be styled along the lines of the Mediterranean architecture. He planned wide, tree-massed streets illuminated by ornamental light standards. There were to be canals upon which gondolas would glide beneath a platinum moon and swept by caroling gondoliers brought from Venice. Nothing resembling Coral Gables had ever been offered to the American public before. Merrick was no tricky promoter after a fast buck. He meant to do exactly what was set forth in his prospectus.

The timing was perfect. Even Merrick, visionary though he might have been, could not have guessed how ready and eager the public was for such a development. The country was prosperous despite a war's tremendous drain upon the national treasury. People were restless, searching for a change, a new way of life. When Merrick went to New York seeking capital for his venture it was literally pressed upon him. Back in Miami he added to his holdings. Streets and sidewalks were laid out, landscape artists brought in. Coral Gables began to take shape. William Jennings Bryan was employed to lend his oratorical talents to extolling the glories of the project. Rex Beach was hired to write a promotional booklet. During the first months of the campaign Merrick sold $150,000,000 worth of lots. Real estate men throughout the state read, watched and thought about what was happening. A fever began to course through the public's veins. Oddly enough the last to believe what their eyes told them was happening were the people of Miami. They either couldn't or wouldn't accept Coral Gables for more than a wild dream.

Coral Gables was the beginning but this was no real estate boom in the usual sense of the word. Those who bought in the lavish subdivision did so with the idea of building and living there. Speculation in land, a game of chance with lots and acres as chips, did not make an immediate appearance. What Merrick did was substantial, practical, honest, beautiful and well thought out. He was, however, a showman of considerable talent. He was aware of the mounting excitement his venture created and had no intention of allowing it to slacken off. He continually sought for new and startling promotional attractions. Johnny Weismuller was engaged to swim through the lagoons and underwater grottoes. Paul Whiteman and his band played "When the Moon Shines Over Coral Gables." Goggle-eyed tourists were lured to visit and look. They stayed and bought. Merrick decided he needed a hotel and built the Miami-Biltmore. He wanted a country club and a golf course. They appeared. Everything he did had grace and solid worth. The name, Coral Gables, was carried on the wind. Housewives and their men on lonely farms in Idaho, the Dakotas, Kansas and Nebraska spoke the words with wistful longing. Families in the flinty states of Vermont, New Hampshire and Maine sat about in their parlors at night and dreamed aloud of the soft beauty and semitropical climate of Coral Gables. Of course they probably couldn't afford anything that luxurious but there must be other places in Florida where a man could make a living, find sunshine, fertile land, a good job. The dream began to shape itself. The appeal of Merrick's Coral Gables was universal and it generated its own publicity. Florida's newspapers wrote glowingly of it. The wire services carried feature stories to every section of the country. Nothing before, save perhaps the gold rush in California and Alaska, had ever so caught and stirred the public imagination. It was a phenomenon without parallel.

In Daytona, Dennis Lathrop packed a bag and took an afternoon train to Miami. At the last moment, more to please his father than anything else, Tod had agreed to make the trip with him. Tod was only mildly curious. He had more than enough to keep him busy. The Citrus Belt Line, both truck and bus service now, had expanded beyond anything he had expected in the three years following the war. His line was covering towns as far south as Fort Pierce on the coast and inland west as far as Leesburg, in the lake country, south to Kissimmee and included DeLand, Sanford and Orlando. Eventually he planned a route to Tampa. Actually there was no reason why the company couldn't operate throughout the entire state. Railroads simply couldn't carry passengers, freight or express beyond their static railheads. There were thousands of towns and communities which were forced to depend upon buses and trucks. The line had, also, secured a local franchise and the buses operated on regular schedules from mainland Daytona to Daytona Beach, Seabreeze and Ormond.

Dennis and Tod sat in the Pullman's smoking compartment. Watching the play of expression on his father's face Tod understood Dennis Lathrop was experiencing the satisfaction of a true prophet. Merrick was doing what Dennis had predicted must come but he had only opened the gates. Coral Gables was for the wealthy or the slightly better than well-to-do. The tremendous buying power of the middle class remained to be tapped. The perfection and careful planning of Coral Gables, Dennis asserted, barely touched the potential.

Tod crumpled the soggy paper cup from which he had taken a drink of bourbon with a little water.

"Are you going to buy in Miami?" he asked.

"I don't know. Not in Coral Gables, anyhow. I just want to look around." He half smiled. "I've been sitting on all that property around Daytona for years. My cash is limited. I'd like to liquidate some of my—our—holdings, but damn it," he shook his head with mock resignation, "I can't make myself let go of anything. Your grandfather is beginning to think I'm a little crazy. He humors me, so maybe I am. The strange thing about it, boy, is I'm not actually thinking about the money to be made. We have everything we need. And," his hand rested on Tod's knee, "I have no wastrel son to support." His eyes brightened with affection. "Are you happy in what you're doing?"

"As far as it has gone." Tod was gravely thoughtful. "I'll have to admit it isn't enough. I want to reach around me and put my hands on a lot of things." He laughed quickly. "I'm afraid I'm something of a disappointment to Grandfather Will. He was looking forward to a fine crop of wild oats through which he could walk hip deep by proxy. I'll get around to that, also, one of these days."

"I've wondered some about that," Dennis admitted. "You haven't shown much interest in girls."

"Oh, I'm interested enough! But I imagine you're talking about marriage. It will come, I suppose."

Dennis turned the cigar between his fingers. "You have a gift, Tod. It's the sure touch of a man who knows where he's going. In a different way your grandfather had it also. He's had a full, rich life doing exactly what he wanted to do. I don't think he ever felt a moment's embarrassment over the fact he lived so splendidly on his wife's fortune. He was proud of his ability to enjoy it and, curiously enough, so was my mother. She was quietly delighted with his extravagances. They kept her young and vital. Will Lathrop made every day a new adventure."

"Grandfather Will wants me to move into the river house with him. Of course, he wouldn't admit to being lonely. He merely suggested, obliquely, we could have a fine time drinking and wenching together in that big house."

"I think it's a good idea."

"What?" Tod was surprised. "The drinking and wenching?"

"Your grandfather's idea of wenching," Dennis chuckled, "is, probably, drinking champagne from a girl's slipper. No. You are much alike. He has always been fond of you although he has viewed your industry with a certain amount of suspicion. I think it would make him very happy to have your company. Give it some thought. After all you will only be on the other side of the river. Your mother and I don't see too much of you as it is. We can always get together."

"I'll think about it. I don't believe the old gentleman would give me much time to myself and right now I don't have much to spare."

Miami was generating its own excitement. In the hotel lobbies, on street corners, brisk, eager young men in white linen knickerbockers talked incessantly of "deals," of "options." Everyone was in a hurry, but it seemed to Tod it was an aimless scurrying. No one had any real idea what it was all about. At the moment little money was changing hands. There was a form of horse trading. A man with a couple of acres or a small house would swap with someone else. The banks were cautious. When the success of Coral Gables was dangled before them as a sparkling example they nodded but held back. Merrick's Miracle. In the bankers' minds it was just that, a miracle. On the balance sheet it seemed unlikely to occur again. They would wait awhile. No one was particularly concerned over their caution. Capital from the North was beginning to show; not in large amounts, usually no more than was necessary to secure an option. What gave the impetus to a growing boom was an almost irresistible tide of optimism. The speculators, those looking for a fast buck and a faster get out, the hurrying "binder boys," suddenly began to believe what they kept telling each other. This was going to be the greatest land boom in history. It had to go. Nothing could stop Florida. It was up for sale and the country was filled with eager money with which to buy whatever was offered.

Real estate offices began to spot Flagler Street. Desk space was rented in hotel lobbies or on the mezzanine floors. The telephone company was pressed to provide additional facilities. Out in the back country the farmers with a couple of acres under cultivation became accustomed to the spectacle of brisk young men walking about the virgin pine flats, measuring distances with their eyes, cautiously skirting a pond or section of swamp. They would halt, standing to gaze in rapt concentration at the marshy stretch. Now and then a surprised Cracker would come out to find a stranger on his rickety porch. Two, three, and sometimes even five hundred dollars would be pressed upon him for an option to purchase his small holding. Few country families had ever seen that much cash at one time. Bewildered and slyly certain they were dealing with lunatics they took the money and signed the papers before a notary.

Despite the humming activity nothing of real importance, other than Coral Gables, had actually happened. One man would sell an option he held to another, pocket his profit and rush off to get "the down money" on another tract. Up and down Flagler Street, in the lunchrooms and restaurants, there was a constant flow of hyperbole with talks of deals, of profits on options held. One free dealer proudly boasted that he had an option on the property of the First Presbyterian Church. Since this was a choice site, as were most of the other churches, there was a rush to tie up all the religious institutions, and bewildered ministers appealed to their congregations to hold fast against the devil, appearing in the form of a binder boy, who was ready to snatch pulpit and altar at the slightest sign of weakening. Trivial as all this was at the moment it did generate an excitement Miami had never before known and it began to sweep through the state. Corporations for the development of property were hastily formed, although they were without assets and held little more than options on outlying tracts. Gaudily lithographed brochures were run off showing what was planned. There were to be wide streets, golf courses, country clubs, swimming pools. Snug homes, secure within their bowers of brilliant foliage, offered security and the good way of life. Happy figures lolled beside the pools while others bicycled on the flower-bordered paths or swung clubs or rackets on courts and fairways. Everyone was young, tanned, beautiful and carefree. They were, of course, also wealthy since they had invested early and made enough money to retire to this perfumed haven. Mailing lists were purchased and the other forty-seven states flooded with enticing literature. Florida's arms were held open. She was ready to embrace the nation. Here was the invitation to share in the bounty.

Tod and his father remained in Miami for three days. The younger man could see the perplexity, and then anger as it gathered within Dennis Lathrop.

"Why," the man finally exploded, "they are nothing but a goddamned bunch of sharks and promoters! There is no intention of building anything substantial. All they are doing is throwing options back and forth. Florida is ready for honest, planned development. This isn't it. This is a crap game with loaded dice." He picked up one of the brochures from the hotel room's desk and tossed it over to Tod. "Just look at that nonsense. Country clubs. Golf courses. Fishing. No one doing a damned thing but lying around having fun. Have you any idea where this heaven on earth is?"

Tod shook his head, quietly amused by his father's passion.

"It's out west of town about twenty miles. I hired a car and it could barely make it through the sand ruts described as a 'fine, broad highway.' There is nothing there but flat pine and scrub land with a stretch of swamp the brochure says is an 'azure lagoon.' In the summertime it will be a hundred and more degrees and the mosquitoes will hang over it in a cloud. No one will be able to live there. A man would be a fool to try. Yet, by God," his impatience caused him to raise his voice, "they call it 'Paradise Acres.'" He snorted. "I tell you if the legislature doesn't step in with some sort of regulation, swindles like this one will ruin Florida and a lot of honest people with it."

"Right now, here in Miami, the honest people seem to be in the minority." Tod poured himself a drink and added a little tepid water from a glass pitcher. "So, not too many persons are likely to get hurt."

Dennis regarded his son incredulously. "You sound as though you thought this was all right."

Tod shrugged. "As you said, it's a crap game. I don't approve or disapprove. It's a matter of choice whether you want to roll the dice." He understood his father's sense of outrage but couldn't share it.

Without comment Dennis pulled a chair to a window. He slumped to his spine, cocked his feet on the sill and stared moodily at the bay.

"Will you have a drink?"

Dennis shook his head but it was not a gesture of petulance. He was disturbed, unhappy and a little disappointed that his son seemed indifferent to what was happening here.

"After all," Tod came to stand beside him, "there isn't anything you can do about it."

"You know how I've always felt about Florida. God knows I've talked enough about it."

"Sure. You've been a circuit-riding evangelist carrying the word." There was an easy companionship between them which robbed the words of any bite. "That or it has been a big love affair. I remember how you talked on that first trip we took through the interior when I was about ten years old." He grinned. "It was as though the land was a girl to be handled gently and taken care of."

"Then damn it," the scowl vanished and Dennis looked up at his son with a tiny smile, "you can't blame me for not wanting to stand by and watch my girl raped by a lot of cheap gamblers."

★ 160

"I don't blame you but I don't know what the hell you can do about it." Tod sat on the windowsill. "I have a feeling something big is about to happen. It probably won't be what you've always wanted—a solid boom and development. But," he gazed thoughtfully at the glass in his hand, "there's going to be action and I'm going to have a piece of it."

"I had an idea it was in the back of your mind." The rebuke was there but tinged with a certain unhappiness. "But, as you said, there isn't a hell of a lot I can do about it. Yes there is." He dropped his feet and stood up. "I can go back to Daytona, take that ocean front property and lay it out for honest building and development. It will be a place for men and families who want homes and not for speculators to gamble with."

"They won't let you do it." Tod lit a cigarette.

"Who won't?" The question was snapped aggressively.

"The fast buck boys. Oh," Tod interrupted the objection he could see gathering in his father's expression, "you can subdivide the tract; put in sewers, streets, lights, water. But you can't control what will happen after that."

"I won't sell to anyone who doesn't intend to build."

Tod was secretly astonished by his father's naïveté. He honestly believed, at this moment, he could dictate the terms.

"So," he continued quietly, "you sell the lots."

"There won't be any of this damned option business."

"Big money is going to come in." Tod studied his drink. "Capital that will be able to put the cash on the barrelhead and buy outright. Everyone swears by his gods he intends to build a home. Then he changes his mind, as he has a right to do, and sells the property to someone else. All you will really be doing with a subdivision is putting more chips on the table."

Dennis mulled this over. "Then," he decided, "I won't sell one damned, square foot. It has been lying there all these years. I can wait a few more."

"I guess you can." There was an affectionate admiration in the agreement. "And you'll end up with a hell of a lot of acreage no one wants. The balloon that goes up is the same one that has to come down. As for me, I'm going to take the ride. I want a hell of a lot of money. It's to be made. What's happening in Miami has shown me that. It's only a matter of timing. Get in and out at the right moment."

Dennis shook his head stubbornly. Then he stood. He gazed at his son and his expression softened. "I think you'd better go and live with your grandfather. Will Lathrop may be appalled by the unnerving experience of your industry but he'll like the excitement. Now," he put an arm over Tod's shoulder, "I'll have that drink with you. Then suppose we go to The Dock for supper and eat a mess of stone crabs."

* XI * *

IN the office of the Citrus Belt Line Tod leaned back in his chair behind the desk and studied the bland innocence of Willie Estes. Then he carefully reread the document before him, skipping none of the involved legal technicalities.

"Why didn't you tell me about this lease before, Willie?"

Estes took a little Gem nail clipper from a vest pocket and snipped at a ragged piece of cuticle on a forefinger.

"You never asked me none about it." He scowled at the offending finger and then carefully replaced the tool in its small leather case. "Besides, it's been in your file all this time if you was interested to see." He looked up with bright pleasure.

"So." Tod mastered a growing anger. "We're tied to this property for ten years at a rental, now, of a thousand dollars a month. And," the tone hardened dangerously, "at the expiration we agree to demolish all structures, clear and grade the land and prepare it for rebuilding."

"I guess so. I didn't pay too much attention. You was away in the Army. We had to move from where we was. Me an' Stilings had the joint powers of attorney. When the lease was up I took it to lawyer Pope."

"John Pope advised you to sign this?" Tod was incredulous.

Willie met his eyes. There was the faintest suggestion of a smirk in the expression.

"If I recollect right he said I could sign it if I wanted to. I didn't go to him for advice about that, see. I just went to get an opinion. Was the lease watertight? He said it was."

"You know this property could have been bought at that time for no more than twelve thousand dollars; what we'll be paying in rent this year. When I came back I asked you what rent we were paying. You told me two hundred dollars a month."

"That's right."

"But," Tod leaned slightly forward, "you didn't say anything about an escalation clause which raises it to a thousand this year."

"You didn't ask." Willie gazed absently out of the window. "Like I just said, the lease was in your file. You could have read it through, comma for comma, whereas for whereas, if you was a mind to. I figured it was no real skin off my ass since you got the majority holdin' in the line. My slice of the operatin' cost don't amount to nothin'."

"This Franwill Corporation we lease from. What is it? Who is it?"

Willie grinned. "Now, Tod boy, you know damn well you're a mile ahead of me already; right this very minute. You got it good in your mind who this Franwill Corporation is."

Tod nodded. "I'd just like to hear you say it."

"It's like I'm married to Francine. My name's Willie. You kind of put them together an' you get Franwill. Francine was real tickled because her part of the name come first."

"We ought to keep Francine happy."

Willie's agreement was immediate. "That's what Francine said."

"So. You're the landlord." Tod mused drily on this. "You lease to yourself and me. When the lease terminates we tidy everything up and move along, leaving you and Francine with a fine piece of business property."

"Not really me," Willie protested. "The Franwill Corporation."

"Have you any idea why I don't kick you the hell and gone out of this office?"

"Sure." Willie was confident. "Because if you did that you'd be admittin' to yourself that you ain't quite as smart as everyone else figures you to be. Now," he sighted playfully over a thumb to Tod's face, "if I'd been you an' come back from the war like you done, I'd a gone over every scrap of paper, down to the last sheet in the toilet, to find out what had been going on while I was away. You sore?"

Tod shook his head. "No, I'm not sore. I can't say I'm standing off viewing you with admiration and pleasure. But, I'm not sore."

"That's good." Willie was benign. "It would upset Francine to have you sore at us."

"The reason I'm not sore," Tod continued, "is because it's my own fault. I let myself forget I was tied in with a real sharp bastard."

Willie stood up, took an ivory toothpick from a pocket and dug between his teeth. "If you ain't sore I'll get along to the shop. We got them new rigs comin' in today." He examined the toothpick, the upper half of which was delicately carved into the figure of a naked girl. "I hear they make these things in solid gold. I'm goin' to get the jeweler, Rowe, to order me one."

Tod waited until Estes reached the door. Then, he called.

"Willie."

The man turned inquiringly.

"Would you mind having your girl call me every morning?"

"Well, sure." Willie was surprised. "What for?"

"Just tell her to say: Good morning, Mr. Lathrop. This is to remind you that Willie Estes is a conniving son of a bitch. Don't let up for a moment or he'll have you gutted and laid out for broiling."

"Sure, Tod boy." Willie beamed with an easy fraternalism. "Hell, Josie don't have too much to do anyhow. She already thinks I'm some sort of a bastard. It'll do her good to be able to say it out loud without gettin' fired." He left the door open as he went out with a jaunty, bouncing step.

Tod snapped at the lease with a flick of forefinger against thumb. Then he began to laugh, softly and with amusement. He'd been had and there was no one to blame but himself. But never again would he take Willie Estes for granted. If he stuck to this the lesson was cheap. He rose and went out to his car, swinging around the corner of Fairfax to Beach Street and then downtown.

The river was filled with dancing lights from the bright sunshine. It was dotted with small islands thrown up where the suction dredges regularly worked along the channel to keep it clear. He wondered who owned these scallops of land; the state or federal government, probably. Enlarged, buttressed by substantial seawalls, filled and raised well above any possible high-water mark, they could be built upon, planted and landscaped. That would be something; to have your own island and a home in the river. He made a mental note to inquire about the title.

He drove idly and without any particular destination, taking a deep pleasure in the familiar scene. The vacant slots of land were slowly filling with one- and two-story buildings for business purposes. The town still hadn't quite made up its mind which direction it should take. It straggled a little here at the northern fringe. There were still residential areas with small frame houses tucked back in their groves of oleander, oak and magnolia. Beach Street had been widened and paved but this ended abruptly down around the Palmetto House and from there on it was a sandy road to McDonald's boatyard. The commercial center was clustered between the avenues of Volusia and Orange.

The changes, small in themselves but collectively shaping the town, had been made so gradually that few persons seemed aware of them. Not long ago, Tod thought, a walk down Beach Street meant a continual exchange of greetings. Everyone knew everyone else; except on Saturday nights when backcountry farmers and the Negroes from Newtown and Waycross came in for the weekly shopping. Now there seemed to be more new faces than old.

Only Commodore Burgoyne's place on the river front defied the years and change. It held fast to most of the square block bounded by Beach Street and Palmetto Avenue and shored at the ends by Oak and Volusia. Tod had no idea how old the residence was. It had been there, dominating the community, when he was a small boy. The Commodore had died a year or two back and Mrs. Burgoyne rarely left the big house. With its drawn blinds the residence offered a titillating aura of mystery, and fanciful tales were spun about the widow who lived in gloomy seclusion. The Commodore, Tod recalled, had been a quietly pleasant man of cultivated taste. Unobtrusively he poured considerable money into the small town. He subsidized winter band concerts, sponsored the Elks Lodge, automobile racing on the beach and the Halifax Yacht Club.

Opposite the Burgoyne place now Tod drew into the curb. He shut his eyes and smiled a little to himself, wondering why the mind should cling to so many trivial things. The incidents were deeply etched and refused to be erased by the abrasiveness of the years.

The small schoolyard had no room for a baseball diamond and the pickup teams played for awhile in the driveway of the Troy House until the guests complained of the noise. Then, a little fearfully, they had marked out a field at the Palmetto Avenue end of Commodore Burgoyne's property. The entire tract was enclosed by a shoulder-high wall of coquina and the games were played with all eyes darting toward the house from which the boys expected to see the Commodore come out and chase them away. Instead, one afternoon, they gathered and gazed with wonder at a couple of workmen who were removing a section of the wall and installing a gate.

"I guess the Commodore got tired of watching you all skinnin' your butts climbin' this here wall." One of the men volunteered the information. "He said to open it up an' put this here gate in it for you to use."

They never saw the Commodore. He never stepped from the house while they were there nor strolled down to watch the play. Apparently, the gardeners had their instructions and they ignored the daily intrusion.

From where he was parked Tod could look down to the corner where long ago the excited shouts and the soggy thump of bat on ball had sounded within the afternoon's long shadows. He laughed quietly to himself. The sound of bat against ball had been soggy. The balls they played with cost ten cents. They were made of a soft cotton stuffing encased in an oilcloth cover with simulated stitching. They rarely lasted more than nine innings before being beaten into a shapeless gob with the oilcloth splitting and the cotton oozing out. Now and then they pooled their nickels and pennies to buy a quarter ball at Dunn Brothers. These were wound and encased in leather and were good for several full games. One year the Brooklyn baseball team held its winter training up in Seabreeze. The club's manager, Wilbur Something, Tod couldn't remember the last name, had sent a dozen almost new, big league balls to the school's principal for distribution. These were regarded as rare treasures and they lasted well through the winter and following summer.

Along Volusia, where the Burgoyne property stopped a couple of hundred feet or so short of the road, there had been a two-story frame building with balconied apartments, a couple of cottages, the tin shop owned by Clarence Nash's father, and the Opera House which, certainly, must have been almost as old as the community itself. During the winter months traveling road companies appeared to offer their melodramatic repertoire. The plays, as Tod recalled them now, always dealt with the mustached villain who was sneeringly about to foreclose on the cottage of a poor widow and her beautiful daughter. It was a cavernous place, heated by two potbellied iron stoves, one placed at each end of the stage in the auditorium and fed from a pile of pine logs. Neither the audience nor the players seemed to mind when the janitor clanged open the doors to feed a couple of pieces of wood to the coals. Tod wondered how and why the Opera House had been built in the first place. It seemed unlikely that the village would have supported road shows at the time of its construction. Tod recalled that the Elks gave their annual minstrel show there but most of the time it was vacant and became a fine place for furtive assignation; used by the town's sports who took their girls in through the unlocked stage door for a little dalliance on the rough pine floor. Tod remembered with a quick grin how he and Rodney Kincaid had caught Oscar Miner there one afternoon. Oscar had his pants down and couldn't chase them away. The girl just lay there and cried until he and Rodney, shamefacedly, ran out.

Lord! Tod thought. The things which came unbidden to the mind. Why should he suddenly remember these seemingly trivial moments? But then, maybe nothing which happened when you were young was unimportant. Added they became the sum of what you were and how you thought.

He pulled away from the curb and drove on down, parking again in front of his father's office. Here, again, was something which caught at him. There had been a Jewish family, he couldn't remember the name. The man ran a small cleaning and pressing shop and his son, about Tod's age, went to the Bay Street School. He was called "Jewisky" by the other children. Who had taught them, at such an early age, that Jews were natural objects of ridicule? How had the seed of intolerance been planted? Who among them had first spoken the word "Jewisky" with derision and why had the other children picked it up? You called a Negro boy a nigger but you didn't dog his steps and shout it after him. You said nigger the way you might say Chinaman. But the word Jew, somehow, managed to carry with it contempt. The cleaning and pressing shop had been next door to his father's office.

Many times, with nothing to do, Tod had sat on the counter and watched while "Jewisky's" father manipulated the machine which steamed and pressed a pair of trousers or coat. His presence had always been accorded a quiet and gentle courtesy and if the man knew Tod was one of his son's tormentors there had been nothing in his manner to indicate a resentment.

Walking into his father's office now Tod realized that the place had grown unaccountably shabby. The small reception room needed painting, a new carpet and furniture. On a couch which sagged wearily old Captain Oliver, Thomas Mears and another man sat and argued earnestly, thumping their canes for emphasis and glaring angrily at each other over a disputed point. They came here each day, appropriating the couch by some unvoiced agreement with Dennis Lathrop. They were not clients, had no business to transact. Tod wondered why his father tolerated them. As he passed, the old men glanced up but did not speak although they all knew who he was. Very little new practice came Dennis Lathrop's way these days but he didn't seem to care. The office reflected this indifference. It smelled slightly musty and appeared threadbare. The large map of Florida in relief still occupied one wall but it was badly in need of cleaning. Opposite it was the skin of a ten-foot rattlesnake Dennis had killed down around Bethune Point twenty-five years ago. It was lusterless, brittle and curled at the edges, held in place by rusted tacks. Tod recalled how his father, scoffing at the idea of a taxidermist, had tacked the fresh skin to the side of Grandfather Will's barn. It had been Tod's job to rub salt into it each day and even now the sight of it filled him with revulsion.

Mary-Anne Finley, Lathrop's receptionist and secretary, looked up from behind her desk and smiled a greeting.

"Hello, Tod. Your father's in court, in DeLand. Anything special?"

"No. I just stopped by to say hello. Why don't you nudge him into fixing this place up a little? It's beginning to look like something out of Dickens."

Mary-Anne shrugged. "Your father doesn't nudge easily. You know that. He doesn't seem to care anymore. Sometimes I wonder what I'm doing here. It's a place to go, I guess."

"Well, when he gets back tell him I came in. I'll go by the house this evening."

"How do you like living with your grandfather?" she called after him.

He smiled. "It's an experience, Mary-Anne. It's a real experience."

"I think he's just wonderful. He never seems to change. He's an old rip, isn't he?"

"He'll be delighted to hear you think so, Mary-Anne. I'll remember to tell him. So long." He waved at her.

In the west corner, on the top floor of the Clarendon Hotel, a small gambling casino had been discreetly opened. Few of Daytona's townspeople were aware of its existence. The police knew and the word was quietly passed here and there but the tables drew upon the tourists and hotel's clientele for patronage.

The community of Seabreeze was a continuation of Daytona Beach. Its residents lived in substantial but unpretentious homes within the groves of gray oaks and magnolia trees on the river front. They were, for the most part, moderately wealthy northerners who came to Florida for five months or so out of the year during the winter. They skirted the raffish atmosphere of Daytona Beach whenever possible. Their children attended a private school. They did their shopping on the mainland and came quickly home in their sedate Pierce-Arrow, Packard or Cadillac, chauffeur-driven limousines. It didn't seem at all the sort of place where even a small gambling room would flourish.

The Clarendon Hotel dominated the area. At night it glowed with a subdued brilliance. The guests dressed for dinner, waltzed or fox trotted in the ocean front ballroom, strolled the terrace overlooking the dunes. By day they played golf or tennis and sunned themselves on a restricted section of the beach where the sand was freshly raked and combed each morning. The hotel was open from December to April only. Those who came to it were of more than average means but they could hardly have been called a "sporting crowd." They were, as someone once remarked, "just this side of Palm Beach." This was a social rather than a geographical classification. However, when the word was carefully spread that a gambling room was open, many of them patronized it nightly. They did so with the slightly self-conscious air of embarrassment of persons caught in unfamiliar surroundings. There were two tables in the central room, one for roulette and the other for dice. Roulette drew most of the patrons since they fancied it to be a much more sophisticated and refined form of gambling. Dice was something bellboys and chauffeurs "shot" and called craps.

In deference to the conservative nature of the Clarendon's guests the rooms were called a Club. After a few minor formalities those who applied were given a membership card along with a key admitting them to the suite. A pretty mulatto girl in saucy, short skirts and long, black silk stockings took their wraps or scarves. A butler and two assistants presided over a buffet. Liveried waiters served champagne and highballs with the house's compliments. For the younger group among the hotel's guests the place offered a welcome change from the rather dreary music furnished by a string orchestra in the ballroom.

Tod stood near the buffet talking with Wright Hilliard. They had been at Princeton together but a class apart. The Hilliards operated the Prince George, a hotel on the mainland's Beach Street.

"I heard you were down in Miami. What's going on there?" Wright was interested. "Is it a real boom or just talk?"

"Right now it's an ant hill with everyone poking a stick in it." Tod glanced over the room. His attention was fixed on a slender, dark-haired girl with an almost Oriental cast of features. He had noticed her before. She always seemed to be alone. "But," he continued, "it looks as though it might break wide open and spread over the state. I'm going to get in on it. I think there's a buck or two to be made. Do you know who that girl is?"

Wright followed the inclination of Tod's head and then nodded. "A Mrs. Lanier. Pettis introduced me one night. She's a guest here. There doesn't seem to be any Mr. Lanier. Widow. Divorcée, maybe. Looks sort of haremish, doesn't she?"

Tod put down his glass and touched Wright's arm. "Let's visit the harem, friend."

There was room at the table. The girl, she was twenty-five or so, looked up and smiled with faint recognition at Wright. Then she put a yellow, ten-dollar chip on the "don't pass" line. They waited while the man who held the dice shook them with an earnest fervor and sent them spinning out across the green cloth. They turned up an eight.

"Eight's the point. Who wants to take it the hard way?" The stickman pushed the dice back with his small rake.

The player rolled a five, a ten and then a seven. He grunted his disgust.

"Seven the loser."

The girl picked up her original bet and the added chip, stacking them on a small column before her.

"Mrs. Lanier? May I present Stoddard Lathrop?"

She nodded to Wright with an easy smile and then coolly studied Tod for a moment. A slight flicker of amusement touched her eyes.

"I know Mr. Lathrop by sight as I'm certain he knows me. How do you do, Mr. Lathrop?" She offered her hand.

"I suppose I was staring," Tod admitted. "But I won't apologize."

"Why should you?" She placed another ten-dollar chip on the don't pass line.

The player rolled a four, a six, a three and then a seven. Again she picked up her single-chip win. The dice came to her and she shook her head.

"I'll pass them."

The cubes went to the player on her left. He cupped them in a hand, blew upon it and murmured the sacred ritual known to all crapshooters.

She glanced up at Tod. "I always feel silly doing that so I pass and let someone else do the rolling."

Tod bought ten ten-dollar chips. "Do you always bet against the player?"

"If it's good enough for the house it ought to be good enough for me."

"The house has the long pull." He rejected the assumption. "And the edge on a dozen other players. You can run into a red-hot roller and get burned."

"Not too badly at ten dollars."

"I saw a man make fourteen passes one night."

"Even so." She shrugged.

"Well," Wright glanced from Mrs. Lanier to Tod, "if no one needs me any longer I'll go and put a few tourist dollars on the wheel."

"The odds are better here." Tod turned.

"I know." Wright nodded. "But I like to see the ball run. Besides, roulette is impersonal. All you have to do is stand, watch and wait. Good luck."

"Thanks, Wright."

"Don't mention it, friend." He walked away.

"Was that for me?" Mrs. Lanier took a small gold cigarette case from her purse. "The thanks."

Tod lit a match, holding it for her. "That was for you."

"It didn't really have to be maneuvered. You could have said: I'm Stoddard Lathrop. As a matter of fact I already knew."

"How?"

"I asked. Anyhow," she inhaled slowly, her eyes not leaving his, "I would have said I'm Julie Lanier. That would have been it. There is, I have discovered, an easy informality among gamblers. By the way, do people really call you Stoddard?"

"Tod."

"That's better although it must have been difficult to outgrow Toddy." She laughed with her eyes.

"I fought my way out of it."

They gave their attention to the table, winning a few bets, losing a few. The play was unexciting. After a few minutes she turned.

"Would you get me a drink? No." She changed her mind. "I'll go with you." With a careless gesture she pushed her chips to the stick-man. "I'll pick these up later, Charlie. Give me a credit."

They crossed the room toward the buffet and Tod signaled a waiter.

"Champagne?" He turned to her. "It's authentic. A boy I went to school with is the hotel's bootlegger. He brings it over from Bimini."

"You made that up."

"No." Tod gave the order.

"You're native, then?"

"Almost. My family brought me down when I was about seven years old." He indicated the buffet. "Hungry?"

"No thank you. Let's encourage your schoolmate's shady business and then, maybe, you'd take me for a drive down the beach."

He grinned. "That's the local equivalent of asking a girl if she wouldn't like to come up and see some etchings."

"I suspected as much." She took a glass from a tray held by the waiter. "What do you do?"

"I suppose you mean for a living?"

"Yes."

"I have a truck line, the Citrus Belt. Also, a local franchise for the city bus service."

"Really?" She eyed him with interest.

"Why the surprise?"

"I don't know. It just seems a little incongruous. A trucker." She tested the words. "You don't fit. A con man. A slick promoter, maybe, but never sweat and brawn."

"The drivers and helpers provide the sweat and brawn. Should we go?"

Under the moonlight the beach stretched like a great band of silver. A west wind had flattened out the surf until the sand was barely washed by small waves which moved upon it with a soft murmur. To the south the lighthouse at Ponce de Leon Inlet held its steady beam.

Tod lounged comfortably on a corner of the seat, holding the wheel with his fingertips. The convertible's top was down and she leaned back, staring up at the star-dusted sky.

"Is this your first time here—in Daytona, I mean?"

"Yes. We used to go to Havana or Nassau in the winter. How far away is that light?"

"Twelve miles or so. For years it was called Mosquito Inlet. Then the Chamber of Commerce decided it was bad for the tourist trade so they changed the name to Ponce de Leon. Where's Mr. Lanier?"

"Is it important?"

"It could be."

She studied him for a moment and then nodded. "Yes. It could be. Well, the last I heard he was in Honolulu with a Scandinavian blonde. He collects them; blondes but not necessarily Scandinavian."

"Divorced?"

"Yes. Divorced. A little wary but not bitter."

"That's good."

"I'm not sure." She was soberly thoughtful. "It might be simpler to be angry. To be only indifferent is sometimes confusing. You wonder now and then how it could have happened. What puzzles you is why. It would be much easier to say he was a son of a bitch and mean it."

"You can't say it?"

"No, not really. Tell me." She veered effortlessly from a distasteful subject. "There is a lot of talk about a real estate boom in Florida. You hear it everywhere. Is it really happening? Would you invest in it?"

"No. I don't think it is that kind of boom." He took a cigarette pack from his jacket pocket and offered one to her. She shook her head. "I wouldn't invest, if, by that, you mean buying and holding. But I'd speculate. I'd trade as I would in the stock market. Get in when it's low and out when it's high. Never take your eye off the ticker."

"I have some money. It was a generous settlement." The statement was made matter-of-factly. "I'd like to put it to work."

"Don't buy anything outright," he cautioned. "It isn't that kind of market; not right now, at least. Money changes hands but it is all in taking and selling options. But," a note of suppressed excitement betrayed him, "the first development on a large scale will touch things off around here as it did in Miami. That's what I'm thinking about. I don't mean an actual development with streets, lights, sewers. It only has to sound and look good on paper and I have a feeling it won't make much difference where it is."

"I thought you had the look of a con man." She laughed softly. "Want a partner? I have a small streak of larceny also."

"I'm thinking of some sort of a corporate setup." It was neither an acceptance nor rejection of her suggestion. "If it looks good you could buy into a piece of it."

"Are you honest, loyal and trustworthy?" There was a mocking note in the query. "If you aren't then I might come in."

"I don't know." He was thoughtful. "I think, maybe, it is better to run alone. I have just been lightly screwed by one partner."

"That was deliberate, wasn't it? The vulgar verb. You wanted a reaction."

"Yes."

"It has been a long time since I have thrown up my hands in maidenly horror. I am not impressed by calculated vulgarity."

He swung the car in a wide circle and headed back for the Silver Beach approach which would take them to the South Bridge.

"Are you taking me back to the hotel?"

"No. I think my Grandfather Will ought to meet you."

"Oh!" She was surprised. "Why?"

He grinned companionably. "You sort of have me backed into a corner. I'm not sure just how you did it. So, this is a diversionary action."

The lower floor of the old house on the river front glowed softly in the night. Tod drove through the rear entrance and then led her up the path of white marl. The ancient oaks spread, a dark canopy laced by shafts of light from the moon.

"How beautiful." She spoke with a small catch of breathless wonder in her voice. "They, the oaks, make you think of Druids at their ceremonies or nymphs dancing at midnight."

"Grandfather Will would have them—the nymphs—if my grandmother hadn't put her foot down."

Wash, his tightly knotted hair a sheer white now but his carriage still erect and vigorous, opened the door before Tod could get out his key.

"I heah you comin', Mistuh Tod." He bowed in Julie Lanier's direction. "Good evenin', miss." His words were directed to Tod as he stood aside, waiting for them to enter. "I say, thank God. Maybe now I kin git some sleep, wid Mistuh Tod home. Mistuh Will keep me up case he want to talk wid someone—which he usually do. He in dat den place playin music wid de Vic-to-ro-la."

"All right. Good night, Wash."

"Good night, suh. Miss."

Tod touched Julie's arm, turning her to the long hall and a corner wing of the house.

"Wash," he explained, "was promoted from sort of a handyman to the post of confidant and companion. I think it's beginning to wear him down. All he ever really wanted to be was a coachman."

Light fell in a narrow lance from a partly open door. A Chopin waltz spun gracefully out from a record on the Victrola. With a half grin of anticipation Tod held the door of Will Lathrop's den for Julie's entrance.

The room had recently undergone one of its frequent transformations. Now it had a musty, academic air. Artificial cobwebs stretched across the ceiling corners. Bookcases filled the walls. Volumes were scattered haphazardly about for effect. It was illuminated by candle-light only. There was a brass, emerald-shaded student's lamp on the desk. It had been wired for electricity but candles burned in the sockets. Will Lathrop wore the flowing robe of an Oxford don. He was slumped in a huge leather chair with his slippered feet on a pile of cushions. A long-stemmed clay pipe was at his hand on a small table. He looked up with surprise as Tod and Julie entered and then arose with a smile of pleasure and welcome. He turned off the Victrola and the music died with a complaining whine.

"Well, boy." The voice was clear. "I didn't expect you home so early and," bright, quizzical eyes fastened and held upon Julie, "in such pretty company." He waited expectantly.

"Julie. Mrs. Lanier. My grandfather, Will Lathrop."

She offered her hand. "Mr. Lathrop." The accompanying smile was warm and overtly amused.

The sharp eyes took in every detail of the slender figure and the dusky beauty. Then they puckered at the corners as though they had discovered something extraordinarily entertaining.

"I sincerely hope you are not of good, moral character, Mrs. Lanier."

"Not offensively so, Mr. Lathrop." She looked about the room and her glance held upon a long, peeled willow switch as it lay at an angle across the cluttered desk. Her attention went back to Lathrop in his gown. "Are you about to birch one of your students, sir?"

"Now." Will Lathrop was delighted. "That's the kind of a woman I like. Show me one who refuses to be surprised by anything and I'll show you a lady of quality." He ignored Tod, took her hand and brought her to a chair beside his. "Will you have some coffee and brandy, Mrs. Lanier?"

"Thank you."

"I told Wash he could go to bed," Tod interposed.

"Naturally, boy. Naturally. If the old fool had any sense he would have packed himself off long ago. He's always nosing about when I don't want him." He beamed down upon Julie. "I suspect I entertain Washington." He turned and opened the doors of a wall cabinet. "We'll make our own coffee. I keep a spirit lamp, kettle and water for just such an emergency." He busied himself for a moment, gathering the robe about him. Despite the extraordinary costume there was nothing grotesque about Will Lathrop. His self-confidence was supreme. Setting out a decanter and brandy glasses he then turned to Julie. "By what good fortune did my grandson meet you, Mrs. Lanier?"

"We were in a gambling hell together."

"You don't say." His satisfaction was obvious. He poured the brandy carefully. "You may as well know, Mrs. Lanier, that I have long and secretly considered my grandson to be something of a problem." He brought the liquor to her. "For years I have extolled the pleasures of the fleshpots to him, pointing out the delights of unadulterated license. In this I have had little success. He is in grave danger of becoming an upright citizen. I shouldn't be at all surprised if he doesn't do calisthenics and take deep breathing exercises in the mornings behind a locked door. Oh," he studied the brandy in his glass, holding it to the light, "I do hear he gambles some and wenches a little here and there but not on the scale I had hoped for."

"I can understand your concern." She winked at Tod.

Will Lathrop ignored this byplay. "It is quite possible he may have developed principles. I find them a little nauseating. Take your brandy, boy."

Tod lifted a glass from the tray and sniffed the cognac appreciatively. There is no one, he thought, quite like this rare old gentleman. His gaze rested with affection on his grandfather.

"Before he becomes completely unbearable," Will Lathrop prattled on with an amiable disregard for Tod's presence, "I should be most grateful, indeed, if you could succeed in corrupting him a little."

She nodded with solemn assent. "It is an attractive proposal. Also," she met his eyes with a quick smile, "it presupposes a certain amount of native corruption on my part."

"Well. Naturally." Will was undisturbed. "Give it some thought, Mrs. Lanier. By all means give it some thought."

They had their coffee and brandy within a warm circle of companionship, spontaneously created. Will Lathrop was at his charming best. His fund of anecdote was inexhaustible. The stories were phrased with a dry, impish humor and his agile mind darted from subject to subject with the flashing movement of a hummingbird. He was stimulated by the presence of Julie Lanier and made no effort to disguise his pleasure. When they were ready to leave he accompanied them to the broad porch with its wicker furniture weathered to the color of old ivory.

"You'll come again, with or without my grandson?"

"I wouldn't miss it, Mr. Lathrop." She was cast in the moon's pale radiance which seemed to create a shimmering aura about her. "You may be sure I'll come again."

For a long moment he studied her and then seemed to reach a decision.

"Wait a moment, before you go." He turned abruptly away and darted into the house. "I have something; put away these many years," he called back over his shoulder.

Julie looked at Tod, who shrugged.

"I don't know," he answered her unvoiced question. "He's unpredictable."

When Will Lathrop returned he carried a sari of exquisite fashioning. It was worked with threads of gold and silver and was so fragile it actually had a luminous incandescence. It seemed to float upon the windless night, detaching itself from Lathrop's hands as he held it toward her.

"A long time ago, in Calcutta, I bought this only because it was beautiful. I would like to give it to you now for the same reason. Half a century has not tarnished its perfection."

Julie Lanier stared at him for a moment and then silently inclined her head. The sari dropped from her brow and she was transformed. The scarf accented the unmistakable Oriental mold of her features, the oval construction of her face. Suddenly, the night seemed to carry with it the sound of small bells, of bare feet upon ancient stones, the soft wailing of a distant flute.

She made no false protestations over accepting the gift.

"Thank you, Mr. Lathrop." It was said simply and in a whisper.

"You wear it with great dignity. Now I know why I have kept it all these years. Good night." He took both of her hands as she extended them and nodded his satisfaction. "Yes. You are the reason for its creation."

Not until they were across the bridge and on Peninsula Drive did she speak.

"I don't believe it." She spoke wonderingly. "He just can't be real."

"He's real enough. Tonight," he shook his head, trying to explain Will Lathrop, "it wasn't entirely a part, a role he enjoyed playing although it's difficult to know where the actor Will Lathrop bows off and the person Will Lathrop returns."

"Thank you for taking me." Her laughter was sudden. "How did your grandmother adjust herself to such a man? I can't imagine him ever being any different."

"I think," he chuckled, "all of her life she was secretly delighted by Will Lathrop. He showed her a world so new, so different, so exciting she never quite believed in it. As a result she lived in a state of quiet enchantment with a man whose humor and imagination bubbled as naturally, as effortlessly, as champagne."

She half turned to look at him. "And what are you really like, Tod?"

"I'm not certain. A little of the old gentleman, some of my father, some I just made up for myself."

"I think I'll stay and find out."

"Good."

Swinging up the steep ramp to the Clarendon's entrance it suddenly occurred to Tod that it had been a most peculiar evening. He hadn't even touched this girl's hand and yet he knew, somehow, they had arrived at an understanding. It was unstated but there. They walked into the high-ceilinged lobby with its towering, white Corinthian columns.

"I'm going to drive out west of Daytona tomorrow and look at some land. Would you like to come?"

"What time?"

This, he thought, this quality of directness is what I like most about her. She never wastes words nor, probably, emotions.

"Ten o'clock."

"I'll be ready." She gave him her hand. "Good night and thank you again for the evening. It was quite an experience."

He waited until she had entered the elevator and the doors closed behind her. Then he turned, walked outside and drove back across the river.

* XII * *

WEST of Daytona the empty land stretched to the horizon. It was unbroken by cabin or farm. No cattle grazed on the tough, wiry grass. No man bent to the hoe or followed a plow. Pine, scrub palmetto, clumps of bay and holly, sparkle berries and fetterbush were spread with a ragged lavishness. Buzzards wheeled in high, sweeping circles, hunting ceaselessly. Over it all the sun spread a warm canopy.

It is not ugly, this flat country. There is about it a strange and compelling solitude. At early morning when the mist, sometimes, lies like a long, wavering scarf it has a beauty. In the evening with the sun cutting into the dark ridge of distant pines it tugs at you a little with its loneliness. For perhaps half an hour before darkness it comes alive with the scattered flight of rice birds, the red-winged blackbird of the north. Rabbits break suddenly from cover and bound away in terror-stricken leaps, brought to panic by some fancied stalker or their own imagination. A crow rasps and a whippoorwill laments and a moon will often dust it with a powdered silver. At midday, though, it is lifeless, asking nothing, yielding nothing.

Tod spread a map over the car's hood and studied it, lifting his eyes now and then to sweep the empty acres. Julie Lanier stood beside him.

"Do you honestly think you can sell this?" She was incredulous.

He looked up. "I don't know. But if people will buy this then they'll buy anything in Florida. They'll buy without looking, seeing or understanding. They'll fight to buy a cigar box full of Florida sand. I'm sure as hell going to find out."

"Who owns it now?"

"It's broken up into sections, half and quarter sections. The parts I want in here are held by a dozen different persons. I have their names and addresses. Whispering Pines." He tested the phrase. "Build your home in Whispering Pines."

She shook her head unbelievingly. "I thought you told me last night that wasn't the way to do it. You were just going to get in and get out and never wet your feet."

"I've changed my mind. Come on." He took her hand and led her to stand beside a drainage ditch. "Do you want a piece of the action?"

She was silent for a moment. "How big a piece?"

"Depends on what you want to go for. I'm going to get options to purchase first but I'm going to buy one small tract right here and put up a big, stucco entrance arch. In wrought-iron letters WHISPERING PINES. Then I'm going to open an office on Beach Street and get together a sales force. The initial investment should be around thirty thousand dollars. You can have a third."

She thought this over. "What are you going to sell, a development, houses, streets, lights, sewers? All the things which go with it?"

"No." He folded the map and put it in his pocket. "I'm going to say, Here it is. No golf course. No tennis courts. No country club. No landscaping. No swimming pools. No palm-lined driveways. It's flat pineland and I haven't the slightest idea what the hell you are going to do with it. But if you want it, it's for sale. No options. No down payment. Cash only."

"All right." She made up her mind. "I'll take that ten thousand dollars' worth. I honestly don't believe you can do it but my investment, at least, ought to give me visiting privileges with your grandfather."

"I'm going to form a corporation. Stalath, for Stoddard Lathrop. I want you to understand," the tone was abruptly and surprisingly decisive, "you are only making an investment. I'm letting you do that," he grinned and took her arm, "only because I expect it to give *me* visiting privileges. But you, in fact no one from here on in, will have anything to say about the operation of Stalath. I'll do things in my own way and any time you don't like it I'll buy you out. Now, let's get some lunch."

No one could possibly have foretold what was to happen within the next twenty-four months. Two and a half million persons were to pour into the state. All of them clutched their money. All of them were certain this was the rainbow with a pot of gold at the end. Not since the gold rush to California had the nation witnessed such mass hysteria. Land prices were to double, triple, quadruple and finally soar to a completely fantastic height that seemed infinite. People would buy anything, and everything was for sale at a price.

Until 1924 the selling of real estate had never been more than a small sideline. It was usually carried on in conjunction with an insurance agency for some reason. So, a man with an insurance office usually added the words *real estate* to the lettering on his window. If, now and then, he made a sale it was considered a stroke of luck, a bonus. The usual procedure for someone who wanted to buy a house or a homesite was to seek out the owner of the property. Between them they made their deal and a middleman rarely entered into the transaction. In Daytona, Bob Smith was the only man who devoted himself entirely to land sales. His slogan—"We Sell the Earth"— was a pardonable exaggeration.

Florida's banks were reasonably cautious with their loans. There was little or no speculative buying. Now and then a tract or a couple of lots were purchased as an investment but such transactions were not considered as a gamble.

For years the communities of Daytona, Daytona Beach, Seabreeze and Ormond had remained more or less static. A couple of attempts at establishing other settlements had been made. One, Ortona, between Ormond and Daytona Beach, never progressed beyond a dozen or so homes. A similar grouping, on the beach side between the Port Orange bridge and the inlet, was called Wilbur-by-the-Sea. This, also, drowsed away in the sun and time with little change. The houses belonged to "winter people" who came south for a few months each year. During the summer and until January they remained boarded and locked while sandspurs and phlox, castor bean plants and weeds choked the yards. The idea that Daytona or Daytona

Beach would ever extend beyond their limited confines was regarded as wild and impractical.

With a quietly enthusiastic determination Stoddard Lathrop moved to secure the options he wanted and made an outright purchase of two hundred acres fronting the DeLand road. The ornamental arch of cream-colored stucco with its wrought-iron designation of *WHIS-PERING PINES* rose to confront each passing motorist. When these things had been done he struck Daytona with the startling impact of the equinoctial storms which boiled out of the Caribbean each year.

He rented the lower floor of a building just south of the corner of Magnolia and Beach. Carpenters, painters and decorators tore away the useless partitions. A heavy-piled carpet of bright orange color was laid. Comfortable lounges and chairs with shaded lamps gave the space a clublike atmosphere. Murals covered the walls and depicted every section of Florida with annotations of historical minutiae. Just inside the entrance an attractive receptionist sat at a desk. At her hand were lithographed brochures of "Whispering Pines. Your Investment in Tomorrow." Four salesmen, brisk, alert but not alarmingly eager, were present to answer any questions. Two Lincoln limousines were parked at the curb to take prospective purchasers to the tract. The heavy, plate-glass windows were lettered simply STALATH CORPORATION. Small groups of townspeople frequently gathered to peer through the windows, and the office became a showplace.

Tod was working fifteen and sixteen hours a day and left the operation of the Citrus Belt Line almost entirely to Willie Estes. He drove up and down the east coast and into the interior taking options on land which was generally considered useless and inaccessible. He drained reserve funds from the bus line and borrowed money from the Merchants Bank on his own credit and the local bus line franchise.

Desk space was rented in the Clarendon Hotel and he called in Julie Lanier to help design a uniform dress for all employees other than the salesmen. The young women he hired were trimly outfitted in a soft gray with an orange insignia on the jacket pockets. Chauffeurs for the limousines were similarly outfitted. The orange became the Stalath trademark.

Dennis Lathrop viewed all these things with a frowning disapproval.

"What the hell are you trying to do, Tod; open a circus?"

"That's about it." Tod was exuberant. "A man will almost always stop for a pretty girl. He'll ask questions and he'll buy. That's all I want. I learned a thing or two about promotion from Merrick, in Miami. If I can I'm going to out-Merrick Merrick right here."

"You know damned well no one is going to build out there on that pine flat."

"I don't care what they do with it. They can chase rabbits, plant a truck garden or put up a house. Nothing is being misrepresented. I'm only saying, Here it is and it's for sale."

He went further into debt, purchasing four of White's newest buses. On their sides were the brilliant orange globes. Two were sent to Jacksonville and parked before the Union Depot's entrance. The remaining two were stationed at the Clyde Line piers.

Visitors to Florida were offered free trips from Jacksonville to Daytona with a way stop at St. Augustine. Box lunches were served by pretty, young hostesses with the compliments of the Stalath Corporation. In a pocket at each seat there was an "Information Kit"; an orange-colored envelope with a map of Florida, a description of "Whispering Pines," a statistical table showing the increase in land prices over the years. There were lightly written notes on the history of Florida: the settlement of St. Augustine by the Spaniards, the hegira of the Minorcans from New Smyrna, the Seminole War and the phenomenon of an unknown Indian by the name of Osceola, the vision of Henry Flagler and the building of the Florida East Coast Railroad. There was also a description of the towns and routes served by the Citrus Belt Line. Lecturers, recruited from the State University and the Chautauqua circuit, radiated a wholesome, serious academic air and they lectured on points and items of interest on the trip south. There was no high-pressure selling. An engraved card was attached to each information kit. It read: *Stalath Corporation. If it's in Florida and you want it we have it. If we don't have it we'll get it for you.*

Calling upon friendships which went back over the years, Tod arranged to have Stalath brochures placed in the rooms of hotels and boardinghouses and on the tables in restaurants. Almost every place the visitor looked he was confronted by some activity of Stalath.

Daily the people funneled into Florida. They came by train and ship and, more frequently, also by automobile. The Clyde Line, operating out of New York with stops at Charleston and Savannah, was booked to capacity for a full year in advance. Tod arranged with the pursers and chief stewards of the two largest vessels, the *Mohawk* and the *Cherokee,* to have Stalath literature placed in the cabins, the writing and dining rooms. A Stalath band blared a brassy serenade of welcome to the passengers as they disembarked onto the Jacksonville pier. Uniformed high school girls, fresh of face and brightly smiling, passed out oranges and Stalath booklets and invitations to board a Stalath bus for the free trip to Daytona. At the Georgia-Florida state line Stalath representatives thrust pamphlets into every car. Within a few weeks it became all but impossible to enter Florida without encountering a uniformed representative of Stalath. The first impression of courtesy, service and something for nothing was a lasting one. The visitors and prospective investors wrote to friends back home and all the letters carried a word about Stalath.

Within sixty days Stalath had sold twenty thousand acres of flatland west of Daytona. The property was staked out into 50 x 100 lots and most persons bought two or three adjoining plots. Stalath banked three quarters of a million dollars. Tod Lathrop reached out for more. He took options on property no one else wanted. It didn't make any difference where it was. He was satisfied to let Fisher, Merrick and the others plunge into high-priced developments, dredge up their islands in Biscayne Bay, build ocean front hotels and lay out golf courses and plan country clubs.

He was on the road constantly, driving the big Lincoln touring car with its silver greyhound ornament on the radiator cap. The Lincoln had become a status symbol in Florida. Roving up and down and across the state he became more and more aware of the scanty accommodations offered the motoring traveler. Save for run-down hotels in the larger towns there was no place for a man or a family to spend the night. Those who drove from the North, and the number increased monthly, were forced into the most miserable of shacks. With roads of unpredictable quality, scattered gasoline stations, miles of uninhabited land, the drive from the Midwest and East was hazardous enough. Those who couldn't or didn't make a town by nightfall were often caught and had to sleep in their cars or rent one of the infrequent cabins by the roadside. These were unheated, flimsy, whitewashed structures without electricity, running water or indoor toilet facilities. They were usually operated by a slatternly couple in conjunction with a crossroads store and were more often used for an afternoon's assignation than anything else. Driving to Cocoa one day an idea began to form in his mind. Why wouldn't a cabin grouping, strategically spotted on the main highway down Florida's east coast, pay off? They would be solidly constructed and of simple design; a single room with twin beds, a shower and toilet. They could be bright, airy and comfortable. Above all, the accommodations would be uniform and a man who spent the night in a Stalath cabin outside of Titusville would know what to expect of a Stalath cabin at West Palm Beach. Maids could be trained and a supervising housekeeper engaged. The idea fascinated him and he began to explore beyond it. Why not add an automobile service station with a trained mechanic to operate it? Why not complete the grouping with a restaurant offering good food, reasonably priced and served by uniformed waitresses? The buildings would be of orange color with gray, slate-shingle roofs. By the time he reached Cocoa the Stalath chain was complete in his imagination. Nothing like it had ever before been attempted. It was a revolutionary concept; as revolutionary as the growing travel by automobile. Hotels for motorists. Motels. The word came without conscious effort. That was it; provocative, short and self-explanatory. He would space them from Jacksonville to Miami, a couple of hundred miles apart.

Back home, three nights later, he had dinner with his father and mother.

"We see so little of you, Tod." His mother reached across the table to place her hand on his. "Is what you're doing so important? I don't think you take very good care of yourself. You look tired. I think you ought to settle down and marry some nice girl."

"I have a nice girl, Mother." He smiled at her. "But, I don't see much of her either."

"But, Tod." The dismay was evident. "She's a divorcée. You told me so yourself."

"That hardly makes her a candidate for burning. A great many persons get divorced these days."

"I'm not sure." The sniff was just short of audible. "A woman who can't keep one husband. There must be something wrong with her. When I was a young girl . . ."

"I know. Things were different. I suppose they were. Marriage was sort of an endurance contest." His reassuring pat on her hand was gentle. "Anyhow, I don't think Julie has any idea of marrying again; not right now and neither have I. We'll just go on the way we are, living in sin."

"Tod!" She was actually outraged and withdrew her hand quickly. "I hope you're joking and even so it's in very bad taste." She rose. "If you'll excuse me . . ." She relented and waited as he came around the table to kiss her. "Will you stop by my room and say good night before you leave?"

"Of course."

He and Dennis remained standing until she had left and then Dennis brought a bottle of brandy and glasses from the buffet and with them a box of cigars.

"What's this new scheme of yours?" Dennis offered the small alcohol lamp for Tod's cigar. "You said you wanted to talk about it."

Briefly Tod outlined the plan for a motel chain, uniform in character and service. Dennis displayed an immediate interest.

"That's more like it, Tod." He nodded his approval. "It's a contribution; a step toward what I have always had in mind for Florida. It's substantial and goes beyond just something which will make more money. Frankly, I don't understand your preoccupation with the putting together of a fortune. I suppose that's your target. We've always lived comfortably. You've never wanted for anything. Your Citrus Belt Line and the local transportation buses must be doing well. Why do you keep driving yourself?"

"You sound just a little like Grandfather Will." Tod laughed. "He's convinced I'm a black sheep. I'll tell you why I do what I do. It's fun. It's exciting. Why does Ford keep making automobiles? He doesn't need the money. Why do the Astors, the Vanderbilts, the Rockefellers, scheme and plot and put together their syndicates and corporations? It's because they'd be bored to hell and gone with nothing to do. As you said, we've always had a reasonable amount of money. When you've always had it then you don't think much about it. No," he shook his head, "it's a game in which you try to outguess the other fellow."

Dennis sipped his brandy reflectively and studied his son's animated features. He drew upon his cigar.

"I have to be honest, Tod. I don't like what you are doing. It's the rankest sort of speculation. This land you're selling. You know what's happening?"

Tod knew well that the lots in Whispering Pines had changed hands a dozen times since their original sale. The first purchaser made his profit. He took the binder money but held the title. Then the option was optioned and with every exchange the price of the land increased.

"I'm selling chips in a poker game." He met his father's accusing gaze. "I'm not taking anyone's paper. I get cash. What happens to the property after that is no concern of mine."

"Well. It should be." Dennis rose from the table and paced back and forth across the room. "The town, the state, the country, for that matter, have gone crazy. Why?" He leveled a finger at his son. "Just the other day that Howard boy, the one who works behind the soda fountain in Peter Paul's drugstore, had the effrontery to ask me if I didn't want to sell some of our river front property down near Burgoyne's Point." His laugh was harsh and unamused. "I asked him if his salary was large enough to make a purchase. He wasn't at all embarrassed. He said no but that he knew someone who was interested."

"I heard about that." Tod couldn't hide the smile although he knew it would further anger his father. "The next day he sold Webster's grocery store—with old man Webster's permission, of course. He quit Peter Paul and is in business for himself now. Joe Howard. Realtor. I understand he has ordered a Lincoln sedan."

Dennis Lathrop dropped back into his chair and shook his head, perplexed and confused.

"I don't suggest that what you're doing, Tod," he continued, "is dishonest. It is simply without value, lasting value. I read one of your Stalath brochures. 'An Investment in the Future.'" He snorted his impatience. "This boom, this frenzy, has no future. It's like one of those damn fool chain letters. When the chain is broken the whole scheme falls apart. I . . . we." He corrected himself quickly. "We own some really desirable property between here and the inlet. It runs, as you certainly know, in large tracts from ocean to river, right across the peninsula. Why don't you take it and develop it the way Merrick did with Coral Gables? You'd have something to be proud of."

"Later, maybe." Tod understood his father's long-standing dream of a prosperous, populated Florida. "The time isn't right now."

"Then tell me what is right for now." Dennis hit his fist on the table and the glasses rattled.

"It's right for what I am doing." Tod was undisturbed. "It's right for the hoopla, the free barbecues and bus trips; pretty girls, smartly dressed; the trading and swapping; the selling and buying. It isn't right for building. No one is interested in that. People are investing in Florida for one reason only: to make a fast buck and turn that buck into three or four. They are all in a gambling sweat. It is all you hear. This is for sale. That was bought on Wednesday for five thousand dollars and sold on Thursday for fifteen thousand. The fact that that much money doesn't actually change hands doesn't cool the fever. Some of it sticks to everyone's fingers and it is used to take an option on something else. It is as irresistible as the pull of gravity. I took an option today on a thousand acres up beyond the Tomoka River, south of Osteen. All I had to put down was a thousand dollars."

"Then you're as wild as everyone else." Dennis Lathrop was wearily resigned to the madness. "There isn't even a cow path through to that land. The only way to get in and out is by a balloon."

Tod sat upright with a jerk and stared at his father with admiration. He drew upon the cigar and took a swallow of brandy.

"That's one hell of an idea. Just one hell of an idea. Free balloon trips. 'Look at your land from the sky.' A balloon, orange-colored, floating along over Florida. 'The sky's the limit.' " He whistled softly. "I wonder if the Army has any surplus observation balloons left over from the war?"

"Are you serious?" Dennis couldn't believe it.

"Of course I'm serious." Tod leaned back and gazed at the ceiling, his mind clicking methodically. "Not even Merrick thought of anything that good." He began to whistle, a little off key, "Come, Josephine, in My Flying Machine."

"Sometimes," and Dennis was serious, "you frighten me a little, Tod. You talk like a carnival operator of a shell game."

Tod grinned. "Julie said I had the look of a con man. Maybe you're both right. But I don't think so." He crossed his arms on the table and leaned upon them, his eyes meeting his father's, steadily and without embarrassment. "I have never"—he selected his words carefully—"or, Stalath has never, misrepresented one square foot of the land it has sold. We promise nothing. All we say is that if you want to invest in Florida land Stalath has it for sale. If you don't care where it is neither do we. I'm not out to bilk the widows and orphans. I'm not out to cheat anyone. A couple of times," the smile broke slowly, "I've told prospects that the land they were looking at wasn't worth a goddamned thing and probably wouldn't be for another fifty or seventy-five years. They didn't even hear me. They weren't listening. It was like saying a hundred-dollar bill was, after all, only a piece of paper. A new breed of trader is moving into Florida. He may not know anything about land but he has the gambler's instinct. He's shrewd. He buys today because he is certain he can sell tomorrow and make a profit. Everyone thought I was crazy when I made a deal for acreage west of Titusville, near Lake Harney. Well, I'm selling it for twice what I paid. If I wanted to manipulate around I could get more. Of course no one is going to build homes there. No one expects he will. What he is buying is a seat at the table where the cards are being dealt. Money is no problem. I can go into the Merchants Bank tomorrow and borrow as much as I want on my signature alone. That is the way things are. All over the state the bankers are standing out in front and calling, Step right in, folks. How much do you want? We're loaded." He finished his brandy. "You hold on to that ocean and river front for six months and I'll get you a fortune for it. I mean that literally. As far as land is concerned you and Grandfather Will have the oysters with the real pearls in them."

"I don't want a fortune." A small expression of regret crossed Dennis Lathrop's face. "And, even if it was in my nature to go after one, I'm getting a little too old for the high jinks you seem to delight in. You're the crapshooter with bills tucked between his fingers and saying, I'll take the action. When people are ready to build then I'll sell the peninsula property." He stood up and Tod followed. They walked into the living room and Dennis put an arm over his son's shoulders. "At least," he continued, "you don't seem to be doing anything for which you should be ashamed."

"Would you have the time and be interested enough to give me a hand with this motel chain? I could use your advice. In time, if they pay off, they could be expanded to lace the country from Florida to California. They will take the guesswork and much of the discomfort out of automobile travel. Florida can be used as a testing site."

"I'm complimented but you don't really mean that, boy." There was affection and pride in the tone. "I'm beginning to understand you a little better. Whatever you do has to be a one-man operation. This Stalath Corporation is Stoddard Lathrop and Stoddard Lathrop is Stalath. They are indivisible. You might listen respectfully to my advice and suggestions but I doubt if you would take them. But, by all means, go ahead. What you have in mind is new, provocative and a real contribution. I doubt, though, that it will raise any enthusiastic shouts from the Florida Hotel Association."

"It's time someone jolted them."

Tod went to his mother's room. She was reading in bed and put aside her book as he entered. He bent and kissed her cheek and she held him with a tight possessiveness for a moment.

"Come and see us a little more often, Toddy."

"You haven't called me that in years."

"Oh! I do to myself." Her smile was wistful. "You were such a little boy. I look at you sometimes now and say, Who is that handsome stranger? You keep in mind what I said. Marry some nice girl and settle down."

"I will when I find one."

"Do you know, I don't think your grandfather is a very good influence. He is a libertine at heart although I must admit he has kept his baser instincts under admirable control all these years."

"I'll armor myself against his temptations." He touched her chin gently with his fingertips. "I'd like to bring Julie . . . Mrs. Lanier . . . down to meet you sometime."

"Are you serious about her, Tod?" The expression clouded. "After all."

"I know." He humored her. "She's a divorcée. But, honestly,

Mother, that doesn't mean she's ready for the stocks and a scarlet letter."

"I find it difficult to adjust myself to the changes which everyone else seems to take for granted. Bring her to dinner." She laughed with a small pleasure. "I promise I will not point an accusing finger or utter the word *fie!*"

He kissed her again and then went out to join his father on the porch. They stood for a moment, listening to the rushing sound of the ocean and watching the brilliant streaks of phosphorescence where the breakers curled and spun shoreward. The headlights of many automobiles cut their paths along the beach.

"Come again soon, Tod."

"I will. Mother just conceded that a divorcée might not be a painted Jezebel. I'll bring Julie down for dinner. She uses a fork and doesn't spit chicken bones to the floor."

"Good. I mean about bringing her to dinner. How is my father, by the way?" He shook his head. "None of us seem to have the time we once had. Are the days, weeks and years really shorter than they used to be?"

"I think we're all just running a little faster and covering more distance." He pointed to the moving cars on the beach. "Do you remember when going to the inlet and back was a day's excursion? Now they drive it in half an hour and are not even aware of where they've been or what they saw. Well . . . good night."

On Main Street he pulled into the curb at Peter Paul's drugstore for cigarettes. The corner was brightly lighted and crowded as usual. Groups of men gathered to talk earnestly and with extravagant phrasing and gesticulations. They drew together, broke up and re-formed. By some mysterious accord Peter Paul's had become sort of a Curb Exchange for real estate. Those who gathered nightly talked of deals and options. Some were local men Tod had known since childhood. The majority, though, were strangers. They had all, save for a few exceptions, adopted a uniform dress—white linen plus fours, Argyle stockings of heavy wool and completely unsuited to Florida's climate, sport shirts open at the throat. The local men smoked cigarettes. Those from out of state invariably chewed upon cigars, rarely lighting them. All, however, gave the impression of being poised on the balls of their feet, waiting for the starter's gun which would send them racing off to snap up an option, put down a binder. They were tense and overtuned; eager to run toward some unannounced goal.

With his huge bulk wedged on a narrow ledge jutting out from one of the windows, Pete Rogers flipped a hand in Tod's direction.

"What do you say?"

Pete's greeting never varied and it was voiced on a shrill note which seemed incongruous coming from a man of such large frame. Tod remembered him with a warm affection from boyhood. Pete had given him his first tennis racket and later, a mandolin. The instrument had been left on the porch of the beach house one night and the following morning it was swollen and split from the dampness. So Tod never had a chance to become proficient. The accident had been regarded by his mother and father as a kindly manifestation of Heaven's constant solicitude. Each morning Pete arrived at Peter Paul's corner, took his place on the ledge and rarely moved from it until evening.

"Hi, Pete—Fred—George," Tod called to old acquaintances. He bought a carton of cigarettes and carried them into a telephone booth. He waited while the Clarendon operator paged Julie.

"Hello?"

"I'll buy you a drink."

"Well! How is my reluctant Romeo?" There was a small suggestion of exasperation in the question. "I didn't think you had time for girls anymore."

"I don't, really, but my mother thinks I ought to get married."

"Oh? Do you have anyone in mind?"

"No. I'm sort of shopping around."

"Putting down a binder here and there, I suppose?"

"I'll buy you a drink or take you for a drive down the beach."

"Hey! That sounds pretty daring. The drive along the beach, I mean."

"We'll stop at Clifton's first and I'll likker you up. Alcohol is supposed to make girls susceptible."

"Oh, I'm susceptible enough! You just don't seem to offer anything contagious. About Clifton's. I'll go but I'm damned if I will eat any of those boiled peanuts."

Chet Clifton had a still somewhere out west of Holly Hill. He retailed his moonshine in pints, quarts and gallons. For friends of long standing he would uncork a jug on the premises. With the whisky he served a large bowl of peanuts, boiled in the shell in heavily salted water. These he pressed upon his acquaintances as an esoteric treat. The reason for boiling unhulled "goobers" was a secret Chet kept to himself. His "shine" was only a few months out of the still but it was carefully made of good corn mash and, with a swallow of Coca-Cola, fairly palatable, but it did nothing for the peanuts.

"I'll be up in five minutes." Tod waited.

"I'll be ready." She hung up.

On the way up to the Clarendon Tod, for the first time, thought seriously about Julie Lanier. There was much to recommend her. She had the poise and assurance of a woman who knows she is beautiful. He wondered why her marriage to Lanier had gone sour. She had mentioned it but once and that on the evening of their first meeting. Their relationship had been casual, friendly. He made no attempt to press it beyond that. This, he mused, had piqued her just a little. There had been plenty of opportunities to move their association onto a more intimate plane.

"You know," she had once said, "I am a perfectly healthy, normal female."

"It never occurred to me to doubt it."

"Well, I'll just be damned." She turned to look at him. "Is there anything wrong with you? I mean . . . you have, as they say in the automobile advertisements, all the usual accessories?"

"Grandfather Will asked me the same question once in a slightly different way."

"This doesn't disturb you? What goes on? Do you have a little seamstress tucked away somewhere on the other side of the tracks or don't I appeal to you? It does something to a girl's vanity when a man doesn't make a pass."

Driving now with one hand he reached over and drew her within the half circle of his arm. She settled against him with a small murmur of contentment.

"This is more like it. I was beginning to worry about you."

"Have you thought about marrying again?"

"Are you making an offer?"

"No."

"You're yellow." She reached up to link her fingers with his. "The worst part of it is I really am fond of you and," she paused, "I think you are going to be able to afford me."

"I'm working at it. Anyhow, I can afford Chet Clifton's with or without the boiled peanuts."

* XIII * *

THE phenomenon of Florida was the fact that it ceased to be regarded as a phenomenon. This was the new El Dorado or the fabled land of Zenu. So, a patient was no longer surprised when a dentist put aside his drill to tell of a land sale he had made, a property purchased or an option taken. A clerk would halt in the act of wrapping a parcel to tell of a neighbor who had sold his house for a fabulous sum. Soda jerks and grocery clerks quit their jobs and went hustling over the dunes and flatlands, looking for something to sell. Land was sold by mail, by telephone, through coupons to be clipped from the daily papers of every town and city in the country. People took their life's savings and trustingly bought lots they had never seen. A magnificent development on Florida's Gulf coast was announced by direct mail and in newspaper advertisements. *Poinciana. The Miami of the Gulf.* Hundreds of thousands of dollars were pressed upon the promoters. Cartographers noted the flourishing community on new maps of Florida which were hastily scrapped when it was discovered that Poinciana was nonexistent. The lots were all under water. There were other revelations of fraud and chicanery. There were cartoons of men and women in deep sea diving outfits holding the deeds to their property, suckers became the butt of vaudeville jokes, and economists warned that the boom was only a fragile bubble—beautifully colored but nevertheless a bubble.

None of these things had the slightest effect on the speculating public. It became literally true that Florida was running out of land. Islands, dredged from the bottom, rose in Biscayne Bay. West Palm Beach, which had been visualized by Henry Flagler as a place where the servants of the Palm Beach mansions might live, boomed into a small metropolis. West of the railroad tracks at Daytona the Negro communities of Waycross and Newtown were invaded by knickerbockered agents and binder money was pressed into the hands of astonished owners of a ramshackle cabin on a few feet of weed-choked, sandy soil.

In other parts of the United States a variety of things were happening. The Prohibitionists seemed to be the only segment of the nation's society which wasn't preoccupied with the fortunes to be made in the peninsula state. They went doggedly about their task. Congress was prodded into concluding a treaty with Great Britain which permitted the search of British vessels within one hour's sailing distance of the coast if they were suspected of smuggling liquor, and W. H. Anderson, superintendent of the Anti-Saloon League, was convicted on a charge of forgery and sent to jail. In Santa Monica, California, four planes of the United States Army Air Service started a flight around the world. Senator Wheeler was indicted in Montana for accepting fees to influence oil and gas permits and the Supreme Court solemnly ruled that beer could not be prescribed as a "medicine" by physicians. Governor McCray, of Indiana, was sentenced to ten years in jail and fined $10,000 for fraudulent use of the mails and a bomb was exploded in the Rhode Island Senate in an attempt to end a filibuster. "Ma" Ferguson was inaugurated as Governor of Texas after "Pa" had fallen afoul of the law, and an earthquake destroyed the business section of Santa Barbara, California. No one paid much attention to these events, diverting though they might be. They were all too busy trying to get a few feet of Florida land.

Riding this tide of unprecedented prosperity and seeing no high-water mark from which it might recede, the banks became prodigal with their money. A loan could be arranged for almost any venture as tracts, parcels and lots changed hands daily. New Buicks, Studebakers, Franklins, Hudson Super-Sixes, and even an occasional Stutz Bearcat were parked out of doors and under pine trees beside the unpainted cottages of small farmers who had sold their fields for building lots. The binder boys roared over the state in their Lincolns and every now and then took their wads of cash, engaged whole parlor and sleeping cars and went off on a binge to New York. They registered for entire floors at the Biltmore or the Ritz-Carlton and their proudest moment came when they paid fifty dollars a bottle for New Jersey champagne and were greeted by the boisterous Texas Guinan with: "Hello, Suckers." Comely young women of elastic disposition were engaged as "bird dogs." It was their job to move in and about the better hotels and strike up acquaintances with newly arrived speculators. They would then "point" them for their employers, who always had a deal ready or going.

Contractors and architects sat hopefully in their offices and waited for the golden shower to fall upon them. Clients were rare, for nothing was actually being built. There was a brisk business in the ornamental entrance arches of stucco or brick which marked every development. Occasionally a street would be laid out and lightly paved with asphalt, and signs went up to indicate where "Jasmine Place" or "Hibiscus Road" would be. The investors all agreed that such improvements as sidewalks, lights, sewage disposal and water facilities could wait. In the meanwhile the trading climbed to new heights of excitement. The hotels were filled and the Clarendon decided to remain open throughout the summer. Liquor was good and plentiful as the speedboats shuttled between Bimini, in the Bahamas, and the Florida coast. Madams from New York and Chicago came south with their coveys of girls and set up shop. This so outraged the local whores that they sent a letter of protest to Governor Martin asking for some sort of protective tariff or a quota system by which the home industry would be secured. The Governor never replied.

The acreage on the DeLand road which Tod had designated as "Whispering Pines" had been sold to the last foot. It had been a cash deal from the beginning and the profit ran close to a million dollars. Part of this Tod left on deposit with the Merchants Bank. He opened an account in the name of the Stalath Corporation in Seabreeze. The bank there, established a few years earlier by a shrewd and conservative Hoosier, Richard Niven, Sr., refused to be drawn into the whirlpool of speculation. You could get a loan from Mr. Niven but your security almost had to be gold bullion. The balance of the money Tod stashed away in a safe deposit box. He wrote a substantial check for Julie Lanier; the return on her investment of $10,000 in "Whispering Pines" remained as it had been. Not so much as a two-by-four had been raised. The land was staked but flat and lonely and the lots were a huge deck of cards which was being shuffled constantly.

Tod wanted to move the Citrus Belt Line into the Stalath Corporation but there was the problem of Willie Estes and his twenty-five percent. Willie refused to sell and Tod didn't want him in Stalath, so the bus, trucking and new taxi service remained a separate operation.

Julie had moved from the Clarendon and leased a house on the beach side of Ormond.

"I thought," she said one evening, "it might encourage you to spend the night sometime."

"I don't want to be involved." He said it simply and without emphasis.

"Damn you, Stoddard Lathrop." She had wheeled angrily. "I'm not suggesting an involvement. If you think I'm getting nesty you're wrong. Can't there be a little tenderness between us? I don't want to move in. I'm not a possessive woman. What goes on inside of you? All I seem to hear is the tinkle of a cash register. After you have made all the money there is to be made in Florida, what then? Where do you go and why should you want to go?"

"Because I must. There's a compulsion to put things together. I don't know where it comes from but it's there. You think I drive myself. I don't. I keep moving because I can't stand still."

"If I had any sense I'd leave here and never look back."

"I'd miss you."

She looked up at him. "That's the first gentle thing you have ever said to me. I'm not whining and complaining, standing on your doorstep with a little shawl wrapped around my shoulders saying, Please take me in, kind sir. I'm cold and have no place to go. Even when you've made love to me I've had the feeling you were thinking about something else."

"I'm sorry." He took her hands. "I mean it. I've never taken you casually no matter what you may think."

Mystified, she shook her head. "I think I'm out of my mind to stay. Why is it I seem to be attracted by offbeat characters like you and Lanier? He wanted to collect dames; really used to bring them home to show me how clever he was at it. You"—she lifted her shoulders in a gesture of resignation—"you're nice to be with. I suppose I could be in love with you but," and her expression was one of wry humor, "you run too fast. I'm out of breath at the quarter pole. To hell with it. Would you like a drink? I have a new bootlegger. He said he used to go to school with you."

"Most of them did. We all learned about boats hanging around the river and McDonald's or the McCoy brothers' boatyards. When prohibition came along they put what they had learned to work."

He splashed some water into the glasses of Scotch and brought them over to the couch where she sat, wedged into a corner with her feet tucked beneath her.

"Do you know anything about interior decorating?"

"Only what my instinct tells me is right or wrong."

"Wait a minute."

He put his glass on a small table and went out to the car. When he returned he carried a rolled sheet of drawing paper which he spread on the couch between them. She watched this with an ironic half-smile.

"I know." It was almost an apology. "You don't need the money but would you like to come to work for Stalath? I could use you."

"Don't talk dirty." She took a swallow of her drink.

He grinned and his features lighted, making him appear inexplicably young and eager for a moment. She stared at him and then relaxed. This was the key to Stoddard Lathrop. The whole thing was a game. He could no more resist it than a youngster could pass a tin can without kicking it or see a fence without wanting to walk it. The money he made was almost incidental save for the fact that it was tangible proof of a can kicked, a fence walked. She moved down to lean against him, looking over his shoulder as he held the paper flat with the architect's drawing of the proposed motel grouping.

"I'm going to put up a chain of these. They'll be uniform in design, construction and facilities. I thought of bright colors; orange with gray shingle roofs. Carry the same combination throughout the interiors." He glanced up for her approval.

She shook her head. "Pink. A soft, pastel pink maybe, with gray."

"Why?" The question was snapped with an unconscious aggressiveness.

"Because it's better."

He turned this over in his mind for a moment and then nodded reluctantly.

"You might be right."

"I know I'm right." She dug into his jacket pocket for cigarettes, lit one and rested her chin on his shoulder. "I have a knit combination, gray skirt, pink sweater. I look ravishing in it if you'd ever take the time to notice."

"Do you want to come to work for Stalath?"

"Not particularly but if the boss will dandle me on his knee once in awhile it might be an inducement."

He released the ends of the drawing and the heavy paper rolled itself into a tube.

"Keep this." He tossed it to a chair. "Figure out a decorative pattern for the interiors—lights, drapes, carpets, uniforms for the waitresses and maids." He leaned back and took a long, reflective swallow of his drink. "The big problem, the one I have to be sure is answered, is where to place these units on the Dixie Highway between Jacksonville and Miami. What's true of automobile travel today will not be true four or five years from now. Roads will be improved, cars will travel faster. Overnight stops will be farther apart. I'm going to start with three; one on the northern fringe of Miami; one around Fort Pierce; and one around here, probably between Kingston and Holly Hill."

She didn't reply but merely shook her head.

"What's wrong with that?" He snapped the question.

"The one here." She ignored the small truculence. "The beach is Daytona's greatest attraction. Will people coming to Florida for the first time stop short of it? I don't think so." She answered her own question. "They have all heard of Daytona's beach and will want to see it and the ocean. I know I would so call me average."

He thought this over. "You could be right. As a matter of fact you are. We might get some trade from the traveling salesmen in their cars. The beach is no novelty to them. But, as you say, the tourists will be heading for the ocean. Maybe I should build on the peninsula side here." He rose and began walking back and forth, talking as he moved. "If I make a mistake in locating these accommodations then the whole thing falls apart." He sat on the arm of a chair and stared pensively through a window. "On the road from Jacksonville to Atlantic Beach there are two open-air restaurants. They serve mostly frankfurters, hamburgers, fried shrimp, French fried potatoes, cole slaw, coffee, soft drinks; the usual picnic stuff. They face each other across the highway but the one situated on the right-hand side of the road as you go to the beach was a failure from the beginning. I've tried them both and there isn't any difference in the quality of the food. They are both self-service so it isn't a matter of indifferent employees. They are almost identical in construction. Yet, one place starves to death with only an occasional straggler buying a Coke or a hot dog. The other is usually packed and with patrons waiting for a vacant table. Do you know why?"

"I think so."

"You do?" He looked at her with quick surprise. "It took me a long time to figure it out."

"Maybe some people are smarter than others." She made the statement with a smug demureness, enjoying herself. "I would think that families driving to the beach start around midmorning and had their breakfast not too long ago. Also, they probably have a picnic basket in the car for lunch on the sand. So, they hurry past the restaurant on the right-hand side of the road. But late in the afternoon, on the way back home, they decide they are hungry again; a hot dog and a bottle of pop would taste good. They stop and eat at the place on their right on the way into Jacksonville. It's handy. They only have to park at the side of the road and step out of the car; no turning, no manipulating. That," she laughed at her summation, "is what might be called anticipating the trend or Julie Lanier's industrial survey."

"Do you know something? You're pretty smart." There was an honest admiration in the statement.

"I try to give that impression."

"Will you take a job with me, with Stalath?"

"Yes—but I'm not sure why. I suppose it's because I'm more than a little fond of you. Also, this high trapeze act of yours fascinates me. It's like the circus. You don't really want to see the trainer eaten by the lions but it would be pretty exciting if it should happen."

He gazed steadily at her for a moment and then nodded.

"Have a talk with John Trainor, the architect. He has an office on Magnolia. I'll tell him you're coming in. Work out the details. You'll have a free hand. Do it your way and if I'm not satisfied I'll fire you."

"You really would, wouldn't you?"

"Of course." The reply was just short of brusque and he seemed surprised she should ask the question.

Atlantic Avenue ended abruptly at the south corner of Main Street and led into a sand-rutted alley, flanked on one side by Van Valzah's Graystone Building and Viall's grocery store on the other. The passageway was little used. Maids and porters on their way to work at the Daytona Beach and Breakers hotels trudged along it and the Model T trucks from the markets whirled through with their deliveries. It had been marked out as an extension of Atlantic when the community was planned and was shown as such on the town maps. No attempt, though, had been made to push it to completion and it was halted behind the Pence home at the edge of uncleared land. There seemed no reason why it should ever be extended. Six miles of stunted pine, twisted live oak, bay, holly and scrub palmetto separated it from the Port Orange Bridge and approach there to the beach. Although the property now was sold and resold almost daily it was considered unlikely that it would ever be cleared for homesites. No one in his right mind would want to live in the center section when both ocean and river fronts were available.

Back from Miami where construction had been started on the first of the Stalath Motels, Tod sat with his grandfather on the porch one evening having a quiet after-dinner drink and talking casually of whatever happened to come to mind. They enjoyed an easy companionship and neither ever felt it was necessary to make conversation or entertain the other.

The big Lincoln swung into the front driveway with its border of huge oaks and after a moment its lights snapped off. There was the sound of a door closing and then two figures passed through the picket fence gate and came up the walk.

"Willie." Tod spoke aloud but to himself. "Willie and Francine." He stood up and moved to the edge of the porch.

"Well, how you, Tod?" Willie did his best to make the greeting sound jovial.

"Hello, Willie. Francine."

"Good evening, Tod." Francine was precise.

Will Lathrop was standing and Tod touched Francine on the elbow.

"I don't think you know my grandfather. Mrs. Estes. Mr. Lathrop."

"My goodness, I guess everybody in Daytona knows Mr. Lathrop; at least by sight." Francine was nervous and her voice betrayed her. It ended in a high, giggling sound which she fought to check.

"Good evening, Mrs. Estes." Will Lathrop drew up a deep wicker chair for her. Nothing in his manner indicated surprise. He nodded to Willie. "Mr. Estes."

Willie laughed. "Hell, Mr. Lathrop. You've seen me around most of my life. There ain't no reason to be formal. Just call me Willie. I used to fix some of your first cars, remember?"

"Of course. And you were very good at it, too."

"I had to be, the way you drove 'em." He settled himself comfortably in a chair.

Tod wondered what had brought Willie to the house. Nothing more than a wary business relationship had ever existed between them.

"Will you have a drink? Francine? Willie?"

"Well, thank you, Tod." Francine glanced up at him. "Maybe some coffee and a little Cointreau." She pronounced the word almost mincingly and with obvious pride.

Tod smiled to himself as he rang the small table bell for Wash. Francine was being cultured. From a reasonably pretty girl of a Cracker family she had flowered into an affected and fragile-appearing beauty. She subscribed to all the fashion magazines, spent hours studying the poses of the models. She went to Jacksonville for her clothes and had regular appointments at Christine's Salon de Beauté. She had reluctantly traveled the thorny road of higher education as far as the sophomore year in high school and then quit to take a job in the "five-and-dime store." Tod suspected that she disliked Willie and considered herself to be her husband's intellectual and social superior. She had a habit of regarding Willie with a mildly contemptuous amusement. But, Tod thought, she had recognized Estes's drive. He was going somewhere and somewhere was where Francine wanted to be. As proof of her status she drove her own La Salle convertible and had a personal maid, a gawky Negro girl whom she bullied relentlessly. Proof of her position in the community was the fact that she and Willie could come this way to Mr. Willard Lathrop's home, unannounced and uninvited. In Francine's eyes Will Lathrop was Daytona's social pinnacle and an almost legendary figure.

Wash came to the porch and Tod ordered the coffee and liquor for Francine, a Scotch for Willie.

"I don't hardly ever see you no more at the Belt Line office." Willie folded his hands over the beginning of a paunch. He made the statement almost a crafty accusation as though Tod had shunted the burden of operation off on him. "I guess this Stalath Corporation you got goin' keeps you busy." A foxy smirk crossed his features.

Tod wondered just what the hell it was Willie wanted and was tempted, for a moment, to ask and have it out in the open.

Wash brought the coffee and the drinks. Will Lathrop rose.

"If you'll excuse me, Mrs. Estes," he was flatteringly attentive with his apology, "I have some correspondence I must take care of."

"Well, of course." Francine started to rise and then caught herself. "I guess, maybe, we shouldn't have come without calling first."

"You come any time you like. It is always a pleasure to see a pretty girl around the house." He turned to Willie. "Mr. Estes." He took his heavy orangewood cane from the table and left the porch, punctuating his steps with a thump of the stick upon the boards. "Good night, Tod."

"Good night, Grandfather."

"He sure don't change much, does he?" Willie waited until the screen was closed.

"There's no reason why he should." There was a faint note of impatience in Tod's reply. Will Lathrop never wrote anyone. Willie's unexpected visit had driven him from the porch and his pleasant meditations. "What brought you down, Willie? Anything wrong at the Line?"

"No. We got more business than we can handle." He swallowed part of his drink and belched with a soft whisper.

Francine looked at him with disgust. He was such a pig. Covertly she regarded Tod Lathrop's hard leanness and wondered why he had never seemed to notice what she had to offer if given a chance. Her reading was confined to the romantic treacle of Eleanor Glyn and from it she had drawn erotic fancies of love trysts, scented boudoirs and what Mrs. Glyn referred to as clandestine meetings and romantic attachments. Francine yearned.

"Them free trips your Stalath Corporation is givin' from Jacksonville on down is cuttin' some into our business but we're operatin' to capacity so it don't make no real difference. No. I come to see you about somethin' else." He unbuttoned his shirt and scratched at his navel. "One of Francine's cousins, Ray Kingston, has got a friend on the City Council. He heard somethin' at the meetin' last night an' told Ray who told me an' Francine. I thought maybe you'd like to know about it. If it turns out to be somethin' good for you then," the eyes became shrewdly innocent, "you might cut me in on a piece of it."

"What is it?" Tod deliberately left the suggestion unanswered.

"The City Commission is goin' to extend Atlantic Avenue all the way to the Port Orange Bridge. That'll carry it right through a lot of property you Lathrops own. More than that, it'll open up all that land there ain't no way to get to unless you want to climb up over the dunes."

Tod was surprised. He had friends on the Council, also, who ordinarily would have passed this information to him. These, though, were no ordinary times. Everyone was acutely aware of how sensitive the real estate market was. The most outrageous rumor of improvement, a new flow of Northern capital, a deal made, was accepted as fact and sent prices off on another skyrocket. An official statement of a road paralleling the beach, cutting through the massed scrub, would bounce prices to the moon and start another hysterical stampede. There would be, he knew, some quiet maneuvering by town, country and even state officials to get option money down through dummy fronts. A public announcement would then be made. This sort of thing was accepted as one of the emoluments of office holding and cynically shrugged off by the voters who were busy trying to make a few dollars themselves. In Tod's mind there was the single thought that this would make a Stalath Motel on the peninsula feasible. There would be access to it from the Atlantic Avenue extension where it crossed Silver Beach Avenue. In time, and his mind ran ahead, Peninsula Drive would be pushed farther to the south and a grid of cross streets from Peninsula Drive to Atlantic laid out. This, he thought, would be the first step toward what his father had always urged—a well-planned community.

"You know," Willie suggested, "I could get a price for this kind of information. I brought it to you because we're already partners. If you've got somethin' in mind now I'd like a piece of it."

Tod certainly didn't want Willie to have any part of Stalath but there was no avoiding some sort of an answer to the man's suggestion.

"I'll see what I can do, Willie. We, my father, may let go of something. I don't know. He's pretty stubborn and won't have anything to do with this freewheeling spree. Maybe I can talk him into letting you have an option. That's all you want, isn't it; something to deal with?"

"No. If the price is right I'd make an outright buy. I've got the cash an' I can always get more from the Merchants Bank. Me an' Fred Niver are like this." He crossed first and index fingers to indicate the intimacy.

Tod merely nodded. He doubted that the bank's head cashier was that close to anyone. He was a small, alert and perpetually worried-looking man who managed to remain aloof from most of the townspeople.

"I'll speak to my father and let you know." He stood up. "Matter of fact, I think I'll run over to the beach house now."

"I thought it would get a bur under your tail." Willie was pleased with himself. "Tell your old man I sort of done you a favor."

Tod walked with them to the front gate. On the way down the marl path Francine managed to sway against him a couple of times with an unmistakable suggestion. He dropped a step behind and wondered what she would do if he said what was in his mind. You have a beautiful, pear-shaped ass, Francine. Instead, when he moved forward and reached for the gate, he slapped her lightly with his fingertips and wasn't surprised to discover she wore nothing beneath the Shantung silk dress.

At his touch Francine turned with the exaggerated hauteur of a Ziegfeld show girl descending the staircase. Then she laughed and eyed Tod with amused and bright-eyed interest.

"What's funny?" Willie, leading the way, half turned.

"Nothing. I was just thinking how long it takes people, sometimes, to get around to something."

"What's that supposed to mean?"

"Nothing." She was annoyed by his persistence. "Nothing at all. Just talking."

Willie shook his head and walked out ahead of her. She darted a quick, inquisitive glance at Tod and then dropped an eyelid in open invitation.

Tod waited until they had driven away. Then he strolled down to the dock and stood, entranced as always by the silence which wasn't really silence but a combination of small, muted sounds which slowly crept upon one's consciousness. A mullet jumped with a silver shower and fell back making the plop of a stone thrown. A light wind riffled through dry palmetto fronds behind him. The ocean whispered ceaselessly from behind the barricade of dunes a mile or more away. He had stood here, on this same dock, as a boy. Now, as a man, he experienced the same wonder and secret delight in what he felt, heard and saw. The years had been gentle with this section of Daytona, and the tide of change was little felt. The same old houses stood as they always had, protected by wide and shaded yards. The same Negro gardeners, or so they seemed, worked quietly among the flower beds or trimmed thick hedges beneath a warm sun. In time, he mused, the pressure of expansion would sweep what seemed immutable away. For a moment he regretted his part in what was happening.

The *News-Journal* carried the announcement in a statement by the Mayor and hard upon it ocean and river frontage jumped another thousand dollars a foot. What only a few years ago could have been purchased for a few hundred dollars was now quoted in the thousands. So real had the Florida dream become that those who walked through it never seemed to awaken sufficiently to realize they really owned nothing. All they actually clutched were pieces of paper representing a ten-, twenty- or thirty-day option.

The land Tod wanted for the Stalath Motel, at Daytona, was a seven-hundred-foot frontage on the ocean. Dennis had bought it years ago for two thousand dollars. Now the property, if Dennis wanted to sell, could easily be listed at that much a front foot. Bounded at one end by Silver Beach Avenue it would have two areas of entrance with the completion of Atlantic Avenue.

"I'd like to buy it from you." Father and son stood on one of the high dunes, their eyes surveying the tract. High sea oats, the golden color of ripe wheat, swayed in a light wind and morning glories were a riot of color upon the sand. "It's ideal for what I have in mind." He squatted on his heels and traced an outline with one finger. "I'll lay it out so every room will have an ocean view; sort of an open square with parking facilities at the entrance." He glanced up at his father for approval.

Dennis smiled. "I have some trouble," he admitted, "in reconciling the boy I knew with the man you are. I'll deed the property to you for the customary one dollar and good considerations. You are the only one who seems interested in building anything. Take it. Don't overextend yourself. Keep your capital liquid. This thing has to snap. There isn't a bank in Florida that hasn't stretched its resources to the breaking point. One of these days someone is going to get scared and start calling in the outstanding notes. No one has the money to pay. The banks will begin closing and the great dream of unlimited profits will turn into a nightmare. How are you really fixed, Tod?"

"I'm all right." Tod arose and brushed the sand from his fingers. "I keep a sizable balance in the Merchants Bank because I do business there. But I've stashed away a cushion in Niven's bank and there's cash in a safe-deposit box. I can ride out almost anything but a national panic."

"Good. Keep it that way. Now, how about coming up to the house and having lunch with your mother and me? She—we—miss you."

"I'd like to but I want to be in Fort Pierce this afternoon and Miami tonight." They began walking back to where Tod's car was parked.

"You couldn't stop even if you wanted to, could you?"

"No." The notion seemed to astonish Tod. "First, why should I? Second. What would I do with myself? It takes a particularly tranquil nature and a mild conviction, such as Grandfather Will has, that the rest of the world is divertingly insane to be able to sit back and survey the antics without being a part of them. I'm not made that way. I have to put things together. I want the Stalath Corporation to be the biggest operation in Florida and, by God, that is what I'm going to make it. When I get everything together here I'm going to move in on the Bahamas. They don't seem to realize what they have over there. The British are as conservative as their food. They think it is bad form to advertise themselves. The strange thing is, they are very fond of money but like to pretend that the acquiring of it is, somehow, vulgar and a fit pursuit only for tradespeople. Well, I don't think it's vulgar. I think it's a hell of a lot of fun."

Dennis nodded. "Sometimes you almost make me believe it."

"Come in with me and I'll show you." Tod put an arm over his father's shoulder.

"No. I think I'll watch. Maybe I can acquire the detached attitude of Will Lathrop."

Tod thought he detected an almost wistful note in his father's voice. He said nothing and they covered the remaining distance to the car in silence.

After he had dropped his father off at the beach house Tod drove up to Ormond. Julie's maid told him, "Miss Julie playin' that golf thing."

He caught her on the seventh tee just as she was hitting down the middle for a good two hundred yards. Everything Julie does, he thought, she does well and with an unconscious grace.

"Hi!" She greeted him with pleased surprise. "Don't tell me you have time for silly games?"

"John D. Rockefeller plays it." He fell in beside her and they walked down the fairway.

"Mr. Rockefeller is no longer in a hurry."

"Well, I am. Want to drive down to Miami with me for a couple of days?"

"Yes." Julie never fenced. She called the caddy. "Take my bag back to the clubhouse, Warren. I won't finish it out today."

They strolled toward the gray-shingled clubhouse. She wore a white silk dress. A scarf of bright, metallic blue bound her hair and this single touch of color heightened the rose dust shade of her complexion.

"You're one hell of a pretty girl." He spoke suddenly. "Will you marry me?"

"No. Well," she amended, "not today at least or even tomorrow. I'll put your name down for consideration, though."

"You're serious." He was honestly surprised.

"To tell the truth I'm just a little confused. Not about you. I'm not sure what I want. Let's leave it that way for awhile, shall we?" Her hand reached for his and found it with a quick, firm pressure.

"All right," he agreed, "but I'll ask you every now and then if I remember."

"I'll remind you. Why are we going to Miami?"

"I want to take a look at the first Stalath Motel. I can open it in a couple of months."

"Motel." She uttered the word with distaste. "I suppose it could be worse. Dew Drop Inn or Kozy Nook. Stoddard Lathrop the Kozy Nookie Bookie. That is what they could be used for, you know."

"Don't begrudge the citizens their pleasures."

"Oh, I'm not! I'd just hate to see you hauled up for operating lewd and lascivious places. How long will we be gone?"

"Two or three days."

"I can be ready in half an hour."

He was studying the rolling fairways and thinking what a site it would make for a development. Ormond was a static community. Nothing was built, nothing changed. The huge hotel was a relic of another era. It would have to give way. In his mind was the thought that he might give it a little nudge.

* XIV * *

No one wanted to step off the merry-go-round.
The faster it whirled the more the public scrambled to get aboard
and take the intoxicating ride. That it was really only going 'round
and 'round without destination was not important. The music was
gay, the lights bright and the pace exhilarating.

Miami, which had first tasted the heady wine of boom, continued
to pace the rest of the state. Carl Fisher threw up his island fiefs
in Biscayne Bay. Hollywood-by-the-Sea was created and a huge
hotel towered on the dunes. The binder boys stood on street corners
holding sheaves of options, waving them invitingly at passersby and
chanting the litany of quick profits and easy money. At Coral Gables
William Jennings Bryan, hired by Merrick, sat in shirt sleeves on a
raft in the middle of a man-made lake, cooled himself with a palm
leaf fan and orated to a gawking public on Florida's golden future,
urging his audience to have a part in it.

What was occurring in Florida was symptomatic of the incredible
era of irresponsibility spreading across the nation. Old values
were thrown away. Gangsters shot each other down in the city
streets. Contempt for the prohibition law bred scorn for all law. In
New York the debonair James J. Walker was elected Mayor and
gave the metropolis a fancy exhibition of political tap dancing which
ended in his removal. Chicago went bankrupt and the city employees

received IOUs instead of salaries. The city's Mayor, Bill Thompson, threatened to "bust King George in the snoot" if he ever came to Chicago. The citizens cheered loudly. Organized crime flowered beneath the warm and benevolent protection of grafting officials and there was more drunkenness in homes, restaurants, speakeasies, offices and streets than there had ever been in the days of the open saloon. Moral standards were swept away in the tumultuous frenzy and the tastiest plum on the public tree was a job with the Treasury Department's Enforcement Bureau. A smart prohibition agent could retire for life after a year's service in such rich orchards as New York, San Francisco, New Orleans or Chicago. The desire for *status* became an obsession. The goal was no longer simply keeping up with the Joneses but of outstripping them. The urge for conspicuous consumption was described by one industrialist as "the divine discontent." Debt was encouraged and made easy. Everything could be bought for a small down payment. Few persons remembered when there was a vague social stigma in having a mortgage on one's home. To owe money, and the more the better, was an infallible indication of a man's credit and, therefore, his position in the community. Factories combined to stuff a giant horn of plenty from which everything desirable in life would tumble: vacuum cleaners, radios, shiny automobiles, new furniture, refrigerators, boats, furs, clothing, jewelry, a cottage retreat for the harassed businessman, a place in the country and a home in the city, swimming pools and steam baths. All these things could be had for the mere signing of one's name on the dotted line. The public laughed and the cow jumped over the moon.

Miami was thrusting out in all directions. There was talk of draining the Everglades and turning the entire swamp into a development of tropical beauty. New projects were announced daily. A thing only had to be said to be believed. When the hotels and roominghouses were filled, private "guest homes" were opened and a spare bedroom rented. The demand for living space constantly increased as the pressure of new arrivals made itself felt.

Just north of what had been the town's city limits the first of the Stalath Motels was opened and was an instantaneous success. The idea was revolutionary. Here a man parked his car outside his unit, carried in a single, overnight bag. He looked about the bright, cheerful, airy room; tried the shower in a glass-enclosed stall; found a reading lamp on the bedside table adjustable to the height at which he would be comfortable. There was no more waiting around in the lobbies of second-rate hotels. There were no indifferent or insolent bellboys to placate and tip; no disinterested clerks to appease; no tasteless food carelessly served in cheerless dining rooms. Boxes with cubed ice were spaced along the covered walkways outside the room. The restaurant, circular in design, with windows opening upon flower gardens, offered a varied menu. The waitresses were attractive in their uniforms of dusty pink and gray. The service was deft, unobtrusive and the food well prepared. The management provided fresh, hot coffee in the morning with its compliments. The brew was delivered in Thermos jugs at an hour designated by the guest when he checked in.

Some of the old, run-down hotels and boardinghouses complained of unfair competition but the Automobile Association's representative was enthusiastic. The organization voluntarily sent Stalath Motel literature to its members.

Tod was delighted with the initial operation. He spent four days going over every detail of management with the couple he had engaged to run the place. He had known Dale and Verna Chastine in high school. Gradually, and as was the case with so many others, they had moved from his orbit. Now and then he encountered one or the other on Beach Street but this called for nothing more than a pleasant hello or a wave of the hand. Dale was a handy man with tools and Verna delighted in the details of housekeeping. For the past few years they had been in charge of a small hotel on Ridgewood Avenue. Looking around for someone to take over the first Stalath Motel, Tod had made them an offer. They were pleasant, soft-spoken, efficient and delighted with the adventure of this new project.

Tod could find nothing to criticize. He prowled over the place, poking into odd corners, talking with the help, inspecting the rooms when they had been put in order after a check-out. He tried all the light switches, turned showers on and off, flushed the toilets, filled and emptied lavatory bowls, tested all the beds and chairs. He sat on a table in the kitchen, gnawing on a chicken leg, watching the preparation of food. He had lured the chef, a giant of a Negro with a delicate touch, out of a secure job with the Bluestone Lodge, in Asheville, North Carolina.

"You come with me, Docker, and I'll make you famous. Where did you learn to cook?"

The man had scratched at his head and broken into a slow smile.

"Well, Mistuh Lathrop, I was one of eight kids. Hit seemed to me we nevah really had enough to eat. So, I said to mys'f, Boy, git you a job somewhere en a kitchen. No mattah what else happen you kin always eat good. Little by little I begin to pick up some knowledgment of how things should be cooked to taste right. I ain' suah about this famous business. Jus' leave me to cook an' pay me regular. That all I ask."

In the kitchen now Tod finished the piece of chicken, dropping the bone on the table. Docker picked it up and carefully put it in a refuse can.

"I never tasted better chicken or deviled crabs and those fried clams you make. Do you suppose you could teach someone else to do them in exactly the same way?"

"Well, suh, that depen' upon th' man."

Tod shook his head. "No, we can't count on that. What I'm trying to get at is a recipe, a cooking time, that won't vary with the individual. I mean, when I get them built and running, I want the deviled crab, the cole slaw, the potato salad, to be identical. When a man checks in at a Stalath Motel in Montgomery and orders fried clams because he liked them in the Stalath Motel at Miami I don't want him to be disappointed."

Docker was skeptical. "You take a good cook, Mistuh Lathrop, he don' follow no receipt. He add a little pinch of somethin' heah, a dibbin of somethin' else theah 'til what he makin' suit him. I don' know ef you could get a cook to follow no rule."

"Anyhow," Tod swung off the table, "we can try. I'll talk with you about it again sometime. There's a restaurant chain in New York called the Automat. The chicken pie in the Automat at Broadway and Forty-seventh Street is identical with the one at the Automat on Lexington Avenue. That's what I'm driving at."

Docker inclined his head. "I'll scheme some ovah hit, Mistuh Lathrop. I'll put my mind to it."

In the suite adjoining the office Tod had coffee with the Chastines.

"I came down," he confessed, "looking for something to raise hell about. I can't find it. You two are doing a fine job and I'm grateful."

"We're glad, Mr. Lathrop." Neither of them ever presumed upon the fact they had all gone to school together and called him Tod. "It's really exciting," she added. "New and different."

Tod studied the printed form she had given him. It was a check list for the maids covering every item in the rooms. On it the girl would note a burned spot in the carpet or table; the need for additional ashtrays; a faulty light socket, burned-out bulb, a switch which wouldn't make immediate contact; towels and washcloths taken as souvenirs, a bath mat missing. With this information in hand Verna made a daily inspection tour of all units.

"We had those printed up in Miami without asking you if it was all right." She was a little apprehensive. "Sometimes it's hard to keep track of everything. Unless a guest reports a burned-out bulb or the maid tries every light in the room the office never hears about it. I guess nothing makes a guest madder than to check in and find the bathroom light doesn't work. With this list, and the girls check off every item on it, we know the condition of every room at any time." She shook her head with mock resignation. "We're going to lose an awful lot of those pretty pink and gray washcloths and towels. The guests just don't seem to be able to resist putting one or two in their suitcases. If we put in good, plain white towels we could cut the loss in half at least."

"We'll charge it off to advertising. They are all marked Stalath Motels. In time, and as the highways get better, I'm going to push this chain from coast-to-coast. Maybe that sounds a little wild right now."

"Coming from anyone but you it would," Dale mused. "But, damned if things don't seem to have a habit of turning out the way you say they will. Everyone said you'd go broke with the Citrus Belt Line. I guess it's a big moneymaker. People thought you were crazy with that flatland on the DeLand road. Now this motel idea. It's just got to go. They all said that people in cars would want to ride right into town, to see what it was like and what was going on. They predicted a man wouldn't want to carry his bag or his wife's from car to room. Hotels had bellboys and porters for that. The funny part of it is they really like it." Dale relit his cigar. "I guess, I'm not sure but I think, maybe it gives them a feeling like they were going into their own home when they close the door behind them. Verna and I have been in the hotel business one way or another ever since we were married. We've had a chance to deal with all kinds of people. When guests check out of here you can see on their faces they are sorry to leave."

"That's another thing we had to do and we did it without asking you first." Verna was almost embarrassed. "We've had to put a limit on the days a guest can stay. With the shortage of rooms in Miami we get people who want to check in and stay for months. Dale and I thought you would want a turnover so more people would be talking about the Stalath Motel."

"That's right." Tod was emphatic. "The motel has to be for transients. I'd like to see all the rooms empty every morning and filled by nighttime." He leaned back in his chair and stared at the ceiling. "I was talking to Docker about standardizing the food. It gave me another idea. As this thing grows we are going to find out we can't get enough of the right kind of help. So, I'm going to start a training school for the Stalath employees—the maids, waitresses, busboys, cashiers, managers and assistant managers." He stood up and began to pace the floor with a characteristic restlessness. "I don't want stereotypes but I do want a uniformity in certain fundamentals. We'll set up courses of four or six weeks and the people we accept will get full salaries while they're learning. I don't ever want to hear any excuses; a maid or a waitress who apologizes for something and says, I'm new here. They'll all be experienced hands when they get their assignments."

"You wouldn't mind a suggestion?" Verna said.

"Damn it, Verna." He was impatient and then checked himself. "I'm sorry. If you and Dale didn't have ideas of your own I'd know you weren't right for the job. What is it?"

"Well, in the dining room we're beginning to get families for lunch and dinner. They're not checking in but just passing through. Others drive out from Miami because they've heard the food is good and it's a change. Sometimes they have children and when the parents order for them they have to take the same portions as the adults. Why couldn't we have, say, half portions at half the price for the youngsters? They never eat it all anyhow. It's a waste and I think the parents resent it just a little."

"A little dissatisfaction is as bad as a lot of dissatisfaction. I think maybe you've pulled a rabbit out of a hat." He was quick with his approval. "I like it fine. Have some special menus printed with perhaps illustrations; something the kids will like to look at and keep as their very own, a souvenir. Go into Miami tomorrow, have a talk with the advertising agency. Tell them to put an artist on it."

"It will cut down some on the restaurant's profits." Dale offered the objection.

"Don't worry about the restaurant's profits. The dining room isn't a separate unit. It's a part of the whole. Things will balance out. I want to make money with this chain but I want to make money because it will prove the operation is sound and successful; something people want. Anything more?"

"Well," Verna was hesitant, glancing at Dale for encouragement, "there is one thing. I guess we better settle it now. We've had several young couples who wanted to check in." She met his gaze with a half smile. "I'm not too old or too long married not to know how it is. I had a pretty good idea what they wanted the room for. I could have been wrong but I said we didn't have a vacancy. I'd like to have you tell me what I should do in the future. I don't think we want that kind of business."

He smiled at her earnestness. "You just go on using your own judgment. If they don't look right turn them away. You'll get fooled sometimes but the word will get around. If it's a quick tumble they want there are plenty of those roadside cabins and no questions. Or," he knuckled his chin, "if you are acrobatic enough, the back seat of a car. I don't recommend the front. The gear shift lever gets in your way. They do say, though, it is one of the few things you can do almost any place except standing up in a hammock. Well, I guess we've covered everything. I'm going to drive into town and have a look around. Maybe I'll go back to Daytona tonight. I'm satisfied with everything I've seen here."

They walked with him to where his car was parked in the driveway of crushed, golden coquina rock which picked up the afternoon's glow from the lowering sun. He stood for a moment, looking around at the neatly trimmed flower beds and hibiscus, heavy with crimson and yellow blooms, the royal palms taking firm root. Everything he saw gave him a warm feeling of satisfaction, of accomplishment. He was sorry his father hadn't come with him. Dennis Lathrop would be pleased with this first unit and proud of what his son had done.

Driving into Miami it was easy to see how the town's population explosion had pushed far beyond the original limits and out into Dade County. Here there were housing developments with row after row of neat, cheaply built but not inexpensive houses cut from two or three patterns. Fruit stands, orange juice bars and open-air souvenir shops crowded each other. There were Bar-B-Q, chili and hot dog stands beneath canvas awnings. Here and there larger and more substantial eating places offered EATS AND ENTERTAINMENT. BEVO. THE NEAR BEER NEAREST BEER. The entertainment was confined to a jukebox which monotonously ground out laments of love and frustration. There was a brash, carnival-like atmosphere along the highway. Signs urged the motorist to stop and watch Seminole Tommy wrestle a giant alligator. "Snake Farms" with a few, torpid reptiles lying in the sun competed with Gypsy fortunetellers and the casters of horoscopes. Grapefruit, tangerines and oranges were arranged in bright mounds and open crates decorated with Spanish moss. Fading streamers stretched across the road offering the visitors to Miami an opportunity to: PICK YOUR OWN FRUIT—WE SHIP ANYWHERE. Small boys raced in shouting competition along the shoulders, waving handbills, thrusting them into the outstretched hands of those who reached out from cars. FLORIDA IS IN YOUR DESTINY. HAVE A PART IN THE SUNSHINE STATE. There were guides to Miami. How to invest in the future. Brochures describing the wonders of MEDITERRANEAN SKIES, just twenty miles south of Coral Gables; single sheets extolling the culinary miracles to be enjoyed at SALLY'S. GOOD EATS. NORTH-ERN-FRIED CHICKEN. WISTERIA ESTATES. LOW DOWN PAYMENT. There was the sound of a hurdy-gurdy, and the voice of the pitchman was heard throughout the land.

Miami's Flagler Street was a noisy, crawling artery of bumper-to-bumper traffic. Pedestrians jostled each other on sidewalks and at intersections. Real estate offices occupied practically all ground floors of the buildings. Buses, their sides gaudily decorated with garish paintings of tropical lagoons, palm trees and hula girls, bore the names of new developments: PARADISE GARDENS; TRADE WINDS PARK; BLUE LAGOON ESTATES. The vehicles were parked in a solid line while barkers, disguised as tour guides, offered free trips to the sites, band concerts, barbecue picnics. Men and women, many of them dowdily dressed, thrust and elbowed each other in a scrambling and perspiring effort to get aboard.

Near the bay front traffic diminished and the raucous sound fell away to a faintly buzzing echo. The park was a miracle of ingenuity; a fill-in from the dredging operations in Biscayne Bay. Care, thought, skill and planning had gone into this retreat. It was a half-mile stretch of heavily massed beauty. Wind sang in the high, feathered cockades of royal palms. There were clipped pines and mounds of heavy floral brilliance. Across the bay Miami Beach shone with a white radiance. A few years ago it had been covered with scrub, jungle matted, spread with sea grape and vine, fringed with mangrove and a haven for snakes and canopied by clouds of mosquitoes. Now, each square foot was contested for hourly. Prices asked and agreed upon soared beyond all sanity. Options were sold upon options and the spiral whirled dizzily upward.

Tod pulled into the curb and parked. He crossed arms on the steering wheel and leaned forward upon them, studying the rippling patina of the bay. Even here, in the quiet of late afternoon, he was aware of the kinetic energy pulsing through the city. The impossible was occurring; the incredible a fact. Business property was listed and selling at $20,000 a square foot. A man who had purchased a corner lot on Flagler Street in 1919 for $25,000 refused an offer of $6,000,000. Land in the flat woods was quoted at $25,000 an acre.

Here, Tod mused, was the action; the real excitement. The gambler in him wanted a piece of it. It was cold-eyed and relentless despite the holiday air in which it was set. Yet, a heretofore unsuspected caution warned him against it. He smiled a little to himself, wondering why he should be listening to the small voice of intuition. Not now. This isn't the time. The lid has to blow off. The pressure was too great, the pace too frantic to be maintained. It has to crack and when it does there will be no shoring it up. The whole structure collapses. With the first faltering a few would stop to catch their breaths and when they did, others would halt to rest and maybe, wonder. Then, he told himself, would be the time. The future of Florida, of

Miami, would not be denied but it lay outside the gigantic crap table which had been set up for the eager, the greedy, the reckless, the shrewd and unscrupulous. Sooner or later someone would say, Cash me in. The stampede to get out with a profit would become a panic. In the panic lay disaster for many; a profit for a few who were in a position to buy at the bottom and hold for the long climb back.

He started the car and drove down to Southwest Eighth Street and onto the beginning of the Tamiami Trail, which was not yet completed. The route between Miami and Tampa had been surveyed as far back as 1916. Construction was started a year later but the war brought it to a halt. Manpower was needed in essential industries. Three years ago a group in Lee County had organized a motorcade. The proposed route was to be traveled by ten cars bearing some twenty-three persons. Two Indian guides were engaged as a safety precaution. The trip, planned to stimulate public interest in the Tamiami Trail, took three weeks and the distance covered was only from Fort Myers, on the west coast, to Miami on the east. The expedition was reported "lost" several times. Finally, seven of the ten cars with their weary and bedraggled pilgrims arrived in Miami. The proposed trail became one of the most discussed highway projects in the country. After the war the State Highway Department took over. Surveyors worked waist-deep in the swamps. Drillers thrust at the rock beneath the mud. Dynamite was hauled in ox carts and when these bogged down, men carried the explosives on their shoulders. Huge dredges followed and coughed up the slime and then the rock which was used for the highway's base. Completion had been forecast as being at least two years away. Now, though, a short section of some dozen miles running west from Miami could be traveled cautiously. The grass-matted muck was being offered as homesites. Phony Seminole villages were set up at intervals and the noble Red Man offered carved objects of lizards and alligators, reed baskets, beadwork and the banded, multihued kilts made in New Jersey. Practically all of the Seminole men adopted the name of Osceola. There was a John Osceola, Tommy Osceola, King Osceola and others although it was never recorded that the Seminoles' war chief of that name ever sired a child.

The sun was low in the late afternoon and spread its flaming color across the green and yellow savannahs. Tod drew off of the paved stretch, shut off the motor and, after a moment, stepped out and walked beside a drainage ditch to where a sweep of a small lake stretched to distant cypress. With the darkly overgrown bottom the water itself seemed to be of a rich, mahogany color, reflecting the light and shade of evening.

There was life, movement and even small sound here, but it could pass unnoticed unless one stopped to watch and listen. A heron, startlingly white, sought its nesting place, fishing leisurely on the way home. Small fish and minnows broke the glassy surface. A water moccasin, head and part of its body lifted like the periscope of a submarine, cut a rippling trail. A crow voiced its perpetual, harsh discontent. Tod lit a cigarette and the scratch of the match on the abrasive tab was rasping and out of place. Here man was the intruder and Tod was abruptly aware of a strange feeling of loneliness. He tried to shake it but the mood persisted. He began to walk slowly and without purpose or destination. For the first time that he could remember he was conscious of standing completely alone in the world of Stoddard Lathrop and it was momentarily frightening. He attempted to laugh it off but the effort was without conviction. He caught himself asking, what is it I want? For the question he had no answer. He had hundreds of acquaintances in and out of the state. There were dozens of homes where, without invitation, he would be honestly welcome. He was, he believed, a good companion. He could talk well and entertainingly. He played good tennis and golf. Such social life as he had time for was full and satisfying. But, and now a vague feeling of uneasiness possessed him, he was close to no one and because of this no one touched him. He cast about for a single name. Who is my friend? Why have I never felt the magic held in that single word? Outside of my family who really gives a damn about Stoddard Lathrop? What put my feet on this barren path? If I disappeared tonight my mother, father and Grandfather Will would mourn a little for me. The others might ask, I wonder whatever became of Tod Lathrop? Then they would shrug and go about their business.

He turned and went back to the car, spinning it around until he was headed in the direction of Miami. He drove at a high speed as though to outdistance the specter of desolation. What is it I really feel the need for? Do I want to marry, to have a home, a family—

Father at the hearthside? He shook his head. Not now. I don't have the time. When he said this to himself he was actually shocked. Why didn't he have the time? What was he afraid of? Where was he going and why could he take no one with him?

He circled Miami, avoiding the city's center. When he was well beyond the extended limits he trod heavily upon the accelerator and the heavy Lincoln powered through the night. He stopped only once, at Cocoa, for a sandwich and coffee. Here, also, the booming tide of speculation washed upon the shore. For years Cocoa had nodded quietly in the warm sun. Orange growing was the principal occupation. An ancient frame hotel on the Indian River drew a few regular guests each winter, all of them of middle age or older who were satisfied to do a little fishing, play croquet and escape the Northern winters. Now wholesale development was freely planned. Home and business sites were offered and persons who had never associated the name Cocoa with anything more than a warming beverage gaily put down their money, confident it would return to them tenfold. Cocoa Beach, across the river and on an estuary called Banana River, with a population of thirty-five persons by official census, was being touted as "The Little Miami Beach." Here the dunes thrust out to form Cape Canaveral and the lighthouse, banded in black and white, offered its beacon to the coastal ships. It was here that Don Pedro Menéndez de Avilés, who earlier had founded St. Augustine, was shipwrecked. Surviving the disaster Menéndez walked to St. Augustine, a distance of some one hundred and seventy-five miles. The Cape was uninhabited, ridged with high, white dunes, swept by the winds and washed by the sea, watched over by gulls and patrolling squadrons of pelicans. Only an occasional fisherman who came to cast his line into the booming surf broke the spell of isolation.

Idling over his coffee and a cigarette, Tod listened to the conversation of the half dozen or so men gathered at the diner's counter. Once they might have talked of baseball, fishing, the price of oranges and the best way to make a home brew. Now they spoke knowingly of options and binders, subdivisions and a proposed multimillion-dollar hotel to be erected on the Cape. They discussed these things, not with wonder but as normal development and to be taken for granted. That the hotel would never be built, the subdivisions untenanted, the options never picked up, were possibilities which did not occur to them.

Tod swung off the stool, paid his check and left. The dark humor which was upon him defied explanation. He was anxious to be away from the sound of voices, the company of strangers. At the moment he had no understanding of himself and was troubled.

Daylight was breaking with the smoky color of a black pearl when he roared through the village of Port Orange. The sky was filled with the first colored streamers of morning when he turned off Ridgewood Avenue, down Live Oak and to his grandfather's house. He left the car in the driveway and went quickly, and without sound, to his room. Will Lathrop had the habit of awakening early and stamping about the house in the hope of rousing his grandson so they might have coffee together. Tod didn't think he could take Will Lathrop this morning.

For a long time he lay, staring at the ceiling, listening to the small and familiar sounds of a new day. He was uneasy, for no answers came to mind to the many questions he had asked himself.

The mellowed red brick of the lighthouse rose like a tapered sentinel on the dunes at the inlet. For as long as Tod could remember someone of the Pacetti family had kept the light here. He could recall a Bert Pacetti, a Gome Pacetti; several Pacetti wives and daughters whose names now escaped him. Also, there had always been innumerable Pacetti children tumbling about the yards, falling from docks into the river, cutting their feet on oyster shells, but somehow surviving to provide an unending line of Pacettis to tend the light when the time came.

Grouped a short distance from the light were a half dozen or so houses. They were all weathered and some of them indifferently cared for. Porches were uneven, screen doors sagged, phlox and sandspur choked the yards. The settlement was called Ponce Park and the residents appeared to have no visible means of support other than the occasional marketing of stone crabs and the selling of live shrimp for bait to fishing parties. A wagon trail, two deep ruts in the heavy sand, straggled through the thick underbrush northward to the beach side of Port Orange. There was some talk now by the state and

225   ★

county of laying out a paved stretch of highway which would open up Ponce Park. Years ago Dennis Lathrop had bought land here, insisting that someday it would provide an ideal site for a fishing camp with a small marina for motorboats large enough to negotiate the tricky inlet for outside angling. He had never pushed his idea, however, and the property, heavily overgrown, had remained undeveloped. The taxes were negligible and Dennis had almost forgotten he owned it.

It had been a year since Tod had been down this way but the rumor of a paved road captured his interest and he decided to look around. He called for Julie and they drove down the beach and up the approach through the dunes.

They stood within a small grove of oak and pine sapling. Beyond, the river, broken by little islands of dark green mangrove, rippled and shone with the incoming tide.

"I don't know." Tod spoke to himself but aloud.

"Really?"

He turned to look at her, surprised by the unmistakable edge in the tone of her voice. On the way down she had been strangely remote and uncommunicative. Wedged into a corner of the seat she had stared indifferently at the beach and sand dunes as they slid past. Once or twice he felt the impact of her gaze and when he glanced at her she was studying him speculatively, almost clinically.

"What?"

"Nothing." She shrugged.

The shoreline was broken into many small coves, heavily ringed with mangrove and reed grass. The air was rich with the scent of sun on salt marsh.

"I used to come down here when I was a youngster. There was a Mr. Howard who owned a hotel, the White House, on Main Street, across from the Keating place. He had an old horse called Belle and a wagon. There are a lot of clams, quahogs, in those tidal flats there. Mr. Howard liked clam fritters. He used to invite me and a boy, Jake Odum, to go with him on his expeditions." He smiled reminiscently. "Come to think of it, Jake, Belle and I were the only ones who did any work. Mr. Howard would sit on the wagon seat, calling out instructions, while Jake and I mucked around down there, digging out the clams. It was a two-day trip. Belle was pretty old and she made about a mile and a half an hour. We'd sleep in the wagon and go home the next morning. Mr. Howard never did ask us to have any fritters with him. Those quahogs are tough. You almost have to chop them with a cleaver. I tried to eat one out of the shell once and my teeth bounced off like it was rubber."

The uncertain popping of a single-cylinder outboard motor caught their attention. They watched as a heavy, flat-bottomed rowboat nosed toward a rickety dock below. A huge Negro, bare of chest and in patched and washed-out dungarees, towered in the stern, his weight lifting the bow to a steep angle.

"That's Jesse." Tod reached for her hand. He led her down the slope, heavily carpeted with the oaks' oval leaves and browning acorns. "Jesse's been around here for as long as anyone can remember. If his stories are true he must be a hundred years old but he looks and acts like a young buck." They picked their way along the rough ground with its outcropping of bleached coquina rock. "This part of the river is posted by the Government as a waterfowl preserve. There's a sign out there which says 'U. S. Waters.' Jesse's very proud of it. He calls the area 'us waters,' meaning it has been set aside for him and a few of those privileged to call him friend."

Jesse was the blue-black of the Ogeechee River Negro. His poll was gray, deep wrinkles were carved into the dark satin around his eyes. When he lifted himself from boat to dock his movements were as lithe as a boy's. He regarded most white men with a friendly tolerance and made a fair living guiding fishing parties. He took no nonsense from the winter tourists, though. When he accepted a client it was with a warning: "Don' you be late gittin' heah en th' mornin'. Don' be stayin' up ahl naight drinkin' en wrestlin' wid wimmen. You late we don' git no fish. Dat don' do my reputation no good." A tardy angler was quite likely to find Jesse asleep in a hammock and no amount of explanation would rouse him. He would merely grunt his impatience and set the hammock to swinging lightly.

As Tod and Julie came out on the dock he squinted and then nodded his recognition.

"Hello, Jesse."

"How you, Mistuh Tod?" He made the boat fast.

"Any smoked mullet?"

"Ah always gots mullets. Hit's a spell sence yo' bin down this way." He regarded Julie with interest and then inclined his head. "Miss."

"Hello." She smiled. There was a courtliness about his manner and a fine dignity. "Tod . . . Mr. Lathrop . . . says you're a hundred years old. Is it true?"

"Well," Jesse chuckled deep within his throat, "Ah'm eithuh a hundred yeahs ol' oah th' things Ah tell is 'bout th' biggest lies a man can think of."

He followed them up the knoll to a neat, sun-bleached cottage. The walk was bordered with carefully tended phlox in mounds decorated with clamshells. At their approach a squirrel raced along the narrow porch, jumped to a Mason jar filled with flowers and suspended on a wire from the overhang. It swung back and forth there, chattering furiously.

"He wan' he lunch. You evah see a fish-eatin' squirrel befoah? Dis one eat swimp, crab, mullets, mos' ennythin' Ah give him 'cept nuts laik enny regulah squirrel." He clucked and the rodent leaped from its perch to his shoulder and rode there as Jesse went inside.

There was a single wicker rocking chair on the porch. Julie settled herself on the edge of the boards, dangling her feet over the side. Tod took a place on the top step. There was an unmistakable constraint between them to which neither would admit. When Jesse came back he carried half a dozen split, smoked mullet on a piece of newspaper. The fish had a glaze of cherry-brown color and carried a perfume of bay and hardwood smoke.

Tod picked out one and passed it to her. "Have you ever tasted smoked mullet?"

Julie shook her head, took the fish and broke it open. The flesh was firm, creamy white, soft and moist to the touch. She sampled it and her eyes widened.

"It's delicious, better than," she sought for a comparison, "better than sturgeon; better than any fish I have ever tasted."

Jesse took a place on the opposite side of the steps and they ate with a rare contentment, licking their fingers and searching out the sweet morsels. Now and then Jesse would break off a small piece and feed it to the attentive squirrel.

"Where do you smoke these, Jesse?" Julie looked up.

"Ah got me a rack out to the back of th' house. Hit's ahl en th' kin' o' smoke. Ah mix up bay, oak en sometime', put dried seaweed wid dem." He was pleased by her interest. "People ahlways aftah me to sell 'em some. I smoke foah myse'f en a few frien's, laik Mistuh Tod, heah, en," he added graciously, "you too, miss."

"Up North the restaurants have a fish called sturgeon and a white fish that comes from the Great Lakes." Tod finished a second mullet. "They can't compare to this. You could make a fortune, Jesse, if these could be smoked in quantity and shipped."

"What would Ah do wid a foahchun? Gots no woman to take cah of, no chillun."

"You mean you don't want a fortune?" The sarcasm bit although the question was asked with a bland innocence. "The Stalath Fisheries, Limited, Incorporated," she continued, "doesn't interest you?"

Tod glanced quickly at her and a small line about his jaw tightened with anger. She ignored his glare.

"Why, you and Mr. Lathrop could probably corner the smoked mullet market."

Jesse smiled uncertainly but there was an uneasiness in his expression. His glance moved between them and then he bent his head and selected another sliver of fish for the squirrel.

"I'm sorry. That was rude of me." She spoke to the man, ignoring Tod.

Aware of this flaring hostility but not understanding it, Jesse remained silent save for the little clucking sounds he made for the squirrel. After a moment Tod stood up.

"Thank's for the mullet, Jesse."

"Hit a plesuah t' see you agin." He gathered up the newspaper, small bones and sections of scaled skin.

They walked back to the car. Tod held the door open and when Julie was seated he closed it with an unnecessary slam.

"What's wrong?"

"You." She was tense. "You're what's wrong. It's an obsession, isn't it? You can't even sit on a man's porch and eat a piece of smoked fish without thinking how it might be turned into a new product or an enterprise for Stalath, Incorporated. It's some sort of a sickness, Tod, and you'd damned well better get over it before everything human in you is killed."

He hesitated and then walked around and slid behind the wheel.

There was, he admitted to himself, a small truth in the accusation. But she made it seem unnatural, grasping and harsh. It wasn't that way at all. Or was it? No. Not the way Julie said it. When he said "make a fortune" he used the phrase only as a handle; something easy to understand. It was a part but not paramount in his enthusiasm to put things together, to watch the well-oiled wheels go around and take a satisfaction in their performance because he had set them in motion.

"I don't think I can explain it so you would understand."

"No, I don't think you can."

They were halfway home before she spoke again. She lit a cigarette and drew upon it thoughtfully, half bent over on the seat, hands clasped, staring at the carpeted floorboard as though to find an answer written there.

"I'm giving up the house and going to New York in the morning. I won't be back, Tod."

"When did you decide that?"

"Just now."

He knew a protest of some sort, even a small, polite expression of regret, was expected, demanded. Yet he could not make it. The words, as he framed them in his mind, were hypocritical. Almost desperately he asked himself, why don't I feel anything beyond a mild regret? And he thought, I'm not even too certain about that.

"Did you hear what I said?"

"Yes."

She shook her head and the smile was forced, wan. "That's all? No 'I wish you would think about it'? No 'I'll miss you'? Nothing?"

"Of course I'll miss you."

"In the beginning it seemed so right. You were fun to be with. You still are. I like so much about you. I tried. I wanted you to like me. It sounds so simple."

"Of course I like you," he interrupted.

"You really don't have room for anyone else. I'm beginning to understand that. Believe me, I'm not too certain about my own heart. Since the divorce I've tried to put out an anchor which would keep me from drifting until I found a course. There's an emotional wrench in the breakup of a marriage; even with such a son of a bitch as Lanier. Who also had charm after his own fashion. I would have settled for an—an arrangement with you. But I don't even think that's possible now. So," she straightened up, "before my emotions take over and I catch myself waiting for you to call me or stop by the house, I'm going to get out. I'm vulnerable and you're not. In your scheme of things there is no place for anyone else. I don't think you are unique. There are other men of single purpose. For all I know that may be enough."

"Will you let me hear from you?"

"No." She snapped the cigarette away. "I'm not one for writing chatty little letters. I'll get over you." Her eyes brightened. "I'm going to miss your grandfather. If he asks what happened just tell him for me that I'm a lass with a roving eye. He'll understand. And," she leaned impulsively toward him and brushed a light kiss against his cheek, "thank you for not protesting. You in the role of a broken-hearted lover would have been too much."

He said nothing for a moment and when he did speak, the tone and words carried with them a certain quiet astonishment.

"I'm really going to miss you."

"Just a little and for a little time. I hope so, Tod. But you'll recover and quickly, too. I should say it will take no longer than the time between when you drop me at the house and reach the Stalath Corporation office on the mainland. By then you will have thought of a new project. I wouldn't be at all surprised if you eventually owned the State of Florida. If that is what you want."

They took the Seabreeze approach from the beach. A few minutes later he pulled into the driveway of the house she had rented. Julie opened the door on her side and was out before he could move to assist her. She reached across the seat for his hand and the clasp was warm, friendly and firm.

"Good-bye, Tod. And," she laughed with honest amusement at the puzzled expression on his face, "don't sit there, mentally stubbing your toe into the ground like an awkward schoolboy. I'm not hurt, really I'm not. I guess my vanity is piqued just a little. The competition is tougher than I thought it would be."

She turned away and walked with a free, swinging stride up the walk without a backward look. When the door closed behind her, Tod drove away.

He was halfway across the Ormond Bridge before he realized how

231 ★

accurate Julie's prediction had been. He caught himself thinking of Jesse, the smoked mullet, and wondering if a fleet of shrimp boats working out of New Smyrna might be drawn into a profitable venture, East Coast Fisheries, a subsidy of Stalath, Inc. Why not?

* XV * *

SPRING comes unobtrusively to Florida's coastal regions. There are no freshets of woodland creeks suddenly released from winter's lock; no sudden flowering of dormant shrubs. The season moves softly. Green nubbins appear on the mulberry trees, the scrub takes on a fresh, pastel haze. The wind displays a restlessness, moving about the compass points, playing from southeast to south, to west, touching the land with gentle fingers.

This year of 1926 was no different from the many others Tod Lathrop had known. He knotted his tie at a window overlooking the Halifax and felt the warm moistness of the east wind upon his face. Below, and at the river's edge, his grandfather stood upon the short dock and tossed small mullet to the pair of dazzling white cranes as they wheeled overhead. They came each morning and at the same hour to circle about the house and then drop to the shallows and stand, stiff-legged and alertly inquisitive, thrusting with long bills at a careless shrimp. Will Lathrop rarely kept them waiting.

This was no casual feeding but a highly stylized ceremony. Will Lathrop came to it freshly barbered from Washington's hands; a small tot of rum warmed his stomach in preparation for breakfast later. This morning he wore a suit of white Palm Beach cloth, black knit tie upon a shirt of fine linen, a wide-brimmed hat of Panama straw. A polished and mottled Malacca cane was hung between wrist and elbow. Wash, as always and with the patience of years, had followed him down. He bore a small silver pitcher and bowl and a monogrammed hand towel. These, by custom, he set upon a piling head. Then from the river he hauled up a bait box of wire mesh. As it came to the surface there was the metallic snapping of the fish as they flipped and tossed themselves in the panic of being taken from their element. The box was stocked each evening by one of the yard boys who worked along the shore with a cast net. One by one Wash would hand the mullet to his employer. Will Lathrop tossed them into the air with a piping cry of "Cranie, Cranie" and the swooping birds caught them in full flight, circling and diving for more. With the last of the mullet Wash lowered the cage back to its resting place on the bottom. Then he filled the bowl with warm water from the pitcher and Will Lathrop fastidiously washed his hands. He dried each finger carefully and waited while the Negro brought a match for his cigar. He would smoke with a deep contentment, gazing now and then at the sky as though to dare God to intrude with wind, cloud or rain upon this perfect day. So completely self-assured was Will Lathrop that this performance, which might have bordered upon the ludicrous, seemed natural and without affectation.

Walking now from the porch and down the path of marl, Tod smiled to himself at the almost youthful swing of his grandfather's arm as he hurled each fish into the air. Time, he thought, barely touches this man. He stands like a rock, forcing the waters of the years to divide at his feet and pass him by. He had never seen his grandfather excited, never heard his voice raised in anger. He carried himself with the serenity of one who felt that the world was being run in an orderly fashion and who did not question his place in the cosmic scheme of things.

At the sound of footsteps on the boards Will Lathrop turned, saw his grandson and nodded.

"Where the hell have you been this past week? I never see you anymore."

"I didn't get in until late last night." Tod moved toward him. "The house was dark. I didn't want to wake you so I had a drink and went to bed. Good morning, Wash."

"Mornin', Mistuh Tod." Wash gathered up the toilet articles. "You en Mistuh Will goin' to have breakfus togethah?"

"Yes. Set a table on the porch. I'd like some fruit, ham and eggs. Corn bread if Louise made some this morning."

After Wash had left them, Will Lathrop studied the birds as they flew in wide, lazy circles.

"You know," he confessed, "sometimes I catch myself thinking these are the same cranes I used to feed here fifty or sixty years ago. Of course they aren't but I like to think they are. I don't know how the hell it ever started. Now I would feel guilty if I didn't come down each morning. Do you suppose cranes talk with each other? Maybe they say, There's a real, easy touch up the river at Daytona, boys. Some old fool comes out on a dock every morning and gives away free fish. Must be some sort of a nut— Do you imagine they say that, boy?"

"I doubt it, Grandfather." Tod seated himself on the top of a palmetto piling.

"Well," Lathrop was unconvinced, "they pass the word around somehow. Otherwise, why does a pair show up here each day at the same time? For as long as I can remember they have always come in twos; never any more, never any less. After they have been fed they hang around for awhile and then go back down the river to Pelican Island. What's happened to your girl?"

Tod had long ago adjusted himself to this habit of his grandfather's. From almost any subject he would abruptly strike out at a tangent and expect everyone to follow his line of thought.

"She went to New York."

"Coming back?"

"I don't think so."

"That's a damned shame and you're a fool to let her go. Let me tell you a girl like that doesn't come along often. What happened?"

"Nothing really. No argument. Nothing unpleasant. I guess she just decided we didn't have any future."

"Well, did you?" The old man eyed him sharply.

"I don't know. I—I liked her better than any girl I have ever known. I guess I was even in love, after my own fashion. We might have had something but it needed care and attention."

"You don't have the time for that, do you?" The accusation was unmistakable.

"No, Grandfather, I don't seem to have the time and I wonder why. I could end by being a very lonely man. I've thought about it. I'd like to try again but I don't think I'll get the chance. I miss her."

"So do I." The words were edged. "She had a spark. There was a gypsy in her. Oh"—he answered the surprise on Tod's face— "she came over to see me several times while you were out of town, tearing around the state. We liked each other. You shouldn't have let her go."

"You may be right."

"Whatever it is you're chasing I hope you catch it, because if you don't you're going to find yourself out of breath one of these days and wondering why you ran so hard."

They walked slowly back up the dock. The sunlight filtered through the varnished leaves of the oaks and a breeze played within the wavering palmetto fronds.

"I knew a man once. He saved newspapers; never threw one away. He said he might want to know sometime what had happened on a certain day. If he did he could look in an old newspaper and find out. He saved newspapers for thirty years; filled all the closets, packed the basement with bundles of them, all carrying date tags. He subscribed to newspapers all over the country. Finally he could barely walk around the house, didn't even have room for a bed. He made little tunnels so he could crawl under the stacks which went right up to the ceiling. Do you know what happened?"

"No, sir." Tod's mouth twitched.

"Well, he was living like a mole, creeping around in those tunnels of newsprint. The neighbors tried to get him out of the house but he wouldn't go. He said that one day he would think of something he wanted to know and would read about it. Finally the Board of Health, his doctor, the police and some old friends got together and took him away. He was stone blind."

"That's a hell of a story, Grandfather."

"Yes sir." Will Lathrop nodded. "That's a hell of a story. It probably has a moral in it somewhere. I wouldn't know. If I were you I'd go and find that girl before it's too late."

"And I discover I can't read?"

"Something like that, boy. Something like that."

Wash had the table laid in a triangle of sun at one end of the porch. He was waiting to take Will Lathrop's cane and hat and hold his chair. There was a deeply rooted affection between these two old men although Wash frequently pretended a resigned desperation. Sometimes, feeling himself too heavily put upon, he would walk around muttering, "Ahl Ah evah wanted to be was a coachman laik dat dere Mark we onct had. Ahl Ah evah ask o' Mistuh Will en th' Lord was a top hat, some o' dem shiny boots en a carriage t' drive. Did Ah git 'em? No suh! Heah Ah em, barely able to keep th' body togethah en I gits me a big house t' tek cah of." He was always quite certain to be within earshot of his employer when this lament was voiced but he pretended to be talking to himself.

Breakfast was brought in a warming cart by a maid but Wash took over the placing of dishes and the pouring of coffee. Then he would leave and wait just inside the door. Will Lathrop cut slices from half a papaya, squeezed lime juice over them and ate with meditative concentration.

"You carry much of a balance in the Merchants Bank?"

Tod looked up, surprised. His grandfather rarely talked of money.

"Some. It's mostly Citrus Belt Line cash. Why?"

"Get it out." The old man added a tablespoonful of brandy to his black coffee. He stared absently at the river. "I've been hearing things. If it's important money I'd close the account or whittle it down to a few hundred dollars. Take the bulk and give it to old man Niven to hold for you. I'd say he has one of the few safe banks in the state. There's a rumor he locks himself in the vault with the money at night but I never really believed it."

"What have you heard?" Tod put aside the wedge of yellow corn bread he had buttered.

"Nothing I want repeated." The warning was explicit.

"You know I don't talk."

"I have friends at Tallahassee. There's just a whisper. If someone raises his voice right now there could be a panic on Beach Street. I hear the Merchants is in trouble. The bank is overextended and the examiners are due next month. Anyhow, if you don't have important money on deposit let it alone. Don't start walking around in the canoe. A run would really slam the doors shut. How's this thing you have going in Miami turning out?" He changed the subject with an effortless finality.

"Fine." Tod cut a piece of ham. "It's going to work better than I expected."

They made small, inconsequential talk. Wash brought fresh hot coffee and Will Lathrop had his second cigar of the morning.

"Do you know, as you grow old you begin to resent change."

"I hadn't thought about it." Tod finished the ham.

"I don't like to drive uptown anymore. I keep thinking I ought to know everyone who passes. All I see are unfamiliar faces, new people. I wonder where the others went. It was a nice little community. When we built this house our only neighbor was Colonel Bullard. I think he was promoted to a general. Damned if I know why since as far as I know he was retired. Anyhow, there were the Bullards, and the Browers had a place on Palmetto Avenue."

Tod wasn't really listening. He understood his grandfather didn't expect a reply to his ramblings.

"Hankins had a little drugstore on the corner of Orange Avenue and Beach Street. There was a grocery store a couple of doors away. Henry Titus had a motion picture theatre, one-reel comedies. It was just a room with undertaker's chairs. He called it The Gator and kept an old alligator in the window. Fitzgerald's newspaper, McDonald's meat market and the Merchants Bank. They were all there together in half a block and that was about all there was to Beach Street."

"I remember." Tod dropped his napkin to the table. "It was still that way when I was a boy." He stood up. "If you'll excuse me I have a couple of things I want to do."

"I thought you probably would have." Will nodded. "What I told you is confidential. Keep it that way. If you don't have an engagement this evening maybe we can have dinner together. Is your father still alive?"

Tod laughed. "Of course he's alive."

"Give him my regards. Tell him I asked." The smile was that of a delighted imp.

On his way uptown Tod realized he hadn't been surprised by what his grandfather had told him. Almost every bank in the state was overextended. Money was easy and the bankers happy with their interest rates. If, as his grandfather had warned, no one tried to stand up in the canoe it probably wouldn't overturn.

He went first to the Citrus Belt Line and called for the bookkeeper.

"Let me know what our balance is at the bank, Joyce."

"I can tell you now. I just finished bringing everything up-to-date. It is thirty-seven thousand, three hundred and fifty-three cents. Out of that we have this week's payroll and operating expenses to meet. Do you want it broken down for an exact balance?"

Tod walked to a window and stood staring out. That was a lot of money to lose.

"Is something wrong, Mr. Lathrop?" His indecision was communicated to the girl.

"No, Joyce. Thank you."

She hesitated for a moment and then left. Tod remained at the window. If he withdrew a sizable amount to protect himself Joyce would have to know. She would wonder. He knew he didn't have to explain to anyone, but Joyce would be curious. She'd think about it; probably mention it to a girl friend, talk about it at home. Why was Mr. Lathrop closing out the Citrus Belt Line account at the Merchants Bank? There was more to it than that. Counting the drivers, the office staff and maintenance crew, he employed some fifty persons. They were local men and women and most of them, he imagined, had small accounts with the bank. If he was going to insure himself against the possibility of the bank's closing then the decent thing to do was to warn them. If he did that, the bank would face a run in the morning which would force the closing. So, he asked himself, what do I do? Take mine and say to hell with you? He shook his head, knowing he couldn't do that. He turned and walked back to his desk, picking up the slip of paper on which Joyce had written the figures. Slowly he tore it up and let the pieces fall into a wastebasket. A thirty-seven-thousand-dollar gesture. You put a high price on your conscience. He thought of Willie Estes and felt a little better. This would hit Willie right in the gut. It would be almost worth it just to hear him scream.

Later, after the first numbing shock had worn off, there were those who would insist they had felt something was wrong from the very beginning of the day. "It was sort of like you were walking through a vacuum." Actually, the morning had been much the same as any other. Men went to their jobs, women to their household tasks. The shining Lincolns were parked on Beach Street before the real estate offices. The salesmen lounged on outside benches in the warming sun or strolled down to the drugstore for a "dope." The stores did their usual Monday business. The sky was bright and cloudless. God was in his Heaven and all was right with the world. It wasn't until late in the afternoon that a few were abruptly startled to realize that, although everything seemed normal, no sales had been made, no options swapped or bought. No prospects had crowded into the reception rooms or waited in line to be taken to a proposed development. No one inquired or expressed an interest about or in a desirable tract or lot. A few telephone calls were cautiously made between friends and associates.

"Hi, Joe! How's everything?"

"Fine. How's it with you?"

"Great. Couldn't be better." The reply was immediate and hearty.

"Good."

The pauses were sometimes long and wary, each waiting for the other to speak.

"You know that piece just west of the railroad tracks in Holly Hill? The one you were after? I have a binder down on it."

"Yeah. I know."

"Well"—and this casually—"I've got a deal on the fire. Something really big. I need extra cash to swing it. So, if you are still interested you can buy my option. I wouldn't offer it to anyone else before I gave you first chance."

"Thanks. But I've got something of my own cooking right now. It's so good I don't want to talk about it."

"Joe?"

"Yeah?"

"What the hell's going on?"

"I don't know."

"We've known each other for a long time. You can talk with me. Have you had any action at all today?"

"No and neither has anyone else as far as I can find out."

"What do you suppose has happened? It's kind of scary. All of a sudden nothing's moving. Your call was the first time my phone has rung all day. I nearly jumped off the couch to get to it. I called some people on a waiting list I have. No one was interested. Last week they were running all over the state looking for anything."

"Maybe it isn't anything to sweat about. You know. The weekend and all. It could just be slow picking up."

"I hope you're right."

"The Holly Hill piece. If you change your mind let me know. We can get together."

"I'll think about it."

The receivers were guardedly put back. The men sat and stared at the silent instruments, their apprehension gathering.

That was the way it ended; as though a curtain was unaccountably dropped in mid-act on a stage, closing out a scene. A reporter from the *News-Journal*, making his rounds of the hotels in search of local items, discovered there had been an unusually large number of checkouts over the past forty-eight hours. On a hunch he put in a call to the passenger agent at the Florida East Coast Railroad depot and found there was no Pullman car space available on the afternoon train to Jacksonville. As a matter of fact, the agent said, all northbound trains had carried capacity both Saturday and Sunday. It looked like one hell of a lot of people were leaving Florida all of a sudden and few coming in. The reporter passed the information on to his city desk and was told to keep the story on ice. There was no sense in worrying everyone with something which probably had a logical explanation. "Don't sell Florida short." It was a rallying cry, but as the days wore on it became thin and plaintive.

No one could bring himself to believe it was all over but options were allowed to lapse. All construction came to a halt. The wind sighed across developments in the flatlands and nagged at the stucco arches until a few pieces of the plaster broke away, disclosing a bony skeleton. Birds shed their droppings on the ornamental street signs and weeds sprouted on Hibiscus Boulevard.

No one had an explanation. They told each other it would all come back but no one really believed what he said or heard. The butcher, the grocer, the druggist, filling station operators and bootleggers who had been satisfied to let their customers' charges run for months at a time began to ask for payment, or at least something on account. The requests were met with a cheerful: "Sure. I'll get a check to you right away. Must have slipped my mind." But no checks were written.

Then the banks began to close after the bankers tried calling in their big loans and discovered no one was going to pay and they had only stacks of paper with which to meet the demands of their depositors. The slamming of the heavy doors echoed up and down the state with the thunder of doom. Fear knifed at everyone.

In Daytona, the Merchants Bank failed and a long line of depositors queued up to stare hopefully at the shuttered windows. The unbelievable, the incredible and the impossible had happened. Many small merchants and shopkeepers with one or two employees were unable to meet their payrolls. No one complained. They all shared the common bond of misfortune. Things couldn't be worse so they had to get better. Some families, whose funds had been in the bank, were actually reduced to scraping the penny jar for cigarette money. The light and telephone companies continued their service since it was understood that to shut off light and communication would result in a near panic. Grocers and butchers were sympathetic but they were frank to admit they didn't know how they were going to pay for new stock when their present supplies were exhausted. Now when a man said he was going fishing it wasn't for sport or recreation. He was after food for the table.

The Lincolns began to disappear from the garages as the finance companies moved in to repossess them. FOR SALE signs sprouted like weeds on choice properties from Ormond to the inlet. There were no buyers. The Negro population of Newtown and Waycross who were dependent upon the whites for their livelihood and employment and who never had more than a dollar or two put aside went hopefully to their old jobs. Their employers told them they didn't have the money to pay their wages but they showed up anyhow. If the white people ate then the servants would eat.

There was a rumor an hour. The bank was being reorganized and would open the next day. The bank would remain closed but depositors would receive fifty cents on the dollar. The federal government and the Red Cross would move to see that there was no real suffering.

Not everyone, of course, had been caught. Niven's bank, in Seabreeze, was on a solid financial rock and those who had been scornful of its conservative policies now saw it as a shining beacon of hope in a confused world. Not everything had gone to hell. The damage, though, was widespread up and down the peninsula. There had been some 271 state banks chartered. Of this number more than half failed. The razzle-dazzle had been hypnotic. Money had been made, of course, by those persons who moved in and out of the real estate market and took their profits at the peak. Others, when the frenzy for buying anything manifested itself, demanded such a large down payment that it made little difference if the purchasers eventually defaulted. There were, also, developments of solid worth such as Coral Gables, and the people who bought into them were in a position to hold their investments. The ones hurt were the small investors, the hopeful gamblers, who made their down payments on purchases from maps or on the strength of lavish promises. Many found that the properties in developments were covered by a blanket mortgage and they had no title to their lots. Others had hovered around the ring of speculation and plumped down their money a day or two before the boom collapsed. They awoke to discover there were no buyers in the once wild market place. The happy realtors, the binder boys, the brisk traders in options, had earned large commissions. These were spent with a lavish hand on new cars, clothes, large homes and cellars filled with cases of fine whiskies, brandies, rum and gin from the Bahamas.

Oddly enough, in Daytona at least, this spirit of carnival persisted amid the wreckage. The sound was muted but there. When the first nerve-grinding shock had worn off, the people looked around and grinned a little weakly at each other as though to say: We sure had one hell of a time while it lasted, didn't we?

Tod Lathrop, coming out of the Stalath offices, was surprised to see an old Ford half truck pull into the curb and Lonnie Heuy step out. At the peak of the dizzy ascent Lonnie had driven a big maroon Lincoln upholstered with cream-colored leather and a conservatively black Rolls Royce, the first ever seen in Daytona.

"Hi, Tod."

"How are you, Lon? How's Margaret?" Tod surveyed the Ford. "Where's the Rolls?"

"*Shhh!*" Lonnie looked up and down the sidewalk with an exaggerated caution, moved closer to Tod and whispered hoarsely, "It's on blocks, locked in the garage. My God! If I drove down the street in that Rolls now the grocer, the butcher and everyone I owe money to would throw rocks at me. This way they just say: 'Look at poor old

Lonnie, riding around in a beat up truck. You've just got to admire him. He's takin' it real good.' " He winked.

"I'm on my way home. Come on down and have a drink." They were old friends.

"I've plenty of drinking whisky at home. Now, if you'd say: 'Come on down to the house and have a meal' I'd be interested. I never thought about being hungry before." He grinned. "I stopped in at Dunn Brothers and got some seeds on credit. Now I'm going to put Margaret to work planting a truck garden right in the front yard on Ridgewood Avenue. Beans, peppers, tomatoes, okra. After they come up I'll catch a mess of crabs for boiling and we'll have crab gumbo every day. Might even open a soup kitchen for the deserving poor who once were rich." He waved a hand cheerfully and went down the street.

The maids and houseboys who worked in homes on the beach side were walking now because they couldn't spare the dime for fare. They straggled across the bridges morning and evening on their way to jobs which weren't paying anything. Just having a place to go gave them a small feeling of security.

The Citrus Belt Line had operated buses for this traffic apart from the regular routes for which it held a franchise from the city. Now, over Willie's protests, Tod had signs put on the vehicles:

FREE BUS TO THE BEACH.

"You're a damned fool. Why should we pay for the gas, drivers and upkeep to give those niggers a free ride? Hell, let 'em walk or stay home."

Willie had been hurt by the bank's closing and Francine's sarcastic contempt was no salve for the wound. She would walk around the house, two fingers crossed, parroting, "Me an' Fred Niver are like this." Her mimicry of Willie was deadly. Save for his twenty-five percent interest in Citrus Belt, Willie was broke. In the last days of the boom he had been unable to resist the temptation and invested heavily in a proposed development north of Ormond, south of Flagler Beach. Now he was part owner of a lot of sand dunes and scrub which no one wanted.

Tod ignored Willie's objection. The free buses operated on a regular schedule, touring Newtown and Waycross in the mornings and waiting at designated loading zones in the evening to take the domestic servants to and from their work. The line's intrastate service was taking a beating. Traffic was close to a standstill and truck cargoes at a premium. Tod cut down on the schedules to fit the pattern. Citrus Belt would take a mild licking for awhile but he was determined to meet the obligations of the franchise and maintain both truck and passenger service.

When the Merchants Bank closed, Tod immediately went to see his father. The two sat on the comfortable porch facing the ocean.

"Were you hurt much?" Tod was concerned.

"No. Your grandfather warned me. But I only had a small account there so I let it alone. I thought maybe if no one began pulling at the plug the keg wouldn't run dry. What about you? I assume your grandfather gave you the same information."

Tod nodded. He was concerned over his father's physical appearance. Dennis Lathrop seemed to have shrunk; literally to have become smaller. Also he was disturbingly apathetic, finding little of interest in anything. Actually, he seemed older than Grandfather Will.

"I let my account ride also." He answered his father's question. "There was quite a bit of money involved but I didn't see how I could protect myself without telling the people who work for me what might happen."

Dennis gazed at the tumbling ocean and the faintest of smiles gave a temporary light to his eyes.

"That's good to hear, Tod. I've been uneasy about you sometimes. You seem to have the instincts of a speculator, a gambler. It is nice to know they are tempered by honesty and a genuine feeling for others. We don't see much of each other anymore. I've missed your company but I'm glad to hear you are the man of the boy I once knew so well."

"If you need anything . . ." Tod hesitated. "I'm solvent. There isn't any obligation due I can't meet. So . . ." He left the offer unspoken.

"You don't have to say it." Dennis put a hand on his son's knee. "I'll let you know. We'll see how things go for awhile." He smiled again. "I imagine that the practice of law will pick up locally. When the people recover they'll start suing each other. It's amazing, though," he marveled, "how everyone seems to be taking this. It is almost as though they were glad the time of extravagant nonsense is over and they can get back to their normal, unexciting lives."

"A lot of them are never going to be the same. After a diet of champagne and caviar, grits and a piece of side meat will be pretty tasteless."

"What do you think is going to happen?"

It was strange, Tod thought, his father should voice such a question to him. Dennis Lathrop had always been so sure of himself and his opinions. Now, he seemed out of touch, groping and indecisive.

"My guess is it will be a long, slow pull back. The real assets of Florida haven't been lost. You can't wipe away the solid development of, say, Miami, Jacksonville, Tampa, St. Petersburg. They have become cities with a character and drive. Everything Florida had is still here; some of it improved. I'm going to put my money on it. When the real estate market really goes to the bottom, and it's almost there now, I'm going to take everything I have, step in with the Stalath Corporation and begin to build." He stood up. "I want to see Mother before I go."

"Yes." Dennis spoke almost absently. "She isn't well, Tod. I sometimes think she isn't happy here. We may go to my father's place near Asheville. He never uses it anymore. How is he, by the way?"

"Grandfather Will almost makes me feel young again." Tod laughed. "He's ageless."

"It's strange," there was a small note of regret in the voice, "but you are closer to my father than I ever was. You seem to understand each other."

"We get along fine. He's given up all hope of my leading a dissolute life. I suspect I amuse him. You ought to stop by the house more often. He would be glad to see you. He doesn't go out much anymore."

"Yes, I suppose so. Some evening when your mother feels up to it we'll call and come to dinner." He offered his hand almost formally. "It's been good talking with you. Now, run along. I know your mother is waiting."

Tod glanced back as he went inside. His father rocked gently in the chair, his eyes upon the ocean, but Tod had the feeling he didn't really see it.

* XVI * *

D URING that first summer following the boom's collapse Florida drew itself together with the groggy determination of a man who knows he has to go to work despite a rocking hangover.

The big dream? The people began to shrug it off. Few of them had taken the high dive into the real estate market's shallow tank. Most of the speculative money had come from out of state. The big developments had been projected and financed by local interests in many cases but those who bought into them, put down the cash, were drawn from outside. From Miami to Jacksonville the natives had engaged in the selling and not the buying. The commissions earned were collected and spent with the noisy enthusiasm of a miner who unexpectedly hits a mother lode. The excursion into town was an exhilarating experience. They had no real idea where they were going but the company was good, the trip exciting. Now it was over. After a few, deep breaths everyone began to look around. When it was discovered no irreparable damage had been done, a curious spirit of community awareness began to assert itself. As the Lincolns disappeared, secondhand Fords or Chevrolets took their places and no one was embarrassed since the readjustment was general. If the mortgage payments on large homes could not be met then there was a small cottage tucked in behind a fragrant hedge of oleander which was for rent and no one felt an explanation was necessary. Clerks and soda jerkers, mechanics and bookkeepers, insurance salesmen and taxi drivers went back to their old jobs where they could find them. The unhurried rhythm of another time began to reassert itself. Life was pretty wonderful after all.

The real hurt lay in the bank failures where the entire capital of many families and small merchants was frozen. There was no money to meet the day-to-day necessities and credit was short. In Daytona a group of the leading businessmen met at the Elks Club to work out a controlled system of extending credit. In some cases there was the pledging of personal assets to underwrite reasonable loans to small merchants: the owner of a candy store, the operator of a one-man magazine and cigarette stand, a cleaning and pressing establishment, the owner of a fish market or a taxicab driver who was behind in his payments. Slowly an order began to establish itself.

Reluctantly, since the Stalath Corporation was, almost exclusively, an operator in real estate, Tod was forced to reduce his staff there. But where the salesmen were local residents, he continued most on half salary until they could find jobs elsewhere. Some of his sales and promotion force was made up of men drawn from the big real estate developments on Long Island, in New York, and the Philadelphia suburbs. Almost all of these went back to familiar ground. Although traffic, both passenger and freight, had been drastically reduced on the Citrus Belt Line he maintained the full complement of drivers, mechanics and clerical workers. These things were done quietly and apart from his participation in the general plan for recovery. To finance everything he was forced to draw upon his personal account to the disgusted amazement of Willie Estes.

"You goin' to run for Mayor or somethin' or have you got a Santa Claus suit at home? If you've got such a damn big bleedin' heart an' so much money, you can give me some."

"I'll buy out your twenty-five percent, Willie." Tod made the offer hopefully.

"Uh-uh." Willie was shrewdly emphatic. "I figure no matter what happens you'll keep the Citrus Belt runnin' because it's your first baby. I look for my share to hold me up in my old age. Just the same you're bein' a damn fool. Half the people in the office, on the road an' in the shop haven't anything to do. They just sit on their butts an' take your money."

"I'll be satisfied to break even for awhile." Tod was undisturbed.

"Breakin' even don't put no steak in my belly." Willie was bitter. "An'," he made the confession unhappily, "you don't have to live with Francine. She never lets me forget how I waited until the last minute an' then put all of my cash into the ground just before everything went to hell. Like last night she says, sweet as you please: 'Willie, honey, let's drive up to Flagler Beach an' look at some of that lovely real estate you once owned. You know, honey, that fifty-thousand-dollar piece where the buzzards are roostin', the snakes are crawlin', the loons laughing their goddamned heads off!' " He spat disgustedly and plodded back to the maintenance building.

By midsummer most of the beach cottages were rented to visitors from the interior and the states of Georgia and Alabama. The town, which had always thought of itself as a winter resort, was steadily attracting a large tourist business. At this time of year the beach was at its best, the climate close to ideal. Now and then the prevailing southeast wind would shift due west and bring with it the oppressive heat of the midlands. But the nights were cool and perfume laden. There were nightly dances at the Burgoyne Casino on the mainland, beach picnics and moonlight excursions on the river. The town was once again noisy and filled with a holiday vitality. Pretty girls from Orlando, Sanford, Atlanta and Montgomery were seemingly without attachment and the local men hunted with skill and success. A pale sand dune made an ideal resting place for a pliant back and there was a soft keening as hymens shattered beneath the moon.

Tod had tried to talk his grandfather into moving to the beach side for the summer. The old gentleman resisted stubbornly and would not budge.

"I like my home here on the river. If I hadn't I damn well wouldn't have built it where I did. Anyhow, who would feed my cranes in the morning? You go on over and do your wenching. I hear it's open season and you don't need a license. You can stop by once in awhile, have a drink and tell me what's going on."

Dennis and Tod's mother had gone to Will Lathrop's place in North Carolina for the summer and the beach house was empty. Tod moved in. A Negro woman came each morning to clean, take care of his laundry and keep a semblance of order. With time and nothing pressing to take him out of town Tod set about rediscovering old friends and renewing acquaintances among the regular summer visitors, and the house provided a setting for a continual party. For almost everyone the heady days of good Scotch, brandy, Canadian rye and French champagne were over. But Bacardi from Cuba was plentiful and cheap and there was always Clifton's still in the backwoods to provide an unending supply of good corn moonshine. Its age left something to be desired but there was no arguing with its effect. With a certain amount of astonishment Tod discovered how much fun there was in just doing nothing or, certainly, no more than he wanted to do. He drank with old friends, made love to pretty girls, slept in the morning and stayed up all night.

Clinton Campbell, who had ridden high on the wave of the boom from the Keys to Jacksonville, moved in with him. The debacle hadn't depressed Clint. He'd shake his head bemusedly over what had happened but he never complained. A slow, engaging and reminiscent grin would appear when they talked of the high-rolling days.

"I just couldn't believe it at first. There everyone was with a fistful of money begging me to take it. You know," the smile broadened, "when I bought my first Lincoln, paid cash for it and drove back from Jacksonville, the only thing I could think of was that damn bicycle we used to ride all over town with me doing all the pedaling."

They would sit on the porch in the late afternoon, drinks in hand, and in a reminiscent mood reach back into their boyhood together for adventures and incidents. There was a bond between them although neither would have expressed it as such. Clint had always been a little different from the other boys. When, as he often did, he took a summer job jerking soda water at Peter Paul's at a salary of ten dollars a week, he would save for two weeks to buy a twenty-dollar pair of shoes. Always he wanted the best and refused to compromise. This had led him into innumerable fights with those who found an unendurable snobbery in his attitude. He was forever reaching for things which the other boys couldn't understand. He was selective in his choice of girls and the acquaintances he made.

"Sure," he had once said to Tod. "My father was a house painter. He was a damn good one and never felt he had to apologize to anyone. We pay our bills when they are due; which is a damn sight more than a lot of people around here can say. I like Johnston and Murphy shoes and I'm willing to save until I can buy a pair instead of settling for something cheaper. I'd rather wait until I can have a suit tailor-made than take one off the rack at Debrow's. Damned if I can see anything crazy about that but for some reason it makes a lot of guys sore and I always have to fight them. They think I'm stuck up."

There had been an interlude while Tod was away at Princeton and later, during the war, when they lost track of each other. The Campbell family moved to Washington. They never attempted a correspondence, both somehow sensing this wasn't necessary. If and when they met again they knew they would be able to pick up where they left off without excuses or explanations. The elapsed years would make no difference. Of such solid material had a boyhood friendship been forged and tempered. That was the way it worked out. During the frenzied days of the boom they had frequently run into each other in Miami, Palm Beach or Jacksonville. Each was wholly pre-occupied with his own projects and ambitions but they had time for each other—a meal, a drink, a long evening's talk. There was never any constraint between them. There was much to remember.

Now, as they watched the first long, violet-colored shadows move upon the ocean, they were quietly thoughtful. In an hour or two people would start to drop in and Bunk Ohler was planning a fish fry. Bunk would arrange these cook-outs on a moment's whim. He liked only a few persons and these he invited, allowing them to add to the guests with their dates or friends. He was a big man, broad of shoulder, heavily muscled but his voice was a high squeak which he could not control. Secretly, he was embarrassed by this but his intimates were so accustomed to the unusual sound that it passed unnoticed.

"You have a date for tonight or are you going to catch something on the fly?" Clint finished his drink and put the empty glass on the porch's railing.

"Fern said she'd be down. She has a real pretty cousin from Plant City visiting her. She's bringing her along. Maybe you'll like."

"What became of that Mrs. Lanier you introduced me to once in Miami? I thought you had something going there."

"So did I. So did she." Tod reached for the Bacardi, more ice and a half of a freshly cut lime. "I guess I wasn't ready for it then. I didn't want the obligation and Julie wasn't a girl to be taken casually. She wasn't insisting on marriage but I was jealous of my time. I couldn't share it. Right now I have just a hell of a lot of time but it's too late."

"Maybe not."

"No." His expression clouded with regret. "I have a feeling it would be like trying to blow on the ashes of a dead fire. A girl like Julie doesn't wait or come around a second time but she left something I can't quite get over." He swirled the ice, rum and lime juice about in the glass. "What are you going to do now, J.C.?" Always Tod had called him by the initials of his first two names, James Clinton. "Want to come in with me? I have big plans for the Stalath Corporation."

Clint shook his head. "No thanks. I stashed some money away, not a hell of a lot but enough to carry me for awhile. For some reason I got smart one day and put it in a safe-deposit box." He leaned back and scratched his scalp against the rough wicker weaving of the chair. "My days of working for someone else are over. I know where I want to go and I'm better off on my own."

"It wouldn't be working for someone else. You know it."

"Yes it would and *you* know it. No one is going to work *with* Stoddard Lathrop. I've watched you and you're going it alone and all the way. Anyone who comes in will work *for* Stalath. Anyhow, I have an idea of my own. I've made a lot of friends. I can get the backing for what I have in mind but it isn't the time now. In a few years, maybe. I can wait because I know what I want. In the meanwhile I'll get along." He laughed softly. "We all will. Thanks just the same. By the way, that motel thing you have going is just one hell of an inspiration. I wish I'd thought of it. You may have to drag your feet for awhile and put off expansion but it's sound. You are going to have a lot of imitators but you're in fust with the mostest."

"I'm going to have them all over Florida and maybe from coast to coast."

By the time the brief twilight had vanished a half a dozen or so cars were parked around the beach house and everyone was crowded into the drinking room, the kitchen. They were all persons Tod had known for years but had lost track of during the hectic period when there didn't seem to be time for anything but the making of money. Now he felt the warmth of old friends who had worn so well. Dick and Nell Niven. Bill and Harriett Freeman. The Mathers from Orlando. Norma Herndon, from Sanford. Fern Wentworth, a lovely girl of exquisite and delicate blond radiance, and her cousin Marlene. Donnie Moore and his wife. Rollie Stevens, who operated a rum running boat out of Bimini, and his girl. As a present Rollie had brought a five-gallon wicker-covered jug of Bacardi. Frances Warner, who was celebrating one of her frequent divorces, breezed in with a new boy friend who seemed a little awed by the amount of liquor being consumed. No one made an attempt at bartending. The guests poured what they wanted when they wanted it; either from what they had brought with them or what was handy. The Victrola, with an automatic return, played "Valencia" over and over without end and no one paid any attention to it over the conversation. People kept dropping in, singly or in pairs. Lonnie and Margaret, Marion Kincaid, Liz Eastman, Jack and Roberta Greene, Jim and Sis Lawrence. They came laughing and talking. Everyone had known everyone else for years and now they were all again once more at ease and without the pressure of a "big deal" to worry and nag. Secretly, they were all a little relieved that it was over.

"Damned if I hadn't forgotten how much fun it could be just being one's self again." Lonnie looked up over a bottle of Scotch he had brought and was opening. "Remember how we used to do something like this before everyone began to worry about getting rich?"

Outside there was the noisy clattering of Bunk Ohler's truck as it shuddered to a halt. In it was the cork-fringed, folded mat of the big seine. Stashed around it were a huge iron kettle, gallons of cooking oil, a sack of water-ground corn meal, salt, ice water, pots of home-baked beans fragrant with the smell of molasses and the squares of crusted pork glistening on top. Bunk had a young Negro boy to take the outside end of the net. He waited, now, on the seat, his eyes shining with excitement.

"How you, Toddy?" Bunk waved to everyone and grinned. "Ah'm the only one Toddy heah don't mind bein' called Toddy by. Now"—he poured himself a dollop of Lonnie's Scotch—"if you all will finish up your drinkin' we'll go get us some fish." He popped his lips with appreciation over the Scotch and winked at Tod.

With dimmed lights the trail of cars followed Bunk's truck down the quiet, hard-packed beach. Bunk stood up, hands on hips, scanning the ocean which had flattened out beneath the west wind. No one was ever sure what he looked for or what he saw but when he decided to make the haul there were fish in the area selected.

First there was the fire to lay and set up near the fringe of dunes where the sand was powdery soft and white. Then boards were laid over a couple of sawhorses to make a table. When the fire burned down a little the kettle was filled with oil and set to heating. Then everyone had another drink and trooped to the water's edge. Bunk, with both bare feet planted firmly, would bend back against the heavy staff of the net's shore end. The Negro boy would wade out and, finally, swim, drawing the seine into a long crescent. When he came to the shallows again everyone would lend a hand, hauling in the heavy pocket. The bright silver fish shone with an almost transparent brilliance as they fought and leaped against the mesh. Quickly Bunk and the boy sorted, tossing away the many fine blue crabs, the small hammerhead sharks, the whiting, menhaden, cat and other trash fish. From the catch they selected only the hand-sized pompano and mullet. These were quickly scaled, gutted, washed, rolled in corn meal and dropped like doughnuts into the boiling oil. Fish, cooked this way and only minutes out of the water, were indescribably delicious. Paper plates were heaped. Everyone ate with his or her fingers, breaking off the brown crusted pieces from small bones.

Tod, lying back with his head in Fern's lap, sighed his contentment. The sky was heavily dusted with the powdering of stars, the moon a slender sickle.

"It's good to slow down again. I had almost forgotten how. This is the way it used to be. Everyone knew everyone else and life was uncomplicated. No one planned very much. Things just happened and when they did it was usually fun." He paused thoughtfully. "All of a sudden things stopped being fun and no one had time for laughter. I'm not sure we made a good trade."

Fern leaned back, resting her weight on one elbow. She and Tod had arrived at a curiously remote emotional attachment which puzzled her. Now and then, when business had brought him to Sanford, he usually called and they had a date. Other than that they saw each other no more than once a year when the family came to Daytona's beach for the summer.

"I thought you'd be married by now." Her fingers trailed across his temple. "I heard there was a girl you were seeing a lot of."

"I didn't really have time for that, either." He bent his head to look up at her. "What about you?"

"Oh!" She smiled. "I shop around a little but I'm selective. I don't want any bargain basement specials, reduced for a quick sale. When it happens I'll let you know. In the meanwhile, it's nice to be with you this way. When you're quiet and not thinking of anything else. Sometimes, when you were in Sanford, I had the feeling of being something like a hot cup of coffee you snatched up between trains with your eyes on the station clock. You're nicer now, easy to be with, relaxed and, maybe, for a little while at least, I'll be your girl and you my fellow. 'We'll kiss and sigh in a daisy's eye and make love on a green, grass pillow.' "

Rollie Stevens had brought his guitar and he sang now; some of the Conch and Negro songs he had picked up in the Bahama Out Islands. The colored boy moved quietly, gathering up the discarded paper plates and cups, the empty bottles. He halted in the shadows now and then to listen to Rollie's mimicry of a Bahamian boatman. Couples and small groups were stretched out around the fire's perimeter. The waves brushed with a whispering sound against the beach and the west wind fretted and played among the yielding clusters of sea oats. There was an aura of contentment surrounding the group. At the moment no one wanted more than he had.

September came and the wind, throughout the long summer months, had moved through all the compass readings and finally settled in the northeast. The seasonal change was all but imperceptible, but there. The air had a small, nibbling bite in early morning. The ocean now frequently reared in heavy, leaden waves and its voice took on a deeper note. The autumnal equinox was shaping itself.

Miami and the other resort towns along the east coast had shaken themselves into a semblance of recovery. Miami in particular was looking forward to a big tourist season. New merchandise stocked the shelves, the hotels were being readied for the winter opening. Everyone, from taxi driver to restaurant owner, spoke hopefully of the visitors who would bring with them the welcome dollars. No one expected a resurgence of the boom, no one wanted it right now. Florida would be happy with a moderately prosperous season and an eventual slow and orderly development. The state, they all felt, had so much to offer.

The Grace Line freighter *New York*, bound out of her last port of call, rode heavily laden. Behind her lay Barranquilla, in Colombia. The first officer had the watch and he looked down from the bridge at the last of the broad, muddy stream of the Magdalena River as it poured out into the ocean. He felt the curiously heavy slap of wind on his cheek as it passed and was gone. Later in the day, in the Caribbean, a fishing boat working in the waters around the Islas de la Bahía was unexpectedly spun about with the sudden force of a wind which seemed to come from nowhere and as mysteriously vanished. The men glanced up at a cloudless sky and shrugged.

Still later, small bits of information could have been put together to form a vague pattern but no one bothered. This was a restless thing, prowling fitfully through the Yucatan Channel and into the Gulf of Mexico where it disappeared. Then, defying all order, it blew up again, whirling through the Windward Passage, between Haiti and Cuba, spinning out across Long Island, in the Bahamas. It was a mild disturbance of unpredictable caprice. For almost ten days it skittered with a lunatic abandon around the Gulf of Mexico. No one could really call it a storm or the threat of one. Then, at daybreak on the sixteenth of September, a boatman hovering over the cranky engine of his boat in the Miami River was surprised to see a dozen or more frigate birds swoop in from outside. They were followed by wheeling gulls and pelicans and they all moved up the river to the sheltered sections. Farther north, on the New River, at Fort Lauderdale, the Halifax and Tomoka rivers around Daytona, the same thing was happening. Fowl which seldom left the ocean or beaches were instinctively seeking a sanctuary.

In Miami the Weather Bureau's barometer dropped to an unheard of 27.61 and warnings were immediately broadcast to all craft and floating equipment. Yachtsmen and small boat owners worked to secure their craft, gazing often at the sky which, as yet, carried no threat. The warnings were repeated frequently throughout the day.

In the coastal towns the people unhappily went about the task of putting up hurricane shutters. Plate-glass windows in the stores and offices were boarded over. Home owners on the beach grumblingly ordered their gardeners to get out the protective wooden sheaths for picture windows and doors. Umbrellas, garden furniture, pads and lounging chairs from the pools were gathered and stacked in garages. As an additional precaution flashlights were checked and someone sent down to the store for a supply of fresh batteries. The food supplies were checked and an order telephoned in to the grocer. Those who had lived through tropical storms before filled bottles and containers with fresh water. Then they walked outside and stood in silent contemplation of the sea, which had begun to rock with a heavy motion.

In the orange groves men walked among their trees and wondered if they would survive a really bad storm. The crop looked good, the market was firm. Every tree represented an X number of badly needed dollars. The operators of roadside souvenir stands apprehensively felt the flimsy canvas awnings, tested unstable counters and wondered whether they should pack everything up—the stuffed alligators, the illustrated booklets, coral necklaces, snakeskin purses, crystallized orange and grapefruit peel, pocket knives inlaid with mother-of-pearl and a picture of a Seminole chief in color. It would be a hell of a job and maybe the storm would veer off anyhow.

As hurricane reports were broadcast people in the towns along the coast gathered on street corners to exchange bits of news and opinions. A bad storm, one with real destructive power, would scare off hundreds of persons who had planned a winter trip to Florida. The loss in revenue might really cripple things again. Why the hell did something like this have to happen now? With an assumed wisdom they held a wet finger to the wind or peered knowingly at the sky. Others, more venturesome, took walks along the beaches. Here the waves seemed to rise straight up and fall with a crashing rumble. Spume rolled itself into flying balls which looked like frosted tumbleweed. They bounced and careened along the breakers' edge. Slowly the force of the wind picked up. It held steady now out of the northeast and the sky was filled with a curious half-light, ominous and disturbingly eerie. Against the yellowish glow the lighthouses at Jupiter and Cape Canaveral were stark shafts, heavily crayoned lines drawn against the horizon.

As the Weather Bureau plotted the hurricane's course it became apparent that Miami would be struck with its total fury. The city braced itself for catastrophe. Most of the people in the metropolitan area and its outlying districts had taken what precautionary measures they could. Now there was nothing to do but wait and hope for a miracle which would turn the whirling monster out to sea. The rain came first in a hail-like curtain. Biscayne Bay steamed from its impact. It swept with a heavy scythe up and down the hissing streets, flooding the gutters, pouring into the drains until they were choked and unable to swallow the cascading torrent. The water began to rise with no place to go. It rushed down the streets toward the bay; spilled up over the curbings and worked its way beneath the doors of banks, stores and restaurants along Flagler. It seemed a deserted city. Only an occasional police car moved cautiously, throwing out broad fans of spray. No pedestrian ventured along the boiling sidewalks.

Steadily, throughout the day, the velocity of the wind rose. Where it had free passage it roared with a blasting rage. It howled and shrieked around the corners of buildings, the sound rising to a continuous whistling on a high, shrill note. On Miami Beach the sea piled higher and higher, eating at the beach and breakwaters. A wind gauge spun so fast it became an indistinct blur and registered a force of over one hundred and thirty miles an hour before it was blown away. Heavy scuds of clouds now marched in a tremendous procession from the northeast and the sun's feeble light was blotted out. The trees which man had planted along the strand were torn out by the roots and propelled through the air like shafted missiles from a giant's catapult. Chairs and tables, neglected or overlooked, were whirled up and out in an insane pattern of deadly shrapnel. Bricks from chimneys were plucked out one by one before the exposed flue collapsed in a shower of masonry. Here and there a shingled roof lifted and sighed back as though the structure supporting it was breathing deeply and expelling the air, forcing off the cover.

All electric power in Miami and the surrounding communities had been shut off. There was no telephone service. The radios were dead. Overhead wires whipped and curled with a lashing fury as they were torn loose from quivering poles. Ditches paralleling the dirt roads in the country overflowed. The volume of rain became so great the sandy soil could no longer absorb it. Flatlands were sodden. Flimsy shingled roofs of farm families were torn away to be spun overhead with sections of fence and outhouses. Chickens and small animals, cats, rabbits, dogs and pigs, were picked up and hurled aloft in an incredible spectacle. Pines were ripped from the earth. The oaks, with their silver-gray drapings of Spanish moss, seemed to take on the appearance of gnarled old men cowering in their shoddy garments.

Along Miami's bayfront the wind ripped and looted. Up from the gentle slope, in the business section from Seventh Street southward, signs were torn from overhead mountings and went sailing through the air. What were once streets had become impassable rivers. Then the storefront windows began to go. They were not blown in but sucked out by the terrific pull of an infuriated Nature.

In a lesser degree the east coast, as far north as Fernandina, near Jacksonville, felt the incredible impact of the hurricane's passing. Palm Beach became a wasteland. The magnificent groves of Australian pines and royal palms were leveled, and carefully tended shrubbery ripped apart in ugly shreds. Debris filled the air and tidal waves rose ten feet above normal. Lake Worth and Hobe Sound were churned and filled with hapless craft torn from moorings and boathouses. The ocean chewed insatiably at the dunes. The world became a vacuum in which it was difficult to breathe and the air had the peculiar odor which arises from a mammoth electrical discharge. Along the Indian River orange groves were flattened and broken, torn by savage hands into a tangle of ruin. Large farming areas were devastated and crops totally lost. Water in Lake Okeechobee rose and overflowed, flooding and destroying rich farming land. Everywhere the destruction was all but complete. Florida, which each year braced itself for the equinoctial storms, and was accustomed to rampaging winds and torrential rains, had never known such a hurricane as this one.

In Daytona waves from the river broke high over the seawall and poured into Beach Street. Few of the business establishments were open but the drugstores maintained a clerk and pharmacist for emergency calls. For awhile telegraph and telephone lines were down and the town was isolated. Now and then there were brief lulls, moments and minutes of dead calm which were almost more frightening than the wind.

Across the river, residents of beach front homes tried to peer out through the opaque shield of rain and flying scud. They could not see beyond their windows. The ocean, with an insatiable appetite, consumed one full line of the high dunes and relentlessly gnawed at a second. Half of the pier extending out from where, long ago, Keating's Casino stood, was torn away and the few remaining black pilings were skeletal remains. Rain, driven by the relentless force of the wind, forced itself beneath weatherstripped doors and windows. Floors were four and five inches deep in sluggish water. Men and women mopped ceaselessly, trying to blot up the flood with heavy Turkish towels or bath mats. They would stop on hands and knees, close to exhaustion, and then grin helplessly at each other. Light pieces of furniture began to float in slow circles. Now and then the residents would say to hell with it and go to the kitchen for a drink, staring bleakly outside. Then they returned doggedly to the all but impossible task. They soaked the towels, wrung them out into buckets and seemed to make no impression at all on the flood.

Lying north of the hurricane belt, Daytona had experienced the seasonal storms. They were, sometimes, bad but marginal. Considerable damage was done to gardens, trees and shrubs. Now and then the roof of a small structure would collapse but there was never any real disaster. Because of this many of the beach residents had come to regard the gale warnings as an excuse to give a party. There would be gatherings in the houses with food and plenty of liquor stashed in the kitchen. Candles and oil lamps were trimmed and readied; an oil stove for cooking brought in from the garage or storerooms in case power and gas were shut off. Everyone was invested with a holiday mood. They drank, made love, scooped or mopped at the gathering water and turned the whole thing into a day and night fiesta. The wind howled, the house shuddered, the rain pelted. The lights went out and there was no current for the radios, so everyone was oblivious of the hurricane's force, destruction or its direction. The elementary power outside created an odd state of excitement which was difficult to explain.

The Lathrop house was overflowing. Everyone had brought "a jug" or two as a precautionary measure against the storm's duration. Beer was tucked into washtubs filled with cracked ice. A large pot of chili simmered on the kerosene stove. Everyone was barefoot. The men had trousers cuffed to the knee and the women gathered their skirts between bare legs and pinned them to form a pannier effect. Now and then when the water rose on the floor they sloshed happily around, attacking it with mops and buckets. The Victrola ground out "Bye,

Bye, Blackbird" or Whispering Jack Smith sang "When the Red, Red Robin Comes Bob, Bob, Bobbin' Along."

Tod replaced the telephone receiver in its cradle. Fern Woodward, sitting on the arm of his chair, watched the frown of concern gather on his face.

"Nothing?"

"No. It's still dead. I wish I knew what was happening down around Miami."

"Would it make things any better?"

"No." He half smiled an acceptance of the truth. "I guess not. But I can't help worrying about the Stalath Motel. I'd hate to lose it. It's my firstborn."

"You're insured, aren't you?"

"Yes, but I'm not certain the policy covers hurricanes. I had Keith write it up and then never read it or thought to ask. That's a pretty stupid admission to make." He arose, took her hand and walked to a window. There was nothing to be seen but the rain as it was slashed by a knifing wind. "If I thought I had a chance I'd get in the car and drive down."

"You'd never make it. Please don't try."

"No. I guess not." There was a high peal of laughter from the kitchen. He smiled and shook his head. "I don't know why, but a storm always seems to loosen the inhibitions. The joint is filled with abandoned wenches and predatory males. Let's get a drink."

Clint glanced up as they entered. He understood Tod's restlessness. No news out of Miami was bad news. The motel was more than a building. It represented an idea.

"Lines still dead?"

Tod nodded and reached for a bottle of rum. The house quivered from an unusually heavy blast. "I'm almost tempted to try and get down there and see what's happened." He poured a drink.

"You wouldn't get across the bridge here." Clint shook his head. "Your car would take off like a kite. Anyhow, I'd think the roads must be clogged with a thousand trees and more falling all the time. Numb yourself a little with some rum and sweat it out."

The hurricane cut its path of destruction across Florida, turned and roared back over southern Georgia and up the coast to strike around New Bern, in North Carolina, before veering out to sea. The damage to Florida was appalling. Hundreds of persons had been killed, thousands injured. Crops were ruined, roads washed out, fine homes along the beach fronts wrecked or so badly damaged they had to be rebuilt. Housing developments, inspired by the boom, were leveled into heaps of unrecognizable rubble. The Red Cross set up emergency shelters to care for the homeless but these were inadequate. Citizens Committees were formed to alleviate the misery. Many towns, which had escaped the fury, voluntarily raised funds and sent them to less fortunate areas.

Tod walked about what was once the Stalath Motel and kicked unhappily at the tangled piles of brick, lumber and mortar. Both wings of the structure had been demolished. Oddly enough the dining room had survived but its gaping windows now stared upon uprooted flower beds, gardens and driveways which looked as if they had been plowed by a bulldozer. Newly planted palms, Australian pines, orange and Chinese plum trees, were stricken and lay atop of one another like a log fortification. Verne and Dale Chastine followed silently as he made the tour of inspection. They halted at the entranceway. The marle drive was gutted into deep furrows. Lamp standards had been blown away and the ground was covered with sparkling shards of glass.

"We were doing so nicely." Verne was close to tears.

Tod turned. "We'll rebuild it, Verne; build it better this time; incorporate some of the things we learned from the first one—larger rooms, different lighting arrangements, tubs and showers instead of just showers."

"I know." Verne was disconsolate. "We were sure you wouldn't give up. Everyone who stopped with us thought it was the most wonderful thing. Before they left most of them made a special trip to the office to tell us how nice everything and everyone had been."

"Well." Tod lit a cigarette and gazed at the sky. It seemed impossible such destruction had come from that bright, cloudless dome. "I'll get a crew out here to clean things up and then we'll start on a new one with double the capacity. The general plan will be the same so I think we can salvage the dining room. To hell with that," he suddenly decided. "We'll build it all new and with an outdoor terrace on the dining room, and maybe a swimming pool. It will be a showpiece."

He was enthusiastic again. "I want you and Dale to stay on during the construction."

"You don't have to do that." Dale spoke quickly. "I mean, Verne and I can get along. We'll find something temporary."

"This isn't charity." Tod waved away the objection. "There will be plenty for you to do. I'll see if I can rent or buy one of those trailer homes. I'd like you to live on or near the premises. When we're in business again I think we'll name this one Stalath Number Two. If anyone asks where Number One is just say it ran away with a hurricane. Number Two sounds more impressive anyhow."

Bent a little by two successive shocks, the east coast of Florida began to rebuild. Millions of dollars in insurance money poured into the state and construction boomed again. Labor became short. Carpenters, masons, plumbers and electricians were forced to ration their services. The tourist season was hurt but not irreparably; people would forget the disaster and when winter blanketed the North they would want to head South. Slowly but determinedly businessmen, hotel operators and home owners moved to clear the ruins and build anew.

* XVII * *

THE signs had been there all along but almost everyone was traveling at such a dizzy speed that few bothered to slow down and read what was so plainly written.

Herbert Hoover had been elected President. Now there was to be a chicken in every pot, two cars in each garage. The stock market was hitched to a skyrocket which had only one place to go, up. Trading moved to new and speculative heights. Everyone from waiters and manicurists to retired admirals and bootblacks had a piece of the action. Housewives, meeting in the markets, no longer talked of the price of eggs. Instead they spoke knowingly of Du Pont, RCA and Standard Oil of New Jersey. It was so simple. You put down a small margin and watched the stock go up. Brokers' loans were made with a free hand and careless gesture. It was all part of the "go now—pay later" philosophy. What had happened in Florida only two or three years ago was now being duplicated nationally. No stock was so obscure, no new issue so shaky that they could not find eager buyers. No one looked behind the curtain to see who was manipulating the strings. The puppets danced and Judy whacked Punch over the head with a board to the delighted laughter of all. A few Cassandras raised their voices but no one listened to their prophecies. Some of the skeptical asked: If this is all so wonderful why are the industrial towns in New England bleak with unemployment and dying? How does it happen that mill workers in North Carolina, laboring eleven hours a day, receive only twenty cents an hour for the unending drudgery? Why are there deep pockets of miserable poverty in the South where the average wage for a woman is nine dollars a week and the men can only earn eighteen? What is happening in places like Gastonia, North Carolina, where the mill hands ask only for a decent living and the State Troops are called out to shove them into docile, beaten lines? Who has the chickens and the cars? Who, for that matter, has the pot? No one had any answers. As a matter of fact few even heard the questions.

Florida had enjoyed two booming tourist seasons. Everyone, it seemed, was loaded. The new and glitteringly magnificent hotels on Miami Beach were crowded. The men, soft, paunchy but determined to live it up, lolled in the shade of their cabañas, smoked two-dollar Havana cigars and put a flame to them with the solid gold Dunhill lighters. They brought with them their wives or mistresses or sometimes, both. The women wore their diamonds to the beach and sighed after the young life guards atop their towers. Gambling casinos were open day and night. Liquor boats shuttled continuously between Nassau or Bimini. Sleek call girls drove to their clients in LaSalle convertibles. Up and down the coast there had been a resurgence of private building. Elaborate homes rose in lush estates. New yachts and speedboats were packed into the marinas while the Stock Exchange ticker tape unrolled, carrying its message of plenty. It became the confetti of a never-ending carnival.

To those who first waded and then dove into the exhilarating waters of the market, the brokers were magicians who held the secret of unbelievable wealth. What one bought today could be sold tomorrow at a profit. Wall Street brokers had loans of almost seven billion dollars—more than the total amount of money in circulation throughout the country. The Federal Reserve Board was urged to curb the speculation by raising the discount rate. It refused. The National City Bank, of New York, offered to loan twenty million dollars to brokers at 15 percent interest. Huge corporations banded together and advanced close to eight hundred million dollars in "call money" to the brokers. The skyrocket soared, colored lights filled the sky. The question: "Is Everybody Happy?" was asked from the stage of the *Ziegfeld Follies* and everyone shouted back: *"Yes!"*

A few responsible persons in Florida who had survived the state's boom and collapse saw the same thing happening to the nation. No one, it seemed, ever learned anything from a disaster. Those who had gone under didn't count. The survivors were again filled with an optimistic fervor. This was no bubble. How could it be? Weren't the most astute financiers in the country making daily predictions of a greater prosperity and a more bountiful way of life for everyone? After all, if men like J. P. Morgan, Charles Mitchell, Andrew Mellon, Charles Schwab and even the President of the United States didn't know what they were talking about, who did?

Tod walked around it all for awhile. But he was the inveterate gambler who knew perfectly well he was going to take a seat; the alcoholic with a bottle in the kitchen who knew he would, sooner or later, pull the cork.

A branch office of a New York brokerage firm was opened on Beach Street. For almost everyone this was a new and certainly more refined form of gambling. Taking their places in the comfortable chairs facing the blackboard they could feel themselves as one with Du Pont, General Motors, A. T. & T. or Standard Oil. They were in the company of tycoons; the industrial giants who shaped a nation. They chewed upon their cigars, ground out cigarettes in silver ashtrays, scowled or leaned forward as a trim young woman chalked frequent changes on the board. They felt themselves to be keen of mind in this rarefied atmosphere where the legendary figures strode. This was no reckless plunging, no wild gambling. How could it be; here in this room with soft lighting, softer cushions, the subdued chatter of the ticker and a general air of solemnity appropriate to a temple of high finance or a mortuary?

Several times over the past three years Tod had considered leaving Florida. He had friends in New York, men he had been with in college. There had to be, he told himself, a market for an aggressive talent, a flair for promotion. Florida real estate moved slowly and in small parcels. Stalath Corporation was little more than a name lettered on the Beach Street office. The motel outside of Miami was profitable but unspectacular. The Citrus Belt received a fair return. He could leave and things would almost run themselves. But this was his home, and deep within him rested the conviction that Florida was firmly rooted with Tod Lathrop's destiny. Experimentally at first, and then boldly and with more confidence, he began moving his capital into the stock market. The trading was astonishingly easy. Stocks were bought on margin, requiring a minimum outlay of cash. What was purchased today increased in value tomorrow. Everyone was making money. Conditions were such that it was all but impossible to lose. If one stock dipped, requiring additional margin, than another rose to supply it. A bright youngster with a grammar school knowledge of figures could play this game.

Now each morning, and usually accompanied by Will Lathrop, Tod took his place in the brokerage office. The ticker, with its direct wire to New York, spoke with controlled excitement. This was the voice of the crap table's "stickman," the chant of the croupier at the roulette wheel, the words of the faro dealer in a no-limit game. It was generally recognized that certain regular customers always occupied the same seats. No one, save an occasional tourist, would think of intruding upon these unreserved reservations. When this did happen, someone would lean over and whisper an explanation. There would be a hurried, and almost embarrassed, exchange of places.

Will Lathrop took no active part in the trading. The morning trips with his grandson uptown were a diversion, for there was little he cared about doing these days. He went, as he said, "just to see what all the damn fools are up to, and because I don't see much of you anymore and you are one of the few persons in whose company I find a certain amount of mystified pleasure."

When the market closed for the day Tod would drive Will home. They would have a drink or two on the front porch and watch evening settle on the river. Sometimes, and without asking the old gentleman's permission, Tod would turn over the South Bridge and down Atlantic Avenue to the beach house. Dennis Lathrop was almost always at home. He was cordial and, apparently, honestly glad to see his father. The old man's vitality never ceased to astonish him. Will Lathrop, he once calculated, must be close to ninety. But his mind was still sharp and he moved freely and without an assisting hand. They had, though, little in common and found small talk difficult.

Once Will had blurted, "Damn it, Dennis my boy, how does it happen you never seem to have any fun?"

"I'm amused in my own quiet way, Father." Dennis refused to be drawn into a discussion of his private life.

The truth was that he found his life almost unendurably lonely and without purpose. Alice Lathrop had died the year before. They had been making plans for the summer in North Carolina. She had looked up and smiled with affection at her husband's enthusiasm and then, suddenly, slumped forward in her chair. The doctor diagnosed it as a stroke, a cerebral hemorrhage. There had been no warning and Dennis was completely unprepared for the loneliness. Once, half jokingly, he had said to her, "Have you ever thought that when all is said and done we don't have anything but each other? Oh, I suppose Tod would mourn a little. Perhaps my father would be momentarily subdued if either or both of us should die. A few friends would say: 'Isn't it too bad about Dennis Lathrop?' Then they would go on about their affairs. But the truth is that if and when we lose each other the one who stays behind will have nothing." The bare fact of this was now a constant companion. After Alice Lathrop's funeral, which Will Lathrop attended reluctantly and with outspoken annoyance over "a damn bad display, a barbaric orgy with a Presbyterian witch doctor," Tod suggested to his father that he move to the river house.

"We can come over here for the summers," he urged. "I really think Grandfather Will would like to have your company even though he'd never admit it. Also, it would make things much simpler. I could sort of shuttle back and forth between you."

"I'll be all right, boy." Dennis had smiled at his son's concern. "I won't say I'm not lonely but the empty place Alice left can't be filled with someone or anything else. Come over when you feel like it but don't think there is an obligation."

Tod told his grandfather of the conversation and Will snorted his impatience.

"Your father was a good boy. He went on to be a good man. Personally, I find such consistency a little nauseating. Of course he's welcome here if he wants to come. But hell, boy, what would we talk about? Somewhere along the road Dennis lost his sense of purpose. I'm not sure when or why. Purpose is important." He caught the beginning of a grin on his grandson's face. "Oh! So you don't think I had one? Well, you're wrong. My purpose was to lead a life exactly as I pleased. By God, I did it too!" He leaned back, eyeing Tod. "I'd say you have a purpose although I'm not certain what it is. You've certainly put out a lot of energy and I can't see anyone doing that unless he had a reason or was feebleminded."

"I'm going to make a lot of money."

"Why?" The question was sharp.

"For the fun of it. You don't understand that, do you?" He leaned forward. "I mean just one hell of a lot of money. The kind of money they talk about in Texas. Well, I'm going to make it here and have fun doing it. It isn't too easy to explain. But if I stand at a dice table and win a hundred dollars I feel better than if I lost a hundred. The hundred in itself doesn't mean anything but I guess, deep down, everyone wants to be a winner. It makes him feel smarter than the fellow who loses. Maybe it isn't an exalted ambition but it's mine, my purpose."

"All right then. Stick to it." Will Lathrop pulled at an ear and his eyes brightened. "About your father. We get along fine with a river separating us. I don't think we ought to press our luck."

So the two establishments had been maintained. There was little, save an occasional inspection tour of the Citrus Belt routes and branch offices, or a run down to Miami to check up on the motel, to occupy Tod's time. He spent two or three evenings a week with his father. They'd have a few drinks, drive down to Gardners, at Port Orange, for fried shrimp or to New Smyrna for stone crabs. They were pleasantly companionable but the real intimacy existed between grandfather and grandson. Will Lathrop had a spirit to match Tod's.

"You ought to get into this market." Tod casually made the suggestion to his grandfather over breakfast one morning.

The old man looked up and over a half of stewed guava he had spooned from a bowl. Then he slid the syrupy, fragrantly pink fruit to his plate and added a squeeze of lime.

"Why? I have all the money I need and no desire to build a fortune for any of my relatives. Let them scratch for it as I did." He cut the guava in half.

Tod screened a smile with a coffee cup. The old gentleman now liked to pretend he had worked his way up from an apprentice boy or chimney sweep. He conveniently forgot he had married into a comfortable fortune. It was one of the poses which Tod found constantly diverting.

"Besides," Will continued, "when this thing blows up as it must there will be a lot of scalded asses around—yours included. I'll keep a little bear's grease for you to put on the blisters." He ate the guava. "Why don't you get out while you're ahead?"

"I'm not far enough ahead, yet. When I am I'll quit."

Will shook his head. "During my life I have rarely seen a man able to walk away from a table while he was winning. It takes character. When I was in college I played a lot of poker. Those who were losing always tried to convince the winners it was unsporting to quit winner. They did their best to set up some sort of a gentleman's code. I said, What the hell is a winner supposed to do; stay until he is a loser and the losers winners? When I had a good stack and felt like it I'd say, Cash me in. I wasn't too popular, sometimes, but by God, I was usually solvent."

"There isn't any reason for me to get out now." Tod glanced at his watch. "I'm not speculating in wildcat stuff. It's all blue chip. A.T. & T., General Motors, RCA, Du Pont. Swift & Co., New York Central, General Electric. Westinghouse. Standard Oil. If those things go under, the whole country sinks."

Actually, he was deeper in the market than he cared to admit but any real danger was almost inconceivable. Values might slip here and there but they always rallied. This was the chance he had been waiting for. When the figures and his instinct told him to get out he could close an account a couple of million ahead. To this end he had mortgaged the Stalath Motel and borrowed on his seventy-five percent interest in the Citrus Belt Line. He knew there were intangible assets in the real estate he still owned. At the moment land was only a small drain. The taxes were negligible. The value was there and he intended to hold everything he had. The stock market, though, was the horn of plenty. With cash he could expand the activities of Stalath. Cuba was offering all sorts of incentives to American capital. The island's tourist trade boomed, and to accommodate it Cuba wanted new hotels and casinos, and outside investment was invited to come in on a ten-year, tax-free basis. The profits here could be enormous. Also, for some time he had been watching the slow buildup of the tourist invasion of the Bahamas. Nassau was all but overrun and there were opportunities for luxury resorts and clubs in the Out Islands. To move into Cuba and the Bahamas he needed ready money. The stock market would supply it. He smiled a little to himself thinking how quickly panic seized those who really had no heart for a big gamble. A week ago there had been a heavy decline. Orders to sell had poured in on Wall Street. Those who were caught short took a licking. Those who had the guts and the cold nerve of a gambler took everything they had, put up additional margin and waited for the hot dice to roll. Sure enough, the big money stepped in as he had been certain it would. J. P. Morgan & Co. voted $240,000,000 in support. Others followed with orders to buy and buy. The slide was checked, then halted. Slowly, out of the confused uncertainty, the market began to rise. New confidence displayed itself. J. P. Morgan certainly must know what he was doing. If he didn't who did? The gamblers were reassured and key stocks were again off on a soaring flight.

Tod rose. "Want to drive uptown with me this morning?"

Will shook his head. "No. I think I'll just sit around and watch the fish jump in the river."

Tod nodded and glanced down at the unread morning paper. The date, he noticed absently, was October 29th. Right now the big sea bass were running in the surf down around the red shell section of the beach across from New Smyrna. For a moment he was tempted to let the market alone for the day and drive down for some fishing. He put the idea aside. There would be other bass runs; other days to fish.

On that black and frightening day in October the impossible occurred. What couldn't happen did happen and an era came to a shattering close. In the panic which seemed to grip all men thirty billion dollars vanished while frantic efforts were made to salvage something of the Golden Dream. Sixteen million shares were traded. Margin calls could not be met. Thousands and thousands of investors caught short begged for time—a few hours. There was no time. Homes, cars, savings accounts, fortunes and even lives were swept away in the tidal wave of disaster as it swelled up out of Wall Street and engulfed the nation. Tickers in hundreds of brokerage offices from Miami to Seattle continued to pound out the message of doom with an idiotic fury. Finally the machines gave up, for they were unable to keep pace with the trading. In homes and offices, on street corners and speakeasy bars, Fifth Avenue shops and rural grocery stores men and women, the small fish who had believed in the miracle, stared bewilderedly at the paper on which they had been figuring their profits. Numbly they realized now that there were no profits, only the paper. The scanty margins they had been able to scrape up, borrow or beg in a desperate effort to hold on had been erased as the market continued to fall. They had no reserves and were closed out. Some stocks dropped as much as fifty points. This was the Biblical flood of terror.

There were millions, of course, who had not ventured into the market's unfamiliar waters. Now they were smug, holding to the opinion that it served *them* right. The *them*, of course, meant the Wall Street financiers. Few realized that the disaster was not limited to that narrow lane in downtown Manhattan. It moved like a poisonous cloud over the country, searing the land and leaving a desert. Banks would fail, homes be lost, evictions commonplace, wages would be cut and cut again. Mills, factories, great industrial complexes and small businesses were to close their doors. The gaudy era of wonderful nonsense was to be followed by a depression so terrible, so destructive both morally and physically, that its total misery would never be fully comprehended. Professional men, architects, technicians and designers, engineers and lawyers were to stand on bleak street corners in New York, Chicago, Detroit, Los Angeles and Philadelphia. Before them a wooden crate would hold a tiny mound of apples which proud men would try and sell to a hurrying passerby for a nickel. College graduates, skilled mechanics, actors, writers, artists, businessmen and the perpetually unemployed were to shuffle together in long lines before the free soup kitchens and Salvation Army centers. For millions of persons life was to revert to the elemental—a hole in which to sleep, a bone on which to gnaw. Haggard men would appear on the nation's streets with a FOR SALE sign hanging by a soiled piece of string around their necks. All of this was to happen despite a President's assurance that "there is nothing in the situation to be disturbed about."

But in the first week or ten days after the walls had come tumbling down, few persons were able to see beyond their own, personal concerns. They moved, walked and talked in an incredulous daze, asking themselves: How could this happen to me?

Tod parked his car high on the beach near the crescent point of the inlet and stared unseeingly at the ocean. It moved with a heavy thunder and the wave crests were whipped away by a cold November gale. He reached for a pint flask of whisky in the glove compartment and then put it away. There was a small, frosty light in his eyes. The flask was sterling silver, encased in a fine pigskin casing. Brother, can you spare a dime?

Every dollar he could scrape together had been fed into the insatiable demand for more and more margin. He refused to believe, as did almost everyone else, that this was the end. The market had to rally. The possibility of the total collapse of a great nation's economy could not be conceived. If a man could only hold on. But a man couldn't. He fell and the pit seemed bottomless.

"You're broke, Stoddard Lathrop. You're flat on your naked ass." He said these things aloud and the words were caught and blown away.

Everything he had so carefully husbanded and salvaged from the explosion of Florida's land boom had gone into the futile effort of trying to cling to what he had for a few more hours or days. Now the banks would foreclose on the Stalath Motel, the Citrus Belt Line, and even the scattered pieces of real estate with their dubious current value. He took out his wallet and thumbed through the bills. One hundred and eighty-five dollars. Stoddard Lathrop. Age 36. Occupation? Assets? At the moment he could find no answer to those questions. Everything, he mused, had been made to appear too simple, so easy. There had been no real test of ability. He had no idea what Stoddard Lathrop's potential was. A well-mannered, decently clothed half-wit could have made money in Florida during the boom. As a matter of fact, and he did smile then, many of them did. But, and this bothered him a little, he had never experienced any real pressure. He had been reared in security and carried this with him unconsciously, like a shield. Even now it provided a certain defense. He was broke but he didn't feel broke or poor or beaten.

He was annoyed because he had been a damn fool. That, also, he thought was all right. A man was entitled to make mistakes but only if he was willing to pick up the tab. He couldn't turn to family or friends and say: Let's split the check on this one. Here and now, alone on the beach, he had to decide what to do. Oh, he was aware that he still had a measure of security. His father's house and his grandfather's were his. But this wasn't enough. He couldn't rock away the days on the front porch waiting for something to happen. I'd better get damn mad about something, he told himself.

A copy of the Jacksonville *Times-Union* lay on the seat. He picked it up. There was a front-page story on the suicides which had followed the market crash. Men, unable to face the ruin, had put a revolver to a throbbing temple and pulled the trigger. Others had leaped from skyscraper windows. The *Times-Union* also reported a current vaudeville joke. A man went into the Waldorf and asked for a room. The clerk wanted to know if it was for sleeping or jumping. A wry bit of laughter escaped Tod. He shook his head, marveling at the macabre imagination which could fashion such nonsense within the cyclone of disaster. There was one thing about living in Daytona. Jumping from a window to commit suicide was almost impossible. There was nothing, except the Clarendon Hotel, higher than two stories.

He snapped on the ignition switch and started the motor. Driving northward he could feel the car sway under the impact of the half gale. Ordinarily the wildness of the scene would have delighted him. Today it struck no responsive emotion. He thought he had probably reached the saturation point of excitement. He whistled softly, meditatively. The first thing to do was to get down to Miami and have a talk with the bank holding the paper on the motel and the Citrus Belt Line and see if the president was open to a little reason. If so he might be able to continue operating. It wouldn't be the same, of course. He would be an employee. The bank certainly didn't know anything about running a motel or a bus and trucking outfit. He would take over on a small salary and the revenue would have to be turned in to reduce the mortgage. The idea cheered him. Hell. It wasn't going to be too rough if he kept a sense of proportion. He still had a lot going for him. The whistle rose on a happier note. From riches to rags and back again. He leaned forward, punching the glove compartment button and taking out the flask. For the second time he returned it. There was no fun in drinking alone.

He drove beneath the pier, past the Clarendon and up to the Ormond approach. John D. Rockefeller had a home here and when he was down for the winter he distributed shiny dimes to the community's youngsters. He wondered if Mr. Rockefeller was hurting just a little. It tickled him to think of a Rockefeller trimming his largess to a nickel and saying, "I'm sorry, boys. This is all I can afford."

Chet still ran his speakeasy on the end of a dock across the river. The police and Sheriff's Office knew of Chet's operation but he had never been raided. As a small concession to the proprieties Chet had placed a sign: FISHING TACKLE—BAIT—BOATS on the frame structure housing his illegal but cozy activities. Tourists, hurrying past in their cars, barely noticed the place but Chet never tired of telling the story of one who did. The man came out on the dock to inquire about renting tackle and a skiff. Expressionlessly Chet displayed a warped pole with a few yards of rotted line on a rusted reel. He pointed out the fiddler crabs on the strip of sand at water's edge and declared they made fine bait. The skiff, he admitted gravely, was more of a problem. He and the almost speechless tourist leaned over the wharf and Chet indicated a half-submerged rowboat, voicing the opinion that it probably leaked a little but if the man was a quick bailer he might keep it afloat. The visitor, thoroughly confused by now, stared at Chet incredulously. Then he exploded with impatient anger. "No wonder you damn Crackers never amount to anything." He strode away muttering the threat to report the whole thing to the Chamber of Commerce or the Tourist Bureau.

Tod parked beneath a palmetto tree off the road's shoulder and walked down the dock. The house at the end was neatly kept and painted white with a green trim and shutters of the same color. There was a square central room and an alcove off it where Chet kept the moonshine, Coca-Cola and ice. His wife had put up red and white window curtains and the tables were covered with the same material. The floor was bare and almost white from constant sanding and scrubbing. The illicitly distilled corn whisky was served in old jelly glasses and the quantity measured by Chet's humor. He had brushed off his wife's suggestion that it would be nicer and give the place a certain tone if he put in uniform glassware. Chet pointed out that if they were ever raided there wasn't any point in supplying good glasses for the agents to break or confiscate. So the establishment remained simple, practical and devoted to a single purpose. A man could get a drink of good corn at a reasonable price. Now and then Chet, when he felt like it, would boil up a mess of shrimp or arrange a stack of smoked mullet on a tin plate. These he placed on a table and proudly invited his customers to help themselves to the buffet. He pronounced the word as it was spelled. He had a card printed. BUSINESSMAN'S LUNCH—AND IF YOU AIN'T GOT ANY BUSINESS IT'S FREE ANYHOW. HEP YO'SE'F.

In a corner, near a window overlooking the river, Willie Estes, Francine and a man Tod did not recognize were seated at a table. Willie and Francine looked up as the screen door slapped lightly against the frame in its closing. Willie lifted a hand in lazy greeting.

"How you, Tod boy?" In the mechanical query there was no suggestion of real interest.

"Willie. Francine." Tod nodded and pulled out a chair at the nearest table.

"Come and sit with us, Tod." Francine beckoned to a place beside her.

"I'm only going to stay for a drink."

"All th' more reason to sit, Tod boy." Willie seemed to be exceptionally pleased with himself. "I like buyin' a drink for a one-drink man."

Tod realized he couldn't refuse without being deliberately rude. He took the chair beside Francine and almost immediately felt the abrupt, demanding pressure of her leg against his. He held back a smile. One of these days, he thought, he'd have to get around to Francine.

"This here is Francine's uncle, Reese Sparks from Alabama."

Willie made the introduction and Tod nodded an amiable acknowledgment. Sparks studied him with an unabashed curiosity. His eyes, cold and shrewdly calculating, were the palest blue Tod had ever seen. They glinted as though flecked with mica and their light came not from a humorous nature but from a sharp and appraising interest. He wore a suit of cheap blue serge and the soiled edges of long underwear protruded like a dirty ruffle from shirt and coat sleeves. The hair, thin and red, grew in scattered patches about his head. His face was weathered but not tanned; reddened from long exposure. An Adam's apple the size of a large walnut moved up and down even when he was not speaking.

Chet brought a drink for Tod. No one ever bothered to order the first one since the establishment offered no variety.

"How you, Chet?"

"Fine, Tod. Want some boiled peanuts?"

Tod shook his head, added a little water to the whisky and swirled it about. He was aware of Sparks' intent scrutiny.

"So, you're Willie's partnah?" The question was asked in a dry, rasping voice which even the Alabama accent could not make pleasant.

Tod glanced at Willie and then at the man. "I guess," he admitted drily, "you might say that."

"Hell, I ain' sayin' it. Willie did. Willie's a liah, though. Did you know that?"

"Uncle Reese came down for a visit." Francine's voice betrayed her nervousness.

The man patted her hand and then squeezed it. "I wanted to see this heah little Francine girl again. She an' her mother, my sister, used to come visitin' me some summahs. A damn many a time I chased her around the barn when she was twelve oah thirteen; a ripe age foah pluckin'. I nevah really caught her, though." Sparks made the admission with a matter-of-fact regret. "I neah had her cornered a couple of times but she was slick an' fast."

"A girl around you had to be slick and fast," Francine smirked, "if she wanted to keep her pants on."

Willie belched, crossed his arms on the table and leaned forward upon them. His eyes never left Sparks' face. There was no resentment in his expression. He followed every word with a bright intentness.

Sparks took a swallow of the drink. "I figured"—for some reason he seemed to think all of this was of concern to Tod—"maybe, marriage had slowed her down an' she'd be easier to catch now. So I just got in my car an' drove down heah to see."

"You'll never catch me, you dirty old bastard." Francine made the statement without resentment. She actually seemed entertained. The pressure of her leg against Tod's became more insistent. "I'd just as soon get into bed with a stinkin' alligator."

Sparks opened his mouth for laughter but there was no sound. It was, Tod thought, a fascinating performance. Deliberately he reached over and put a bony, blue-veined hand on Francine's breast. She pushed it away impatiently but not with anger. Willie's glance moved back and forth between the two, his eyes lighting with attention. Tod had the uneasy feeling that he was somehow involved in something dark and obscene which he couldn't understand.

"You know why she don't slap my face, Mr. Lathrop?" He thrust his head forward and his breath was that of decaying offal. "You want to know why Willie don't object?"

"No." Tod was annoyed. "I don't really give a damn."

"It's because Francine and Willie know I got me about a million dollars an' they're figurin' how to get some of it. That's the reason I can feel her titty like I did." He turned abruptly to Willie. "Ain't that right?"

Willie pretended he hadn't heard. He continued to lean on crossed arms watching Sparks with a slack-mouthed pleasure.

Tod finished his drink in a hurried swallow and started to rise. Sparks reached out and put a hand on his wrist. The fingers were strong, talonlike.

"Don't rush off, Mr. Lathrop. I been wantin' to meet you." The voice was wheedling. "I'd sure like to know how you evah got into somethin' with a fella like this heah Willie. It just might be impo'tant."

Despite himself Tod rested back in the chair. There was an ambivalence here he couldn't explain. This foul and grotesque man astonished him. He was so completely repellent, so consummately evil in mind, so ruthless in his goading of Willie who seemed oblivious of what was happening.

"Willie heah," Sparks continued, "figures to screw me out of some of my money. Hell. I don't mind that. Almost everyone's got the same idea. Francine's about the only close kin I got but Willie can't wait foah me to die an' leave her some. He got to have it now."

The astonishing thing about this monologue was that neither Francine nor Willie made any attempt to deny the words. Willie even nodded a slight acknowledgment of the charge.

"Right now, with most of the country flat on its ass, I figure I'm in a good spot for dickerin'. Now, I would share some with Willie if Willie would share some with me." He squinted playfully at Francine.

"You'll never get any of it, you dirty old bastard." Francine was pleasantly entertained. Her knee nudged Tod's with playful intimacy.

"You know somethin', Mr. Lathrop?" Sparks put a match to the ragged end of a long, twisted stogie. "Right now you're wonderin' why you're sittin' heah, listenin' to me instead of gettin' up an' walkin' away like you really want. I'll tell you why. It's because you never come across anyone like me before." He leaned back and drew upon the stogie with satisfaction. "I take to you, Mr. Lathrop, an' that's a fact. I got a feelin' that between us we could screw up a lot of folks an' that's what I like best. I don't mean girl screwin'. I mean people screwin'. I just like to give it to 'em an' then watch 'em squirm on the end of the shaft. It's my real pleasure. You know how I got a million dollars?" He didn't expect a reply. "The Sparks have been livin' in Alabama for maybe two hundred years. They all settled around a little place called Stith. So, between all of them the Sparks had a thousand acres or more. I had me a grocery an' general store an' damn neah every Sparks in the county owed me money. I give 'em all credit an' when the bills run up to moah than they could evah pay I took a little piece of paper, kind of like a mortgage." He cackled happily and his voice warmed with satisfaction. "Then one day," he stared dreamily at the ceiling, "some fellows come with equipment an' say they want to make some land tests. I told 'em there was nothin' but rocks underground but if they wanted to test go ahead an' test. Then I got to thinkin'. They must know what they're lookin' for an' if they're testin' it's because they think there's somethin' down there I don't know about. So I get myself humpin'. I begin to foreclose on all them othah Sparks. I run 'em all right off their land. By damn, you could heah 'em yell all the way to Montgomery but I don't pay no mind. Well, them testin' fellows found about the biggest by-God iron deposits in Alabama. I screwed them Sparks good an' ended up with a million dollars from the steel company an' some royalties to come besides." He tilted back in his chair and stared raptly at the opposite wall.

Tod had been listening and watching Willie, whose attention was riveted upon Sparks. As the man talked Willie kept moistening his lips, licking them as though each word had a particularly satisfying flavor.

"You see how Willie theah," Sparks spoke absently, "keep wettin' his mouth like he's tastin' somethin' good? That's because he's countin' on me to help him screw you some, Mr. Lathrop."

Willie was jerked out of his half-mesmerized contemplation by the bald statement. His eyes darted with a sudden apprehension from Reese Sparks to Tod.

Tod stood up. "Willie's been trying to do that ever since I've known him." He was pleasantly indifferent. "We understand each other."

"Hell, Tod-boy. Sparks here's just talkin'." Willie made an effort to laugh.

"No I ain't, Mr. Lathrop." Sparks ignored Willie and made the statement without emphasis. "Like I say. I take to you but that wouldn't stop me from helpin' Willie give it to you if there was some profit to be made. Like I said. That's my pleasuah. There wouldn't be any hard feelings on my part." He actually wanted Tod to sympathize with his predicament.

"That's nice to know." Tod pushed back his chair. "Francine. Willie. Mr. Sparks." He inclined his head to the trio as he named each in turn. "Thanks for the drink." He turned from the table.

On the way out he scooped up a handful of Chet's boiled peanuts and cracked one between his fingers. At the door Sparks' voice all but halted him.

"Don't forget what I said, Mr. Lathrop. I take to you. I really do. You remember that."

Tod let the screen crack softly behind him. As he walked down the dock he wondered what Willie was up to. It didn't occur to him to question what Sparks had said. Idly he tossed some peanut shells into the river and watched as a crab came slowly up from the bottom to investigate.

"Hello, Willie," he said aloud to the blue-shelled scavenger.

The sheer absurdity of the remark made him feel better. He laughed and threw the rest of the peanuts into the water, brushed his hands together and went on to where his car was parked.

* XVIII * *

IN a Miami hotel room high above Biscayne Bay, Tod strode restlessly up and down, pacing off the distance between windows and door with a tight anger he fought to control.

Once he halted, surveyed himself in a mirror and laughed with a harsh absence of humor. He had delayed the trip to Miami for almost two weeks, feeling confident that his obligations to the bank could be worked out with a minimum of difficulty. Bankers were interested in money, not properties. Show them how they could get their money, with its accumulating interest, and they would string along. No one was going to be unreasonable. The assumption had seemed valid.

The meeting with the institution's president, Benton Chase, had been precise and impersonal despite the fact he and Chase had known each other for several years. This had surprised Tod a little but then, he decided, the ways of bankers were sometimes inscrutable; particularly when you owed them money. Chase had led him into the somber privacy of the board room and with an assumption of congeniality waved a hand toward the silver boxes with their Havana cigars, the bourbon and a Thermos of iced water on a side table. Tod refused, lit a cigarette and made the expected, polite inquiries about the Chase family. After a couple of minutes he realized that Chase was uncomfortable, almost unwilling to discuss that which had brought Tod to Miami.

"What's wrong, Bent?" He was puzzled.

"Wrong? Nothing." Chase tapped a pencil's eraser soundlessly on the table.

"O.K. Then let's get to it. You know I took a licking in the market. So did a lot of other people. I can pull things together but I need a little time. Time and credit."

"The bank tries never to be unreasonable."

Tod stared at him. "For God's sake, Bent, stop saying *the bank* as though it were written in italics. As far as I'm concerned you're the bank. Will you go along with me for awhile? That's all I need to know. You hold my paper on the Citrus Belt and the Stalath Motel. The notes are due. I can't meet them. I'll assume that the bank—" He smiled a little at his own employment of the word. He also put it in italics. "Anyhow, this impersonal thing, the institution, the bank, hasn't any desire to get into the trucking and transportation business or the operation of a motel. So let's work out a deal. I'll run them for you at a nominal salary. The profits can be used to reduce, and eventually, pay off the notes. That way I'll be able to hang on and the bank will get its money. Does that make sense to you?"

"Naturally, Stoddard." Chase had never called him Tod. "Money is our business. I'm sure we can come to a mutually acceptable agreement on the Stalath Motel. I don't see any difficulty there."

"Good." Tod felt easier. "Now, what about the Citrus Belt?"

"Well . . . I . . ." Chase allowed the words to trail away.

"Well I what?" Tod straightened up from his position of comfortable lounging.

"The truth of the matter is, Stoddard . . ." Chase stared at the heavily draped windows. "Well . . . we don't hold your notes on the Citrus Belt." He saw the incredulous anger gathering on Tod's face. "There was nothing unethical, you understand. We advised you by registered letter that the notes were due."

"I know that." Tod was short. "It was routine. I knew you understood the situation. Or," a note of irritation crept into his voice, "did I?"

"You have to understand our position, Stoddard. Money is short. We have to protect ourselves and our depositors. You know how

★ 282

things are. When we had an offer from a third party we sold your notes, taking a small discount. That was practical business and not at all unusual."

"You son of a bitch." Tod stood up.

"Now, Stoddard." Chase drew upon the dignity of his position with an effort. "There was nothing furtive about the operation. It's common practice."

"I still say you're a son of a bitch." Tod bit the words off one by one. "If it was so open and aboveboard why didn't you pick up a telephone, call Daytona and let me know what was going on?"

"You're offensive, Stoddard. I'll excuse it because I know you're under pressure. If I had called would you have been able to do anything about it?" There was a flash of corresponding temper in the question.

"I don't know but neither did you." He leaned over the table, resting his palms on the mahogany's cold surface. "Who holds my notes now or is it too unethical and too open and aboveboard to tell me that?"

"No." Chase framed his reply slowly. "Naturally you're entitled to know. I'm honestly a little surprised you haven't already been notified. Is there any reason why someone wouldn't want you to know?"

Tod shook his head and then a sudden comprehension illuminated his eyes.

"Of course." He spoke with wonder. "It couldn't be anyone else. The bastard would want to play it that way." He turned to Chase. "Willie Estes?"

"Yes. You know him?"

"I ought to. He works for me. I cut him in for twenty-five percent when I had to have him during the war while I was in the Army." He turned away, went to the cabinet and poured himself a drink. "So Willie finally pulled it off. That old bastard Sparks wasn't fooling, was he?"

"What?" Chase was mystified.

Tod faced him again. "I'm talking to myself. It isn't anything you'd understand."

"I'm sorry, Stoddard."

"I don't think you really are, Bent." There was no rancor in the statement. "I don't think it makes a damn bit of difference to you. The bank has its money. That's your job. I still think, though, it could have been handled differently."

"We didn't hear from you." Chase was honestly concerned. "The obligation was due. I hope you're not sore, Stoddard."

"You're damn right I'm sore." The anger flared. "Wouldn't you be? I built that line up from a couple of trucks. It's mine and no conniving bastard is going to take it away. All right," he put the glass back on its tray, "you have a talk with the bank, whatever that is. See what can be worked out with the motel. I need a favor but I'm damned if I'm going to beg for it."

"Hell, Stoddard." The tone was sincerely friendly. "I—we—don't want to push you to the wall. The Stalath Motel is a good operation. There isn't anything like it in the state. I'd like to see you finish what you started. We'll come up with something satisfactory to everyone concerned. I'm sorry about the Citrus Belt. I mean it."

"Forget it." Tod was impatient. "I'm going back to Daytona this afternoon and maybe kick someone's ass around just for the fun of it. You know how to get in touch with me."

Now, as he paced in the hotel room, the threat seemed juvenile and ridiculous. Nothing would be solved by letting his temper get out of hand. He halted at the writing table and picked up a copy of the hotel's house organ. It was a handsomely lithographed brochure in color, listing the hotel's dining rooms, pool, nightclub and services. Among the advertisements the Citrus Belt carried a full page. He looked at it almost absently. It was a good ad with the orange symbol, the truck fleet, the buses with their uniformed drivers standing at attention at open doors. He started to drop it back on the desk and then his expression was suddenly transformed into one of complete, unbelievable astonishment. Then he began to laugh, almost hysterically at first. Why hadn't he thought about that before? It was the key to everything and without it Willie had nothing but a damned big stone around his neck.

With a gesture of exuberance he tossed the brochure into the air.

"I'm going to give it to you, Willie!" he shouted exultantly. "I'm going to give it to you good. That," and his words mimicked the tone of Reese Sparks, "is my real pleasure. I'm going to get you on the end of a pole and watch you squirm."

Willie Estes, feet on desk, leaned back in the chair and pretended to read the *News-Journal*. His eyes, though, constantly shifted to the windows opening on Fairview. He was waiting, confident this had to be the day. He wriggled a little with the pleasure of anticipation. From an adjoining room Tod's secretary brought in the morning's mail and carefully placed it on the desk, just out of Willie's easy reach. He could feel her resentment and it pleased him. He was in Lathrop's office with his feet on Lathrop's desk. Only, and he hugged the secret knowledge to him, they were no longer Lathrop's desk or office, his secretary or, and it was all Willie could do not to laugh, Lathrop's Citrus Belt Line. He would have a sign painter come in later and have WILLIE ESTES lettered in gold on the door. He wanted to see the name on every truck, bus, advertisement and piece of equipment in the shop.

He knew Tod had gone to Miami and learned from the bank what had happened. He also knew Tod had returned two days ago. What mystified him was the fact that Tod had not come to the office, telephoned or raised the hell which Willie would have considered normal. This puzzled but did not worry him. It only delayed the moment of triumph. Sooner or later Tod would show up. It was for this appearance Willie waited and he controlled his impatience with an effort.

Willie had made no overt move. His first inclination had been to call the Citrus Belt Line employees together and tell them he had taken over the company. He discarded the idea reluctantly. Let Mr. Stoddard Lathrop tell 'em. Let him stand up and say: I'm out of the Citrus Belt Line. Mr. Willie Estes owns it. Take your orders from him. Say Mr. Willie Estes from now on because if you don't, Mr. Willie Estes will throw you out on your ass the way he did me. By God! Willie smacked his lips. That would be something to hear. Of course, and the admission was made grudgingly, it wouldn't happen that way but they'd all get the word. From a grease monkey in the shop pits to the auditor they'd damn soon know who was running things. Now it was Mr. Willie Estes who would be invited to address a Rotary luncheon. Mr. Willie Estes' picture would be in the paper with a caption identifying him as one of Daytona's most energetic businessmen.

A slight frown touched his expression. In all of his calculations, he couldn't afford to forget it was really Reese Sparks who owned the Citrus Belt. Sparks had put up the money. The notes had been purchased in Willie's name but Sparks had demanded and received Willie's note in return. It was call money and so Reese could shut him out any time he pleased. He'd have to be careful how he walked around old Sparks.

Francine's uncle was a bur on Willie's hide and Willie was sure the constant pricking was deliberate. They had given him their best room, catered to his whims and urged him to stay with them for as long as he liked. Francine's attitude toward her uncle was one of breezy insult. She appeared to be unimpressed by the fact he had a million dollars, goading him constantly with ribald comment, teasing him with her body. She would appear at the breakfast table in the sheerest of negligees and take a brazen pleasure in his open hunger as his eyes lingered on her breasts.

"Stop chewing me up, you old bastard, and eat your breakfast." She'd stick her tongue out at him and laugh.

Sparks actually enjoyed her taunts. "By God, Francine! Just give me a chance an' I'll eat 'em without no syrup."

"You don't have teeth enough to chew a nipple, you old crow. It's all you can do to gum that milk toast." She'd wink at him as though they shared a lewd secret and the old man would snort his delight.

They usually ignored Willie. Sparks was always reaching out to touch Francine. Sometimes she permitted his hand to linger for a second. At other times she pushed it away.

"Not for a whole million you couldn't get it."

"That theah is a lot of money, Francine," he complained mildly.

Her insults were deliberate and they worried Willie. The old man might just take so much. She was always critical of his appearance.

"One of these days I'm going to get a can opener and cut you out of that long underwear. How many years have you been wearing it without a change? You smell like an old wet dog. Why don't you take some of that million dollars and buy yourself some new clothes so a girl could look at you without wanting to puke?"

The surprising part of it was that Sparks actually made an effort to improve his appearance. He bought new lightweight suits and shirts with soft collars at Debrow's; went to a barber instead of hacking at his spotty hair with a pair of scissors in front of a mirror. He even cleaned and cut his fingernails.

"You're sure getting to be a dandy." Francine scoffed at the change. "Next thing you know you'll be using a toothbrush instead of a piece of twig."

Alone with Francine, Willie voiced a worried objection. "You ought to be more careful with what you say. That old man ain't a fool. He'll get real mad at you one of these days an' that'll be the end."

"Not that old bastard. I know him. I've known him all my life. He's been after me ever since I was eleven years old. He isn't going to stop now."

When Sparks agreed to put up the money so they could move in on the Citrus Belt he left Willie in no doubt as to where he stood.

"I don't want you to get any wrong ideas, Willie." He had jabbed a long, dirty finger into Willie's soft belly. "I don't really like you worth a damn an' I surer 'an hell don't trust you. This looks like a good thing. That's why I'm layin' out the money. I really take to Mr. Lathrop. I wisht it was him an' me givin' it to you instead of the othah way 'round."

It puzzled Willie that Sparks always referred to Tod as Mr. Lathrop.

"When we call them notes," Sparks continued, "an' Mr. Lathrop can't pay then you step in an' run things. But," the pale eyes were frosty, "don't you nevah forget you're runnin' them for me. An' another thing. Don't make no mistake about Mr. Lathrop. You always got to be careful when you go to do dirty to a gentleman. A right-bred man don't lower his head an' swing away when he fights. He thinks things ovah an' decides on a place to stick it in you. It don't often pay to pick a fight with youah betters."

"Who's better?" Willie had taken a couple of drinks and they made him incautious and belligerent. "Who says he's better?"

Sparks scratched himself. "Why, almost anyone, Willie. Just almost anyone you an' me can think of."

Out of the corner of his eye now Willie saw Tod's car roll up to the curb. He whistled softly to himself and watched eagerly while Tod stopped for a moment to talk with one of the drivers. He was smiling and Willie wondered just what it was that Stoddard Lathrop had to smile about this morning.

When Tod came in he showed no surprise at seeing Willie in his chair, feet on desk.

"Hi, Willie." He nodded pleasantly and riffled through the stack of mail. He picked out a couple of envelopes and tossed the rest back. "Those belong to you."

Willie stared at him uneasily. Didn't the damn fool know what had happened? He searched for an opening, something to say which would bring everything out where it should be.

"I heard you were down to Miami." This was tentatively, almost hesitantly stated.

Tod nodded. Still standing he opened one of the letters, humming quietly to himself as he read.

Frustrated and bewildered by Tod's seeming indifference Willie tried again.

"Then you know about the Citrus Belt Line?"

"Yes." Tod continued to read.

Willie was baffled. He could feel himself sweating. This wasn't what he had expected or wanted. Tod should have come storming in, shouting and raising hell. This would have given Willie the real satisfaction of the moment.

He made another effort and there was a small note of desperation in his tone. Something had to provoke the outburst.

"You know," he was casual, patronizing, "you can always have a job here, Toddy-boy. I ain't goin' to be hard nosed about things. You can stay on."

"Doing what, Willie-boy?" Tod was agreeably interested.

"Well, hell." Willie's confidence returned. "I got me a line to run. You know it all from the top. We could work together like always only things would be some different. You'd have to know that right off."

"What line?" Tod seemed not to understand.

"The goddamned Citrus Belt Line. That's what." Willie's frustration spilled over. His voice rose unsteadily. This wasn't the way things were supposed to go. Tod should have been doing the yelling. Willie felt cheated. "You know damn well I got it." There was almost a question in the statement and Estes stared hopefully at Tod. He wanted his declaration confirmed.

Tod folded the letters, put them in his pocket. Then he lit a cigarette and his glance roved indifferently around the office.

"I know you have the Citrus Belt Line, Willie. But," Tod pretended to untangle a riddle, "I just don't know what you are going to do with it."

"I'm goin' to run it, you damn fool. That's what I'm goin' to do." Despite an effort at control Willie's voice rose again.

"I just don't know how you are going to do that, Willie." Tod was sympathizing with Willie in his dilemma. "Where are you going to run it?"

"Now, by God, you cut this foolishness out." Willie's mouth was dry. He was being maneuvered and he knew it. Instead of dominating the situation he was being forced to explain it. "I'm going to run it where it's always been run. The buses, the trucks and the whole service." He glared defiantly.

"No, Willie." The correction was made regretfully. "No you're not."

"What the hell are you talking about?" Estes dropped his feet to the floor and stood up. "Who says I ain't?"

"I do."

Willie tried to laugh but the sound was a feeble croak. "I'd like to see you stop me." He made an effort to strike an attitude of pleased defiance.

"All right, Willie." Tod reached out and thrust one hand against Willie's chest, all but throwing him back into the chair. "I'll stop you right now, here, today."

"You're crazy." Willie clung to the arms of the chair which had spun wildly with his impact. "You got nothin'."

Tod seated himself on a corner of the desk and studied Willie with a relaxed pleasure.

"I'll tell you what I have, Willie. I have a city and county franchise; an exclusive franchise with five more years to run. That means you can't so much as run a bus across the bridge. Well," he amended, "you can, of course, but you can't charge a fare. If you and Reese Sparks want to operate that way, free rides, no one will stop you. But," and the warning was unmistakable, "if you try it any other way I'll knock you down with an injunction within twenty-four hours.

289 ★

I'll tie you up in a lawsuit for an infringement of franchise. I'll beat your brains out, Willie."

"You're bluffing." Willie searched his face. "That franchise is Citrus Belt."

"Uh-uh, Willie." Tod dropped the cigarette on the floor deliberately and stepped on it. "When the franchise was granted I didn't even have a name for the line. It was awarded to Stoddard Lathrop. I've read it and checked it out with the city and county attorneys."

"Where the hell are you going to get the equipment to operate?"

"That's another thing." Tod was amiable. "When I started, truck and bus routes were something new. The franchise was pretty loosely worded. It requires me to furnish regularly scheduled, adequate transportation at stated fees. Nothing is said about the type of vehicles to be used. So, that leaves me free to put into service any reasonably safe conveyance I select. I'll scrounge up the equipment, Willie, if I have to use rickshaws and pull them myself. That's how it is, Willie. That's really how it is. Now, you go ahead and sit on the Citrus Belt Line until your ass is sore. Then I'll talk business with you and Reese Sparks."

The contest was short lived and mildly diverting to those who watched from the sidelines. Tod moved with a determined confidence and for the first time he exerted pressure where it was necessary. He had friends in the Mayor's office, the City Council, the Sheriff's department and State Motor Vehicle Bureau. Now he called upon them. Some owed him a return of favors. Others acted out of friendship and others because they disliked Willie Estes.

Without being asked, Dennis Lathrop mortgaged the beach house and deposited twenty thousand dollars to Tod's account.

"I didn't want you to do that." He was sincerely moved by his father's action. "This is something I should work out by myself." He sat across from his father in Dennis's office.

"Let's just say I wanted to do it." Dennis studied his son's face with a smile. "I'm not going to sit by and watch something you put together go by default. I still don't know how you're going to operate, though."

Tod laughed, shaking his head bemusedly. "I have the damnedest transportation fleet you've ever seen. A dozen or more persons I have known all my life—some I haven't been closer to than a wave when we passed on the street—came up with offers to loan me their cars for as long as I need them. I have Buicks, Cadillacs, a couple of old Reo tourers, an air-cooled Franklin and a Metz roadster. That Metz belongs to Mrs. Bemis. You remember her? I gave young Bemis a job in our Orlando office when he got out of jail and no one else would have him around. I put my Lincoln into the pool and use the Metz. It's chain driven, would you believe it? Anyhow, I never knew I had so many friends. Jameson Thorpe, he's a contractor in Ocala, called to say he could let me have a couple of trucks. I rented four old buses from the School District in Jacksonville. Everything is moving. The bus service here with the Daytona-Daytona Beach and Seabreeze routes is uninterrupted with the use of passenger cars. Six of Citrus Belt's drivers quit their jobs with Willie to come with me. I can hold on to the intercounty runs with the equipment I can borrow and, thanks to your loan, rent. We'll just have to see who can hang on. Willie must be having his troubles. I have an idea old Sparks is cutting him into small pieces."

Sparks was chopping at Willie. He camped in the Citrus Belt Line's office and was obscenely furious with Estes.

"Just lookin' at you should've told me better," he railed. "You're a damned fool but I'm a bigger one for not lookin' into this thing real good before I let you go ahead. Now, by God, you get us out of it."

"We can wear Lathrop down. He can't last. All we got to do is wait."

"There ain't no we. I'm the one who's got to wait an' that's against my nature. You settle this thing quick."

Willie did his frantic best. He moved the orange and gray colored buses along the scheduled routes but they all carried the humiliating sign: FREE BUS. Then all sorts of mysterious difficulties began to manifest themselves. His drivers were continually cited for speeding. They were ticketed for the smallest traffic violation. Motor Vehicle inspectors found fault with the mechanical condition of the vehicles. The buses ran out of gasoline on the bridges and trucks broke down on lonely stretches of road. His drivers were late for work or their wives reported them sick. In an unreasoning fury Willie fired them and found replacements difficult to get. There were long and inexplicable delays, and passengers who had been delighted by the offer of free transportation between beach and mainland became impatient and boarded one of Tod's cars. Drivers of Willie's buses would pull into a filling station and spend half an hour drinking a Coke and talking with the attendant. Small acts of untraceable sabotage occurred in the shop. Sand was discovered in the drums of oil, tires blew out from overinflation.

Willie screamed. He took his complaints to the City Manager, the police and Sheriff's Office. They were met with courtesy and the assurance they would be investigated. But the delays and frustrations mounted and Willie searched desperately for a way out of his predicament.

Tod Lathrop maintained his franchise. There was no interruption. He operated on regular schedule fulfilling his agreement. A great many persons seemed to enjoy the novelty of riding in the Lincolns and Cadillacs, and the Negroes, who supplied the heaviest morning and evening traffic, called them their "limousine service." Tod discovered what almost amounted to a quiet conspiracy of agreement. People meeting him on Beach Street would grin and wink as though they had a share in the contest. Time and again he was met with further offers of assistance. "If you need a car for the rush hours take mine. Just have it back so I can take the old lady to the movies. I sure like to watch that Estes bastard bleed."

Although he presented a breezy and confident front Tod was secretly worried. His gesture of defiance was just that, a gesture, and he was certain Reese Sparks was shrewd enough to know it. Sparks, if he wanted to, could outlast him. Sooner or later something would have to give; people would want their cars back; with the tourist season mounting to a peak he simply would not be able to meet the demand for transportation and his franchise would be voided. Then, unexpectedly, the break came.

Without any preliminary negotiations Sparks appeared one evening at Will Lathrop's home. He waited on the porch while Wash went back inside to announce him. When Tod came out he was still standing as though uncertain of his reception.

"How you, Mr. Lathrop?"

"Hello, Mr. Sparks. You wanted to see me?"

Sparks nodded. "Yes, sir." His voice was a dry whisper. "I suah guess I want to see you oathehwise I wouldn't be heah."

"Well," Tod indicated a chair, "sit down." He noted the old man's appearance—the new suit, well pressed and spotless; white shirt, blue knit tie, polished shoes. He wondered who or what had made him clean up. "Will you have a drink?" The courtesy was instinctive.

"Latuh maybe, Mr. Lathrop." His eyes didn't waver and the tiniest suggestion of a smile appeared about his mouth. "Time foah drinkin' is aftah business not befoah." He studied Tod openly, making an estimate of their relative positions. Finally, he settled himself into one of the wicker rocking chairs. "You got spunk, Mr. Lathrop, but you know damned well I can outlast you."

"I suppose so. But do you know something? Right now I'm betting you won't try."

Sparks inclined his head in agreement. "If I was plannin' to I wouldn't be heah." He paused. "I take to you, Mr. Lathrop. I did from the very first day. I told you so then. Sometimes you can look at a man, a dog or a horse an' know right off he's got the breedin' in him. It's somethin' that shows through. I take to that. I like to be around it." He pursed his lips and squinted at Tod. "Do you think you an' me could do business togethah?"

Tod wasn't prepared for this. "I don't know, Mr. Sparks." He moved cautiously. "What do you have in mind?"

"Well, first off I'd want you to take back ovah the Citrus Belt Line. I got a demand note on little wet-nosed Willie. I can close him out any minute. So suppose we quit this wrestlin'? You come on back. I'd still hold the papuh on you but you could have all the time you need to pick it up. Pay me the intrust regular, cut down on the note as you go along. How does that sound?"

"Generous," Tod admitted. "But it makes me wonder. Why should you do it?"

"Foah one thing I'm out of patience with Willie. Second, when a deal goes bad I want out of it. I cross it off an' go to somethin' new. Willie ain't the man foah me. He got no brains an' no real heart foah cuttin' up people. He's cocky outside but theah ain't no real fiah in him."

"The trouble is, Mr. Sparks, I'm not sure I like you."

The eyes lighted. "I'd say you got moah damned company in that than any one man needs. I ain't made foah likin'. If I was to

293 ★

think about it theah ain't one person in this whole world I could rightly call a friend. It used to bothah me some but it don't no more. Like me oah not, this heah I'm offerin' is business. Youah a fool if you don't see it thataway." He fumbled in his pocket for one of the black, twisted stogies and lit it. He watched Tod over the flame.

"You'd have to stay out of the operation, Mr. Sparks. There can't be any question of your participation."

"It ain't my intention to meddle." He examined the stogie. "It'd pleasuah me none to have a hand in runnin' things. If it did I'd out-wait you an' take ovah the line."

"All right, Mr. Sparks. You have a deal."

There was a rare smile. "I figgured I did oah I wouldn't have come to you." He sniffed with audible pleasure at the night's air, opening his mouth a little as though to taste the garden's perfume. "This heah is a good place to live. Theah ain't no reason foah me to go back to Alabama. I'm thinkin' of buyin' me a house an' settlin'. Get-tin' me a good, young housekeepuh to take care of things an' me. Outside of a little huntin' with a good dog I got no hobbies. The real pleasuah I get is dealin' an' dickerin' an' this looks like a right good place foah it. I got a fine stack of chips an' a hankerin' to sit in a game. Now, Mr. Lathrop, if you've still a mind to offah it I'll take that drink."

Tod called for Wash and told him to bring the bourbon and water. They sat in meditative silence each knowing, somehow, there was much to be said between them.

"We'ah goin' to make a pair, you an' me, Mr. Lathrop." The state-ment was made matter-of-factly.

Thinking about it later Tod realized he had not been moved to contradict Reese Sparks and what should have been his astonishing declaration. There was, he knew, an unstated agreement and he had the curious sensation of walking with a new and most unlikely companion.

Feet on his desk in the Citrus Belt Line's office, Tod watched Willie Estes through the open door. All morning they had been in-dulging in a game of elaborate pretense in which Willie refused to admit Tod Lathrop existed. When Tod, with a deliberate casual-ness, strolled back into the shop Willie immediately dropped into one of the pits. There he pretended a minute examination of the underside of a truck until Tod walked away. Now he stood, wiping his hands on a wad of greasy waste, examining the sky with skeptical interest.

Tod waited. He had sent his secretary to tell Willie he wanted to see him. There was no way for the man to refuse. He might delay the moment of accounting but that was all. Watching him Tod thought wryly, This is pretty small stuff but I'm really enjoying it. He knew Sparks had told Willie he was pulling out, leaving Estes with empty pockets and that Willie, now, didn't know exactly where he stood. After a moment Willie balled the waste and stuffed it into the hip of his coveralls. He set his shoulders at what he thought to be a jaunty, to-hell-with-you attitude and strode into the office.

"You want to see me?" The tone was belligerent. When Tod didn't reply immediately he shifted uneasily. "I guess maybe we got things to talk about."

"Not so much, Willie." Tod squinted as though taking aim across the tips of his shoes. "You're fired."

"Like hell I am." The small pale eyes were suddenly hot. "You nor no son of a bitch can fire me. I got a piece of this here line an' you know it."

"The way I look at it," Tod was pleasantly conversational, "this isn't the same line. You see, it's changed hands a couple of times. Once it belonged to me. Then you stole it or tried to. Then I took it back. So I figure it's an entirely new operation. You'd hardly recognize the old place. It's under new management and you don't have a percentage. You just don't have a damn thing, Willie."

"The hell I don't. We have an agreement."

"We had an agreement."

"I'll sue you, by God. I'll sue you in every court in the state. I'll sue you an' that old bastard Sparks."

"Well." Tod dropped his feet and stood up. "You do that. I'll wear you out. Now." He moved a couple of steps toward Estes. "I'll tell you something. Every now and then in a man's life he gets an opportunity to do something which gives him real satisfaction. It may be trivial in itself." He was smiling happily. "The motive may be petty but the gratification is complete. I've wanted to do this for a long time. I can't understand why I put it off for so long."

Tod's arms shot out and his hands fastened on Willie's shoulders, spinning the man around. He planted a foot in Estes's twisting buttocks. Tod couldn't bring himself to kick Willie but he shoved with all the power of his leg. Estes was propelled through the door and out into the shop on a staggering run which almost tumbled him. He screamed and yelled his obscenities, turning to face Tod with contorted fury.

"Don't stop, Willie," Tod called. "Keep going because if you don't, I'll do what I promised to do a long time ago. I'll kick your ass from here to Beach Street." He turned away and went back to his chair.

His secretary, who had remained at her desk, wide-eyed and secretly delighted, watched him. He was a little ashamed now of what he had done and pretended to examine some letters.

"Mr. Lathrop?"

"Yes, Josie?"

"I just wanted to say," she hesitated and then started to giggle, "I just wanted to tell you to forget my Christmas bonus this year. I've just had it."

* XIX * *

DURING the years which were to pass, Stoddard Lathrop would recall many times the talk with Reese Sparks and marvel at the association which followed. That they became, in a sense, partners was never suggested orally or verbally sealed with a contract. That they also, without effort or ever feeling the necessity to say so, became friends was all the more incredible. Yet time made these things self-evident.

From the beginning it was a most unlikely alliance and yet it rooted itself firmly. Each contributed an element missing in the other. Tod had the energy, the drive, the imagination. Sparks was a shrewd appraiser of things and people. He was seemingly without emotions; never permitted himself to lose sight of the target or allow his aim to stray through the intrusion of personalities or sentiment. Slowly, and a little reluctantly, Tod was forced to revise his first impression of the man as he had seen him that day with Willie and Francine Estes. What he had believed to be an inherent and unmitigated evil turned out to be something quite different. Sparks could be ruthless in a business deal but his inflexibility had a detached, impersonal quality. He had small patience or compassion for a loser. Yet he never actually seemed to take any pleasure in the misfortunes or lack of acumen in others which yielded him a profit.

297   *

"I do purely love to put it to someone, Mr. Lathrop," he remarked once, "but that's because it makes me feel good an' not them bad."

He was, by any standards, an all but illiterate man who had probably read nothing but an occasional newspaper since he left a backwoods grade school in Alabama. He was vulgar but this, again, Tod was to learn was calculated and deliberate. He resorted to a sudden, explosive coarseness to push an opponent off balance. It was a strategem which frequently produced surprising results. The average person wasn't temperamentally prepared to cope with the crude assault. It left him shocked and without a ready defense. Sparks usually walked off with the scalp. In this manner the old man would tilt a deal in his favor.

He had, Tod understood, no real need for money—big money. His desires were few. Yet he was unable to resist the fascination of making it. There was a Florida land crab which youngsters call a "robber" because of its habit of dragging off any bright and shiny object, no matter how useless. That was Reese Sparks. He liked the glitter of things and the triumph of acquiring money which shone best of all.

Sparks kept his word. Stoddard Lathrop took back the Citrus Belt Line and the old man made no attempt to intrude or force a relationship. Only once did he come to the office.

"Like I told you once, Mr. Lathrop"—he refused the offer of a drink—"I got me about a million dollars. In ordinary times this maybe ain't such a much. But right now, with the country on its ass, it's as good as ten million. I like the way you handled me an' Willie on that bus line. You do the kind of fightin' it's nice to watch. Now I don't want to suggest nothin' beyond a business deal. You're short right now. I ain't. When somethin' good comes along you can't swing I'd be obliged if you'd come to me instead of a bank." He snickered soundlessly. "I don't figure the banks to be turnin' loose with any speculatin' money anyhow. We can work out things between us. I talked around some. The Lathrop name in Florida is as good as a shining gold piece. Nobody knows me. So we could put together what we both got an' take us some pretties home from the Fair."

"That sounds like more than a fair deal to me." Tod nodded. "I'll keep my eyes open."

"There's likely to be some ripe peaches ready to drop to the ground." He picked up his hat from its place on the floor beside his chair. "Now, you can say this is none of my busines an' you'd be right. But if I was you I'd fire Willie. I sure wouldn't have no hungry dog hangin' around the market."

"I already have. This morning. I needed time for a replacement."

"Good. You give a dog a taste of porterhouse, what was what Willie had for awhile, an' he's likely never to be satisfied with a naked bone again." He lit a stogie and the smoke was rank and acrid. Sparks breathed it as though it were the finest Havana leaf. "I bought me a house on the peninsula waterfront, down by a place they call Burgoyne's First Point."

Tod inclined his head. "That's fine property. I always liked the oaks and the river there."

"Now, I need me a young mulatto housekeeper oah a maid to keep things goin'." He bared his teeth in a wolfish grin of anticipation. "That's one thing about the white Southern gentlemen. They may not like the nigger but they sure'r'n hell like their girls." He sighed with a gusty piousness. "I've purely admired, all my life, the Southern gentleman's ability to make that distinction. Yes sir, I surely have."

Tod kept his face expressionless with an effort. He was well aware of Sparks' sanctimonious hypocrisy. It tickled him and offered another facet of the man's character which Tod was learning to respect.

"Just one moah thing." Sparks stood up. "If it's all right with you I'd like to have a look at that motel thing I heah you got goin' down to Miami. It's somethin' new, ain't it? The whole idea. Like a self-service hotel?"

"I didn't carry it that far. Just eliminated some unnecessary things. You drive right to your accommodations and carry a bag five feet or less inside. Beyond that there is all the service a man could want."

"You don't mind if I go down an' have a look?"

"Why should I? Check in. Pay the rate. Stay as long as you like."

"You got a good deal worked out with the bank? I mean good for you?" It was an unstated offer.

"I have full control of the operation."

"That's good." Sparks was disappointed. "Keep it that way. If they get to breathin' down youah neck, let me know. Well—I bettah be goin'."

Tod took a Citrus Belt Line card from a small rack on the desk and scribbled on it.

"Give this to the manager when you check in at the motel. It'll get you complimentary room and meals." He handed the card to Reese Sparks.

Reese took it with an avid pleasure. His smile was one of childish delight. He turned it over and over between his fingers as though it were a magic talisman beyond price.

"Well now, sir." He beamed. "Ef theah's one thing I do like gettin' its a bargun, a suah-enough bargun. This heah looks like a good one."

These were the long, the uncertain years when the fears of men crowded upon them, dogging their footsteps and flitting through their dreams at night. Those who once had little now had less. Those who had a lot—so much that the rock on which they had built did not tremble—were in a position to make more. The stocks of great corporations fell to unbelievable lows. Who, with any judgment, could doubt the eventual survival of General Motors, Standard Oil, A.T. & T., Western Union, Bell Telephone, United States Steel and the others? Yet their shares lay on the bargain basement counters. Those with ready cash gathered them up and so became wealthier. For, they reasoned, if these things failed then the nation was a failure and that was impossible to conceive.

He was damned as a wild-eyed Socialist, a maverick and a false Pied Piper. He was hailed as a Saviour. But there was magic in the Roosevelt vitality. No one could deny this and an order began to assert itself. The banks were reorganized and men breathed a little easier. One federal bureau after another was created and they seemed, at times, to threaten the alphabet from which they drew their designations. Congress brought back the saloons under the more chaste name of "bar and grill." "Happy Days Are Here Again" was blared out by hastily organized WPA bands and the musicians saw a weekly check once again. An all-out planned economy was blue-printed through the National Recovery Act and the Republicans screamed that when the national debt reached fifty billion dollars the country would be bankrupt. The Securities Exchange Commission made plunder and rigging in the stock market all but impossible. Child labor decreased, despite the opinion held in many quarters that the youngster was being deprived of a God-given right to work fourteen hours a day for a dollar and forty cents if that was what it wanted to do. Labor unions inched toward collective bargaining. The AAA set out to do something for the farmer. Even its sponsors admitted that paying rural families something for planting nothing was a crude piece of legislation. But it worked; the glut was removed. In one year farm income rose over three hundred million dollars. Recovery. The nation crept toward it slowly while in Europe a new World War was being planned.

Florida was badly hit by the depression. Along the resort coasts where the economy was based upon a now nonexistent tourist business the situation was acute. The big hotels were empty, the beautiful sweeps of beach unpeopled; golf courses lay idle. There were a few visitors, of course—at any time there are always a few with money —but these provided the merest trickle. Press agents were hired, drums beaten and few heard the call. The big money, those who had always had it, came south in the private yachts, went to private estates in the Bahamas or the elaborately expensive fishing clubs in Florida's keys. They did little to relieve the economic pinch. Choice real estate was for sale at ridiculous prices; vast acreage of rich farm and cattle land in the interior could be picked up by paying the tax liens. Who wanted land when no one had the money with which to build, no one cared to farm, no one had the capital to put together a herd? Florida was a beggar, standing on a street corner asking: Who'll buy me?

Dennis Lathrop died in the fall of that year, 1938, without ever seeing even a small fragment of his dream becoming a reality. Sometimes he had been angry and bitter, feeling, somehow, he and the dream had been cheated. He had planned well in his mind. But where were the ordered, self-contained communities; the homes of simple but solid design and construction? Where were the people; the man and wife on a retirement income; the dentist and young doctor, seeking a better life than the crowded warrens of the cities? Where were those who wanted a little more; sunshine, a better existence, a community where they could practice their skills and professions, marry their girls, rear their families? They had been run over and trampled. The completely artifical values created by the boom had made such modest communities impossible. With the collapse had come the depression and panic. He had talked of these things with his son many times.

"Someday," Dennis was sitting on the front porch of the beach house, "someday you'll see it, Stoddard." He drew the light blanket tighter around his knees. "I hope you have a part in it."

It was a curious thing, Tod reflected, that as his father had grown older he no longer called him Tod. He drew upon a new formality. It was always Stoddard now. Actually, when he thought about it, much the same thing had occurred in Daytona itself. Few persons ever hailed him as Tod and those were of old acquaintance. It was either Stoddard or Mr. Lathrop. They had all changed, he, the people, the town.

The long, curving line of the beach was dotted with cottages and larger homes from the pier to the inlet. There were still vast sweeps of empty dunes and of the green-gray scrub but a hundred or more persons had built where once there had been nothing. Even so the peninsula still had a ragged, half-wild quality which he found good and disturbingly exciting. It still waited for man to put his hand upon it.

"Someday," the thoughts of Dennis Lathrop sometimes wandered now but his voice was clear and steady, "you'll see I was right."

"I never doubted it, Father." Tod's words were gentle. He could feel the old man's anger. "I remember the trips we took together and the things you said. They excited me. They, the ideas, still do. The times have never been right. They are not right now. The country is groping for stability but there is another war on its way and surer than hell we'll be in it. Maybe after that . . ." He shrugged. "Who knows?"

"When it comes I hope you have a part in it, Stoddard. Not the war, of course," he smiled at his small attempt at humor, "the building as we once talked about it. The building, Stoddard, not the speculating." He was suddenly vehement. "I wouldn't like to go out this way feeling so little of what I believed in would eventually be accomplished without a Lathrop having a hand in it."

"You aren't going out now." Tod was shocked to realize his words were without conviction.

Dennis shook his head. His eyes were fixed on the rearing line of breakers as they piled upon the offshore sand bar.

"I think so, Stoddard. A man gets a feeling. I won't say it is a premonition. It is a feeling that you are suddenly intolerably tired. This I had heard but never really believed. It is true. You get a feeling that you're not going to make the effort when the mind asks: Shall we go on a little longer?" He leaned back. After a moment he spoke again. "Your grandfather came over to visit me last night." He smiled again, eyes closed. "It is a curious thing. I never say my father; always *your* grandfather. I wonder why?" He brooded silently for a moment. "We haven't always understood each other, have we, Stoddard?"

"Not always. But I don't think that's unusual. The relationship between father and son isn't too easy. It is made more difficult by people taking it for granted. There is the assumption that two adults will be compatible simply because one is the parent, the other the son."

Dennis nodded. "Of course, you're right. My father and I don't dislike each other. It is simply that we don't understand each other. I don't see any change in him." There was a flicker of interest in the voice. "He appears to me to look much the same as he did thirty years ago. He and that Negro man, Washington. The two of them may just go on living forever. I wonder why?"

"Wash says he's over a hundred. Grandfather Will refuses to discuss age."

Dennis rocked gently in the deep chair. "Why," he asked finally, "why haven't you ever married, Stoddard?"

"I don't know. It isn't that I don't find it pleasant to have a girl around. I've had no monastic life so far. It's just that I don't talk about it. This is a small town and I've tried to be discreet."

"You haven't answered my question. Why have you never married?"

"I answered as honestly as I could. I don't know. Maybe there's no room for a permanent attachment in my life. I've yet to meet the girl who made me want to say: Without you I cannot get along. I can get along very well. I know it and the girls I have known have sensed it. Also, they have been intelligent enough not to try and force me into a domestic mold where I wouldn't fit."

"That was highly commendable of them." Dennis smiled drily. "Believe me, I am not becoming a doddering sentimentalist. I have no wish for grandchildren to be crawling and mewling all over the place. It just struck me as odd that such a personable, successful man had escaped matrimony. I use the word escaped advisedly. But I'm only making idle talk, trying to prolong your visit because I enjoy it. Would you get me a cigar and let's have a little brandy together before you go."

Dennis Lathrop was buried in the family plot in the cemetery atop the ridge which was once known long ago as Mount Ararat. It surprised Tod to discover how many friends his father had. Dennis Lathrop was never a joiner. He belonged to no clubs, no civic groups. Yet, more than a hundred persons came to stand beside his grave on that windswept day.

Will Lathrop steadfastly refused to attend the chapel services or the interment.

"Why the hell should I go around, peering down into the face of a dead man?" He held a glass of warm toddy between his blue-veined hands. "It isn't that I don't grieve a little for my son. But let me do it in private. Let it end there without any mawkish display at the graveside."

Following the funeral Tod drove away without any particular destination. He crossed the tracks at Volusia. Memory fled back to their arrival in Daytona with Grandfather Will, Grandmother Felicia and the shining barouche to meet them. What a place it had been for a boy. Each day a shining thing filled with wonder and an almost unbearable excitement. It was something never again to be recaptured. What had been a village was now a town. Where once the deer ran there were streets and houses. He halted for a moment, eyes traveling over the pleasant lines of the depot. For years Mr. Flagler had every building along the railway painted a bilious yellow. Idly, Tod wondered if the paint had been cheap or Mr. Flagler liked the color. Now the station was pleasantly hued and a flowered mound spelled out the word DAYTONA BEACH in blossoms.

He started up the long slope toward Ridgewood. Here, once in a meadow, he had picked violets for his mother and then, diverted by some game, carried them about until he had only a small, wilted bouquet to give her. Back there had been the bottling works where soft drinks had been splashed into glass containers. He and a boy, Delos Blodgett, used to go to the plant because they sold a bottle of pop for three cents, if consumed on the premises, instead of the nickel it cost uptown. The Blodgetts lived in a big house on Ridgewood and used to have the soda delivered in case lots. They could have had all they wanted in the house or in the yard, but somehow it tasted better at the plant.

Turning left on Ridgewood he followed the avenue through Holly Hill and Kingston. Here the years had left their mark. It was once a tangled area. Now there were homes, small markets, little communities like cells within the larger one. He went on to the bridge at Ormond. Beyond lay the curving bends of the Tomoka River and along here, during the years of Spanish occupation, the King's Road had run to St. Augustine.

Crossing the bridge the realization came to him that the linked towns no longer offered him the opportunity he was seeking. Oh, he admitted, there was plenty of room for development but it would follow prescribed lines. He wanted to strike out with something new. The conventional no longer had a power to capture his imagination. Quite suddenly he decided to transfer the activities of Stalath to Dade County, in and around Miami. He might go farther afield, to the west coast, around Tampa or Clearwater. With his father dead there was no one to hold him here except Will Lathrop. His grandfather appeared quite content to live alone and in the manner which suited him best. He swung about and turned toward Daytona, knowing now what he intended to do.

The following years ground slowly through the most terrible of wars when Germany, for the second time in a generation, almost beat the world to its knees and the United States fought for its life with Japan.

Then, as all wars must, it ended and the nation struggled to readjust itself. Everyone had a great deal of money and there was what amounted to an almost nationwide restlessness. People were on the move and the tide began to wash once more upon Florida's shores.

Tod had moved the Stalath headquarters to Miami, leaving the Daytona office with only a secretary in charge. In Miami he had found a heady vitality, held under leash by the strictures of a war. The energy was there. It was something to be felt.

Although more and more of his interests were being consolidated in Miami and throughout Dade County, Stoddard Lathrop never abandoned the idea of a Stalath Motel somewhere outside of Jacksonville. Now, with the war over, people were on the move. The national trait of restlessness was displaying itself again. They took to the road in every conceivable type of vehicle and came to Florida by all routes. The war had curtailed building and there was a continual scramble for accommodations. If he was ever going to build, now, he felt, was the time.

Over the war years he and Reese Sparks had shared half a dozen profitable ventures. Most of them had been modest but they had all yielded a return. The best had been an investment in a new process for the extraction of resin and acids from pine so it could be used for the manufacture of paper. As usual, or what was becoming usual, this was the result of what Sparks, with a certain amount of awe, called the "Lathrop gift"—the incalculable luck which seemed to follow everything he touched.

He was planning to go to Gainesville to look at some timberland which he had heard was on the market cheap. Before leaving he had talked it over with Reese.

"If what I hear is true we can pick it up for almost nothing. The owner is in trouble. He's land poor. The funny part is he won't do business with any of the large timbering interests. A few years back, during the depression, one of them foreclosed on him and took his home, along with several thousand acres of farm and grazing land, for little more than the taxes. He hates all big business."

Spark's features lighted with a slow, lazy expression of pleasure. "Well, then let's you an' me go up theah like a couple of poah boys with th' seat of theah pants out. That ought to make a good impression."

They had driven to the university town and inspected the property. It ran flat with a solid stand of fine timber. The huge pines stood straight in their green and bronze magnificence. The wind playing through the tops sounded like a whispering organ. They stood without talking, both caught by the cathedral-like hush.

"Well?" Tod finally spoke.

"I say let's you an' me buy it, Mr. Lathrop, just because hit's suah pretty ef foah no othah reason."

"You're getting soft, Mr. Sparks." Tod smiled.

"Hell, I always bin soft. I only act mean to covah up some."

That evening Tod called an old friend from the hotel. The man was head of the university's science department. He immediately asked Tod to come over for a drink and some talk.

Earl Hallowell was a bachelor who lived alone in a small, neat cottage set among a mass of shrubbery off campus. He welcomed Tod heartily. They had been friends in high school and he was one of the few persons Tod had kept contact with. They sat in the warmly furnished living room talking, with bourbon and water between them. Hallowell had a second visitor—a young, slightly vague, bespectacled young man who was shy to the point of inarticulateness in Tod's presence.

"Harvey," Hallowell made the introduction, "is a graduate student. A brilliant chemist. He had a chance to go with Du Pont but turned it down. He's working on something of his own."

Harvey Brewer blushed, squirmed uncomfortably and twisted a button from his worn jacket. He dropped it into his pocket as though it were a scorpion.

"I just don't like to work for anyone else," he mumbled and stared at his shoes as though surprised to find them on his feet.

When they left Hallowell, Tod and Brewer walked together down the silent and deserted street.

"What are you working on, Mr. Brewer?" Tod had an inquisitive and acquisitive nature. What interested someone else interested him.

"Oh, it's just something to do with pine pulp." He found it easier to talk in the semidarkness. "Maybe nothing will come of it. I have an idea for a new machine to reduce the wood to pulp and a new formula for taking out the pitch. All I have is some drawings. I don't have the money to build a model or get it built."

At Tod's urging they went to Brewer's room where they went over the mechanical drawings together. Tod studied them and listened carefully as Brewer explained, asking questions as they came to mind.

"How much do you need to have a model built and be able to devote your full time to it?"

"Oh . . . I don't know." Brewer was unhappy at having to answer such a personal query.

Tod had written a check for five thousand dollars.

"I always like to have a piece of the action." He smiled at Brewer's obvious embarrassment. "It's in my nature. You have the model built. Perfect the formula. If it works we're partners. I'll handle the business end."

The model and formula not only worked but the process was better, faster and cheaper than anything so far tried. It revolutionized the industry in the South where the preponderance of timber was pine.

Sparks, with time on his hands, frequently drove down to Miami. He never came to the Stalath offices without an invitation. This was achieved by an almost apologetic telephone call when he would tell Tod he was in town. They had no social contact beyond an occasional drink. Reese called Tod Mr. Lathrop and Tod spoke to him as Mr. Sparks. Behind this façade of formality, however, there was a small gleam of humor. They were both aware of a situation and each was pleased in his own fashion.

On one of the visits Tod mentioned the plans for the second motel.

"Ah'd suah like to have me a piece of that motel with you, Mr. Lathrop." The suggestion was made with open envy.

Tod shook his head. "The motels are my babies. Anything else Stalath gets into we'll talk it over. The motels I'm going to keep for myself. When the name is well enough known I'm going to work out a franchising deal. I'll lease the name providing I set the operating standard. In return I'll take a share of the profit. I'll keep the restaurants as separate units for lease. It ought to work."

"You're goin' to go to the bank, ain't you, for this second one?"

Tod nodded.

"Well then, I don't see why you should be givin' a bank all the profit in interest. Borrow some from me. I got plenty. Let me have the interest. As a part backer I ought to be able to get me a motel discount."

"All right. I'll take two hundred thousand from you at the current rate."

Reese Sparks had taken out his checkbook and laboriously filled in a blank.

Now, in Jacksonville, Tod was intent upon finding the site for the new Stalath Motel. He had checked in, as always, at the Seminole despite the fact that several new hotels had been built in the city. The Lathrops had always stayed at the Seminole. At the newsstand he bought cigarettes and turned away from the counter as the elevator doors opened to discharge the passengers. Halfway across the lobby she halted, stared and then with a smile of pleasure came to meet him with hands outstretched.

"Tod, how wonderful."

"Hello, Fern." He bent to kiss her lightly on the cheek and then sniffed with an appreciative smile. "You know," he continued to hold her hands, "few persons have names which actually suit them. Yours does. You always smell of something like wood violets or a mossy glen in the sunlight and shadows. Fern is the perfect name for you."

"Thank you, sir." She managed a half curtsy and then took his arm with a warm possessiveness. They walked toward the entrance and he felt the pressure of her hand.

"What are you doing in Jacksonville?"

She looked at him with a half grin. "I told myself I had some shopping to do, things I couldn't get in Sanford. The truth is I just wanted to get away from home and all the other Wentworths for awhile. I thought about going to Miami and calling you. Is it true you just bought Dade County?"

"No, but I'm working on it."

They halted on the sidewalk in the bright sunlight. The doorman touched his cap.

"Good morning, Mr. Lathrop. Your car will be right around. Good morning, miss."

"Have you any plans, anything that can't wait?"

She shook her head. "Not really."

"I'm looking for a place, it has to be the right one, for a new Stalath motel. I'd like your opinion, your advice."

"Isn't that unusual? Stoddard Lathrop asking for someone else's opinion?"

"No-o-o." He led her to the curb as the car came up. "I just don't always take it. I want to go out to the Georgia line and then drive back. Come along?"

"Of course." She studied him for a moment and then laughed quietly.

"I knew a girl whose boy friend traveled for one of the oil companies. Every now and then she'd slip away and they'd go to Savannah. But when they reached the Florida-Georgia line he always made her get out and walk across so that the Mann Act law wouldn't get him."

"I don't believe it."

"It's true. She told me."

"I promise you won't have to walk."

They drove out Main Street and to the broad highway leading to Savannah and Brunswick, Georgia. Where the stucco arch marked the dividing line between the states he turned and drew to the shoulder.

"On the way back," he lit cigarettes for them both, "try to imagine you've been driving from Savannah. It is late afternoon or early evening. You're tired. Where would you like to spend the night?"

"With you." She said it with elaborate demureness but her eyes brightened.

"That's funny but the same thing occurred to me when I saw you in the lobby. Right now, though, we're looking for a place to put a motel."

He began to retrace their route. After a mile or so she spoke with an affected, plaintive squeak.

"Daddy, when are we going to stop? I'm tired. The children are tired and Johnny just wet his pants again."

"Wring him out." He was gruff.

"Let's find a nice motel, one of those Stalath ones."

"How about there?" He pointed to an empty stretch of land.

"No. If we stay here then we'll have to drive into the city in the morning with all the traffic. Let's get through Jacksonville tonight and have it over with."

He reached over and took her hand. "I was hoping you'd say something like that. I'm sure you're right. People would want the city behind them with an easy, fresh start in the morning." He accelerated and the heavy car surged forward. "Outside of the city, South Jacksonville is the place. I'm certain of it now. You've been a great help."

They crossed the high bridge over the St. Johns River and wound through the maze of streets leading out of South Jacksonville.

"When I was a boy there was no bridge here except the railroad one. You went over the river on a ferry. Every now and then the spirit of adventure would take hold of my grandfather and despite everyone's protest we were all loaded into a big yellow car he owned and he would drive us to Jacksonville. Once he damned near ran right off the end of the ferry. It was a full day's trip from Daytona in those days. There wasn't any road; just a couple of sand ruts."

Three miles outside the Jacksonville suburb there were long, empty stretches of flat pineland. Tod checked the speedometer and when they had covered four miles he pulled off the road.

"What do you think?"

"I'd say yes, Tod. It's far enough out. It will be quiet, restful. The pines are wonderful. With some additional planting and landscaping it can be beautiful. Put in a pool. I think this is where people who are going farther south the next day would like to stop and spend the night."

He left the car, went around to her side and helped her out.

"Let's walk over it. Sometimes I get something from the feel of the land. I'm sure you're right. I'm certain of your instinct." He smiled a little embarrassedly. "Particularly since it coincides with my own."

The brown pine needles made a heavy fragrant carpet. They walked hand in hand. The sun was warm, and dappled the ground in golden coins. The wind drifted silently above the treetops, which seemed to pierce the white clouds.

"We haven't seen each other in a long time. I don't know why," he confessed. "I get busy and there doesn't seem to be enough time even for those you really like."

"A couple of times, during those summers I used to spend at Daytona, I thought maybe we had something going for us; something really good."

They halted within the long shadow of a pine. She turned to face him and he bent suddenly and kissed her. They clung together for a moment and her breath came in a quick gasp.

"Tod?" She spoke softly, reluctantly. "Why has it always been this way with us, casual? I'm not at all a casual girl. Yet I am with you. I used to think I was in love when we were together in those summers, but now I don't think so. It's just something I can't help. Or maybe I don't want to try. So I always sacrifice a little pride, even a little self-respect. It's so one-sided because I don't think you give anything."

"I'm very fond of you. You know that."

She stared almost angrily for a moment and then shrugged. "Oh, all right. I don't know why I should expect anything more. You give what you can, I suppose. At least you've always been honest."

They walked back toward the car.

"Tell me." He stopped and looked around. "If you were building a motel, what is the one thing you would do?"

A half grin of mischief touched her lips. "You really want to know?"

"Of course."

She hesitated. "I'll tell you what I'd do. I'd put hooks in the bathrooms for douche bags." She was emphatic.

He looked at her incredulously. "You're joking."

"Why should I be joking? It's as much a part of ordinary cleanliness as taking a bath or brushing your teeth. Certainly it's nothing to be coy about. But there's never a hook in a motel or a hotel. So—you hold the damn thing in the air like a perching Statue of Liberty. That's what I'd do, Stoddard Lathrop, if I was building a motel." She flushed a little and walked ahead of him to the car.

He laughed silently a couple of times back and glanced over at her. She kept her eyes steadfastly ahead on the road.

"All right. You have them."

"Good." She refused to look at him but her lips twitched.

"Let's drive out to the Country Club and have lunch. Will you have dinner with me, also?"

"Of course. How could I resist a man who makes me part of an industrial survey or whatever it was we have been doing?"

"What room are you in?"

"Six ten."

"I'm on the sixth floor, too."

She turned to look at him then.

"How convenient for us both." She said it almost sadly.

South of Tampa Bay there stretches a series of narrow islands. Santa Maria Key, Longboat Key, Casey Key. Below the dark thread of the Miakka River, some eight miles inland from the coast, there stretched a broad expanse of undeveloped land. Here the pines and the scrub, with an occasional grouping of palmetto, lay untouched. The sun rode high and hard upon it but the prevailing winds from the Gulf of Mexico lent a pleasant freshness.

With Reese Sparks beside him in the jeep Tod drove through the high savannahs. Save for the vehicle's motor there was no other sound. Now and then a rabbit bounded ahead of them and overhead the ever-present buzzards spun their wide, circular courses. Tod pulled to a halt within the shade of a stand of palmetto, cut the engine and leaned forward on the wheel to study the land.

"What do you think of it, Mr. Sparks?"

Reese selected a stogie from the breast pocket of his seersucker coat, bit the end and chewed thoughtfully on the morsel of tobacco.

"It depends on what you got in mind, Mr. Lathrop. Surer'n hell it's big an' empty." He lifted his head and sniffed at the warm scent of dry reed grass.

"What I have in mind is something no one has tried before. The Levitts, up in Pennsylvania and on Long Island, have inched toward it but they're still a long way from what I can see." He lit a cigarette. "A long time ago my father talked about a development. What he had in mind was revolutionary, new; a preplanned community. To it people would come and pick out their sites. For their choice there were to be half a dozen different designs for homes. People who bought with the intention of building could select any one but they couldn't build outside this pattern. The houses were all to be within the ten to twelve-thousand-dollar range; reasonable but not cheap in construction. A dollar's worth of value for every dollar. The community was to have its own shopping center and eventually small businesses to serve local needs. It was to be self-contained as far as possible. I have something of the same idea in mind."

"How much land is hereabouts an' what's the dickerin' price?"

"Ten thousand acres if we want them all. I don't think so to begin with. Five thousand to start and a two-year option on the rest. The only thing it's practical for now is grazing and there are no large herds this side of Kissimmee. It's cheap because no one knows what to do with it."

"But you do, Mr. Lathrop?"

"You're damn right I do."

"Oh, I believe you, Mr. Lathrop. I just like to hear you say it." Sparks allowed his gaze to rove over the landscape. "What you got in mind is goin' to take millions by the time it ends. That's more money than you an' me got togethah."

"Once we own the land I'll get the financing. I'll get it in Miami, Jacksonville, New York." There was no suggestion of doubt in the statement.

A brace of quail, startled by some unseen movement, rocketed out of the high sear grass. Sparks followed their flight and made the double popping sound of an imaginary gun with his lips.

"Well, now, Mr. Lathrop." He drawled the words and his eyes lighted. "I'll say one thing. If we buy the land an' you find out latuh you ain't goin' to get no financin', then you an' me are goin' to own the goddamndest shootin' acres two men evah whacked up between them."

Tod laughed at the fancy. He dug into his coat pocket and found a small pad and the stub of a pencil.

"Look here." He began to mark the pad. "We have a triangle made up of the Seaboard Air Line and the Atlantic Coast Line railways. There are three secondary country roads there, there and there which we can lead into. Here, along the coast, the state is planning a paved highway that will run from Venice to Bradentown. We'll have plenty of access. But," he made a double line, "here, from this neck, I want to dredge a fifty-foot-wide canal from the Gulf to bisect the property. People can dock their own small boats in what would be the front yard. We'll build a marina and advertise waterfront lots. People always gravitate toward the water. We'll bring it to them."

He looked up to find Reese Sparks studying him. Their eyes held for a moment and then suddenly they both grinned like a couple of kids, knowing well they understood each other and were in agreement.

"No one has ever tried anything like this before. It is as new as the first Stalath motel and most people said that wouldn't go. It went because I made it go. This isn't just a real estate development."

"It sure as hell ain't, Mr. Lathrop."

"Well?"

Sparks lit his stogie now, taking an inordinately long time with the flame. He let the smoke dribble from his mouth with pleasant reflection.

"You knowed the answer to that, Mr. Lathrop, about five minutes ago. I couldn't say no even if I wanted to; which I don't. Whatever you've got is catchin'."

Tod laughed and crumpled the paper on which he had been drawing.

"Let's get the land, Mr. Sparks."

"You do that, Mr. Lathrop."

Tod started the motor. "It's not all clear yet. Details keep adding themselves. By God, Mr. Sparks, I'm going to build a town! I'm going to build it and name it after my father. Denniston. Denniston, Florida."

Sparks whistled and gave a small nod of assent.

"Someday, when I'm sittin' an' rockin' in the poorhouse, I'll think of you, Mr. Lathrop. I'll think an' remember you as a man who thought real kindly about his papa. I surer'n hell will an' that's a fact."

* XX * *

DENNISTON, Florida, was a spectacular success from the day the acreage was opened. The Stalath Corporation, with the financial backing of two insurance companies and a Miami bank, launched a million-dollar advertising campaign and the results set a pattern for Florida development.

There was no high-pressure, get-rich-quick promotion. No one was promised a fast buck, a high return. No one was asked to invest in the future. This was for today. Speculation in the land was discouraged. It was impossible to control, of course, but most persons who bought did so with the idea of building and living on the property.

Those who came first were elderly couples who had retired on a small income or annuity. They wanted out of the crowded cities, the burgeoning suburbs or bleak Midwestern plains. They were anxious to take themselves from the not always patient sufferance of their children with whom they lived and shared expenses. They read the advertisements, sent for the literature and were reassured by the fact that no one was promising anything more than seemed possible to deliver. There were no free trips, no picnics, no barbecues, no band concerts, no rushing salesmen. Here was a planned community of broad, well-paved streets thoughtfully planted with palms and cedars. Utilities were in and underground. Sidewalks had been laid. Plans, without an architect's fee, were available. With eight different designs to choose from those who built were able to break the monotonous conformity which afflicted most large-scale developments. The down payment was modest, the interest terms reasonable. For those who wanted, and could afford, something extra there were lots on the broad waterway connecting with the Gulf of Mexico. Just that name alone, the Gulf of Mexico, kindled the romantic imagination of most persons. A man could own a small sailboat, a canoe, a skiff with an outboard motor and go from his own dock right down to the Gulf and watch the sun set or do some fishing within the shelter of one of the Keys. Each lot had a palm, two hibiscus shrubs in front and two orange and two grapefruit trees in back. Sprinklers were already installed for the lawns and there was room for a small truck or flower garden in the rear. The climate was agreeable and an insect and mosquito control plan was already underway.

By mail and through personal visits and inspections the money poured in. Within two years Stalath had liquidated its debts and taken up the option on additional acreage and began looking around for another homesite to develop.

Imitators trailed Stalath but few had the imagination or the integrity to duplicate Denniston. They were after the quick dollar and had neither the patience nor the inclination to make the long-term investment.

One of the first houses to go up in Denniston was a two-bedroom ranch style home with a flower-decked patio. It was built at the canal's edge where the water's dark surface mirrored it in the afternoons.

Stoddard Lathrop designed it for himself for it suddenly occurred to him he had never had a home. Always he had lived with Grandfather Will or at his father's house. Also he needed a base here in Denniston, for the development was taking more and more of his time. He had a small plane now in which he flew back and forth between Miami and the peninsula's west coast. He had a landing strip cleared and surfaced and upon this the little plane settled as lightly as a moth.

He superintended every detail of the house's construction down to the laying of the flagstones for an entrance walk. When it was finished he found himself coming down every weekend even when there was no real need for his presence. He had a power dory moored to a dock in the canal. Sometimes he loafed down to the Gulf for some fishing. Other times he would take the jeep and drive over the developing acres. Sometimes he would just lie in the patio's sun listening, as he told himself, to the flowers blooming.

He rarely felt the need for companionship. He actually enjoyed the solitude. He understood himself well by now and knew he was not a lonely man. The drive within him occupied his thoughts and energy. An outsider, an uninvited visitor, would have been an intrusion. Oddly enough, and this always astonished him, he found a pleasure in the company of Reese Sparks.

Reese Sparks, on his part, seemed unable to stay away. He came down diffidently to sit beside the shining canal and throw an occasional rock into the water. He never intruded upon Stoddard's privacy and went to the cottage only when invited. The communion between the two men developed now on a plane of mutual respect. Much of Reese's crudeness had worn away. He no longer indulged himself in the deliberate vulgarities which had repelled Stoddard Lathrop at their first meetings. He accepted this new security of his position with a certain half-embarrassed grace but he never attempted to ingratiate himself.

One weekend when he had driven over from Sarasota he had accepted Stoddard's invitation to stay at the cottage. They sat in the shaded patio with rum, limes and soda on a table.

"We got a real good thing goin' for us heah, Mr. Lathrop. I been learnin' a lot just watchin' you go at it. I been readin' a little, too; readin' about them what made themselves a pot of millions." He grinned almost shyly. "Readin' don't come too easy to me, neither. But it looks to me like them that makes money does it by borrowin'. They get somethin' like we got. Then they borrow on it an' put that money into it so's it's worth more. Then they borrow on that an' go on to somethin' else."

"I'm going to put up an apartment building on Miami Beach."

"By yo'sef?" Sparks managed to sound shocked.

"Not if you want in. We've gone this far together. I'm getting used to you."

"I take some knowin', I guess."

Tod reached for the bottle of Bacardi and splashed some of the rum into his glass.

"I'm going to build an apartment house and buy some property on Flagler Street. Stalath needs its own building. This works out better than you'd think. I, well we, put up an office building. We keep what space we need for ourselves and rent out the rest. But right away we begin what they call 'accelerated depreciation.' We start to write off a hundred thousand dollars a year as depreciation. Say we get a hundred-thousand-a-year rental income. The Government says this isn't income at all. We're just breaking even with our depreciation."

"The Government says that!" Sparks sat upright in his chair and eyed him wonderingly. "You can do that legal?"

"Something else I've been investigating. Savings and Loan. Say we get a charter for a Savings and Loan institution. Right away the Government insures all deposits up to ten thousand dollars. Then, most of the real estate loans we make are insured by the Veterans Administration or the Federal Housing Authority. So, if you own a savings-and-loan outfit you just can't lose. You're insured by the Government at both ends. It's hard to go wrong with a deal like that. The only thing I really yearn for right now is a few oil wells. I'd surely like to have that twenty-seven and a half percent depreciation allowance the Government passes out."

Sparks whistled, a long, low note of astonishment.

"You mean all this heah's been goin' on an' I'm just hearin' about it?"

"I'm afraid so."

"Well." Sparks finished his drink with a single gulp. "Let's you an' me get into the parade, Mr. Lathrop. Looks like we been out of step." He lit a stogie and drew upon it in thoughtful silence for a moment. "You satisfied, Mr. Lathrop? You satisfied with what you're doin' an' what you've got?"

"I guess so." Stoddard was vaguely annoyed by the question. "This is what I want to do."

"I was thinkin' maybe you wanted more. You're a man in his fifties now. It's most too late for a wife, children; things like that. I got nothin' neither. No one who really gives a damn. You an' me could end up by bein' a couple of the wealthiest an' lonesomest men in Florida if we ain't careful. Maybe we already are but don't know it yet. It's a hell of a thing to think about."

Seemingly without effort on anyone's part the Stalath Corporation began acquiring properties far outside the real estate interests upon which it had been founded. Most of them resulted from the insatiable curiosity of Stoddard Lathrop.

In a drugstore on Flagler Street one morning he halted at a counter and picked up a small bottle from a little pyramid on display. The attractiveness of the package was what first caught his attention. Against the deep, rich brown of the glass there was a label and illustration in gold. Reclining against a palm tree was a scantily clad girl. Beneath this, in script lettering, were the words COCOA TAN.

"Is this any good, any different, from all the other suntan oils?" He questioned the young salesgirl whose tan was a startling bronze in contrast to her blond hair.

"It's really wonderful." She was enthusiastic. "And it's made right here in Miami, actually at Perrine. We could sell a lot more but it must be a little plant and they don't make very much. All the girls I know use it."

"Well," he nodded his appreciation of her youthful attractiveness, "you're a good advertisement for it."

Instead of going to his offices in the new Stalath Building as he had intended he drove south, through Coral Gables to the little town of Perrine on the main highway. An inquiry at the local drugstore led him to a small, one-story frame building on Perrine's outskirts. Here in one large room, in an atmosphere rich with the scent of coconut oil, a light perfume and something which had the faint odor of iodine he found a young man. He was bare of foot, shirtless and wore an old pair of patched and faded dungarees. He was stirring at a large tub with a wooden paddle while a Negro boy drew off the mixture and filled the Cocoa Tan bottles by hand.

"I'm Stoddard Lathrop."

The young man nodded pleasantly. "How are you? I'm Jeff McCausland. You in the market for some suntan oil? It's goddamned good. I ought to know. I make it. Put a tan on a yellow pear."

"A young lady in a drugstore up in Miami said it was good. What's in it that makes it different?"

"Hell, Mr. Lathrop." McCausland laughed and his teeth were a white streak against his tan. "If I told you what was in it you'd likely enough go off and begin making your own. Then where would I be?"

Tod smiled. "Up the creek without that paddle." He nodded toward the wooden sweep which glistened from the oily mixture.

"You're damned right." The agreement was cheerful.

"The girl in the drugstore said she could sell more if she could get it. Why don't you increase your production?"

"You hear that, Rose?" McCausland spoke to the Negro. "The gentleman wants to know why we don't make more." He turned to Lathrop. "That's really his name. What the hell do you know about that? Rose Rose. He's got a brother named Geranium Rose."

"Wukkin' my ass off raight now." Rose Rose was mildly interested. "Fillin' these little bottles. Tolt Mr. McCausland us ought to git some machinery. Wukkin' my ass off."

"I think this could be a big product if it was properly marketed and exploited. I like the package. Who designed it?"

"I did." McCausland was thoughtful. "You got a proposition, Mr. Lathrop? I know who you are. I guess everyone in Florida does."

"Sixty percent for the Stalath Corporation. Forty percent for you. We'll do all the exploitation and advertising. If you want a job with Stalath you can have it managing the plant."

"I don't think we want jobs, do we, Rose?"

"Nossuh. Wukkin' my ass off raight now."

McCausland thought for a moment and then nodded. "All right, Mr. Lathrop. We've got us a deal and I'll take the job managing the plant. When do we start?"

"Now. I'll have the papers drawn up. You can show them to a lawyer. Sign and we're in business."

"I don't expect the Stalath Corporation is out to cheat me. When the papers are ready I'll come in and sign."

That was how it started and Cocoa Tan became a nationwide product, available at every retail outlet. Tod turned loose every trick he could think of for exploitation. Outside of Miami, on the two main arteries leading in from the north and on the Tamiami Trail, from the west, he had the Outdoor Advertising Company erect two huge billboards with a slanting platform. The prettiest girls he could recruit from the high schools and the University of Miami were engaged to recline on beach pads in the sun and tan themselves with Cocoa Tan. The girls were alternated every hour and their briefest of bathing suits created a sensation among inbound tourists. Additional girls passed out samples from the roadside while others were engaged to parade on Miami Beach. There they carried spray guns filled with Cocoa Tan and gave the sun bathers a free coating of the product. The novelty of this idea was picked up by press photographers and their pictures with the Cocoa Tan sprays were nationally and internationally circulated. Stalath duplicated these exploitation tactics outside of Jacksonville, Charleston, Atlantic City and the beaches around New York and began working along the California coast. It became almost impossible to get anywhere near a beach without encountering a Cocoa Tan girl.

In the first year, Cocoa Tan grossed five million dollars and the end of the market wasn't even in sight.

In much the same fashion Stoddard Lathrop picked up a small box factory outside of Fort Lauderdale. It was a family affair and a father and three sons put together orange crates by hand and bought their wood from a local lumber yard. They made a quality product for the packing of what was called "the souvenir trade"—the crates of especially selected grapefruit, oranges and tangerines which were purchased by individuals and shipped to relatives or friends in the North. It was a small business and the family was satisfied with small profits.

Stalath had just acquired five thousand acres of pine timberland west of Fort Lauderdale. Tod was driving back one afternoon, on his way to Miami, when he passed the small factory housed in a galvanized iron-sheathed building. On an impulse he turned around and went back. Stalath now had a lot of timber. Maybe, he reasoned, it ought to use it instead of selling it off.

He sat on a bench and talked with the owner, a John Dill.

"I know what you're making here are specialty boxes. Stalath has a hell of a lot of timber I bought but I'm damned if I know what to do with it right now. You have a lot of goodwill and a small market. Stalath will come in, put up a modern plant and we can make both kinds of crates—the regular run-of-the-mill for commercial packing and the specialty crates you are turning out."

"Why don't you just go ahead and set up your own plant? The

Stalath Corporation is big enough, I guess, to knock off any compitition." The man was curious.

"Stalath doesn't want to knock off anyone. You're making a quality product for a limited market. You have a lot of goodwill. Stalath would like to invest in that with profit to everyone and expand the operation. I'd like to have you and your sons stay on and manage the operation."

They made the deal and Stalath spun off a lumbering corporation to handle the raw material. In the same way Lathrop acquired an orange juice processing company and then built an ice plant to facilitate the freezing of the juice. Stalath expanded beyond all normal expectations. It added its own legal department and the office and clerical staff increased threefold. Stoddard Lathrop had a sure touch and an instinct. Everything interested him and he found himself traveling constantly around the state and working fifteen or sixteen hours a day. He thrived on it and his enthusiasm was unquenchable.

It was Reese Sparks who voiced the question which he sometimes asked himself.

"Damned ef you don't weah me out just watchin' you, Lathrop. Do you really want it all?"

"I don't know, Mr. Sparks. I wonder, sometimes. I'm wound up and I guess just have to keep going until I run down. It isn't only the money, although that's important. It's taking something little, like Cocoa Tan, and making it the biggest thing of its kind in the country. That's exciting and without that excitement I think I'd suddenly turn into an old man."

* XXI * *

DENNISTON acquired an almost immediate stability. Those who bought and built were, if not exactly senior citizens, well into middle age, retired on moderate incomes. They had not overextended themselves in their purchases and were confronted by no monthly crisis in the matter of meeting their payments. Some had bought outright. Others had financed their homes through mortgages.

They quickly fell into a community spirit. They formed gardening and landscape clubs; laid out shuffleboard courts, bowling and putting greens, croquet and badminton courts. Many of the men were handy with tools and with time on their hands they built benches around the landscaped plaza. They had fishing tournaments, putting matches, community cookouts, baking contests and a variety of activities which kept them from becoming bored. Because small businesses were wary at first to participate at this stage Stalath spun off a wholesale grocery corporation, established a shopping center complete with meat market. Then one of the residents opened a little novelty store and soon there were half a dozen enterprises—a cleaning and pressing establishment, a fix-it shop, a general repair service which did everything from fixing a balky toilet to repairing a toaster. Sometimes in the evenings, over a weekend, Stoddard Lathrop would stroll about the community feeling a warm glow of paternalism and very much the benevolent country squire.

Although he didn't realize it at the time, Denniston was unique. It came at the right time and attracted the right people. Tod began to think more and more of a similar but larger development on the east coast. He had made a trip to Daytona Beach, which he visited infrequently these days, and talked over his idea with Reese Sparks.

"I'm going to duplicate Denniston on the east coast. There's land north of Miami's city limits which can be bought reasonably. If you want a piece you can have it. If not, Stalath will do it alone."

"Now," Reese had drawled, "you know I want in. Bein' around you is like watchin' a fella juggle a dozen balls at once. I always figure you to drop one but you don't. Just the same, we could get a little extended on this thing. There's a bottom to the gold mine you discovered."

"I haven't seen it yet. Anyhow, people are on the move. They're looking at new horizons. Look at Denniston."

"I got a feelin', an I don't know why, that that there Denniston is in a class by hitself. You get a different kind of people, somehow, on the west coast. They're older, more settled. They already run the race. Now they're willin' to settle down. Here, on the east coast, they're younger, tryin' to make it. They're new married an' up to their necks in small debts. Oh, they'll probably buy your houses but I ain't sure they'll be able to pay for them. That's all I'm thinkin'."

"I'm not begging you to come in. I'm offering it." Tod was impatient. "Stalath can swing it for as much as seems prudent. Stalath will buy the land, and the banks and insurance companies will put up the rest. I can get all the money I need."

Sparks nodded. "I expect you can, Mr. Lathrop. But count me in for a piece. You made us a lot of money an' the chances are we'll make moah. I just got a feelin', though, the east coast ain't right foah what you got in mind. At least it ain't now."

"All right, Mr. Sparks. I'll be in touch with you." He walked to the door of the Citrus Belt Line's office with Sparks. "I'll be in town for a few days, maybe longer. My grandfather isn't feeling too well and I think I ought to stick around for awhile. He's a pretty old gentleman."

Back at his desk he signed orders for six new buses and four trucking rigs. Year after year the Citrus Belt had turned in a fair profit. There was competition now where there hadn't been before in the distance hauling. Several new companies had been formed in Miami, Tampa and Jacksonville and these cut into the freight business but Citrus Belt held on to most of its old customers. He had hired Jim Burnand away from the Inter-State Trucking offices in Jacksonville. Burnand was competent and imaginative and he ran Citrus Belt as well as Tod ever had. The office staff, drivers and shop mechanics were all local people who were interested in seeing that the operation was profitable, thereby securing their jobs. Daytona Beach and Ormond had renewed his bus franchise and the line offered no problems which couldn't be handled without his personal attention. Once every two or three months he came up and these visits were made principally to see his grandfather.

He put his signature to the last order and called Burnand on the interoffice phone to see if there was anything he wanted to talk about. When Burnand said no he went out to his car and drove down Beach Street. The town had grown amazingly but he knew he had outgrown the town. This was a new era Florida was entering upon and the pulse, the vitality, lay in Miami. Things were happening all over the state— some good and some bad. The imitators who had attempted to duplicate Denniston were without Stoddard Lathrop's integrity or vision. They built cheaply, advertised falsely, made down payments preposterously low and foreclosed immediately when anyone fell behind in a mortgage payment. The shoddy houses were sold again and again. On the other hand there were developments which were planned for the upper middle class. There were building restrictions, the homes were separated by a half acre of land on either side. These were for the moderately wealthy who came to settle in Florida and not simply live in it for three or four months out of the year. Most of the owners had flourishing businesses in the North. They spent part of their time in New York, Philadelphia, Boston and Chicago while their families lived in Florida year around save, perhaps, for a couple of months when they went to the North Carolina or Virginia mountains to escape the heat. Then, also, the big money was coming to Florida in increasing numbers. They came in their private yachts or by train or car to pick up their boats which were berthed at Miami, Fort Lauderdale or Palm Beach. They moved in a tight, exclusive circle to their private fishing clubs on the Keys. But the big change in Florida, the thing that was making Florida history, was the migration of the great middle class and the young people, in particular, who were looking for something better, a new way of life. The very wealthy were the transients and few of them were looking for investments in Florida. A few had made contact with Stalath because they were interested in the Stalath Motel franchises but most were satisfied to keep and manage what they had. They had though, Tod discovered, one thing in common. A lively curiosity as to how someone else was making money even though they had no need for more. Money fascinated them as jewels intrigue a woman. They never discussed money itself, only the means of making it.

One afternoon, at Key Largo, he sat on the afterdeck of a hundred-and-twenty-six-foot auxiliary schooner talking with the owner. They had both been bone fishing from different skiffs in the grassy flats and later struck up a conversation across the distance separating them. Highballs in hand the conversation veered around to Stalath with which the visitor seemed well acquainted.

"I like your motel idea, Mr. Lathrop. I have a subsidiary company which operates half a dozen hotels. We'd be interested in a West Coast, California, franchise." His name was Gailbraith.

"I don't see any difficulty there. When you come back to Miami let's have lunch together."

"Have you ever thought about moving into the Bahamas? Not with motels, of course, but with an exclusive club. I should think it would be right up Stalath's alley."

The suggestion hadn't meant much at the time but every now and then it would recur in Stoddard Lathrop's mind. He stored it there for future use.

Now, driving south on Beach Street, he thought about it again. "Why not?" He spoke aloud. First he wanted to acquire the land outside of Miami for a second Denniston. Then there would be time to put together some ideas for the Bahamas. More and more tourists, he knew, were visiting the islands but the people who would be attracted to such a club as he was mentally building were such people as Gailbraith, men with unlimited resources. He wondered if the Bahamian Colonial Government could be induced to permit gambling on one of the Out Islands. He wouldn't want a casino in conjunction with the club he was envisioning but a casino attached to a hotel on another island—Chubb Cay or Lyford Cay or Bimini—would attract the sporting crowd now going to Havana. It was worth making inquiries in Nassau where he had several influential friends who could get the Government's ear.

On the porch of the house by the river Will Lathrop sat in a deep wicker chair, tugging irritably at a light blanket spread across his knees. He had grown frail and seemed to have shrunk. His skin had the transparency of porcelain. Beside him Wash tried ineffectually to put a small pillow behind his employer's back.

"I don't want any damned pillow. Stop clucking over me. By God, you're older than I am! If anyone needs a pillow it's you."

"Yes suh," Wash agreed in a melancholy tone. "Ah suah enough do only Ah ain' got no one to put hit theah."

Wash was bending slightly with the years. His poll was the purest white as were his eyebrows. Veins and cords ridged his hands and he shuffled a little when he walked. Watching him through half-closed eyes Will Lathrop thought, two old men, grown old together, waiting for the scythe to cut them down. This is a hell of a way to end. Will Lathrop, who had always been meticulous in his speech, found that he was growing more and more profane in thought and word as the years crowded him. He was mildly astonished by this.

"Are the days getting colder, Wash?" He peered at the river which sparkled in the sunlight.

"Ah ain' suah, Mistuh Will. Sometime Ah think so. Ah git a chill to th' bone. Hit do seem coldah." He turned at the sound of a car swinging into the front driveway. "Heah cum Mistuh Tod."

"I know damned well it's Tod." He could see the figure but dimly as his grandson came up the walk and onto the porch. "Hello, boy."

"Hello, Grandfather. Wash, how are you?"

"Poorly, Mistuh Tod. Poorly."

Tod took a chair next to his grandfather. "Get me a drink, will you, Wash? Some rum, a lime and water."

"I'll have a hot toddy." Will Lathrop struggled into a semi-upright position.

"Now, Mistuh Will. You know what th' doctah say," Wash objected.

"Who the hell pays your salary? Dr. Rawlings?"

"No suh," Wash replied wearily. "You does, Mistuh Will. Whin you think of hit an' that ain' often no moah." He went into the house.

"I'm going to fire that boy one of these days." Will glared after Wash. "He's getting fresh and if there is anything I can't stand it's a fresh nigger."

Tod looked at him, surprised. "In all the years," he said slowly, "that's the first time I ever heard you use that word."

Will Lathrop was silent for a moment. "Yes. I guess so. I don't think I ever said it before. I'm angry, Tod. I'm an angry old man because I'm dying and I don't want to die. I don't particularly want to live either. It's a hell of a situation. I can't get used to it."

"You're not dying." There was little conviction in the statement. "You'll be around for a long time."

Wash brought Tod's drink and Will Lathrop's toddy steaming in a silver mug with a wooden handle. They sipped and Will sighed appreciatively.

"It's a curious thing, boy, how a man's ego asserts itself when he knows he's dying. He says: How can everything go on as it has, just as though nothing has happened, and I'm dead? The wonders of the world will continue without interruption. People will laugh, sing, cry, drink, make love, battle their fears and cherish their hopes and all this time, while this is going on, I'll be underground with the worms crawling in and out. It doesn't seem fair, somehow. It doesn't seem possible. The mind rejects it. I suppose that is why man invented Heaven. The mind stops short of accepting finality. He had to find a substitute so man turned to something as preposterous as immortality and Heaven."

"I wish you would come down to Miami with me. We could close the house. Wash could come with you. I'll put together a four- or five-room suite at the Stalath Motel or we can rent a house if you prefer. I don't like the idea of your being alone."

"I'm not alone, boy. There's the memory of a lot of fine years to keep me company. I have Wash and Cynthia in the kitchen. The three of us have added up the years together. I'm better off here." He put his toddy aside and then picked up and studied the mug again. "I bought these in Sweden fifty or sixty years ago. Felicia was with me. We had just begun to spend her money." He smiled. "I've had the best of everything, boy. But the knowledge doesn't make it any easier to leave. I only hope you're enjoying your life as much as I have mine. Sometimes I get the idea you're lonely."

"I don't have time to be lonely. Oh, I'll admit I've thought several times I should have married and raised a family. It might be pleasant now. You know. The pipe and slippers business and a fire on the hearthside. Time slipped through my fingers."

"You're not too old. Find a fine young woman who is good in bed. You'll see. It's not hard to become domesticated."

Tod shook his head. "I know any number of fine young women who are good in bed. But the idea of adjusting completely to one of them scares me. I don't think I could do it. A night, a week, a month even. That is all right. Anyhow, I don't think a fine young woman would put up with me for very long."

Will Lathrop was nodding in his chair. The toddy had made him drowsy. Tod watched for a moment and then rose, pulled the blanket up slightly, left the porch and went to his room. It faced the river and he stood at the window looking out upon the pewter sheen. The Halifax was linked with his earliest memories. He had fished and played in its waters from the time he could remember. Memory tugged at him. Over there, near the Gamble house, he and Jake Odum had found a canoe. Someone, one of the winter families probably, had abandoned it. The canvas was torn in places. It leaked and needed painting. They sewed the canvas with an upholstery needle borrowed from Ferd Bracey. Then they begged some tar from men who were roofing a house. They coated the craft liberally with the tar and when it was dry took their savings and bought two gallons of marine paint and a quart of varnish to complete the job. It was a fine, watertight canoe when they were finished and they rigged it with sideboards and a mast. It gave them a wonderful sense of freedom to have a boat and every day after school found them on the river. One night he had sailed it from the beach side to the mainland and Burgoyne's Casino where the weekly dances were held. His arrival by canoe created a sensation among the boys and girls his age, he remembered. Helen Hotchkiss was so impressed she voyaged across the narrow stretch of water to City Island where, for the first time, she let him make love to her on a bench in the dark. He remembered now he had thought it must be a great thing to be a sailor if this sort of thing went on in every port.

With a reminiscent smile he turned away and stretched out on the bed, arms crossed beneath his head. There was no question but that Will Lathrop was dying. It was almost possible to see the day-by-day disintegration of the body. The old gentleman's mind, though, remained sharp and filled with an acid humor. When Grandfather Will was gone he would have no one; no one who really gave a damn. The thought depressed him. He had few intimates and the pressure of his manifold activities prevented his seeing much of the few persons he really liked and felt comfortable with. Money, and he was edging into the really big money now, created its own wall. Those without it were uncomfortable in its presence. They either wanted something or were fearful of being suspected of wanting something. He thought of an incident which had occurred in Miami a few weeks ago.

The new Stalath Building, on Flagler Street, was a structure of sheer beauty. It rose twenty-five stories and was so artfully designed and constructed that it seemed to be made entirely of glass. Sometimes, feeling a little embarrassed by what he was doing, he would drive downtown on a late moonlit night and stand admiring its shimmering magnificence.

Entering it one morning he moved into the crowded elevator, nodded to the operator. Then he caught a glimpse of a vaguely familiar face. He stared for a moment and then recognition came.

"David. David Herndon. How are you?" He extended a hand.

"I'm—I'm fine—Tod." There was a moment's hesitation.

He and Herndon had been in high school together, played on the basketball team. They had never been close. But now Tod suddenly discovered he was glad to see him.

"How have you been?"

"Fine, Tod." Again the curious irresolution.

"Look." It was impulsive. "We haven't seen each other in a long time. If you're not doing anything for lunch come up to the twenty-fifth floor around twelve thirty and have it with me."

"Well . . . sure, Tod. If you want to."

They had an incomparable lunch in Stalath's private dining

room. The talk had been almost guarded on Herndon's part and it consisted mainly of the "do you remember" variety. Now and then Tod caught what he fancied was a sly humor in Herndon's expression. It was disturbing because he couldn't account for it.

They finished their cigars and brandy and Tod arose.

"I have an appointment, David. Sorry this has to be so short. We'll get together again and spend a little more time together. Call me the next time you're in the neighborhood."

"Hell, Tod"—there was just a suggestion of defensive arrogance in Herndon's manner—"I'm mostly in this neighborhood. I work in the accounting department for Stalath. I guess you didn't know, did you?"

"No, I didn't, David."

For a moment he had been coldly outraged, made furious not by the furtive and almost insolent manner but by the fact that Herndon had thought the deception necessary. He actually seemed to take a small, malicious pleasure in the trick. He could have said in the beginning he worked for Stalath and Tod would still have extended the invitation. That Herndon had chosen to make the occasion one of cheap deceit made him angry now.

"I hope you're happy in your job."

"You're not sore." Herndon was apprehensive. "I mean, I didn't know how to tell you. You know, things being the way they are. They're not the same as they were when we were in school together." He was worried now about his job.

"No. Why the hell should I be sore? I hope you're happy in your job. If there is anything I can do let me know."

He carried the distasteful memory of this encounter with him all day. He could not dismiss it and, strangely enough, felt guilty. It wasn't his fault but he resented the implication that he would have acted any differently if David Herndon had told him he was a Stalath employee. From the incident the truth became self-evident. Fitzgerald had once put it succinctly. "The very rich are different." They were. They had to be and there was no point in attempting to evade the truth or the responsibility. Still, he resented the wall which was invisible to corresponding wealth but was an impassable, psychological barrier to those without it. He found the idea depressing.

★ 332

I think, he told himself now, I need Grandfather Will's suggestion. A fine young woman who is good in bed. His mind ran through several names, here in Daytona Beach, in Jacksonville and Miami. Finally he rolled to his side, reached for the bedroom extension phone and put in a call for Fern Wentworth, in Sanford.

"Hello. Will you marry me?"

There was a brief pause. "Don't you think you ought to tell me who it is first?"

"Tod Lathrop."

"Have you been drinking, my rare lad?"

"No. All of a sudden I found myself feeling lonely. My grandfather suggested I find a fine young woman who is good in bed. You meet all those qualifications admirably in addition to being beautiful and smelling of wood violets."

"Thank you, sir. I'm going to do you a favor and turn down the proposal—assuming you really meant it."

"I meant it then, for a minute. I'm scared now."

"Don't be. I won't take you up on it. I like you too much to marry you and spoil it. Where are you?"

"Daytona Beach. My grandfather isn't well. I think I'd better stay around here for awhile. If he's better I'll be back in Miami next week."

"Want me to come down?"

"Yes. I'll tell you what. I have some business to attend to first in Miami. After that we'll take the *Skipjack* and go to the Bahamas. I want to have a look around for something I have in mind. We'll cruise the Out Islands. Appeal to you?"

"Very much. I told you once before I could be in love with you without much effort. But don't worry. I'll keep my flaming passion under control."

"Good. I'll call you from Miami and send a plane for you. Goodbye—and, Fern—"

"Yes?"

"Thanks."

He hung up, half laughing, and wondering what the hell he would have done if she had said yes. Dropping back on the bed he began thinking of the Bahamas. They'd have a wonderful cruise. He had a new boat, a sixty-eight-foot cruiser, the *Skipjack,* which, save

333   ★

for an occasional trip down to the Key Largo Angler's Club, he rarely used. A week or two lazing around the Out Islands with Fern Wentworth was just what he needed. Already he was building the new club there on one of the islands. He knew exactly what he wanted —low, rambling, comfortable and with mooring facilities for the largest of yachts. No more than a hundred members and these would be hand-picked. First, though, he wanted the property outside of Miami. Then when the development was established he'd go to work on the connections he had in Miami to have the city limits extended to include the land. Once he had the property he could set about arranging the financing for construction through the banks and insurance companies. What should he call this one? Maybe, he thought, after Grandfather Will. Willton. He tested the name, saying it aloud. Willton. It was good, short, easy to remember. That was it. Willton, Florida.

He swung up and off the bed, eager to have things moving again. Willton would be different in character from Denniston. He sensed this and Reese Sparks' opinion confirmed it. Denniston attracted the retired, the elderly. They seemed to gravitate to the west coast. Here he needed good but low-cost housing for the thousands of younger people who were migrating to Florida and settling in and around Miami, filling and creating jobs. He wanted no dreary wasteland of identical houses side by side but he would plan them carefully to take advantage of every square foot. Two- and three-bedroom homes with a carport or attached garage and each with a small garden space. He'd put in a supermarket and around that other things would grow.

Will Lathrop died the following Tuesday. Dr. Rawlings, who had been the family physician for years, came in response to an emergency call.

"He just ran down, Tod. There was nothing anyone could have done. The machinery wore out. It was a good way to go; no pain, no suffering. Will Lathrop died as he would have liked to, without causing anyone any trouble."

After the funeral Tod had a talk with Wash and the cook, Cynthia. They were red-eyed from crying and sat in silent, rocking misery in the kitchen.

"My grandfather provided for both of you in his will. Neither of you will have to work for someone else. The bank will mail you a check every month. I'm going to close the house. I don't particularly want to sell it. Maybe someday I'll put up an apartment building here. Right now we'll let it stand."

Later he saw Wash alone in Will Lathrop's den.

"I'd take you to Miami with me, Wash, but I don't know what you'd do. Right now I'm living in a motel apartment. Someday I'll probably build my own home down there."

"That's all raight, Mistuh Tod. Ah done put en a lifetime wukkin' foah Mistuh Will. He gone to he res' now an' hit ain' goin' to be long befoah Ah go to mine. Now Ah go back to Newtown to my own people an' sit out th' day 'neath a chinaberry tree in the sun. Ef whin you gits up heah everah now en then hit would be a real pleasuah ef you come to see me. You turn into a fain man from that little boy Ah knowed such a long time ago."

He turned everything over to Will Lathrop's lawyer. As he had suspected there wasn't much left of Felicia Lathrop's considerable fortune. Will Lathrop kept his promise. He lived well and extravagantly to the end. The annuities to Wash and Cynthia and the riverfront house comprised the holdings. There was nothing more for Tod to do and he drove back to Miami at the end of the week.

The tract north of Miami's city limits was some eleven thousand acres stretching north and west along the highway. It was flatland, lightly timbered with pine, live oak and scrub palmetto and was in some twenty different parcels, the smallest of which was two acres. Tod set about buying it through intermediaries. Once the word was passed around that Stalath was interested, the price would jump all out of reason. Even so there were rumors, for Stalath had moved so aggressively within the state that almost any development was credited to it.

The land was gathered slowly. There was bargaining to be done. Owners of small pieces were sometimes reluctant to part with them for no particular reason other than they just didn't need the money or imagined by holding out they could get a better price. While the negotiations were going on, Stoddard Lathrop had architects, engineers and landscape artists at work on their drawing boards planning the community. A tremendous amount of money began to flow into the project, which was still in the planning stage.

Reese Sparks invested half a million dollars in the development. He came down to Miami, not because he was concerned over his investment but, like Tod, he couldn't keep away when things were moving.

"I'll have to figure out what your share is later when I know what Stalath's total investment is."

"I ain't worried about that, Mr. Lathrop." He stood with Tod at the edge of the highway, his eyes sweeping over the acres which were in the process of being put together. "If this one goes we got us a real gold mine an' that's a fact."

"It will go, Mr. Sparks. I'll make it go." He smiled. "It will go because I say it will and that's as close to an egotistical statement as you'll get from me."

* XXII * *

ELUTHERA is a crescentlike link in the long chain of the Bahamas. To the west lies New Providence and Nassau and to the northwest Great Abaco, the Abaco Cays and the Little Bahama Bank. Separated by a short stretch of water is the small settlement of Spanish Wells. The *Skipjack* put in here.

They walked hand in hand through the sandy roads of the tiny community. The houses were all frame, neat and well tended with, usually, a border of polished conch shells along their entrance paths. The schoolhouse had mellowed to a soft, pastel pink.

"It's another world, isn't it?" Fern looked about her with delight.

"It really is. In the school there the boys, and some of the girls, begin studying navigation at eight and nine years of age. They take their living from the sea and are more at home on it than the land."

They had lunch at the St. George's Hotel whose balcony over-looked the incredible expanse of blue, green and indigo colored water of the Atlantic.

Fern sampled the fresh conch salad and her eyes widened with appreciation.

"It's delicious."

"It's supposed to be an aphrodisiac."

"Well, what do you know? Let's order some more."

After lunch they went to the balcony, pulled wicker rocking chairs into the sun.

"I can't understand how a place this size can support three churches." Fern leaned back, a cigarette between her fingers.

"I wondered about that also when I first came here. It's the same throughout the Out Islands. Finally I figured it out. They don't have any other amusement, so they go to two or three churches on a Sunday night to hear a different sermon. Sort of a double or triple feature. The ministers stagger their church time." He laughed quietly. "The missionaries out of England and the United States are forever at their proselytism. The first time I came to Spanish Wells I met a couple of Bible whackers from some mountain sect in North Carolina. They were all but illiterate, walked around with toothpicks in their mouths. They had been sent down by their church to scout the place. The way the A & P might send out a field team to see if it was worth while opening a new store in a town which already had several. They had a guitar and an accordion and sang hymns to a hillbilly beat. Anyhow, we were all seated at the same table here and I started to eat. One of them bellowed at me, 'Do you mind if we say grace first?' I stopped eating and said, 'No. Go ahead.' I waited until they finished in chorus and then had my lunch. Later I was on the porch here. One of them came out and sat beside me. The way you are now. He rocked back and forth for awhile and I could see what was on his mind. Here was the infidel who could be their first convert in Spanish Wells. Even one soul saved would be something. Finally he said, 'Mr. Lathrop, are you a religious man?' I told him no but I wasn't antireligious either. He rocked some more and then said . . . I'm not exaggerating." He caught her smile. " 'Don't you want to get right with God?' I told him that as far as I knew things between God and me were fine. After a minute or two he went on. 'Wouldn't you like to stand on the far distant shore someday with your loved ones?' " Tod laughed again, amused by the recollection. "By this time I was pretty fed up. I said to him, 'If by my loved ones you mean my relatives, well, I couldn't stand the bastards when they were alive and I certainly don't want to spend eternity with them.' It wasn't true, of course, but I had to say it. He jumped out of his chair as though it was a rattlesnake nest. The next day they left. I don't know whether they ever built a church here."

Fern wiped away the tears of laughter. "I don't believe it."

"It's true. I give you my word." He lit a fresh cigarette.

"Why do they call it Spanish Wells?"

"I don't know. I suppose the Spaniards found a well here. That's the most logical explanation. It's the only island in the Bahamas where there are no Negroes. No one seems to know why. All of the others have large populations, the descendants of slaves. Here, on Spanish Wells, most of the families are related. The people who own this hotel, the Pinders, are probably the most important if importance can be measured here. The original Pinders came over around 1650 with the Elutheran Adventurers, from London, and settled on Eluthera. We'll be going over there tomorrow."

She leaned back, lifting her face to the sun and gentle breeze.

"It's been a wonderful four days, Tod. I've never been in Nassau before. It's pretty touristy but nice. What was the name of your friend at the Royal Victoria? Hickman?"

"Denis. Denis Hickman. He signs his letters Denis Hickman, Innkeeper. He really loves that old hotel and he tries to keep it as it is and has been since the Civil War. I wouldn't stay any other place. It was famous in its day with its dashing Confederate officers, in Nassau to buy war supplies for the Confederacy. Also, a lot of Southern belles and their mamas were sent over by the large plantation owners to get them away from the war. Denis tries to preserve the atmosphere." He was silent for a moment. "We can stay here, ashore, tonight if you want to."

"No, I'd rather be on the boat. It makes me feel so abandoned. It's good for my libido, whatever that is. Anyhow, it has something to do with sex. When we get to some of the Out Islands where there aren't any people I want to go swimming naked in that incredible-looking water. You know," she closed her eyes to the sun, "this is really a lotus blossom land. *Dolce far niente*. Or something like that."

"That's it." He spoke with quick interest. "I've been wondering what I wanted to call the club I'm going to build. I didn't want the usual names. Coral Club. Anglers Club. Out Island Club. That sort of thing. The Lotus Club will do. It will do just fine. Do you know, I think I'm going to charge a million-dollar initiation fee."

"You won't get many members at those rates."

"No," he said happily. "I won't, will I?" He stood up and reached for her hand. "Let's go down to the boat."

"Is that conch salad having any effect?"

"I don't know but I think it's just you, the sun and the islands."

Eluthera is almost a hundred miles long and not much more than two or three miles wide save at the extremities. It has lakes, rolling hills, woodlands and valleys with some of the most beautiful of all beaches where the sand is flour white and soft.

They cruised the west side, down to Southeast Point, then back up to Powell Point and into Governor's Harbor. Tod had brought the *Skipjack* over to the islands but in Nassau he hired a captain, a taciturn Scot who had lived in the islands all of his life. He knew every cove, cay and "niggerhead" in the waters. Tod turned the operation of the boat over to him while he and Fern, wearing little more than was absolutely necessary, lay about in the sun forward.

Fern was astonished and delighted by the island Negroes. They walked straight and proud with, sometimes, a colorful basket of fruit on their heads. The girls and women wore their hair in tightly rolled spindles which stuck straight out from their scalp. Their speech, with a curious accent, was frequently completely incomprehensible.

"You don't see any mulattos." She was astonished.

"No, I don't remember ever seeing one. They have managed to keep their blood line clean. It is a little astonishing when you think about it, since their ancestors were all brought here as slaves by the British, first, and later the settlers from the American colonies after the War for Independence. God knows the Southern gentlemen impregnated enough of their wenches on the mainland. It is strange that they apparently gave up the practice here."

For all his attitude of carefree indolence Stoddard Lathrop was searching for something. He knew what he wanted, how it had to be. First, he needed deep water and a sheltered anchorage for the members' boats. Second, he wanted land. As the original idea for the club developed he began to envision it with guest cottages, tennis courts, swimming pool and a golf course. Not everyone, he reasoned, was a fisherman. Almost everyone was a golfer of sorts. Once again he would build a community but this was to be for the very wealthy. No one else would be able to afford it. He had only been half joking when he told Fern he might charge a million-dollar initiation fee. It was an exaggeration, of course, but he almost wistfully thought he would like to have it a fact. Anyhow, the membership would be limited. Not too many would be able to afford it.

He found what he wanted at Rock Sound. Thereafter he had only one thought in mind—to get back to Nassau, put the project in the hands of the Christie real estate people, and see how many acres could be secured. With this and Willton under way he was going to stretch Stalath's resources to the limit, but the knowledge didn't disturb him. There was the element of risk in every venture. That was what made it exciting. Stalath was sound and its assets liquid. It couldn't remain static. He had built it and it was his to take chances with.

Because Fern seemed to be enjoying herself so completely he curbed his impatience to talk with people in Nassau. Leaving Eleuthera they cruised Exuma Sound the length of the Exuma Cays. They put in at small settlements to buy a freshly killed chicken, some tomatoes, other vegetables and oranges. They swam and fished and made love on the white, warm sand of deserted coves. Fern did the cooking and they ate on the afterdeck with the three of them washing the dishes later.

"I could have brought a boy to do this," he apologized one evening. "But I thought the fewer people we had along the more fun it might be."

"I like it this way." She lay within the crook of his arm in a deck chair. "If it wasn't for Captain Muirland I'd run around naked."

"You almost do. It's very easy to forget the years with you, Fern."

"Don't talk about them. It seems we have known each other for such a long time but we really don't know much about each other, do we? I've always been the girl you could call up when you couldn't think of anything else to do. It isn't very flattering. Sometimes I resented it but," she smiled a little ruefully, "not enough, I guess."

341 ★

"What happened to your marriage?"

She was silent for a moment. "I don't know. I really don't. It just didn't work out and it should have. Don was good to me but the truth is we bored each other. I don't know why we didn't realize that before, as they say in the society pages, we plighted our troth. What is a troth anyhow?"

"It's short for betroth—betrothal."

She sat up in surprise. "How did you know that? I didn't."

"I don't know. It's part of a lot of useless information I have stored away."

"Well." She settled back with a comfortable sigh. "What do you know?"

Tod spent an entire morning with Christie in Nassau. They went over the requirements for the Lotus Club together.

"This isn't going to be cheap, Mr. Lathrop."

"I didn't expect it to be. I just don't want to be taken."

"I'll get to work on it and be in touch with you. I like your idea fine. It will be good for the islands and what is good for the islands is good for Christie's."

On the way back to the mainland instead of going into Miami Tod turned south and headed for the keys.

"You remember Clinton Campbell from Daytona Beach, don't you?"

"Of course." Fern was perched beside him at the wheel.

"He owns the Key Largo Angler's Club. I thought we might run down. He's the only really close friend I have. It goes back a long time but we don't see much of each other. Are you in a hurry to go home?"

"I'm never in a hurry to go to Sanford and I'm without kith or kin. Well, not exactly kin. I suppose you know what kith means, also?"

"No." He smiled. "That isn't included in my store of useless information.

"Why do you always call Campbell J. C.? Everyone else calls him Clint."

"I don't know." He mused over this. "It started way back when we were kids. I never called him anything else. His full name is

James Clinton. I used to call him that at first as sort of a joke. Then it was shortened to J. C. It's been that way ever since."

On Key Largo, Campbell had built what had always been his dream—the private club he had talked to Tod about years ago. Now it was a reality. Tod was never sure how it had come about or where he had acquired the original financing. But J. C. had pursued his goal, never losing sight of it for a day. Now the club's membership roll read like a copy of *Who's Who*. The members lounged about in faded dungarees, went bone fishing on the tidal flats or ran out through the tortuous passages to the ocean and fished for sail which played about the edge of the gulf stream. Having achieved what he wanted in life J. C. was completely unimpressed by Lathrop's almost spectacular success. He managed to view his old friend with a quiet, twinkling humor as though the whole thing wasn't real anyhow and because of this they shared a secret joke. When Tod came down to Key Largo, J. C. always found time to be with him. The years had brought no change in the unspoken affection which existed between them.

After dinner Fern went to her room early and Tod and J. C. took a couple of handlines and some pieces of shrimp and went down to the end of one of the docks. They sat, dangling the lines, fishing for grunts, small snapper or a sheepshead around the pilings. This was kid fishing as they had done it years ago when they both were very young. They talked of whatever came to mind and felt no compulsion for words when they wanted to be silent. The communion between them was complete.

Tod told him what he had in mind for the Bahamas. "It's going to be different from anything they have there now. I'm surprised you didn't move in there."

"I have all I can do to run this the way I want it run."

"Want to come in with me?"

J. C. shook his head. "You're a loner. We both are. You don't really want a partner." He laughed softly. "Not even that old rip Reese Sparks or whatever his name is. What's become of him anyhow?"

"He's around, up at Daytona Beach. Every now and then he comes down to Miami. You know," and his words were colored by a little wonder, "I actually enjoy the old bastard. Sometimes I imagine I'm

343 ★

getting a little like him save for some surface polish. He has his house, his money and a more or less permanent guest, Francine Estes."

"The hell you say." J. C. lit a cigarette. "What does Willie think about that?"

"I don't think anyone asked Willie's opinion. I have an idea Reese just went out and bought Francine—with Francine's willing cooperation. Anyhow, from what I hear Willie broke out in a mild rash of prosperity. He opened his own garage on the beach side and a week or so later Francine moved in with her uncle. It seems to have done them all good. Sparks is as frisky as a goat. Willie has his own business. Francie has a new car whenever she wants it, all the clothes she can buy and a personal maid. I'm not sure Willie even has visiting privileges."

J. C. whistled softly. "Is it true you're putting in a development north of Miami, something like Denniston?"

"Yes, but keep it to yourself. Every time someone mentions Stalath the price of the acreage I want goes up. I'm buying it through several different persons but somehow the word gets around."

"Aren't you stretching yourself a little with that and the Bahamas too? It's sometimes hard to get—money I mean. But it's fairly easy to lose. Don't get in over your head."

"I'm a pretty good swimmer. I like the deep water. There's no fun in wading."

J. C. wound in the handline and snapped his cigarette out into the darkness over the water.

"Well," and J. C. smiled, "if you ever get too wet there'll always be a room here for you to dry off in."

"I know that but I don't intend to go broke. The way things are set up with the Government, the F. H. A. and the Veterans Administration, you have to work at it to lose money. The club in the Bahamas is a different matter. I could take a licking there but I don't think so." They began walking back up the dock. "I'm going to start looking around and build my own home. Do you know, I've never really had one. Most of my life I spent with my parents and Grandfather Will Lathrop. It's about time I had a place of my own."

"Why don't you get married?"

"Ever since I've been twenty-one people have asked me that. I don't want to get married. It takes time and I don't have the time."

"I thought, maybe, you had something going with Fern. She's a fine girl and I think a little lonely. Running off to the Bahamas with you for a week or so isn't the answer. You could do a lot worse."

"I don't want to do worse or better."

"All right, my friend, but you'll find yourself rattling around in a house. I've tried it."

Fern and Tod went back to Miami in the morning. On a high stool beside him at the wheel she leaned forward, resting her chin on cupped hands. They passed a channel marker on which a lone and melancholy-appearing pelican roosted.

"They always appear so wise. I wonder if they really are?"

"I have an idea they are like the owl. They just sit and say nothing and this makes people think they are smart." He laughed suddenly. "There was one. I remember as a kid. Someone called him Mose and the name stuck. George Holland's father ran a fish market on the street level of what was then Keating's Casino and Pier. I don't know how this pelican figured it out but he stopped fishing with the other pelicans. Every morning, while his friends and relatives were cruising up and down over the ocean looking for something to feed their hungry bellies, Mose would arrive at Holland's fish market and sit on a railing outside. He just sat there, looking sad and forlorn. Now and then Mr. Holland would throw him a fish head or some scraps. After awhile the people who came to the market would pay four or five cents for a small mullet and toss it to Mose on their way out. He got so fat he waddled when he walked and could barely take off from the railing when evening came. Mose never did a lick of work. He just sat there, his pouch full of fish, swallowing one when he felt a small pang of hunger. Now and then he'd turn around and watch the other pelicans at their endless business of trying to get enough to eat. Mose had settled all of life's complications. He apparently never told any of the other pelicans about his soft touch and he never brought a friend to share the bounty. One day he didn't show up and no one ever saw him again. It was Mr. Holland's opinion that he ate himself to death. I guess," he said with a smile of reminiscence, "there's a moral in the story of Mose somewhere. I'm not just sure what it is."

She reached over and covered his hand with hers. "You're fun to be with, Tod Lathrop. It's been a wonderful trip. I guess a little sin now and then can be a very cleansing thing."

"When I get the land I want on Eluthera," he was enthusiastic over the idea, "we'll go again. I'll have drawings then and show you what I have in mind."

"You never stop, do you?"

"No." He reflected. "I wouldn't know how. That's the truth."

She linked her fingers with his. "I'm very fond of you and have no ulterior motives. We'll leave things the way they are."

From the yacht basin in Miami he drove her to the airport where Stalath's light plane waited. He helped her in and stood watching until it disappeared in the west. Then he drove back to downtown Miami and the Stalath Building, anxious to find out what was happening with the acreage he wanted for Willton.

Stalath occupied the top four floors of the twenty-five-story building. Tod's offices, a vast, almost cathedral-like room with anteroom and adjoining space for his secretary, took in the corner of the twenty-fourth floor overlooking the bay and Miami Beach. In chairs at one side of the huge desk three men—Stalath's auditor, the head of the legal department and John Trevor, a real estate broker—waited patiently. Tod stood, staring out of the window.

"What the hell does he want? More money? Offer it to him." He turned.

Trevor shook his head. "He says he doesn't want anything."

"Everyone wants something." Tod dismissed the statement as nonsense. "Do you mean to sit there and tell me Willton has come to a standstill because some damn fool Cracker is sitting in the middle of the proposed tract, holding on to twenty-five acres he won't sell? We have land all around him." He grinned suddenly despite his annoyance. "By God, we've got him surrounded like Apaches circling a covered wagon! I'll build around him if I have to." He turned to the lawyer. "Have you spoken with him, Bill?"

The attorney nodded. "He says he doesn't need the money, doesn't want to sell. That's all there is to it."

"There has to be more. Maybe he doesn't need the money. Then again, maybe he does and is holding out to squeeze us. He must have figured Stalath is behind the project. There's been a lot of talk, rumors. Even the Miami *Herald* has hinted at it. What's his name any-how?"

"Jess Samish. He runs a general store at a crossroads just outside Apalocka. You know the type—worked hard all of his life, suspicious of everyone, a little crafty and greedy."

"Why should he be suspicious? We've offered him a fair price, haven't we?"

"He's suspicious by nature. Everyone is out to do him," Trevor answered. "I offered him a fair price and even upped it a little."

"There must be something we can put our hands on, a lever to budge him." He sat on the corner of the desk and lit a cigarette. Finally, he reached for the telephone. "Get me Mr. Reese Sparks in Daytona Beach."

His eyes lighted with amusement as he waited for the switchboard to put the call through.

"Hello, Mr. Sparks. Stoddard Lathrop." He was casual. "I wonder if you'd give me a little help? I've run into a fellow down here by the name of John Samish. Now he seems to be just about as mean and contrary as you are. My people, they're delicate, aren't able to handle him. It occurred to me you might do better. You know how it is, Mr. Sparks. One contrary son of a bitch dickering with another contrary son of a bitch. One of them has to give and I'm willing to bet on you. That's right." He listened intently for a minute. "He's sitting on a twenty-five-acre tract right in the middle of our activity and won't budge." He listened again and nodded. "That is right. Of course, Mr. Sparks, it's business. Naturally I wouldn't expect you to pay your own expenses. Stalath will pay them." A smile began to creep over his face. "For two, Mr. Sparks? Oh, I see. Naturally Stalath will be delighted to have you bring your ward. We'll pay Francine's expenses also." He was silent, listening, and his expression was one of incredulity. "Goddamn it, Mr. Sparks. You'll certainly never go broke. Yes. If you can close the deal Stalath will pay you the regular broker's commission of ten percent. All right. I'll be expecting you." He hung up and sat with a bemused air, shaking his head. "The son of a bitch wants all his expenses paid plus a commission for helping out on a deal into which he has already put a half a million dollars. How do you like that?"

When the attorney and John Trainor had left, Tod settled himself behind the desk and regarded his auditor expectantly.

"What's on your mind, Ron?"

"I just wanted to get some sort of an idea how large you expect Stalath's investment in Willton will be."

Tod leaned back. "I don't know for sure. Five million for the development. Another couple of million for national advertising. This is the biggest thing anyone has ever tried on the east coast. I'll borrow what I have to but I don't like paying interest. Maybe Stalath will carry the whole load."

"All right, Mr. Lathrop. I just wanted to know."

"I'm going into the Bahamas, also, Ron. Maybe for ten million. I'm going to build the damnedest private club anyone has ever seen." The telephone rang. He picked it up. "Yes? Oh, fine! Send him right in. It's Keith Harper." He rose and went to the door, opening it. "Come on in, Keith."

"Morning, Mr. Lathrop." He nodded to Ron Davis. "Morning, Mr. Davis."

"Morning, Mr. Harper." Davis left, closing the door.

Harper unrolled a large elevation drawing. They spread it on the desk and weighted the corners. Tod stood looking down at it.

"That's it, Keith." There was enthusiasm in his voice. "That's the way I want it done."

The drawing showed the houses in the forefront in detail. Those in the background lacked the detail but the entire development was laid out, complete to the small fire department station, a central plaza, the planting and ornamental lights with streets and sidewalks and a supermarket.

"I'm sort of happy with it myself, Mr. Lathrop."

"You've caught what I wanted. We're not going to duplicate Denniston. This is young, vital. It looks that way just in the drawing." He began to walk up and down. "Here, in Willton, we're going to do the building instead of letting the purchasers select their own plans. That way I can get the diversity I want. If there is anything I'm not going to have it's a dreary stretch of duplicating houses. It will be more expensive this way for us, but it's worth it. When a man comes home in the evening I don't want him to look around and say, 'Where the hell is my house? They're all alike.' But Willton is going to be too large to let people build on their own. We'll give them good, airy, solid and attractive homes but we'll tell them what they want." His features were animated. "This is going to make Florida history, Keith. For the first time in large planning someone is taking into account the new Florida. The old image of a place for the wealthy or the retired faded slowly. The state is on the stepping-off point. I can feel it. My instinct tells me I'm right. What we're dealing with is a different, a new, generation. They're young, they're eager, they're going someplace and taking Florida with them. They want families and homes, not showplaces on the beach or at Coral Gables. This is suburbia. Willton is for the young professional man just starting a practice, the junior executive reaching for the top, the artisan and clerk, the owner of a filling station, the small store owner, the branch manager for a large merchandising concern. They are all here and more will be coming. I'm going to build for them, Keith. They'll find what they are looking for in Willton. We'll make the prices right, the payments easy. The construction will be honest. I'm not just after a buck. I want homes and a development people can be proud of. Once Willton is established, Miami will extend its city limits. It has to. It's stretching at the seams now. Willton is the answer for a Greater Miami—a Greater Florida."

After Harper had left, Tod, with a secretary's help, tacked the drawing into the cypress paneling of his office and then, alone, leaned back in his chair and studied it with rapt attention.

For three days the routine of Reese Sparks didn't vary. Each morning at exactly eleven o'clock he pulled to a halt beneath a scraggly, bootjack palmetto at one side of Jess Samish's general store outside Apalocka. His car was a new and expensive Lincoln convertible but dirt-spattered and uncared for. Inside the store Reese bought a wedge of yellow "store cheese" from the small wheel covered with cheesecloth. With it he purchased a bottle of Dr. Pepper and borrowed an old jelly glass. Outside he mixed bourbon with the soft drink, sat on the narrow board porch, munched his cheese and drank his strange highball with complete satisfaction. He never spoke to anyone or entered into the conversation with the few loungers who came to spend a little time in the sun. When he finished he carried the empty bottle back inside the store, put it on the scarred counter, nodded indifferently to Samish and left.

On the third day Samish came out and stood watching Sparks pensively, canting against one of the four-by-six uprights which supported the overhang. He was lean to the point of being emaciated. His Adam's apple jumped convulsively when he spoke or swallowed. He was hard bitten and dried by the sun and time and wore faded overalls on long underwear year in and out. Finally his curiosity overcame a native taciturnity.

"What the hell are you wantin' here, mister?"

Reese Sparks looked up with complete innocence and pretended to misunderstand the question.

"Well, thank you kindly but I got 'bout all I want right here." He indicated the cheese, the bourbon and Dr. Pepper. "That's a right good combination for a hungry man."

"What I mean is," Samish's features seemed to sharpen, "that there cheese nor the Dr. Pepper, neither, ain't so special a man would come drivin' out here each day in an expensive car just to get 'em an' eat an' drink on my porch. So you gotta want somethin' more. I'd justly like to know what."

"That's a hell of a way to talk to a regular customer." Sparks was mildly wounded by this lack of hospitality.

"I talk to my customers any damn way I like an' if they don't like it they can go someplace else."

"There ain't no place else around here for them to go, is there?"

"No, there ain't an' that's why I can talk to them any damn way I like."

Reese broke off a piece of cheese and ate it with relish, washing it down with his drink. He stared off at the distant stand of young pine.

"I hear you got a boy who's in trouble up in Alabama; stole a car, broke into a filling station."

Samish started and then his expression grew mean and hostile. His tough hands knotted.

"What the hell's that to you? He's doin' his time. You the law or somethin'?"

"No."

"Then I ask again, mister, what the hell's business is it of yours?"

"It ain't no real business. Now an' then I hear things. I remember 'em. Sometimes they come in handy."

"Now you get the hell off my porch an' don't come back. I got me a twelve-gauge scattah gun inside an' I'll wholly blow your ass off if you come back."

"That ain't no way to talk to a man who comes to you with Christian charity in his heart."

"I don't need none of your goddamned Christian charity nor no other kind neither. Now you get."

Reese Sparks didn't move but he watched Samish carefully.

"I was figurin'," Sparks appeared unimpressed by the threat, "that on account of your boy, you an' me might do a little dickerin'. When I heard about him I said, Reese Sparks, maybe you can help that man."

"I don't want no he'p."

"Yes you do only you're so goddamned mean you won't admit it."

"Why should you go out of your way to he'p me?" Samish softened a little.

"Because you got somethin' I purely want. Say I do somethin' for you. You do somethin' for me. That's fair, ain't it? Now, why don't you sit an' have a touch of that corn likker an' we can talk friendly like."

After a moment Samish, half reluctantly, took a seat on the porch's edge, reached for the bourbon, wiped off the neck and pulled a long swallow.

"How'd you find out about Tom if you ain't the law?"

"You know how it is. People just naturally talk." He smiled amiably and with sympathetic understanding. "I mention your name in a pool hall in Apalocka. First thing you know someone says somethin' about your boy."

"Sons of bitches."

"The world's full of 'em," Sparks agreed.

"What you want from me?" Samish was mellowing slightly.

"Well, it's like this. I'm interested in some acreage you own on the Miami Highway but folks say you don't want to sell. Now wait a minute." He held up a hand to forestall Samish. "I figure to do you a good turn. You do me one an' let me buy that land off you."

"What are you goin' to do?" He was suspicious.

"I come from up to Alabama. I got friends there. Some not many."

"I'm damn sure of that." Samish chuckled raspingly and reached for the bourbon.

"That's right. I ain't got many but I got kin too an' I got a cousin kin who's the head guard at the State Prison where they got your boy. Now if I was to write Purdy Sparks likely he could make it real easy for your boy up there. Get him to be a trusty, maybe. An' when the parole board sits he could put in a word or two. That way your boy would have it good an' even get a parole before his time."

"You can do that?" There was hope in the question.

"I can do it through my cousin Purdy. He stands high with the Warden."

"About that acreage. You're the third or fourth fella that's been around. What's so special about them acres?"

"I got a friend who's puttin' in a development. You're sittin' right, smack dab in the middle of it. You'll get a fair price, maybe a mite above the market."

Samish took another swallow of the bourbon. He stared at the bottle in silent concentration.

"If you can do what you say to he'p Tom an' I heah straight from him he's been made a trusty then I'll loose that acreage to you. First, though, I got to heah it from Tom. Until then I don't turn over so much as an inch no matter what you pay. I got to heah it from Tom himse'f an' how your cousin is goin' to put in a word to the parole board."

"You got a deal." Sparks rose, wiped his hands on his trousers and then extended one to Samish. "I call my cousin tonight. That there's a promise."

In Spark's suite at the Stalath Motel, Tod listened with growing amazement as Reese told the story.

"I thought you once told me you screwed all your relatives in Alabama."

"Mr. Lathrop," Sparks was aggrieved, "that ain't no nice word to use in front of my ward."

In the filmiest of negligees Francine reclined on a couch, flicking at her richly hued fingernails with an emery board. She looked up and smiled at Tod.

"Isn't he a real son of a bitch?" There was a note of pride in her voice. "He's about the biggest son of a bitch I ever knew and I've had some experience."

"Well." Sparks accepted Francine's remark as a compliment. "I never did get around to screwin' Purdy Sparks because he never had nothin' to begin with. So he's about the only relative I've got in Alabama to be on speakin' terms with."

"You think he'll really help the boy?"

"Of course he will. We Sparks always help one an' another if it's asked. I'm goin' to call Purdy tonight." He leaned back and stared at the ceiling. "If there's one thing Purdy Sparks always wanted all his life it's a yellow Cadillac convertible car. Now, I think it would be a nice thing on the Stalath Corporation's part if it had an Alabama dealer send one around to Purdy's house. Don't make no explanation. Just have the man drive it up an' leave it in front of Purdy's house with the keys and a bill of sale. I'll tell Purdy tonight he can expect it. A little thing like that will sort of cement our kinship."

Tod shook his head bemusedly and laughed with quiet appreciation. Then he nodded to Sparks.

"You give me the address before I leave. I'll take care of it."

"You understand, Mr. Lathrop, this Cadillac yellow convertible car don't come out of none of my commission nor my share of the deal. This is just purely a generous thing you're doin' on your own. I figure you're gettin' off cheap."

Tod reached for the bourbon, added some to his glass and dropped in a couple of ice cubes. Francine cocked a leg up and her negligee fell away to the thigh. She made a pretense of replacing it and winked at Tod.

"Mr. Sparks"—Tod spun the ice cubes about with a finger—"you are one of the rich and rewarding experiences of my life."

* XXIII * *

THE tall figure of Stoddard Lathrop striding along Bay Street became a familiar sight in Nassau, and even in this conservative and clannish community strangers would nod a pleasant recognition as he passed.

These days he seemed to be in a perpetual hurry. A new, twin-motored Beechcraft had been fitted with pontoons and he flew back and forth between Miami and the islands as casually as another man might walk around the block. There were innumerable details in connection with the preliminary construction at Hatchet Bay. These might well have been left to the superintendent but Stoddard Lathrop was incapable of sitting passive on the sidelines. Nothing was too small that he would not give it his full attention. He planned with a great sweep of imagination and enthusiasm, dismissing such a petty item as cost.

Once the land on Eluthera had been secured it was necessary to begin the assembly of a labor force. For this he drew upon the Negro population of the Out Islands. Then there was the earth-moving equipment to contract for. To his pleased surprise he discovered the latter was not the problem he had expected. Bulldozers, Caterpillar tractors, scrapers and packers, looking like great antediluvian monsters, had been stored after the United States Government had finished laying out the lend-lease bases in the British possessions during the war. He was able to rent them and they were carried to Eluthera on barges and their skilled operators flown in and quartered temporarily in Gregory Town.

For the unskilled labor he built a neat, semimilitary camp on the site. Concerned that the men might stray back to their homes over the weekends he allowed them to bring in their women. This way he could keep the force intact without having to round them up every Monday. With the women and girls the camp took on the appearance of a small domestic community. Bright washing hung on the lines, pots bubbled on outdoor fires, for the women preferred this to the large central kitchen with its oil stoves. Despite the openly voiced fears of the residents of Gregory Town and Alicetown, there was rarely any trouble and when it came it was settled quickly and within the camp's confines. Tod engaged three former members of Nassau's police force to maintain order and keep discipline. These men were Jamaicans, as were all the Nassau police. They had no ties of kin or friendship to keep them from enforcing the regulations which had been drawn up and read aloud to the workers.

Liquor, usually rum, was sold only on a Saturday evening and the drinking was confined to the central compound area. The people of Eluthera never had a reason to complain. The men worked hard all week and on Saturdays relaxed.

The entrance to Hatchet Bay was an artificial cut through sheer cliffs, and the bay—or "The Pond" as the natives called it—was virtually landlocked. Tod kept the *Skipjack* anchored here and used it as office and headquarters and he found himself making excuses to stay in the islands over the weekend. When night came he would have dinner on the cruiser and then go over the plans for the Lotus Club changing something here, and then, making additions and deletions, redrawing the docking facilities, jotting down notes for the architect and engineers. On Saturday evenings he would go ashore and unobtrusively take a place just outside the circle of light. The flames were reflected on the dark, shining faces. The sudden laughter was gusty and rich in sound. At first the men and women were made self-conscious by his presence although they never spoke nor did Tod offer a greeting. Little by little they began to accept his presence.

Many of the men were self-taught musicians. They had brought their guitars, their gourds, their corrugated strips of metal which they stroked with a polished stick. They fashioned tympanum and a form of xylophone from empty oil drums. The music and dancing usually started slowly and, apparently, was spontaneous. Someone would brush out a few notes on a guitar. Before they died away the gourds, the tympanum and the xylophone would join in mutedly. Little by little the tempo and the sound would increase. They all played by ear and what they wrought was barbaric and compelling. Then a man and a girl would rise and move out into the circle, their bare feet slapping at the hard-packed earth, their bodies swaying and a curious, moaning sound coming from their throats. Before long others would join them and the entire camp would be possessed by the atavistic beat. What they chanted was unintelligible but it was as primitive as Africa itself. The melody and the words were, it seemed, composed as the dancing progressed. Yet there was never a false note, a broken rhythm. Then, as unobtrusively as it had started, the dancing would slow, the music trail away. The men and women resumed their places in the circle around the fire and a bottle of rum would be passed from hand to hand. They were silent for the most part now, seeming to be drained emotionally. After awhile, and in response to no visible sign, the music and dancing would start again. Lying awake sometimes in his cabin aboard the *Skipjack* he would be oddly stirred by the music, the sudden wild shouts which reached far back into their ancestry and springing from a savagery they barely understood. At this hour there was no place in the camp for the alien white man.

Had anyone asked, Tod would have cheerfully admitted he was having the time of his life on Eluthera. There was first the excitement of creating something and watching its daily growth. He rode the bulldozers and the Cat, learning to operate them with a fair amount of skill. The ground plan of the central clubhouse was taking shape. The building was to be low with spacious verandas facing the sea. About it would be the cottages. Island stone was to be used for the facing. He was building into the project every conceivable luxury. When properly staffed there would be nothing like it in the Bahamas.

Now and then he would take time off from trying to oversee everything and go fishing with one of the native boys in Gregory Town. They would take handlines and pick up a couple of conches for bait. The fish they were after were not much larger than his hand.

Through a glass-bottomed bucket he could look down through the incredibly clear water and see them playing about on the coral-strewn bottom or through a waving tangle of dark green weeds. They were silver with streakings of blue and yellow and when rolled in corn meal and fried in deep fat were indescribably delicious. Most of the time, though, he wandered over the club's site clad only in slacks. His chest, arms and face were tanned to the dark color of mahogany and he had never felt better in his life.

He was constantly torn between the Bahamas and what was happening to Willton. The final acres of the huge tract had been secured and the ground was being shaped and prepared for the community as he envisioned it. On the main highway, fronting the tract, a large sign had been erected. Gold letters, four feet high, on a field of sheer white announced simply:

WILLTON. A STALATH PROJECT.

Nothing more was needed. It met the eye of every passing motorist. An advertising campaign of national scope had been carefully planned and decided upon. This would be put into effect when construction was half completed. The streets had been laid out and named with ornamental signs in wrought iron at each corner. The utilities were in and underground. Miami was extending its city limits which now would incorporate Willton. Soon the houses would begin to rise. The setting was perfect, shadowed by giant pines and ancient live oak. It was within easy commuting distance of Miami proper where most of the residents would be employed. Eventually, he thought, the Florida East Coast Railway might build a small station for Willton as it had for Hialeah.

What Stalath was doing touched off a moderate boom. Other developers moved in upon the vacant flat pineland, all intent upon the fast turnover and the quick buck. They built cheaply and without imagination. The small houses, with their tiny plots of ground planted in quick growing rye grass which would die as abruptly as it had sprung, stretched in identical rows. Where the streets of Willton curved to take whatever advantage there was of the lightly contoured land, the hastily created subdivisions were gridded with pavement and streets in a deadly monotony. Because the construction

357 *

was shoddy, these developments outpaced Willton and their homes were on the market long before anything in Willton was offered for sale. The new tracts all bore the familiar names of an earlier boom. Linda Vista. Pinewoods Manor. Tropical Gardens. Seville. The houses were offered on dangerously low terms with the usual "No Down to Veterans." Those who bought, in many cases, were actually unable to pay for what they had purchased but they moved on a high wave of optimism.

Watching what was happening on these hastily thrown-up subdivisions Tod began to realize that there was a danger in this "new Florida"; the overextension of people who could not afford what they were buying. At Denniston, on the west coast, the purchasers were older, established and possessed a certain amount of security. The people moving into these east coast developments were younger and far less stable. Everything they had was being bought on time. They lived from one weekly pay check to the next. As long as they held their jobs they were moderately solvent. But an unexpected lay-off, a strike which kept them away from a trade union job, the loss of a position, caused immediate hardship. They fell behind in their payments, tried to hide their cars from those who would repossess them, engaged in a quiet war to hold on to the television set, the washing machine, the new dining room furniture. There were quick foreclosures in Linda Vista, Seville, Pinewoods Manor and Tropical Gardens. The houses were sold and resold, the new owners seeming to have learned nothing from the old. This was the sort of operation Stoddard Lathrop wanted to avoid.

"It's different, like I told you it would be." Reese Sparks, his curiosity getting the better of him, had come down from Daytona Beach to see how Willton was progressing. "Those are kids movin' into the cheap subdivisions. They never learned to say no nor have anyone say it to them. Everything is up for grabs. They read things like 'no down payment, take thirty-six months to pay' without lookin' what's behind them slogans. They just say, 'Goodie, let's get us one of those.' They don't stop to count that thirty-six months is three years an' the car they are buyin' will be wore out by then an' they'll have to go into debt all over again to get a new one. It's like they are on a treadmill. If they don't keep walkin' they go backwards. That there is what we got to watch with Willton. I'm for sellin' less homes an' have 'em sold than for sellin' a lot an' havin' 'em back."

"I'm not going to make it too easy to own a home in Willton, Mr. Sparks. But we're going to sell where we can. I'm not sure we can't or shouldn't carry the financing load. We have the F.H.A. and Veterans Administration to back us up. Why should Stalath let the banks have all that interest?"

Sparks remained unconvinced. He thought he saw another dangerous boom coming; one which would again wreck Florida. But his investment was small compared to what Stalath was pouring into Willton. There was, he told himself, no sense in arguing against the "Lathrop touch." It had already worked small miracles and probably could again.

As usual Reese Sparks had brought Francine with him and they shared a two-bedroom suite in the Stalath Motel. Sparks made no secret of his delight in Francine. Tod stopped by in the early evening to have a drink.

"What's this thing you have goin' in the Bahamas?" Everything Tod did was of interest to Sparks. "You're bein' mighty cozy with it; never suggestin' it might be nice to have a partner."

"I'm not even sure I can afford the Lotus Club, Mr. Sparks."

"Sir," Francine spoke with a small girl's voice, "I've never been to the Bahamas."

"You see, Mr. Lathrop, how my ward Francine is just thirsty for knowledge. It'd be a nice thing if you took us over an' showed us around."

"Why not? After all, there's your ward's education to think of. A trip to the Bahamas could be very instructive."

Francine stuck her tongue out at him and he grinned back. They must, he thought, make special clothes for girls like Francine. In everything she wore, such as those shorts and blouse, there was just a little less material than was actually needed. They provided the barest minimum. He glanced from her to Reese Sparks. This improbable alliance seemed to be good for both of them. Until now the realities of life had never quite caught up with Francine's dreams. Now she had everything which, to her, seemed important—clothes, jewelry, furs, cars. He knew her arrangement with Reese must have caused talk in Daytona Beach but she was, apparently, indifferent to it. Well, why not? As for Reese, Francine's influence was obvious. He no longer wore the flaming ties, the striped silk shirts, the sloppy seersucker suits and a battered hat. Some of the thick, Alabama backcountry accent was disappearing from his speech. He said *I* instead of *Ah* and the word *it* was no longer *hit*. He still retained, though, the blithe spirit of a confidence man about to take a sucker. Such changes as Francine had wrought had not robbed him of his salty character. Looking at the two of them Tod experienced a curious rush of sentiment. They really had things just the way they wanted them. For a moment he felt a little envious.

"You understand," he continued, speaking to Reese, "when we're over there, you're just looking around. I don't want a partner in the Lotus Club."

Sparks regarded him with a hurt expression. "Now and again, Mr. Lathrop, I get the feelin' you could be a real mean man was you to put your mind to it. However, I would surely like to see what you're doin' over there."

"I'm building the damnedest place you ever saw." Tod's enthusiasm kindled. "It's going to be the greatest thing of its kind in the islands. I like it so much right now I'm not sure I want to divide it up with any members. I'm only talking, of course. But the members will be hand-picked. I'm the admissions committee. It will be like J. P. Morgan and yacht. If you have to ask how much it costs, you can't afford it. When I finish on Eluthera, I'm going to look around and find a place of my own."

"In the islands?" Francine glanced at him with surprise. "I always thought you might go back to Daytona Beach."

"No-o." He spoke almost regretfully. "Daytona Beach belongs to another part of my life. Stalath is here, in Dade County, and where Stalath is I want to be." He stood. "Thanks for the drink. I'll pick you up about eleven in the morning. We'll have lunch in Nassau and then go over to Hatchet Bay."

Outside he glanced at his watch and then instead of going to his own rooms he went to his car and drove downtown. It was a little past six. The afternoon traffic had ebbed and the evening hadn't started. The Stalath Building would be all but empty. He liked to go there at this hour when few persons were around. The Stalath Building, Denniston and now Willton and the Coral Club were enduring monuments, and he often felt as though he had fashioned them with his own hands. He was proud of what had been accomplished. Looking back now and then he often wondered how it had come about. When the Florida boom collapsed he had been broke; really flat save for what his father had so generously offered. Then, little by little, things had begun to fall into place. First, Reese Sparks had made the unexpected move of giving him back control of the Citrus Belt Line. From that point on everything had moved as though on a predetermined schedule. He would never forget Reese Sparks' gesture and often wondered what had prompted it. In the years since then he had made a great deal of money for Reese Sparks. The old man, though, never had any real need for it until Francine came along. It was a game to him, and therein lay the understanding between them. It had been a game for Stoddard Lathrop, also.

Tod parked his car in front of the Stalath Building and the lobby watchman came to open the heavy bronze doors.

"Evenin', Mr. Lathrop." He touched his cap.

"Good evening, Tom. How is the family?"

"Fine, thank you."

The automatic elevator lifted him silently to the top floors. The offices and central rooms were empty and yet, as always, he had the feeling that by pushing a button on his desk he could throw the entire operation into motion. Lights would go on, the offices would fill, messengers would go from floor to floor with memoranda, the switchboard would illuminate itself and telephones would ring.

In his own office he stood at the window watching the Nassau-bound ship as it moved out upon the bay. She was late, he thought and then smiled. What difference did it make? Below him lay the gridded lights of Miami's streets and in their center stood the Stalath Building. Stalath, he thought, was impregnable. It was as sound as the building bearing its name. Only a national disaster could shake it. There were corporations within the corporations and they all functioned smoothly. Each year he combed the universities for the best available talent, eager, bright young men. To them all he said the same thing. "Your future here is what you make it." He would show them a secluded reception room. "This is the nut room. Usually a dozen persons a day show up with an invention, a process, a new way of doing something better. Most of them are wildly impractical but I want you to listen to them all. Every now and then someone will come along with something of value. When that happens I don't want you to miss it. If the thing has any merit at all Stalath will develop it. At least we'll investigate."

Stalath, he reflected, was one of the very few substantial results of Florida's ill-starred boom. Out of its collapse the corporate structure had risen. The keystone, of course, had been the idea for the Stalath motels. Now the corporation operated fifteen outright and had franchised twenty more. His own operation included one on the Atlantic Avenue extension of Daytona Beach. This one had sparked others until that area was dotted with a variety of modest and luxury establishments. He had pushed the Stalath motels into Georgia, South and North Carolina, Virginia and Alabama and franchises had extended the chain to California. The Stalath name carried with it a tremendous amount of public confidence and goodwill. It was a guarantee of quality and service which the motoring public had never before encountered. Through what was either incalculable luck or a sure instinct for doing the right thing at the right time everything Stoddard Lathrop touched prospered. Stalath was now interested in such a variety of enterprises that Tod sometimes found himself hard pressed to remember them all. It was time, he told himself, to begin moving some of the younger executives into places of more responsibility. Sooner or later someone would have to take over part of the increasing burden. At the moment the vast and complex organization was his and his alone to direct. "Mr. Florida." He smiled, knowing that was what some people called him, through either envy or respect. What he had actually done with such enterprises as Denniston, Willton, the lumbering and manufacturing interests the corporation had acquired, was to point the way. Florida was on the move and the road lay straight ahead. As the money had poured in, Stoddard Lathrop had been generous. He made large contributions to the universities of the state, set up scholarship endowments and made substantial donations to hospitals and clinics. When the Lotus Club was finished and in operation he already had plans for building a hospital on Eluthera where one was badly needed. These things, he thought, are my children since I have none of my own. He was not filled with the zeal of a do-gooder. What he did for the state arose out of his awareness of a debt for what it had given him.

He went to a cabinet and poured himself a small brandy. He had been serious when he told Francine and Reese Sparks he wanted a place of his own now. At first he had thought about the ocean front. He had always been irresistibly drawn to the sea. It was so irrevocably linked with his earliest memories, his father and grandfather. Miami Beach, though, was acquiring a garish, neon-lit character. One huge hotel after another were being constructed and it was apparent that resort structures would eventually drive out the private homes. To the north lay Hollywood-by-the-Sea. This again was a tourist community. Southward lay the Florida Keys. He might, some-day, built a small fishing lodge there but not a home. There were, he knew, about three thousand acres outside of Coral Gables. He had thought about them before. They could be developed into an estate of surpassing beauty. On an impulse he downed the drink hurriedly and left the office.

He drove down Flagler Street to Biscayne Boulevard and then out the Dixie Highway toward Coral Gables. The tract was sparsely wooded, scrub pines but with a few fine, old oaks and magnolia trees. The bay was almost a mile away.

He parked the car and walked along the boundary. The house, he thought, would be of the Mediterranean type. Where the old water tower stood he would have erected a miniature campanile. There would be room for greenhouses, tropical gardens and an aviary. He would have a channel dredged in from the bay and build a marina for the *Skipjack* and the Beechcraft. Then, he told himself, I'll take time off and travel as did Grandfather Will, bringing back some of the beauty of the Old World and transplanting it here. After that? He wondered. It didn't seem enough, somehow. He had a wide and varied business acquaintance in a dozen states but ac-tually, few friends, persons whose company he really enjoyed.

363   *

Without being aware of it he had moved far outside the orbit of most of those he had known for years. They no longer had anything in common. He doubted if it was possible to reorientate himself to pick up old intimacies. My God, he thought. Am I going to end up with only Reese Sparks for company?

He turned about and in a depressed mood went back to the car.

* XXIV * *

WHEN the last house was finished in the huge development which was Willton, Stoddard Lathrop called a meeting with the director and staff of Stalath's public relations department to lay before them the plans he had.

"What I'm going to ask you to do is a little out of your line." He studied the half dozen attentive faces. "When we open Willton I want a circus promotion; some razzle-dazzle; a beauty contest, Willton Queen; bands playing, the Governor speaking. Not," he added, "at the same time, of course." He could sense their mystification growing and smiled to himself. These were all serious young men accustomed to dealing on a high level with the press. Those who were with him at the time had been secretly shocked by his outdoor promotion of Cocoa Tan. They glanced uneasily at each other now. "I want," he continued, enjoying himself, "national publicity on this. We have just one hell of a lot of houses to sell and if half-naked girls, parades and dancing in the streets will sell them that's what we'll have. If you don't think you are prepared to handle it I'll call in some theatrical press agents who are more familiar with this sort of promotion." He waited.

George Perry, the department's head, glanced quickly at his assistants and then he, also, smiled.

"We can do the job, Mr. Lathrop. I'll admit it will be a new experience for most of the staff but we can do it. Have you a general idea of what you want or would you like us to draw up a plan for your approval?"

"Of course I know what I want." He studied Perry sharply, wondering if he had made a mistake in the man. "This isn't to be a one-day, one-time shot. Let's spread the opening over a week. Call it any damn thing you like. Willton Week or Come Help Stoddard Lathrop Sell Houses Week. I want the Mayor, the Governor and a Senator to help kick it off on the opening day. Then I want the prettiest girls you can find for a beauty contest. The winner will be the Queen of Willton. We'll give her an automobile as a prize, a flashy convertible. I want," he started pacing up and down the room, "a couple of name bands to play for outdoor dancing on the mall. I want a barbecue with whole steers being roasted over the pits. I want anything the photographers will take pictures of and the papers will print. See if you can get the outstanding French chef to come over and supervise the barbecue. Or," he snapped his fingers, "better still, get the White House chef to do the job. Borrow him from the President." He halted, slid to a seat on the top of his desk and lit a cigarette. "None of you were around during the big Florida boom. Then the promoters created quite a stir by offering free bus trips and box lunches. This time we'll fly people in and put on the damnedest picnic anyone ever saw. There are two things picture and city editors find irresistible—pretty, half-dressed girls and animals. Have plenty of both around." He could see the bewilderment growing on their faces. "Forget about the dignified posture of Stalath for awhile. You are circus press agents. This is the old razz-a-matazz. See if you can get a motion picture star. We'll make him Honorary Mayor of Willton; have his picture taken with the beauty queen. Put them in bed together if you want to. Any questions?"

"What's the budget on this, Mr. Lathrop?" Perry offered the query.

"There is no budget. Spend what is needed to do it right. Put together a junket for feature editors and writers; take a couple of floors at one of the beach hotels. I want pictures of Willton to hit every newspaper, newsreel and news magazine in the country. I don't give a damn what it costs. Stalath has put millions into Willton and another five hundred thousand dollars for promotion doesn't amount to anything. Do it right. Don't skimp anywhere. Figure out some sort of a contest to give a house away with all taxes paid for the first five years. Give it to the oldest couple, the youngest couple, the first couple to get married or have a baby. Hang it on any peg you like. Order prize beef for the barbecue. A fifty-thousand-dollar Black Angus served al fresco has to make the papers. Figure out how much each barbecued rib costs and have pictures taken of the Governor chewing on a thousand-dollar piece of beef. By the time you have finished I want everyone in the country to know what and where Willton is. Now, get to it. Let me have a detailed schedule of what you are going to do and how you are going to do it."

He waited until they had filed from the room and then laughed with honest amusement. He had watched the astonishment grow on their faces as he talked. They took themselves and their careers very seriously. When they had come with Stalath it had probably never occurred to one of them that he might be called upon to supervise a beauty contest. Well, he thought, this will shake up their livers and do them a world of good. He wondered why shaking up one's liver was supposed to create some sort of a therapeutic miracle. It was an expression he had heard all his life. He stood, looking down into Flagler Street. At the moment he regretted having to turn the promotion over to Perry and his boys. It was the sort of thing he would have liked to do himself. He glanced at his watch, surprised it was still early. He had ordered his plane for two o'clock, planning to fly over to Eluthera and spend the night on the *Skipjack* after looking over the progress of the Lotus Club. First, though, he wanted to run out to Willton.

Driving northward out of Miami he passed miles of motels of all sizes and degrees of accommodations. Some were small, unpretentious. Others had swimming pools, tennis courts, pitch and putt golf courses. What Stalath had started had grown into a phenomenal business and knocked the hell out of most of the small, badly run hotels. The idea, which had once been revolutionary, was taken for granted now. Few motorists were aware of how radical the concept was twenty or so years ago. Chains, such as the Stalath franchised units, stretched from the Atlantic to the Pacific coast. Their names became a guarantee of quality and there were accommoda-

367 *

tions to fit every traveler's budget. Stalath, he thought with a warm glow of satisfaction, had started it all; had pointed the way and shown how it should be done. It had created a new industry.

A few miles south of Willton he began to pass the hastily put together developments. Already they were showing the signs of decay and shoddy construction. The streets, covered with the lightest coating of asphalt, were pitted and filled with chuck holes. The ornamental signs were rusting. Weeds grew in the yards of empty houses. Everything pointed to indifference. The houses, with "No Down Payments to Vets," had been bought by the young and hopeful who were fascinated by the glitter of chrome and the sheen of new varnish, sparkling paint, a flowering hibiscus plant. They were without the experience to look into the specifications and find out what had been built into these dream homes. They were stuck now with houses from which the stucco was breaking, walls that cracked, floors that warped and buckled, plumbing which was inadequate, cement walks and driveways which were breaking up because there was too much sand mixed with the concrete. He knew, from inquiries, how rapid the turnover here had been. Everyone had been urged to buy without a thought of how the payments could be handled. A family was foreclosed on today and the house sold to another couple tomorrow. There was a constant coming and going of the hopeful and the disillusioned.

By contrast Willton looked almost like a great private estate. The entrance was marked by two towerlike structures flanking large, double, wrought-iron gates. In one of the towers there was a small comfortable office for the gatekeeper and watchman, who was on duty day and night. He had telephones with direct lines to Miami's fire and police departments. Another phone could be rung by any of Willton's residents by simply pressing a button. Although Tod had changed his mind, deciding to hold all the homes off the market until after a ceremonial opening, the watchman's corps had been installed for training. As families moved in, the enormous tract would be patrolled by private police. There were public playgrounds, a recreational center for adults, a shopping center. Willton was to offer surburban living at its best. The streets were wide, the lighting unobtrusive. Planting had been expertly done and already there were small riots of color in the yards. The pines had been thinned out but not destroyed and the high tops made green magic against the sky.

Tod drove through the gates, returning the watchman's salute with a wave of his hand. He allowed the car to roll slowly up one street and down another. All about him Willton was spread. Its houses were tight and secure, well and honestly made to the last nail, the final stroke of the painter's brush. The contractors who had done the job were outspokenly critical of the specifications.

"You're putting too much into these houses, Mr. Lathrop. Quality is one thing but you're going overboard. Houses like these are what a man might build for himself."

"That's exactly what I'm doing." He was undisturbed. "I'm putting them up as I would if I intended to live in them."

"Well," the contractor had been unimpressed, "to break even you damn well may have to price yourself out of a market. I don't know what figure you have in mind but you'd better sit down with a paper and pencil and see how you are going to come out. Individual houses are one thing. A development like this is another. You could stick to the building code and come out with a nice profit. Instead you've insisted on superquality beyond anything the code calls for. No one else is doing it."

Even Stalath's auditor was concerned. He came to Tod's office carrying a sheaf of papers.

"Have you any idea how much money you're putting into Willton, Mr. Lathrop?"

"I have you around to tell me." Tod grinned at him. "When I hired you I said to myself: 'There is a congenital worrier. A misplaced penny will keep him awake all night. He's the kind of man I need to do my worrying for me.' Sit down and relax and tell me how thin the ice is."

"I guess it's all right if you keep moving fast enough." The man seated himself almost reluctantly. "I have some figures here. You ought to take some outside financing instead of letting Stalath carry the big load."

"I don't see any point in paying interest for what we can get along without."

"How much is the Lotus Club going to cost?"

"I don't know but whatever it is we'll carry it."

369 *

"Then," the auditor was honestly concerned, "let's sell off some of Willton as the houses go up. No one tries to do it the way you are. When a place is finished put it on the market. That way we can keep the operation liquid."

"No." Tod shook his head. "I don't want to do it piecemeal. I want the entire development finished. Then the tract will be opened as a unit. I want it as a showplace."

That was what Willton was. Looking at it now he was impatient to have it opened. He felt like a kid waiting for the Christmas tree to be lighted. Cutting the motor he leaned forward on the wheel, surveying the ordered perfection of the acres. He was proud of what he saw. Of all the Stalath enterprises, Willton and Denniston gave him the greatest satisfaction. All over the state there were cheap imitations of what he had done and the fraud made him angry. There was no excuse for the claptrap contruction. In a few years most of the hastily erected developments would have degenerated into little better than slums. The promoters were promising future value for something which had no value when it was new. He lit a cigarette and inhaled deeply. He wished Dennis Lathrop could see Willton and Denniston on the west coast. Here was the realization of all he had dreamed of for Florida years ago before the words "boom" and "development" were even thought of for the state. Without realizing it he had taken Dennis Lathrop's vision of what Florida could and should be and expanded it far beyond anything his father's imagination had created. Denniston was the model. Whether it could be duplicated here on a more lavish scale was the question. Reese Sparks didn't think so and was outspoken, although not critical, in his opinion. Most of the real estate brokers in Miami were skeptical. Well, Stoddard Lathrop was unmoved. It was his money and he was prepared to risk it.

After Willton he intended to go back to the west coast, somewhere around St. Petersburg. Here was a great, untapped reservoir. What he had in mind was comfortable, low-cost housing for the elderly who had migrated to the sun-washed city on the tip of a peninsula extending into Tampa Bay. Here they had crowded into apartments and lodging houses, spent their days on municipal croquet and shuffleboard courts, or sat on the city's benches idling away the hours. He would give them something better—a community of their own at prices they could afford. A Stalath project here would carry with it the same guarantee of quality that the Stalath Motels so exactingly demanded. This done he intended to explore the possibilities of similar developments around St. Augustine. Jacksonville was too far north. There were days during the winter when the temperature brought a sharp chill to elderly bones. Then, there were the vast reaches of the interior. Here the communities straggled through the pine flats with only a store at the crossroads. Something better could be planned. Dennis Lathrop had been fascinated by the idea of complete, self-sustaining rural communities. Stoddard Lathrop had made a start with Denniston. Now was the time to expand the vision and make it a reality. With Willton a proved success, he would turn his energies toward these new developments. But first Willton had to go. He was determined to make it a model for upper-middle-class housing despite a general skepticism. It would go because he would make it go. He was indifferent to the fact that with Willton and the large investment he was making in the Bahamas he was stretching his resources. There was magic in the name of Stalath. Of this he was convinced. Willton and Denniston were constant rebukes to the badly planned, hastily created "suburban slums" which were beginning to ring Miami and other areas of Florida.

Once embarked on the Willton project, and recovering from the surprise at what it was doing, Stalath's public relations department shed its inhibitions and put on the gaudy coat of a carnival pitchman. The opening of the development was a circus in which most of Miami, much to its astonishment, found itself involved.

One of the plans called for a parade, originating on Biscayne Boulevard, moving up Flagler Street and then out to the highway and Willton. Tod had crossed that off on the schedule.

"A downtown parade only advertises Miami. That's the job of the Chamber of Commerce. By the time a motorcade reached Willton the photographers would be out of film. Get me a couple of bands, a corps of drum majorettes with their short skirts flipping, all the pretty girls you can round up. Let them wander around Willton, pose on the lawns and in the doorways of the houses. I don't want pictures of Biscayne Bay or Flagler Street. This is a Willton promotion; start and end everything there. Anything happening outside the gates is wasted effort."

Full-page advertisements were taken in Miami's newspapers, supplementing the national campaign which was already scheduled. On the opening day the state's governor, a couple of senators and congressmen, not one of which was quite sure why he was there, Miami's city officials—all gave a hand to the ceremonies which began early in the morning. A leggy, photogenic brunette was selected as "Miss Willton" and pictures were taken of her seated, cross-legged, on the roof of a Cadillac convertible as the Governor handed her the keys and received an enthusiastic kiss in return. In what was to be a combination park and children's playground, complete with swings, slides and game courts, tables had been set, barbecue pits dug. There were great tubs of salad, mounds of rolls and enough barbecued beef for all of Dade County. A prize Black Angus had been roasted and the Governor photographed happily gnawing on a "thousand-dollar-rib."

At one minute after midnight on the day of Willton's opening a baby girl was born to the young wife of a service station manager. There were bedside pictures of mother, child and slightly bewildered husband as Stoddard Lathrop presented them with the deed and tax receipt for a Willton home.

Orchestras alternated on the mall where the concrete had been sprinkled with corn meal for dancing. Colored lights were strung overhead so darkness would not intrude upon the festivities. People arrived early in the morning and spent the entire day, turning their children over to attendants who supervised their play. By mid-afternoon the highway was packed on both sides with parked cars. Thousands of persons roamed through and inspected the detail of Willton's model homes.

Reese Sparks, who had come down from Daytona Beach, bringing Francine with him, stood with Tod and surveyed the animated scene.

"Everyone is sure enough havin' a hell of a time," Reese agreed. "But I don't hear the cash register goin' none. No one is layin' cash on the line for a house. That there is what I would like to see."

"We're not trying to sell anything today, Mr. Sparks. This is publicity. Goodwill."

"Well," Reese drawled the word, "maybe so, but what I call goodwill is when a man takes a dollar from his pocket an' puts it in my hand. That there is a real goodwill gesture an' nothin' makes me feel more kindly disposed."

"I don't have a salesman on the tract today. After all of this hits the papers, together with our advertising campaign, everyone in the country will know what and where Willton is. Then we'll begin selling. Our market isn't confined to Miami."

"I hope you're right, Mr. Lathrop." Reese permitted himself a faint smile. "I'll say one thing. You usually know what you're doing. Right now I'd like a good drink and then put my teeth into some of that prize beef."

"We have a bar set up in one of the houses. Come on, we'll have that drink together—and stop worrying about your investment."

Reese Sparks looked at him with surprise. "I wasn't," he said slowly, "worryin' about the little I got tied into this here thing, Mr. Lathrop. I'm a little worried about you an' that's a true fact. I ain't exactly sure you can tell people what they want an' make 'em believe it. If you can't, then this here Willton could be a pretty expensive monument."

The Miami Weather Bureau had marked it down as a "tropical disturbance." It moved erratically off the coast of Yucatan, flirted harmlessly around the Gulf of Mexico, bringing some heavy rain to Brownsville and the Corpus Christi area, and then sidled off toward the Florida Straits. Suddenly, and without warning, it generated a destructive power, spun around and lashed heavily at Cuba in the vicinity of Candelaria. Here it leveled the cane fields, tore the roofs from houses, gutted the countryside with torrential rains. Having cut its path of destruction, it moved out again into the Straits.

As the fourth storm of the season she had a name now—Dora. The Forecasting Division cautiously plotted her course in a northeasterly direction which would bring her across the Keys, and probably out to sea where she might lose herself in the vastness of the Atlantic. It was too early to tell so precautionary warnings were sent out to all shipping around Key West.

On a stool at the Blockade Runners' Bar in the Royal Victoria Hotel, Stoddard Lathrop sat with a Scotch and listened to the radio broadcasting the latest word on Dora. She was working herself into a

373   *

full-grown hurricane but as yet was following no predictable pattern. She was carrying winds up to eighty miles an hour and these were expected to increase.

Only part of his mind was occupied with Dora. Actually, he was deeply disturbed by what was happening to Willton. The development had been open for only a little short of six months and no more than half a dozen houses had been sold. Somewhere, something had gone wrong. He knew the answer but would not admit it. Willton had been designed for the upper middle class but these people—in and around Miami, at least—wanted to design and plan their own homes. They disliked the idea of having someone else doing it for them. The lower income brackets of the middle class couldn't afford the Willton houses. And those in the high-income scale were just not interested in preplanned development. They wanted estates. The class for which Stoddard Lathrop had built simply did not exist in the Miami area. Now he was confronted by the choice of hanging stubbornly to his original idea or making a drastic reduction in the price of his houses and taking the inevitable loss. He knew better than anyone how deeply Stalath was tied into the Willton and Eluthera operations. The prospect of losing everything he had built was there but he refused to admit its presence. He had been broke once after the collapse of Florida's boom but on the wreckage had built Stalath. He had no intention of letting it go now.

Denis Hickman came into the bar and stood beside him, listening as Miami resumed its weather report. There was an abrupt distortion of sound as a Cuban station rode in on the wavelength and shut out the Miami station.

"I don't know how true it is"—Denis nodded in the direction of the radio—"but Bill Pope told me about a radio dealer on Bay Street. He sold a small, battery-powered set to an Out Island Negro. A couple of weeks later the man brought it back saying he wanted one that 'spoke English.' It seems the Cuban stations were blanketing the ones on the mainland and all he heard was Spanish." He ordered a drink for himself. "Are you staying over?"

"I don't know. I got in the way down at Eluthera as much as I could and left before the foreman threw me out. I was going to fly back but maybe I'll stick around and see what the storm does. I've never been in the islands during a hurricane."

"It's an experience you can get along without. A couple of times I thought Nassau was going to take off and go sailing through the air. Somehow, though, we always survive."

Tod finished his drink and walked outside, down the steps toward the pool and the winding path leading through the Victoria's gardens. The centuries-old trees here were only lightly brushed by a small wind. From some the long, brown flat pods the natives called "women's tongues" fluttered and clacked against each other with a whispering of furtive gossip. There was no hint of storm or danger in the burnished and cloudless sky. Somewhere out there Dora was working herself into full force. She began moving toward the Keys, traveling at about ten miles an hour. Warnings had been issued to all shipping and coastal towns from Key West to New Bern, in North Carolina. In Miami merchants and homeowners were resignedly putting up storm shutters and making preparations to withstand the onslaught. Boats were moved up into the protective reaches of the Miami River. The city and outlying districts braced themselves. Everyone had been through hurricanes before. They were a part of the changing season. The question, though, was always present. How bad will this one be?

Along Nassau's waterfront the Out Island boats rocked sluggishly beneath a pewter sky. These were broad-beamed, serviceable craft badly in need of paint and new canvas. They were seaworthy, though, and on them the Out Islanders traveled back and forth from their island homes to Nassau bringing in the fish, the fruits and vegetables for sale in the city markets. The ocean was their highway and when they journeyed to New Providence the boatmen usually brought along their families and an assortment of dogs, goats and pigs. The animals were tethered on the decks and were as much at home on the water as the land. The dogs roamed free, prowling the shore or lying with muzzles flat on the warm deck planking. Sheep and goats and pigs were sold and the Out Islanders made a holiday of these excursions to Nassau.

Tod walked along the seawall listening to the liquid, throaty voices of the men and women as they called back and forth. Braziers were glowingly alight on the decks and pots of rice, beans or conch chowder simmered. Children played or dove over the side with screams of delight and then clambered back to dry themselves in the sun. The wind, when it came, was in fitful gusts and spent itself quickly, carrying no hint of a storm. As he strolled Tod watched the boatmen. Now and then they would halt in the repairing of a net or line to stand erect and scan the sky with a speculative expression. They seemed to sniff at the air, detecting a distant disturbance. Their heads would turn slowly as though they sought for some visible sign of the thing they felt. An instinct told them of the approaching storm and they had no need of weather bureaus or radio broadcasts.

In the marketplace near the piers and close by the Vendue House where their ancestors had been sold as slaves the "basket women" talked and commented endlessly. This was not the tourist season and there was little call for their wares. They came each day, however, to set up and display their stalls with baskets, mats, slippers, hats and woven purses. What they said to each other was all but unintelligible to the passerby. They laughed, joked and sometimes argued and seemed indifferent to the fact there were no customers.

Tod walked back up the long slope to the Royal Victoria. Nassau's waterfront had always fascinated him. He had visited and revisited the old forts commanding the harbor. He had sighted over the ancient cannon and wondered whose hand had put a match to fire a ball against the craft of a roving buccaneer. RESTORE COMMERCE AND EXPEL THE PIRATES. That was the motto on Nassau's shield. This had once been a wild and tumultuous place, contested by the Spanish, French and English.

He had lunch at the hotel's poolside, listening to the news on a small portable radio. Dora was still moving at a comparatively safe distance from the mainland. If nothing diverted her, she would pass harmlessly out to sea. Miami and the Bahamas, of course, would get the peripheral winds of high velocity but might be spared the crushing impact of the hurricane's full force.

Reaching from his chair to the table he turned off the radio. He was restless, unwilling to sit out a storm here in the Bahamas. He could fly back now without any danger of encountering the storm's lash. Abruptly he arose, left his lunch unfinished and strode up the slight incline to the hotel's entrance. He checked out and called for a cab to take him out to the seaplane base.

Airborne later he could feel the mysterious forces tugging at the

★ 376

light plane. There were invisible currents, hills and valleys into which he bucked or slid. Still far from the hurricane's whirling motion the air where he rode was disturbed. He could feel its restless motion through the controls and marveled a little that the power could be invisible. He rode through a seemingly placid and cloudless sky and soon was in sight of Miami's skyline on the beach where the great hotels rose in shining tiers, crowding each other for space. This was a spectacle which never ceased to amaze him. It seemingly defied all logic, but the supply never seemed to catch up with the demand for accommodations along the stretch of white beach. Easily within his memory it had been an all but deserted strand of scrub and mangrove which almost everyone agreed was without value. Now the grains of sand were like gold dust.

He made a wide turn to the left and began dropping down for a landing.

For almost twenty-four hours Dora remained all but static, churning the waters of the Florida Straits, whipping out to lay a warning lash on Key West. Her forward motion was temporarily arrested. Then she began to move again, creeping up to about twelve knots.

Along Miami Beach the wind was whipping at the wave tops, sending them flying in gray scud. The ocean heaved, seeming to be convulsed from below instead of running in true breakers to the shore. The air now was filled with a faint, keening sound as though the wind was playing upon high-tension wires.

Throughout the day and night the hurricane advanced upon a broad tangent course. The Weather Bureau again predicted she would move out to sea after slashing across the Keys. Most of Miami breathed a collective sigh of relief. Along Biscayne Boulevard the palms began to bend. Water rose in the bay and began breaking over the seawall. Even on the edge the storm had a frightening power. Cars moved cautiously along the rainswept causeways and streets. Pedestrians hurried and ducked for shelter within doorways as the winds raced across the city. Flights from the airport were canceled. All Miami and the surrounding communities could do was wait and hope the Weather Bureau was right in its forecast.

It writhed out of the sea at the hurricane's perimeter, a black and ugly thing which twisted into a giant waterspout linking the heavy, ominously dark clouds with the sea. It almost seemed as though the sky had opened a cavernous mouth to suck in this tremendous draft of water. The huge pillar was awesomely menacing in its tormented fury. Then, instead of linking with the storm and collapsing of its own weight, it began moving relentlessly toward the land.

On the beach there were a few adventuresome persons who had bucked the winds and rain because they found a strange excitement in a rampaging nature. They saw the column first. It was inky, spiraling and a spectacle of black terror. Those who had been bending themselves into the gusts, plodding heavily along the beach, mildly excited by the contest between themselves and the storm, now began to run, frantically seeking shelter in the nearby hotels. In a moment the shore was deserted. The waterspout had now become a sea-born tornado, carrying with it an incredible power of destruction. There was a roar which beat against the ears and the earth seemed to shiver beneath the rumbling of a thousand freight trains. The monster struck across the beach, drawing with it a huge core of seawater. Everything within its four-hundred-foot path was destroyed. The velocity flattened houses and small buildings or tore away their sides. Hundreds of windows were shattered and the shards were deadly missiles. As roofs went the interiors of buildings were gutted. Entire rooms of furniture or equipment were plucked out. Roofs, some of them miraculously intact, flew through the air. Automobiles, docks and garden walls were hurled aloft in splintered wreckage. Within the space of a few seconds tons of water were loosed upon Miami Beach, but the velocity of the monstrous thing itself did not abate. It raged across Biscayne Bay and struck the mainland, causing appalling destruction. Miami had long ago adjusted itself to the seasonal hurricanes but never before had it witnessed or suffered the impact of a tornado. Nothing in its path survived. Heavy trucks, fully loaded, were tossed up and carried away as a child's toy might be thrown. Houses, motels, roadside stands, simply disappeared. They were wrenched apart. Bricks, stones, telephone poles, water towers, cars, trees and pieces of buildings were hurled about in an unbelievable spectacle. Those who were caught simply vanished. It moved across the highway, sweeping everything in its path, and struck, dead center, upon the development of Willton.

The ornamental entrance pillars simply dissolved. The watchman, trapped inside, was hurled through the air in a grotesque sprawl. House after house in the development was flattened or torn to flying bits by the implacable thing. Willton ceased to be, seventy-five percent of its houses reduced to rubble. No shrub or tree remained. The path of devastation was complete. Within little more than a minute Willton was reduced to shredded debris. It was as though a gigantic roller had moved across the tract, leveling everything before it. The tornado spun on, crashed into the outlying pine flats and moved into the center of the state before spending itself.

From a window in his office high above Flagler Street, Stoddard had watched the tornado as it was darkly inked against the sky. It was well north of Miami proper, crossing the beach somewhere between the Miami shore and Hollywood-by-the-Sea. There was no question in his mind as to where it would strike the mainland. Willton lay in its path. It was only a matter of how close to the churning center the tract lay. It was difficult to believe what he was seeing. Tornadoes were things of Kansas and the plains. He had only a vague idea of what would happen to Willton when it had to bear the full brunt of that devouring twister.

It was late afternoon before the Highway Patrol opened the north- and southbound roads to traffic. By that time Tod had a police report of the damage done. Willton was gone. When it was possible he drove out slowly. The incredible path was plainly visible. For several miles there was nothing to indicate that Miami had been struck by a tornado. Then, as sharply as though cut by a giant scythe, the lane of destruction was revealed. A small house was intact. A hundred feet north of it everything was leveled.

Standing at the edge of what had once been Willton, Stoddard Lathrop stared at the wreckage. Twelve persons had been killed, trapped within the few houses which had been sold. Searchers were still combing the tract for bodies. The injured, most of them workmen who had been employed on the tract, had been taken to the Miami hospitals. Crowds of the curious were gathering, their cars canted off the shoulders of the highway. Everywhere people stood, gaping in silent awe at the freakish results of the twister. Along one side, houses were untouched. A few yards away there was nothing but debris.

For a long time Tod stood gazing at the development which had been at once his pride and the partial fulfillment of a long-cherished dream. Now he was not certain he wanted to build here on the wreckage. Finally, he turned away and walked thoughtfully back to his car.

Seated across the desk from Stoddard Lathrop, Reese Sparks carefully put a match to the grizzled tip of his stogie. He drew with deep satisfaction and his eyes never left Tod's face.

"It sure don't give me no pleasure to say it, Mr. Lathrop, but that there big wind and the insurance money you got comin' really took you off the hook with Willton."

Just a trace of a smile touched Stoddard Lathrop's eyes. "You're right, Mr. Sparks. It isn't easy to admit a mistake. I was in almost over my head and ready to go deeper."

"I had a feelin' from the beginnin'. An' it ain't because I think I'm smart. Somehow I never shet myself of the notion this wasn't the place for a development like Willton. Maybe the time ain't right. Miami can go in almost any direction. Maybe it's the people. I got a feelin' it's a little of both." He leaned back in his chair. "What I come down to say could have been said on the telephone but I wanted to say it in person. Whatever you got in mind for the future I'm with you all the way. Whatever I got an' you need is yours. I don't recollect," he grinned, "I evah said that to ary othah man."

"Thank you, Mr. Sparks." Tod rose and walked across the room, standing in front of a large glassed frame on the wall. He studied it intently for a moment. It was an enlarged aerial photograph of Denniston. "Come here a minute, Mr. Sparks. Let's look at something together."

Sparks crossed to stand beside him.

"I went wrong with Willton," Stoddard Lathrop spoke slowly, "because I didn't stay with something I knew was good. Denniston. It's sound because it's in the right place at the right time for the right people. I don't know why I didn't realize it."

"It would scare the hell out of me, Mr. Lathrop, if you was to be right all the time. With Willton you were reachin' for a buyer who wasn't there. Like I said, the people who could afford it don't want somethin' shoved at them like it was a take-this-or-nothin' deal."

"Suppose you and I fly over to Denniston today, Mr. Sparks. We'll just sit in the sun, catch a few fish. Denniston is right. I want to get the feel of it again. After that you and I will resurvey the state. We'll build Dennistons wherever there's a need for them. My father had the idea of self-contained communities long before anyone else thought they were possible. I'll do what he never lived to see completed."

"You sure you want me along, Mr. Lathrop?" Sparks regarded him quizzically. "Stalath has been pretty much of a one-man operation."

"I find you're good company on the long trip, Mr. Sparks."

"What about Willton and that there project in the Bahamas?"

"I'll clean up the Willton tract and we'll sell the remaining houses if and when we can. Maybe, in a few years, the time will be right and I'll come back to it. The club on Eleuthera can wait for a while. Let's you and I have a drink."

He went to a cabinet, took out a bottle of bourbon, glasses and a Thermos of water. He waited as Sparks filled a small glass, ignoring the carafe.

"My grandfather," he poured his own, "always said it was a test of a man's character to see what he did with good whisky. If he put water in it he was a man to be careful of and watched."

They drank in silence and Stoddard Lathrop lit a cigarette.

"By God, Mr. Sparks!" He spoke with a growing enthusiasm. "You and I can come damn near building us a whole state if we put our minds to it. What Dennis Lathrop didn't live to do we can do for him."

"I'll just have another touch of bourbon on that, Mr. Lathrop. I surely will."

Standing before a full-length mirror now, Stoddard Lathrop knotted the black tie, squared the ends precisely and regarded his reflection. It pleased him although he was not a vain man. The erosion of time, he thought, was not too apparent. The years were there. He wouldn't pretend they weren't. But they did not weigh too heavily on mind or body.

On a small table there was a square crystal decanter of brandy. He poured a small amount into a balloon glass and swallowed appreciatively. He marveled at the mind's ability to flash back over the years with the speed of a camera, retracing a lifetime within so short a time.

Sharon had asked how it had been in Florida. Well, that was the way it had been—wild, ragged, wonderful and exciting. It had been a challenge and he had met it with imagination. Now a great part of the state bore his mark. There had been many turnings along the way; side roads he might have taken. He could have, as had other men, settled for only a moderate success. Instead he had pursued a vision. Now he could survey Florida with a proprietary air and say: I created this. Because of me this community is here and its people have the good life. Florida is no longer for the privileged few. What had been accomplished had been undertaken not for money alone although, he admitted, money was a pleasant commodity to have. He had built his Dennistons, rebuilt a new and different Willton, finished the Lotus Club in the Bahamas and the Copa de Oro here at Boca Raton. He had wanted something of beauty for the few who could afford it; comfort and security for the many.

He turned and strolled outside to his private balcony. Across the Sound the lights on the craft moored there were topaz yellow. Behind them was the dark, gigantic hedge of palms, foliage and gardens in which the fine homes were hidden. Over it all the sea murmured with its eternal sound. The stars were bright, icy crystals in the sky and their light danced along the waves. His eyes swept over the club's grounds and then held to watch the approach of a cruiser. She was a thing of beauty in the moonlight, sleek and shiny as a wet dolphin. Her searchlight swept across the slips and buoys like a searching finger. From a switch in his office the dockmaster turned on the floodlights. There was a short blast of thanks from the cruiser's horn as she picked her way daintily in.

He knew the craft. She belonged to the Thomsons, of Beaumont. He watched as she moved into the slip and the dock boys took her lines. Then he turned away and walked down the balcony to have dinner with Sharon Ward on her birthday.

DATE DUE

GAYLORD			PRINTED IN U.S.A.